Voyage of ATONEMENT

Brian D. Ratty

Sunset Lake Publishing
89637 Lakeside Ct.
Warrenton, OR 97146
503.717.1125
#93-1015196

First Edition published in May 2016

ISBN-13: 978-0692454282
ISBN-10: 0692454284

Create Space Title ID: 5510106
Printed in the USA

For my Grandchildren and all of us
who enjoy a good seafaring story!

Contents

Author's Note

The English word "atonement" was coined in the 1500's by William Tyndale, and translated the meaning of the Hebrew word "Kippur," which means "reconciliation". **Atonement** meant 'at-one with God.'

Today Atonement means: *Something that makes up for an offense or injury. Webster's*

Somewhere between heaven and hell is a place called life. It is not for me to advocate another's life. I must judge, I must choose, I must spurn, purely for myself. Life gives us all choices: good ones and bad ones, right ones and wrong ones. We all must choose for ourselves. And in the end, we all must atone for those choices. So it was in Europe in the closing months of World War II. With Germany crumbling on all fronts, the fanatical Nazis dreamt of 'wonder weapons' to win the war, while planning their escape from the inevitable. These were desperate times, filled with desperate choices, for millions of people.

Voyage of

Atonement

The Tainted Treasure

by Brian D. Ratty

Chapter One

Berlin, Germany

14 November 1944

The whistle shrieked as the train approached the Central Station. Moments later, in a cloud of white steam, it rolled to a loud, rumbling stop.

The first off the front carriage was an SS Colonel wearing a gray wool overcoat, and dressed in his black and silver uniform with twin lightning bolts on his collar and a skull emblem on his cap. He carried but a single suitcase as he stepped down onto the station platform. Turning and walking toward the crowded terminal he noticed snow flurries drifting down from above. Glancing skyward, he saw the problem; the once beautiful, massive glass dome was in shambles from the Allied bombings. *What a shame*, he thought. *Lehrte Station was one of the jewels of Germany.* Pushing his way through a mostly uniformed crowd, he approached the station entrance and found an SS Sergeant holding a placard with his name on it.

Approaching the man, he said in a firm voice, "I'm Colonel Kobl."

The Sergeant instantly snapped to attention, clicking his heels together, while giving the Nazi salute. "Yes, sir. I'm Oberscharführer[1] Schmidt, your driver. Let me have your bag, sir, and I'll take you to the General."

The two men pushed their way through the hordes of people in the station, and walked outside to a parked black Mercedes. In the dim afternoon light, the Sergeant held the rear door open, and the Colonel slipped into the back seat. As he did, Schmidt noticed his youthful face, cold blue eyes and a jagged ruby scar that ran from above his collar to just under his left ear. The Oberst[2] Kobl had

[1] Sergeant

[2] Colonel

tasted war first-hand, and Schmidt knew immediately that this was not a man to be trifled with, but he was so young to have become such a high-ranking officer.

In fact, at just twenty-eight years old, Rolf Kobl was the youngest Colonel in the entire SS. With the help of his influential family, he had risen through the ranks quickly. But now, with most of his relatives dead and their power tarnished from political infighting, he worried about his future. Why had he been called back from the Eastern Front?

With a light dusting of snow on the roads, Schmidt maneuvered the sedan towards the downtown district.

From the backseat, the *Oberst* asked, "Are we going to headquarters?"

Without looking back, Schmidt answered, "No, sir. The General is working from Lion's Lair, these days. It's much safer. There is a thermos of hot coffee in the seat pocket, sir. It will take us about an hour to get to his estate."

With the hot brew in hand, the Colonel stared out the car window and watched the neighborhoods go by. With a light blanket of snow, Berlin looked almost pristine, the sidewalks filled with bundled-up Berliners moving along the avenue. Then his eyes glanced up to the jagged dark skyline, and he was appalled to see the outline of so many crumbling buildings. While the main thoroughfares were passable, many of the side streets were closed, littered with rubble from all the bombings.

Two years had passed since he was last in Berlin, and much had changed. When he had arrived on the Eastern Front in July of 1942, he had found only victories. Country after country, town after town, had fallen under control of the Nazis. His orders had been to oversee the final solution to the 'Jewish question,' so his SS units had built hundreds of concentration and labor camps, and filled them with enemies of the state. Today, all he found on the Eastern Front was defeat, and his SS units were engaged in scorching the earth, leaving nothing for the advancing Russian armies to find. As he glared at the skyline, even Berlin now looked defeated. He sat back in his seat with a scowl on his chiseled face. *How can this be? The Third Reich was to last for a thousand years.*

It was dark by the time the Mercedes pulled up to huge iron gates guarded by two enlisted SS soldiers. His orders and identification were checked with a flashlight by the sentries before the sedan was allowed to enter the compound.

Once the car had pulled up in front of the large, darkened manor, the Colonel got out and walked up the long, snowy flight of stone steps toward the front door. Looking skyward, he could just make out the silhouette of Lion's Lair, the General's estate.

A grin stretched his lips. He had been here many times before, as a child, and he had only fond memories of his uncle, the General, and his home. So why had he been recalled?

The Sergeant was at his heels, and the front door was opened before they could knock. Standing just inside the darkened foyer was a matronly looking woman, holding an oil lamp.

"Come in quickly," she said in a firm voice.

As soon as the men crossed the threshold, the door was closed and the interior lights turned back on.

Putting her lamp on a table, the woman gestured toward a set of closed doors. "Colonel, the General is waiting for you in his study."

Removing his overcoat and straightening his uniform, Kobl knocked firmly, slid open the large oak doors, and entered the room. Once inside, he paused and closed the doors behind him before turning again to face the room. Coming to attention, he clicked his jack boots together and gave the Nazi salute, saying loudly, "Colonel Rolf Kobl reporting as ordered, sir."

The Commanding General of the SS, the Protector of the Third Reich, Reichsführer[3] Karl Hanke stood up from behind his enormous desk and returned the salute. "Heil Hitler," he said, just as loudly.

The General was in his early sixties, dressed in an open grey tunic and tan jodhpurs. A monocle covered his left eye. He moved to the front of his desk and then towards the Colonel with his hand extended.

"Good to see you again, Nephew," he said, shaking Kobl's hand. "But you're late. I expected you this morning."

His grip was firm and friendly. "We Germans don't seem to keep our trains on schedule anymore, sir," Rolf replied with a smile. "Anyone would think there was a war on."

---

[3] Highest rank of the SS

The General pulled his nephew close and gave him a hug.

As they embraced, the Colonel looked around the large, familiar room. On the left were three tall windows that faced the front of the manor, covered with black-out curtains. Across the room was a large crackling stone fireplace, with the family crest hanging above the mantle. On the right was the General's massive oak desk, covered with papers and files. Behind the desk, on the wall, hung a twenty-foot Nazi flag. The other sparse furnishings in the room rested on polished wood floors covered with plush rugs.

As they parted, the General stared soberly at his nephew for a long moment. "I tried to help my brother, your father, but he had gotten in too deep. The Fuehrer was determined to make him an example. After his execution, your mother collapsed and died from a massive stroke. There was nothing I could do, lad."

Kobl stared at his uncle's wrinkled, weathered face and finally, sadly, replied, "You and my sister are the only family that I have now, sir."

"You also have the Comrades," the General replied. "The SS is also your family."

"Yes, sir," Rolf said grimly. "But you are safe here at Lion's Lair, and she is safe in Stockholm with her diplomat husband. So, Uncle, why am I here?"

The *Reichsführer* gestured to a single chair in front of his desk. "Have a seat, Colonel. We have much to cover, and only a few short hours."

As the men came to rest in their chairs, the General reached into a desk drawer and brought out a bottle of Cognac and two glass snifters. As he poured the nectar, he asked, "So, Rolf, how is your Spanish?"

"A little rusty, sir," Kobl answered, startled.

The General smiled broadly as he handed the Colonel his drink. "Well, you will soon be fluent." Then his expression darkened. "Tell me, Rolf, how have things been going on the Eastern Front?"

There was no honest way to soften the truth. "Horribly, sir. The Fuehrer's 'scorched earth' policy has my men distracted from their work at the camps, and thousands of the Jews linger on. The skies are full of Russian planes. Where are the wonder weapons promised by Goring?"

With some hesitation, the General replied, "There is a new jet aircraft being flown by Luftwaffe, but it is a dangerous machine to fly and we have only a few veteran pilots that can fly them. Our new rockets, the V-1 and V-2's, are now raining down on England, but they have no guidance system, and so they often only fall upon farmer's fields. A new fleet of advanced U-boats is being built, but that is happening slowly. Only a handful are now on duty in Norway. We had planned a battle for the Western Front, using the latest King Tiger Tanks, but the supporting troops were too few and too inexperienced, and they have no proven leadership.

In 1942, we should have finished England off first, made peace with America, and then invaded Russia," the General finally stated, with a long face.

"What are you really telling me, sir?" his nephew demanded.

"Have another drink, Rolf." The General handed the Cognac bottle across the desk to the Kobl, then shook his head. "The war is lost. And, from the ashes of the Third Reich, *we* will build the Fourth Reich."

Pouring the brandy slowly, the Colonel could not believe his ears. His eyes darted around the room as he wondered whether they were being filmed or recorded. But no, the General's treasonous words must be true; no one would dare entrap *Reichsführer* Karl Hanke. He was the third most powerful man in Germany.

The General went on to explain, with a sadistic smirk, how the SS had looted hundreds of millions of Reichsmarks from the Jews. "First we confiscated their businesses, and seized their bank accounts and investments. Then their homes and all their belongings were sold off. But we kept their jewelry, art, and all their valuables. Hell, the SS has an art collection bigger than Goring's. Then we sent them off to the camps where we took their clothes and whatever else they tried to smuggle in. Next, we worked them to near death for the Fatherland. Even in the pigs final butchery, we took the gold from their teeth and their hair for rope. Half of all this booty we shared with the government. The other half, the SS kept. That money is now secreted in numbered banks accounts in dozens of other countries. Our only regret is that we ran out of time before we could complete the Jewish solution.

But time is a luxury we no longer have. Now, we must save our own."

The General leafed through a stack of papers on his desk and pulled out a thick manila folder. "With the war lost, we have formed a secret brotherhood called the Odessa[4]. It will provide money, new identities, transportation and safe-houses all around the world for thousands of SS officers and men who need to escape the grasp of the Allies. These soldiers will become the vanguard of the Fourth Reich. You and many others like you will be the keepers of National Socialism, the future of our Fatherland." The General handed Kolb the folder. "I will not order you to take this new assignment, as I realize it is a direct violation of your oath to the Fuehrer. However, if you agree, here are your new orders. Read them and commit them to memory."

Rolf opened the folder and found written orders, along with new identity cards, passport, birth certificate, airplane tickets and a wallet with a few thousand Argentine banknotes. All of those documents bore the name of Axel Garcia, but the picture on the passport was one of himself, dressed in civilian clothes.

"Why Argentina, sir?" the Colonel asked.

"The Argentinean government will welcome Odessa warmly, as they want to take back the Falkland Islands from the British, after the war. We just might help them with a few of our newest U-boats."

"Have the Fuehrer and Himmler signed off on this, sir?" Rolf asked.

"Nein. They are zealots who believe the war is still winnable," the General said. "But Deputy Führer Martin Bormann and a few other high ranking officers have done so. Will you join us?"

Rolf swirled his Cognac glass, lost deep in thought. He hated Hitler for what he had done to his family… but he loved his country. "Aye, sir" he finally said firmly. "The Odessa is my family now. Send me as many Aryan brothers as you can. "

The Colonel was given a suitcase filled with business clothes that fit him perfectly. He was told to establish safe houses not only in Argentina, but in Paraguay, Bolivia and Peru as well. That was to be accomplished by using a front business, called the South

---

[4] Organization of Former SS Members

American Mining Company, and four million dollars, stolen from the Jews, which he would find waiting in a numbered account in the Bank of Buenos Aires. "The bank codes are in your orders. Memorize them, and then destroy them. Set your networks up carefully, Colonel. Always stay close to the local German communities, as they can be trusted."

Within a few hours, Rolf Kolb, dressed as businessman Señor Axel Garcia, was back in the Mercedes, rushing to the Berlin station to catch the express train to Zurich.

Colonel Rolf Kolb had made his choice: The Odessa.

Baltic Sea
10 March 1945

With a loud *slap,* the bow of the boat sliced through twenty-foot sea swells under a steel-gray sky of early evening light. On the sail-bridge, with a stiff wind blowing sea spray, stood Captain Hans Miller, the boat's Navigator, Karl Fritsch, and two lookouts. All of the men were dressed in foul-weather gear.

With binoculars pressed against his young face, Captain Miller searched the horizon for trouble. He had taken command of the submarine a year earlier, and had trained his crew to be an efficient killing machine. Now, at age twenty-six, he proudly wore the 'white cap' of a U-boat skipper. He was tall and lean, with light brown hair, sharp green eyes and a clean-shaven, chiseled face. To be without a beard on sub patrol was quite uncommon, as it meant that he shaved each day using only cold seawater, which was a painful endeavor. But he relished that little sacrifice to keep himself neat and tidy. On *his* boat, all things were shipshape.

Captain Miller had been ordered from the boat bunkers in Trondheim, Norway, to the shipyards at Kiel, Germany, for repairs to his battled-ravaged U-boat 493. He and his crew of forty-four men had been stationed in Norway for the past ten months, and had sailed on three battle patrols to the North Atlantic. The last trip had been quite disappointing, as his boat had sunk only one merchant ship. With fuel running low, they had made a long and stormy dash for home. When they finally arrived in Norwegian waters, they had a run-in with a British destroyer. During the six-hour battle, the destroyer had dropped over fifty depth-charges on U-493, causing two of the boat's torpedo tubes to leak, damaging the snorkel that had just been installed, and bending the dive planes, making it difficult to trim the boat.

After some hours of brilliant maneuvering, Captain Miller and his submerged submarine had slipped from the grasp of the destroyer and found their way back to Trondheim. But, upon their arrival, they learned that the extensive repairs they needed could only be carried out back in Germany.

It had taken four days for Captain Miller to break through the Norwegian British blockade, but now his boat was finally in the Baltic Sea, where he could surface to fix his position.

"Well, Karl," the Skipper yelled over the howling winds and curling seas, "did you get a fix? I don't want my ass hanging out on the surface very long."

The Navigator removed the sextant from his eye and turned his sea-sprayed face to the Captain. "Yes sir, I think I know where we are. A few more hours on this course and we should be just off the Kiel lighthouse."

"Good," the Skipper replied. Turning his gaze to the lookouts he shouted, "Lookouts below." Then, turning his head to the open conning tower hatch, he yelled down, "Prepare to dive."

Within moments, U493 sank below the surface of the turbulent Baltic Sea.

A few hours later, Miller and his Executive Officer, Lieutenant Max Kogel, were in the cramped Captain's nook, drinking coffee. Max had just poured himself some brew, and stood leaning against the cold steel bulkhead. He was young and thin, with an unkempt black beard that needed trimming. He wore a blue wool stocking cap on his head, and his wrinkled shirt and sweater were stained with salt sweat. At twenty-nine years old, he was nicknamed 'the old man,' because he was the oldest of the crew. Lieutenant Kogel had started in the boats in 1938 as a young Ensign and, after six years, had only risen to an Executive Officer rating. He should have had his own boat years before, but a disgruntled crewmember had accused him of making anti-Nazi statements, so now he had a black mark on his Navy records. Everyone aboard knew his story, and no one really cared, including

Max himself. Politics was a verboten subject aboard U-493, and the Skipper considered Max not only a friend, but the best Executive Officer in all of the boats.

"You look tired, my Captain," he said, sounding genuinely concerned.

With the boat swaying in a strong underwater current, the Skipper sat at his tiny desk with a white porcelain mug in hand. "I'm war-weary, Max," the Captain answered with a serious face. "I'm tired of being shot at and chased by the British. I'm tired of eating rotten food, and the stench of this boat. Now I know why they were called 'pig-boats' in the first war." He took a drink of coffee and continued, "Once again, I would like to smell the perfume of a Fraulein, taste her sweet red lips and have her long legs wrapped around mine. Am I asking too much?" he concluded, with his eyebrows raised.

"No, sir," Max quickly answered. "Maybe all of that can be arranged when we get to port."

"Ah yes... shore leave. We all need it. How's the crew holding up?"

"Three members have families in Hamburg, and they are worried," the Exec answered.

"And you, Max, what about your family in Cologne?"

Max shook his head with a sad face. "Nothing since we left for Norway. I'm worried sick."

The overhead intercom blasted with the Navigator's voice. "Captain, we should be approaching the lighthouse."

Hans got to his feet and clicked a lever. "Alright. I'll be right there." As he turned to leave the nook, the Skipper noticed his friend still had a sour look on his face. "I'll do what I can to get the men shore leave," he told him. "We'll be laid up for repairs for a few weeks, anyhow."

Under the cover of a moonless night, after the soundman had given the all-clear, the boat surfaced. The Captain and his Exec rushed up the ladder to the sail-bridge, with lookouts following. By now, they rode a lazy sea and were still many miles away from Germany. Silently, both officers scanned the dark horizon with their binoculars. In the general direction of Kiel, they saw many yellow-orange flashes, and heard the muted roar of explosions.

"The Navy yard is getting it tonight," the Captain finally said, with the glass still to his eyes.

"Aye," Max answered. "We shouldn't approach until we know the raids are over."

From above, a lookout shouted, "Three planes ten miles out, behind us!"

The Captain twisted his binoculars aft and quickly saw three British Lancaster bombers, low on the horizon, scanning the waters with their powerful search lights. "Alarm," he yelled. "Dive! Crash dive!"

The lookouts and Max slid down the open hatch in one fluid motion, with the Captain pausing on the bridge to watch one of the planes headed in their direction. Cursing the Lancasters, with his middle finger in the air, the Skipper was the last down the hatch, pulling it shut and secure, just before he slid down the ladder to the conning tower deck.

Within moments, U-493 was twenty meters underwater and sinking like a rock. As the Chief of the boat struggled to gain control of the damaged submarine, two explosions rocked the boat from a few hundred yards astern. Moments later, two more were heard, but far off on the port side. Then there was nothing, only the sounds of the sea rushing against the thin skin of the submarine. Finally, the Chief had the boat trimmed at 50 meters, and reports of flooding started coming in.

"Chief, bring her up slowly to 10 meters and get the pumps running. Keep the boat heading towards Kiel, and call me when you have the lighthouse in view."

At 0100 the boat surfaced again, a half-mile from the totally dark beacon that was the Kiel lighthouse. From the bridge, the Exec used a small signaling torch to tell whoever was inside that U-493 was entering the long waterway to the navy yard. Their message was acknowledge by two faint flashes from shore.

The dockside was in shambles and still smoldering from the bombings as the boat approached the concrete sub bunker of the shipyard. Using the handheld light again, a recognition signal was flashed ashore. Quickly, a small red light turned green, a warning horn sounded, and a massive cement-and-steel door slowly opened to a dimly lit sub pen. With a docking crew standing by, the boat slipped through the narrow opening.

The door was closed, and the overhead lights came back on. The U-493 came to rest on a concrete wharf forty feet wide and two hundred and fifty feet long. From the sail-bridge, the Skipper shouted docking orders while looking around the massive bunker. There were no brass bands to greet his boat, no Admirals or pretty girls. Those were the good old days, when U-boats ruled the Atlantic, and submariners were German heroes. What he saw now was only four lone boats docked inside a bunker built to hold thirty.

As he glanced at the other submarines, his eyes were drawn like a bolt of lightning to the boat next to them, on the other side of the quay. It was a new Type XXI boat. He had only seen one other Type XXI submarine, through his binoculars a few weeks before, in Norwegian waters. Now he could almost reach out and touch one of the promised new 'wonder weapons.' This new kind of boat was as sleek as a gazelle, and camouflaged much like the animal itself. Its length and beam were much the same as his type VIIC submarine, but that was where the similarities ended. The new design was radically streamlined, with smooth lines that made the boat look like it was moving even when it was docked. The large, tall conning tower was teardrop-shaped with an assortment of sonar, radar and radio antennas. There were two new types of periscopes and a redesigned low-profile snorkel. The sail-bridge had small white painted numbers near the top, U-3521. The hull itself was smooth and graceful with few protrusions, and on the bow he could see retractable hydroplanes. This was an amazing submarine to behold, and the Captain felt frozen in place as he stared at it.

Max broke his train of thought. "All docking lines are secure, sir."

"Aye," the Skipper replied. "Do you see what's next to us?"

The Exec turned his attention to the wharf, and saw a beehive of activity. The new submarine was being loaded with supplies, fore and aft, by a large detail of sailors.

"Maybe we'll get one of these new wonder weapons someday," Max said, his gaze fixed on the new submarine. "In any event, it looks like the boat is about to ship out."

"You get us secured from patrol, while I go ashore and have a look," the Captain said, moving towards the sail-bridge ladder. "If you hear from headquarters, give me a shout and I'll return."

Captain Miller found the Chief of U-3521 on the aft deck, supervising the loading. From him, he learned that the boat had just completed sea-trials and was about to go on its first patrol. The Captain was ashore with most of the other fifty-six-man crew.

"We expect them to return from their transit quarters late this morning, sir. We are to get underway at nightfall."

"Is the Exec aboard?"

"Yes, sir. Lieutenant Kaplan is below, making up his duty roster."

"Would that Josef Kaplan?" Miller asked, surprised.

"Yes sir, do you know the Lieutenant?"

"Yes. I served with him back in '39 aboard U-166. We were both young Ensigns, back then."

"He'll be in the officers wardroom, sir, just forward of the conning tower."

A large grin chased across the Captain's face. "This boat has an officer's wardroom?"

"Yes, sir," the Chief replied loudly and proudly.

Captain Miller found his old ship-mate hunched over a table in a small, brightly painted nook that was used as the officer's lounge. They shared a cup of coffee and reminisced about the old days when being submariners meant fame and glory. It was a nice reunion, and Lieutenant Kaplan offered to give Miller a tour of U-3521, to which he quickly agreed.

The tour was impressive. They started in the forward torpedo room and worked their way aft. The boat had a range of over 15,000 miles and, thanks to a new hydraulic reloading system, could fire 18 torpedoes in less than twenty minutes. These new boats could do 32 knots submerged and 28 knots on the surface; they were faster underwater than on top. The radio, radar and sonar systems had been completely redesigned, which made the submarine almost impossible to detect and sink. The hull was pressurized, the hydrophones had been moved to beneath the bow, and the low-profile snorkel could recharge the massive battery system within a few hours. Everything aboard was new and shiny.

There were even two toilets and two showers aboard, and a freezer in the galley! Captain Miller had never seen such a boat, or heard of such advancements. With a small fleet of Type XXI boats, the battle for the Atlantic would be won by Germany.

When Miller returned to the U-493, with his mind still swirling with thoughts of victory and a burning desire to return to the glory days, he found himself repulsed by the stench of his own iron coffin.

Later, Max found the Captain in his nook, drinking from a bottle of brandy. "A message has arrived from headquarters, sir."

"Come in, Max, and have a drink. I have just seen our future and it is bright."

The Exec entered the nook and handed the message to the Skipper. Miller poured him a drink and handed him the glass. Then he opened the message and read it. "I'm to report at 0900 this morning. The crew is to remain aboard until I return. They want a complete list of our needed repairs." The Skipper gave his friend a sly look. "That should be a very long list!"

Max noticed the twinkle in the Captain's eyes, and suddenly he felt refreshed. "Now, what was that about our future sir?" he asked with a curious grin.

7th U-boat Flotilla, Kiel, Germany
11 March 1945

Commodore Heniz Krug was a legend from the First World War. As a famous sea-wolf, he had helped create the strategy of attacking convoys by using a large number of U-boats working together. In the early days of World War II, these 'wolf-packs' had brought much death and destruction to the Allied shipping lines. Now, well past middle age, red-faced and fifty pounds overweight, the Commodore fought the war from his plush offices at Kiel headquarters.

Upon arrival, Captain Miller was surprised to find Lieutenant Kaplan from the U-3521 seated soberly in front of the *Kommodore*'s desk. He wore his winter black uniform, and he looked dejected.

Heniz Krug got to his feet as Miller entered his office. The old gentleman gave the Captain the Kriegsmarine salute while saying,

"Heil Hitler," neatly turned out in a blue wool coat, with sleeves covered in gold piping. The Captain returned his salute and removed his white cap.

"Have a seat," Krug said, gesturing to a chair next to the Lieutenant. "We have much to discuss and little time. I understand you know Kaplan."

"Yes, sir," the Captain replied. "We shipped together on U-166, many years ago."

"Good. It looks as if you'll be shipmates again. We had a horrific tragedy here, last night. One of the Lancasters scored a direct hit on our transit barracks. Everyone inside was killed or wounded, including most of the crew of U-3521."

Lieutenant Kaplan fixed his sad-eyed gaze on Miller. "We lost over forty brave souls last night, sir. I had the Chief of the boat and a dozen crewmembers with me on loading detail. We are all that remain."

"So, Captain Miller, I'm giving you command of the U-3521," the *Kommodore* continued. "You will blend your crew with what remains of her crew, and be ready to depart on a secret mission, tonight."

"That's impossible," Miller heard himself say. "It will take weeks to train my crew on how to sail such an advanced boat. And they have been on patrol for over ten months. They need shore leave, sir."

The *Kommodore*'s round face got beet red. "We have no time, Captain! The war is nearly lost; the Allies have crossed the Rhine. They could be here at the shipyards within a few weeks. Take on your passengers, load your cargo, and get the hell to sea by nightfall. That is a direct order!"

"I can train your crew, Captain," Lieutenant Kaplan said with an earnest face.

The room went dead silent for a long moment; only the muffled sounds of distant artillery firing could be heard.

"Sir, I understand your urgency," Miller finally said sheepishly. "But what mission? What passengers? What cargo? I don't understand what we are talking about, sir!"

Captain Miller's questions started an hour-long conversation about the true scope of his mission. First, he learned that his new boat had a sister ship, U-3520, that had departed on a similar mission ten days before. That boat carried the Japanese Ambassador and his family back to Japan. It was to make port in Bergen, Norway, to pick up three German nuclear scientists and all of their experiments on making heavy water for atomic bombs. The submarine was then to depart to the North Atlantic and take the long southern route around Africa and into the Indian Ocean, finally depositing their passengers and cargo on Japanese-controlled Rabaul New Guinea. Once the Ambassador and the scientists were safely ashore, the boat was to proceed to Santa Cruz Island, part of the Galapagos Islands, off the coast of Ecuador, where a supply ship would be waiting with fuel and provisions for the last leg of their mission: rounding Cape Horn and delivering the U-3520 to the Argentinean government. Once that was accomplished, the crew would be given the choice of staying in that country or returning to Germany.

"This mission is defensive, not offensive," the *Kommodore* insisted. "You will attack the enemy only if it is a matter of your own survival."

Miller's boat, U-3521, was to transport a Japanese naval attaché and his family. The attaché would be carrying important documents and plans from the German Admiralty. They would also transport an SS Major named Schmidt, who would oversee the safe delivery of the boat's cargo to the German Embassy in Buenos Aires.

"And what is our cargo, sir?" Hans respectfully asked.

At first, the *Kommodore* dodged his question, but Captain Miller asked again. Finally, after a third inquiry, he learned that their cargo was to be twelve tons of Reichsbank gold bullion.

"That's crazy," Miller said, filled with foreboding. "Twelve tons of dead weight on a submarine is asking for serious trouble." He turned to Kaplan. "And where were you planning to stow this cargo, Lieutenant?"

Kaplan looked surprised by the question, "In the aft engine room, sir."

"What armaments are in there now?" Miller asked.

The Lieutenant thought for a moment. "Four extra torpedoes."

"Those will have to be off-loaded. That will at least take care of six tons of weight. What's in the forward torpedo room?"

"Eighteen torpedoes sir."

"We'll keep fourteen. Off-loading the others should save us another six tons. And stow the cargo both forward and aft, to keep the boat balanced."

"You might need those torpedoes," the *Kommodore* asserted with a serious look.

Captain Miller smiled at him. "Our mission is defensive, not offensive, sir."

The old man looked at the young Skipper with a grudging grin, acknowledging that U-3521 was in good hands with Captain Miller.

As the meeting went on, they were interrupted a number of times by an older Captain who was the *Kommodore*'s adjutant. He brought in papers to be signed, as well as messages from the Admiralty and several requests for Landurlaub[5]. On one occasion, when Commodore Krug was busy in the adjoining office and Lieutenant Kaplan was out of the room, Hans rose from his chair and walked toward the office window.

As he strolled past the desk, he noticed an open desk drawer that contained a stack of green, endorsed shore passes. He stared at the stack with his mind racing. Then, tempted beyond his ability to resist, he pocketed a handful of the passes. He had crew members with families. With the war nearly over, why should they be sacrificed? That he could not – would not – do. But Hans himself was a young bachelor whose family had been killed in train accident in 1940. He was weary and wanted a final solution to the war, but he also hated the British, feared the Americans, and loved Germany, so he would carry out this long, dangerous mission as ordered.

Captain Hans Miller had made his choice: Duty.

Fairview Estate, New Jersey
21 December 1962

Dutch Clarke stood in front of the flickering fireplace in his study. His blue eyes brimmed with unshed tears as he stared at the dancing flames, his mind wandering the far reaches of his memory. He seemed to be lost in time and space.

---

[5] shore leave

The wooden mantle above the firebox held an assortment of pictures, mostly of his family, past and present. Long ago, he had etched these images into his brain, and he knew he would never forget them. There was the old black-and-white picture of his Uncle Roy and Grandfather, taken at Dutch's graduation from high school. Those two men had been the patriarchs; they had founded a family business, Gold Coast Petroleum, which prospered for decades. They were both dead now, and so was their business. Grandfather had died in 1940. Uncle Roy had passed away just three years ago, in 1959. The business they created had been declared dead, earlier on this cold winter's day. And now night had fallen...

Farther down the mantel stood the only picture Dutch had of his mother and father. Their fading black-and-white wedding photo had been taken outside of Fairview, this fine old house where he now stood. They had died in a traffic accident when Dutch was very young. He could no longer remember much about his parents, other than the inescapable fact that they were dead.

His favorite picture was the full-color wedding portrait of himself, Laura, and her young son, Edward, taken at a small chapel in Seattle on September 14, 1946. It had been a grand wedding, with Dutch dressed in his Captain's Marine uniform, Laura in a beautiful, pale-blue dress, and Edward still in short pants. Their faces were full of hope, love, and wishes for a bright future. Uncle Roy had given them a two-week honeymoon at the Ahwahnee Lodge in Yosemite. Those had been the best of times…

But Laura had died from breast cancer, two years ago. In fact, standing here now, Dutch felt as if a death cloud hung over Fairview like a shroud. Of all the people on the mantle, only he and Edward were still alive. All those years ago, he had escaped death many times during the war. Now he longed for it.

The grandfather clock in the empty foyer struck the hour with nine loud chimes. Its mournful rings brought Dutch's mind back to reality, and he turned from the fireplace to his desk. As he came to rest in his chair, his eyes were still fixed on the flames. He shook his head sadly as the tears stung his eyes. *Where had all the years gone?*

At forty-two, he was still technically in his prime. Sure, there was some gray hair around his temples, and some wrinkles in his face from years of working under the hot sun, but he didn't look all that different from the young man in the wedding photo, with his chiseled face and that deep dimple in his chin. He had added some weight, maybe ten pounds too much. Still, all in all, he looked pretty much like the Dutch Clarke in the picture. It was the man inside who had changed. Right now, his mind felt disjointed and he suspected he wasn't thinking all that clearly. The tragedy of losing both his uncle and wife within one year had taken a toll. And now the humility of losing the family business felt like the last straw.

Dutch reached for the stack of legal sized papers folded on his desk and opened them. He had picked up the judge's Final Decree from the courthouse, earlier that afternoon, and had already read the documents twice. The first part of the proclamation had to do with the management of Gold Coast Petroleum during its break-up and bankruptcy. The next part was instructions and exhibits concerning the sale of all the assets of the company, and distribution of that money to the rightful creditors.

The last few pages dealt with his personal bankruptcy. There was a list of every asset he owned, spelling out which creditor each had been pledged to as collateral. The list included all of his personal banking, investment and retirement accounts, his automobiles, the family jewelry, and the other large items of value. It also included the land and house known as Fairview Estates, with all its furnishings and fixtures. The list was long and ruthlessly comprehensive. The bottom line was that his creditors would get it all, even the fifty-thousand-dollar life insurance settlement from his wifes death. At the very bottom of the ruling was the judge's signature, along with bold red type that declared that the decree was to take effect on January 1, 1963.

Dutch stared at the document, rereading the entries, slowly shaking his head. *How can this have happened?* That was the thought that kept repeating in his head. He had been so happy, so much in love with both Laura and her son. He had even legally adopted Edward, many years before. Roy had been in charge, running the business and the family. Dutch had been the field man, searching the world for the black gold known as oil. He had traveled most of the world, with Laura and Edward at his side.

Then Roy died. *How dare he!* Dutch thought in angry grief, for that had been the beginning of the end. When Laura got sick,

Dutch had brought in a new CEO so that he could stay home and care for his wife. The man's name was George Hughes, and he had come with great references and lots of experience in the oil business. In the end, though, he had turned out to be a crook, a clever one who had embezzled millions from the company.

The grim thoughts enraged Dutch. He threw the papers down and opened his desk drawer, pulling out his Marine-issue .45-caliber sidearm. He would kill Hughes if he ever saw him again! But the miserable coward had escaped to Europe, and would likely never be seen again. Still, something about the cold steel of the gun in his hand soothed him. Hughes was gone, but the weapon might yet be the answer. A way not to have to face the humility of defeat…

Ring-ring.

The summons of the phone echoed suddenly through the empty house.

No. Dutch didn't want to talk to anyone. He sat stonily as it rang twice more.

But then he thought of his son, Edward, safely enrolled in the Naval Academy at Annapolis. Did Edward need something?

On the fourth ring, he picked up. "H'llo?"

"Dutch? Is that you, lad?" a strong male voice answered loudly.

It was Laura's father, his father-in-law, Skip Patterson, calling from Ketchikan, Alaska. "Yes, it's me, Skip." He cleared his throat and replied more strongly, "What do you need, pal?"

"Thought I'd check in," Skip answered. "I just got off the phone with Hank Clobber. He tells me you fired him and his wife, Helen, on Monday. Hell, boy, those folks have been with your family for almost twenty years. What's going on, lad?"

Dutch felt a wave of shame rush though his body. He didn't know what to say. Finally, with a knot in his gut, he answered his father-in-law. "Six months ago, the company was forced into bankruptcy. Over the years, I've pledged my personal wealth as collateral, so I've had to file for bankruptcy, as well." He swallowed again the bitter taste in his mouth. "The creditors got it all."

There was dead silence on the line for a long moment. Then Skip said, "Jesus, boy, why didn't you tell me? I could have sold my fishing trawlers to help out."

Dutch sighed into the mouthpiece. "Thanks for the thought, Skip, but it wouldn't have helped. I was short over three million dollars to the banks. That's why they came after me."

"Damn! That's a lot of money," Skip replied, sounding shocked. "They took every-thing?"

Dutch wished he hadn't answered the phone. It was mortifying, having to talk about his failures. "Well, not quite everything," he said in hopes of ending the conversation. "I got to keep an old F100 Ford pickup we use around the estate, and fifteen thousand dollars that the court called my 'homestead exemption' for losing the house. And my clothes, except for the formalwear. That had to be sold by my creditors. But they couldn't legally get their hands on any of my boy's college trust funds, thank God." He heaved a sigh. "The oil business is a big crap shoot, and I'm just as happy to be done with it, but that's why Hank and Helen had to be let go. I'm dead broke, Skip."

After another long pause, his father-in-law said, "There's another asset they didn't get."

"Oh yeah? What's that?" Dutch asked dully.

"That boat you bought in 1957, the *Pacific Lady III.* I've got the title for her in my lock-box."

The boat was a twenty-four-foot sailboat that Dutch had bought for his wife and had given to Skip for safekeeping. He had forgotten all about her. She was a sleek and sturdy craft, perfect for sailing on Alaska's inland waters. The family had spent many enjoyable summers sailing her around. Just the mention of her sent good memories flooding into his mind. "Can't believe you still have her," Dutch heard himself answer.

"Sure. She's been in a heated warehouse for last three seasons. Why don't you fly up? We'll take her for a cruise."

Dutch shook his head. "It's the middle of winter, pal. No sane sailor would have her out in your weather. Listen, Skip, I've got to run, but we can talk about this later. And thanks for reminding me about the *Lady*."

"All right, lad," he replied. "You and I can take her out, when spring comes. Merry Christmas – and don't do anything foolish. Bye."

The renewed silence seemed deafening. Dutch hung up the phone walked to the liquor cabinet, where he poured himself a large whiskey before returning to his desk. He sat down again and picked up his sidearm, took a big swig from his glass, and slipped the magazine clip from the gun, letting it drop to the desktop with a *thud*.

Dutch lowered his weapon and picked up the clip, carefully emptying the magazine. The seven bullets dropped, one at time, on top of the legal documents.

He looked carefully at the clip. Then, using both hands, he reloaded the ammunition into the magazine. His actions were more mechanical than emotional, his gaze unfocused, his mind sinking again into the cold morass of pain, shame and despair. The clip slid back into the gun, and he pulled the breech back, loading the weapon with a loud *click*. A single bullet entered the firing chamber, with the hammer cocked and ready.

Laura, raised a Catholic, had held strong opinions against suicide. But Laura wasn't there to feel the misery he was experiencing now. He would ask for her forgiveness. His cheeks wet with tears, Dutch raised the gun and placed the barrel to his temple. Then, with a blank stare and a silent prayer, he squeezed the trigger.

Nothing happened! Steeling himself, Dutch pulled the trigger again.

Still nothing.

With a shuddering sigh, Dutch lowered the weapon and examined it.

The damn safety was still on!

A tiny ghost of a grin chased across his lips. "Okay, Jack Malone. I get the damn message," he said aloud.

This had happened once before, during the war. His unit had gotten into a battle with some Nips, and a sniper had risen out of the grass to shoot Dutch. The man had hesitated for a second, giving Dutch enough time to raise his Thompson machine gun and pull the trigger. But nothing had happened. His safety had still been on! Jack Malone, just behind him, had used his own weapon to kill the sniper, saving Dutch's life.

But Jack himself had not made it back alive from the Pacific. When Dutch got home and learned of his friend's infant son, Jack Jr., he had pledged that he would be the boy's godfather and look out for him for the rest of his life. And now here he sat, trying to kill himself!

Shaking his head and thanking the Lord, Dutch threw the weapon across the room.

When the gun hit the floor, the safety slipped off, and the pistol fired one loud shot into the ceiling above Dutch's desk. As small particles of plaster rained down on him, Dutch began to laugh. This was crazy! It was time for him to get busy living, or get busy dying. No more feeling sorry for himself. He had been a fool to forget his two boys.

After cleaning up the mess, Dutch poured another drink, this time adding ice cubes to his glass. As he turned to go back to his desk, the doorbell rang.

Bewildered, Dutch went out to the foyer, where the clock showed that it was half past ten. *Who the hell's calling at this time of night?* Dutch wondered, as he opened the front door.

There, with snow falling on the shoulders of their gray cadet Naval Academy uniforms, were his son Edward and his godson Jack Jr. The smiling boys were carrying boxes of food and drink. Dutch stood there, speechless, hardly believing his own eyes.

"Merry Christmas, Father!" His son bellowed, grinning. "We came to spend the holiday with you. Skip and Louise will be here from Ketchikan on Saturday."

"But I talked to him on the phone just tonight; he didn't say a word about it."

"And my mom will be here from California, tomorrow," Jack Jr. added. Then, turning, he gestured toward a cab in the driveway. "And look who we found along the way."

Getting out of the car, also carrying boxes of food, were Hank and Helen Clobber, his household staff. Dutch nodded at the couple through the snow, his heart swelling with joy at the sight of them.

"And don't worry about the cost, Dad. We have you covered until the first of the year," Edward said, his uniform beginning to turn white.

"Yeah, our college trust funds are worthless, with the Navy paying all the bills," Jack added.

With dewy eyes again, Dutch stepped out into the weather and hugged his two boys. By God, how lucky he was!

Dutch Clarke had made his choice: Life.

Three men had chosen their destiny, and all three would have to atone for their decisions, in ways that might change the course of history.

Chapter Two

Buenos Aires, Argentina

20 November 1944

Señor Axel Manuel[6] sat nervously in his airline seat as the DC3 made its final approach to the Buenos Aires airport. As he looked out the window at the sun-drenched city below, he realized he had traveled from the brutal winter weather of Europe to the middle of the South American summer in just four days; the wonderment of air travel! But, it had been an arduous journey. To begin, he had traveled from Berlin to Zurich via train and then flown Swiss Air to Lisbon. From there, he had boarded the Pan American Clipper to Brazil, where he changed planes to an Aero Argentina flight for Buenos Aires. Everything had gone as planned; his forged papers had been checked numerous times, with no problems. Even his rusty Spanish had improved, once he boarded the Clipper in Portugal. His confidence was building, but he was still nervous and tired. The last hurdle was yet to come: Customs and Immigration at Ezeiza Airport.

When the plane came to rest at the International Terminal, the passengers disembarked down outside stairs and were herded inside along a dingy corridor to the Customs area. As Axel walked along, carrying only his single suitcase, he felt a bead of cold sweat run down his forehead from his Panama hat band. Stopping to take out his handkerchief, he blotted the moisture dry, reminding himself not to talk too much and not to look anxious. Resuming his march, he kept a nonchalant expression on his young face.

The government room was big and bright, with a long row of tall desks in front of Customs Agents, with armed guards watching the arriving passengers. Axel got in line and patiently waited for the next official. When his turn came, he approached a skinny fellow in a wrinkled and stained uniform, with a long, bony nose and wire-rimmed glasses. Handing the man his passport, Axel chuckled under his breath; all bureaucrats looked the same, no matter the country.

---

[6] aka SS Colonel Rolf Kolb

The official didn't look up from his passport, and checked the back pages for customs stamps.

"Anything to declare?" he asked, with his nose still down.

Axel answered indifferently, "Nada."

The official held up the photo page of his passport and looked at him carefully. Then, lowering the document, he quickly endorsed one of the back pages with both a customs and an immigration stamp. "Welcome home," he said, handing the passport back.

Axel took the papers and placed them in his valise, then turned and started to walk away. He had only taken a few steps before the agent said loudly, "Señor, I have a question."

Twisting back to the official, Axel answered, "Yes?"

The agent pointed to the left side of his own neck and asked, "How did you get your scar?"

Without hesitation, Axel answered, "Esgrima[7]."

The agent nodded his head with a grin. "Have a good day sir."

Axel pushed his way through the hordes of the main terminal and soon found himself outside in the bright late-morning sun. He stopped curbside and reflected on what had just happened. It was as if a load of bricks had been lifted from his shoulders. He had completed the first part of his mission: he was safely inside Argentina. But now what? He thought of hailing a cab for downtown, and finding a hotel room where he could sleep.

A whispering German voice came from behind him. "Good morning, Colonel. I have a car waiting. But we speak only Spanish in it."

Axel quickly did an about-face and found himself facing a lady in a red, floppy, felt hat. With her auburn hair, high cheekbones and deep-set green eyes, she was a strikingly beautiful woman. Her complexion looked suntanned or Latin, with bright red full lips, little makeup and a shapely figure covered by a conservative feminine business suit. Axel was momentarily speechless.

Finally he mumbled, "Who are you?"

The lady flashed a grin and whispered back, "General Hanke asked me to take you under my wing. I will explain everything at

---

[7] Fencing

your hotel. Let's get in the car. And remember – speak only Spanish."

Her German was faultless and she sounded native-born. Axel decided to trust her, but only because she had used the Reichsführer's name.

Their taxi sped down a few highways for La Plata, a small community a few miles south of Buenos Aires. From the backseat, their Spanish conversation was limited and only staged for the ears of the driver. When they got to the small town, Axel noticed that many of the street and business names were in German. The lady told him that the area had a large colony of German Nationals who had immigrated to Argentina after the humiliating defeat of WWI. The Colonel liked the news, as it made him feel a little more at home.

The hotel was a four-story white stucco affair, with red roof tiles and black wrought-iron verandas. The street that fronted the hostel was shade-tree lined, with cobblestoned sidewalks that were as clean as a starched bed sheet. Coming from war-torn Europe, Axel was impressed by the picturesque setting of La Plata.

After the driver was paid, the couple walked into the hotel together. The lady had already registered him and had paid for a one-week stay, with another week as an option. All that was required of him was to sign the registration form.

At the front desk, she whispered in his ear in a provocative way, "Your new name."

The desk clerk gave them a strange look, and for the first time the Colonel signed his new name, Señor Axel Garcia. He was handed a key for a room on the third floor, and the couple moved towards the stairs.

"You go on up," the lady said. "I have to make a few phone calls."

Axel found his room large, dark and stale, but clean. All the curtains had been pulled, to keep the heat out. These he swiftly opened and then walked around, opening several windows and the door to the veranda. The apartment quickly brightened, and the musty smells soon dissipated. A few moments later, as he was finishing up in the bathroom, there was a knock at his door.

Opening it he found the lady in the hall, with her index finger to her lips. She shook her head and mouthed, "No talking." Pushing past Axel, she entered the room and started looking under lamp shades and behind pictures. She even unscrewed the mouth piece for the phone. Then she went out onto the balcony and looked around at the neighborhood, two stories below.

Returning, she said in German, "We can talk freely."

Axel took a chair next to a built-in desk, and looked up at the lady. "Who the hell are you, Fraulein?" he demanded.

The lady walked to the room door and locked it, then came to rest on a white, overstuffed chair. Taking off her hat, she crossed her long, shapely legs and asked, with a disappointed look, "You don't remember me, Colonel?"

"Nein," he sternly answered. "And no more games."

The Fraulein took an ivory cigarette holder from her purse and placed an American Camel cigarette in it. She lit her smoke with a silver lighter and then tossed it to Axel.

"Look at the inscription, Colonel."

Axel looked at the lighter. One side was engraved with a swastika; the other side, twin lightning bolts. He had one just like it! It was a handcrafted Swiss Zippo, given to all new SS officers when they were inducted into the Brotherhood. "How can this be?" he asked, confused.

"We have met before, Colonel. You, Himmler, and your father attended my swearing-in ceremony in 1941. I remember it well. To have Himmler, your father who had the ear of the Führer – and you, a handsome young SS Lieutenant, in the audience had my class on Cloud Nine!"

The Colonel worked his memory and then, with a bright face, chuckled. "Yes, I remember now. Heinrich told me that it was the first time a few women were allowed to join the Brotherhood."

"And I was one of them," the lady said proudly.

"The Reichsführer also told me that all the women had outlandish nicknames."

"Mine was Scorpion, and it is still my code name."

"The spider that kills its own."

"I prefer the eighth sign of the Zodiac. It doesn't sound so deadly," she replied with defiant eyes.

"Either way, it is not much of a compliment for such a pretty Fraulein. What is your given name?"

"Nicole López is my Latin name; Nicole Lang is my German name. My father was a low-level Argentine diplomat in Berlin after the First War. He married my German mother in 1920. I arrived shortly after that."

"Where is he now?"

Her expression soured, and she looked away with a frown. "It doesn't matter. He was a man of little intelligence and less importance. After his posting expired, we moved to Argentina. Some time later, he was killed by a political rival, after which, Mother took me back to Germany, where I was raised."

"How did you end up back here?"

"Simple enough," she answered, with authority written on her face. "The SS posted me here in '43. I'm the Government Relations Envoy for the German Embassy."

"Why all the cloak and dagger behavior?"

"The current government has a secret police that rivals our Gestapo. They like to know what's going on, so being cautious is a way of life here."

There came a knock on the door, and muffled Spanish words, which startled the Colonel. Nicole smiled at him and got up from her chair. "I have taken the liberty of ordering you some lunch," she said, walking to the door. "I know you must be tired and hungry."

The bellboy pushed a white-tableclothed cart into the room and set it up next to the open veranda door. Nicole paid him and he was swiftly out of the room, after which she locked the door again.

The Colonel got up and moved to the cart. Looking down at it, he saw an ice bucket with three brown bottles of beer, some condiments and a single plate covered with a cloche. Removing it, he found a thick roast-beef sandwich on rye, with sauerkraut and pickles.

As Nicole walked over to the table, he asked, "Are you not joining me?"

She shook her head. "Nein. I have another engagement. You eat while I tell you about my role in your mission."

The Colonel wasn't sure he liked her superior tone, but he was famished. Moving quickly to his chair, he sat down and opened a bottle of beer.

"You will find the Argentine beef outstanding, the bread marginal, and the sour cabbage good. But it is our beer that you will enjoy the most," she said, and then launched into a long, detailed account, pacing the floor as she talked, and smoking one cigarette after another. She had a direct, secure communications with Germany, she assured him. All messages the Colonel received or sent would go through her. Axel's code name, she said, would be Condor, just as hers was Scorpion, and his outgoing messages would be limited to ten words, mostly code words. She knew the general details of his mission, and she would act as the security officer for the Argentine Odessa. "You will tell me everything you know, and when you learned it," she demanded.

"Why is there a need for a security officer?" the Colonel asked, spreading mustard on his sandwich.

Scorpion smiled broadly and raised her left arm, pushing back the short sleeve of her blouse. "Do you still have your blood type tattooed under your arm? I do not."

"Yes, it is an SS custom."

"Those identifying marks, and any others, such as the scar on your neck, will have to be removed. There is a local doctor who we can trust to erase them, but that will take some time. And Odessa wants no trouble from the current Farrell government. They are not our allies, as yet. But next year there will be an election, and the current Vice President, Juan Perón, will be elected the new President. Then we will have an ally we can trust. Until then, Colonel, you will need a security officer." She continued with a long list of general warnings, then changed the subject to the next few weeks. Her first objective was to secure a small local villa where he and other brothers could be trained and live safely. Then they would find a small office for their front company, the South American Mining Company. "Along the way," she said, stopping to stare at the Colonel, "I will also clean up your atrocious Spanish. Your words are filled with a German accent. For that reason, when I leave here today, you will not go downstairs or walk around the neighborhood. Use room service, and we will begin with lessons in the morning. Do you understand me?"

The Colonel, just finishing his sandwich, glared up at her. Opening the second bottle of beer, he asked, “And what SS rank do you hold?”

“Captain,” she replied proudly.

“You might want to remember that, when you address me in the future. I am not accustomed to taking orders from subordinates.”

Annoyance filled her face. “Listen, Colonel, I am your lifeline here in Argentina. You will not cross me, nor order me about. Give me your passport. I have something to show you.”

The Colonel got up, took his passport from his valise and handed it to her.

She opened the document to the picture page. “See the Argentine crest here, and what is behind it?”

He looked closely to where she was pointing and replied, “Two capital letter S’s.”

“Yes,” she said quickly, “SS’s means something special to us, and here in Argentina it means ‘Special Selection.’ All of our brothers will have passports with double S’s. That designation means ‘allow-in’ to every Immigration official in Argentina. That bribe took me almost a year to arrange, and cost many thousands of Reichsmarks. So you need me, Colonel, a lot more than I need you. My authority is not to be questioned.”

With his ire up, he replied, “What happens if Germany is defeated?”

With a sinister grin, she remarked, “I will stay in Argentina, as I have dual citizenship.”

She was one insolent bitch, and the Colonel was disappointed with her status. Her return to Germany would have taken care of the problem. But her words were true. “Very well, Captain. You will have my cooperation, but walk softly with your disrespectful tone. Do not trifle with me.”

Nicole glared at him for a moment, then reached for her hat. “I have to go. Do you need anything? Cigarettes? More beer?”

“I don’t smoke. It’s a filthy habit. And I don’t usually drink, so nada.”

Nicole turned for the door and unlocked it. But as she opened it, the Colonel asked, “Tell me about Argentina and its people.”

She closed the door again and looked back at him. "It is a country of poor people and peasants, governed by the rich who live here in Buenos Aires. The ruling class is as corrupt as the government itself. I know where the landmines are, and where the bodies are buried, so you are in good hands, Colonel. I'll tell you more tomorrow, when we get started setting up *our* Odessa network." She opened the door again and walked out, saying in Spanish, "Lock the door behind me."

The Colonel bristled and stared at the closed door for a long moment. Scorpion was an unforeseen wrinkle in his mission. While she was easy to look at, she was hard to tolerate. He didn't like her, and wouldn't trust her. But he did need her. Like the Jews, her time would come. There was no place in *his* Fourth Reich for impertinent women. Women like her were only good for giving birth to more Aryan babies.

Finally, he got up from the table, walked over to the door and locked it. Turning back to the room, he found the ashtray she had been using. Taking it back to the cart, he removed the longest cigarette butt and put it in his mouth. Lighting it, he reached for the last bottle of beer in the ice bucket. He *did* smoke and drink, but only privately. All bad habits were a sign of weakness, and he would not share his with anyone.

Submarine Bunker, Kiel, Germany

11 March 1945

Under the dim lights of the cement and steel bunker, with repair sounds echoing off the walls, Captain Miller stood on the aft-deck of U493, addressing his crew. Next to him were his friend and Executive Officer Max Kogel, and Breiner the Chief of the Boat. The crew, all forty-two of them, stood in three rows that filled the deck. They were a shabby-looking bunch, with unkempt beards, pale and dirty complexions, and uniforms that were mostly rags.

"As you all know, I have just returned from a meeting with the 7th U-boat Flotilla Commander, Kommodore Krug." The Captain paused, and then continued more loudly. "All of you have noticed the Type XXI boat, moored across the quay. She is the U-3521, and she is the true wonder weapon we all have been waiting for. She was to depart for her first battle mission later this evening.

Unfortunately, last night the shipyard came under a heavy bombardment from the British. The transit barracks took a direct hit which killed or wounded the majority of the new boat's crew, including her captain. Kommodore Krug has ordered me to take command of the sub, and to blend my crew with what remains of hers."

There were gasps and talking in the ranks, with surprised faces all around.

Miller raised his hand for quiet and continued. "I did not seek this promotion, nor did I volunteer you. It was a direct order. What remains of the crew of U-3521 will train you on the operation procedures for this new type of submarine. The boat *will* depart at 2100 hundred hours tonight."

A dark gloom hung on every face and angry words could be heard.

"There are showers, sinks and washing machines behind the bunker. These facilities *you* will take advantage of. Then pack your sea bags and report aboard the U-3521 no later than 1700 hundred. That is all."

The crew stood frozen in place, staring at their Captain until finally, from the ranks, a voice called out, "Where are we going, sir?"

Miller shook his head and replied, with regret, "That I cannot tell you. The crew is dismissed."

After the men scattered, the Captain asked Lieutenant Kogel and Chief Breiner to join him in his nook since it was clear to him that they, too, were shaken by the news.

Once inside his small compartment, Miller pulled the curtain closed and reached for what remained of his brandy. Taking three glasses in hand, he poured the balance of the bottle.

"Am I no longer the Executive Officer,"Kogel asked, taking his glass. Breiner asked the same question while taking his.

Reaching into his pocket, Miller pulled out a small piece of paper. "You two and these four other crewmembers will get packed and cleaned up. However, when you report aboard to the U-3521, you will be on standby. An hour after we depart, I will make an unscheduled stop and release you six for special duty."

Kogel looked at the names on the paper. "We are all family men."

"Yes," Miller replied, drinking his brandy. "Unfortunately, there are four others aboard that I just couldn't help."

"What is this duty?" Breiner asked.

"That you will soon learn," the Captain answered.

Miller went to the showers and, for the first time in weeks, shaved with hot water. Such a luxury! Then, returning to his old boat, he changed into his best uniform and packed up his sea bag. Walking through the old conning tower for the last time, he recalled all the missions he had completed aboard the type VII boats. He had been lucky, while so many others had perished. *Why*?

Crossing the wharf, he walked aboard the U-3521 for the first time as the new Skipper. He prayed his luck would hold and that their ludicrous mission would be a success.

Moving through the narrow, well-lit aft companionway, Miller found Lieutenant Kaplan in the Captain's cabin. And what a stateroom it was, twice the size of Miller's old nook.

"Just cleaning out his personal effects," the Lieutenant said, looking up from placing items in a box.

"Were you close to your Captain?" Miller asked placing his sea-bag on the bed.

"No, not really sir. He was a demanding Skipper with little patience for his officers or crew."

Miller took off his white cap and placed it on the desk. "Being a U-boat Skipper is not a popularity contest. The demands of command are something few of us can satisfy."

"What do you expect of me, sir? Am I still the boat's Executive Officer?" Kaplan asked with an earnest face.

"Aye, you are. I have a special detail for my old Exec and five others. One thing I do expect of you is keeping the daily logs. Nothing fancy, just position, fuel consumption, weather and the like. If something else of importance happens, I will instruct you to log it. Understand?"

"Aye, sir," Kaplan replied, his tone firm and confident.

"Have the torpedoes been removed?"

"Yes, sir, and space provided for our cargo."

There came a knock on the door. Miller opened it and found a short, olive-skinned sailor standing in the passageway. "Yes?"

"The Kommodore has come aboard, sir. He is in the wardroom, asking for you."

The Captain nodded. "Tell him I'll be there shortly," he said, and closed the door. Turning to the cabin, he asked, "Who is that sailor?"

"That's Oliver, sir. He is Greek, and the officer's steward."

Miller shook his head with a grin. "This boat has a steward? Mein Gott! Let's go and see the Kommodore. I want you to hear it all."

Krug had brought aboard a dozen navigational charts applicable to the mission. The three men huddled around the wardroom table for over an hour, discussing the details of the voyage. Fuel and supplies were a big issue, rough timetables and rendezvous grids were mapped out for each of the supply ships. Krug hoped that Miller would meet up with U-3520 before both boats were deep into the Pacific. He also expressed concern that Japan might want to commandeer the two wonder-subs. He warned Miller to stay alert and not to trust the Japanese.

As the men were finishing up, the steward poked his head into the room and announced that the cargo and passengers had arrived from Berlin. Captain Miller sent Lieutenant Kaplan to supervise the cargo loading.

"What of the passengers?" Kaplan asked.

"For now, put them in the crew's mess." Miller poured himself more coffee. "We'll do something more permanent with them after I have inspected the cargo."

"Aye, sir," Kaplan replied.

When the Captain returned to the table, the Kommodore folded up the maps, placing them in a thick pouch that the boat would retain. He looked old and tired, with dark circles beneath pale eyes. "Oh, before I forget," he said, looking across to the Captain. "I brought you and your officers a case of schnapps. Your steward put it in the officer's pantry. I thought you should know, since these Greeks can be thieves."

Miller regarded the old gentleman with respect. "Thank you, sir. My officers and I will toast your health, on the rare occasions that I allow drinking." He shook his head in wonder. "These new boats are certainly impressive."

The Kommodore looked around at the brightly painted, well-lit room and nodded. "Not like the old pig-boats I drove in the First War. But then, that was back in the glory days."

The two men reminisced for a long while. Miller was pleased to spend this time with such a legendary captain. Finally, however, Oliver returned and informed them that the cargo was ready for inspection.

In the forward torpedo room, the Kommodore and Miller found Lieutenant Kaplan, several crewmembers and two SS men standing by a large stack of wooden crates. Both of the SS men were dressed in black and silver uniforms, bracing themselves as the Kommodore entered the compartment. The SS Officer introduced himself as Major Wolfgang Schmidt and his Sergeant as Arnold Beck. Both carried Schmeiser burp-guns and holstered Luger pistols. The stocky Sergeant was gray haired, with a weathered face and sad eyes. The Major moved with a limp in his right leg and used a polished black walking cane with a silver skull as a handle. He had a young face, with deep-set eyes, and projected an aura of arrogance.

The Kommodore introduced Captain Miller to them, and he was given the Nazi salute. He returned it with a casual Kriegsmarine salute and looked down at the large stack of boxes. They all looked the same, in both size and markings. On top of each crate was the stenciled eagle emblem, with the Nazi insignia.

"Do we have a bill of lading?" Miller asked of his Exec.

"Aye," Kaplan answered, handing him the documents. "Fifty crates in all, sir. They are numbered on the side of each box. The first twenty-five are in the aft engine room. These are the last twenty-five."

The Captain reviewed the papers carefully. Everything looked official. There was even a Reichsbank logo on each page. Each wooden box was listed as holding twelve gold bars, except Crate 50, which contained only nine bars and what was listed as 'other assets.' There were 597 gold bars in total. Miller walked around the stack of crates, verifying that the count was right for this half of the cargo.

Pointing to a top box, he said to Kaplan, "Open Forty-Nine."

A seaman with a crowbar approached the cargo, but the Major shouted, "That is not possible! No one is to disturb this shipment. That is a direct order from Reichsführer Karl Hanke."

Miller glared across the cargo at the Major. "I am the Captain of this boat. Under Maritime Law, the Captain is required to inspect each and every cargo that comes aboard. This is not open to discussion."

The Major unshouldered his burp-gun and placed his right hand close to the trigger, staring back at the Captain without blinking.

"You have two options, Major. I look inside these boxes or you reload your trucks and return to Berlin. Which will it be?"

The Major's finger drifted towards the trigger of his machine gun, his expression one of contempt.

The compartment seemed frozen in time. Only the low hum of the overhead ventilation system could be heard.

"If you shoot me, Major, your cargo goes nowhere, and you'll be hanging from the yardarm before the smoke clears."

"The Captain is correct," the Kommodore said in a firm, loud voice. "Only a fool challenges one of my sea-lions. They have nerves of steel and hearts of stone.

Ever so slowly, the Major lowered his weapon and shouldered it again. A small grin chased his lips. "What the hell is a yardarm?"

"The spar of sail where old sea Captains hung their trouble makers from," the Kommodore answered while concealing a small Beretta pistol back into his coat pocket.

Miller nodded at the old gentleman with thankful eyes.

As soon as the box was opened, the Captain pulled away the wood-shaving packing material. Gazing down, he saw a row of four gold bars, with two more rows beneath. Each bar was stamped with the Swastika and twin lightning bolts of the SS. When he lifted a single bar up into the light of the compartment, its glitter was almost mesmerizing.

"Why the SS emblem?" he asked Schmidt.

"I have no idea."

The box was nailed shut again, and the Captain told the seaman to open Crate Fifty. Inside, he found nine bars and, in the void space, three fat leather pouches, which he opened. The first held hundreds of diamonds of all sizes. He poured a few out onto his palm and showed them to the Kommodore.

"What the hell?" was his only comment.

The next bag held other types of precious stones, also in various sizes. There were rubies, emeralds, sapphires, pearls and many other types. Their color sparkled in the palm of his hand as he showed them to his Exec.

Wide eyed, the Lieutenant commented, "My wife would like a few those, sir."

The last pouch held what seemed to be small raw gold nuggets. Pouring a few out, he soon realized he was wrong, for each nugget had a hollow in it. "What the hell are these, Major?"

Schmidt shook his head. "I have no idea."

The Kommodore moved closer and took one from the Captain's hand. "Damned if these things don't look like gold caps and crowns for teeth."

"Well, Major?" Miller asked soberly.

"You're asking me questions, sir, but I do not know. I have been busy protecting the Fatherland from the Jewish threat. Remember, though, that much of the Reichsbank loot came from Russians. You know how savage those Bolsheviks are."

Quickly, Miller returned the gold work to the sack and secured it. "Why don't I believe you, Major?"

Schmidt said nothing, but he glared at the Captain as the box was nailed shut again.

Finally, the Captain turned to Lieutenant Kaplan. "Secure the shipment, fore and aft. Use cargo netting and steel cables to lash the crates down to the deck cleats. I don't want these boxes moving around if we have to do some fast maneuvering. And confiscate the guns from the Major and the Sergeant, if you please. Unload them and secure them in the firearms locker."

"That will not happen," Schmidt replied firmly.

"Listen, Major, don't get into a pissing match with me. I will always win. Again, you have two choices, surrender your weapons or return to Berlin. Which will it be?"

"General Hanke is an old family friend," the Kommodore added. "Shall I telephone him and tell him of your inability to take orders?"

Scowling, Schmidt and his Sergeant unshouldered their machine guns and placed them on top of the cargo. Removing their holsters, they added their pistols to the stack.

"For your information, Major," Captain Miller said, watching them, "this submarine uses a pressurized hull. When we are submerged, which is most of the time, if one of those weapons went off and pierced our hull, the boat would collapse in upon itself from the weight of the sea. That is not a way you would want to die." Turning to the Kommodore, he continued, "Shall we meet our Japanese passengers, sir?"

As the two men turned to depart, Major Schmidt asked, "Where are my quarters?"

Miller turned back to him. "In the aft engine room. You'll find hammocks in the lockers."

"I demand officer's quarters," the Major answered.

Fuming, Miller turned back and said curtly, "I'll take it under advisement."

They found the family having tea in the crew's mess. Commander Naokuni Nomura spoke impeccable German, while his petite young wife and child spoke only Japanese. On the deck, next to them, the Captain noticed that they had brought large canvas bags of food and an oriental wok for cooking. There were also two family suitcases and the Commander had one large case next to him that he said were the papers from the German Admiralty.

They seemed like a pleasant family, and the Captain told them that their quarters would be in the forward torpedo room. "I will send my steward to help you move. It is a very large space, and you can use the cargo boxes as a table."

The Kommodore looked at his watch. "I have to go, Captain. Walk me out."

When they got to the top of the gangway, Kommodore Krug looked at Miller with sad and serious eyes. "There is no doubt that you are the right man to command this boat. I was very lucky when you stumbled into my port. But this SS Major worries me. He is going to be trouble. I've seen these types before, zealots with no common sense. 'Jewish threat' indeed."

"What do you suggest I do about him, sir?" The Captain asked.

The old gentleman grinned. "Well, you can't kill him, not unless you absolutely have to. But there are a lot of deserted islands out there. Maybe he and his sergeant would be happier on one of them. And give them that bag of gold teeth. Maybe they will find atonement, as well."

The two men shook hands, and Captain Hans Miller reflected that he was fortunate to have the old gentleman as his commander.

By 1700 hundred hours the entire crew had reported aboard and formed ranks on the aft deck. Captain Miller, Lieutenant Kaplan and Chief Huffman stood before the crew, passing out duty orders and bunk assignments. They also gave out news about the Japanese passengers and the two SS soldiers, and informed the men that a special departure meal would be served at 1800 hundred hours, after which the crew was to report to their duty stations and prepare the boat for getting underway. The Skipper was last to speak. He gave the men a rousing talk about teamwork and the importance of the upcoming mission. In the end, he was quite pleased with the first muster of his patched-together crew.

Just before departure time, Captain Miller walked into the control room and asked Chief Huffman to 'spark-up' the diesels. As he started up the ladder for the conning tower, he looked back and said with a smile, "Let's see if we can depart the shipyard without embarrassing ourselves."

Standing on the bridge, looking down on all the gadgets and instruments, the Captain felt as nervous as a new bridegroom. For the first time, he questioned his ability to skipper such a new wonder-weapon. He had much to learn.

From the open hatch below, Lieutenant Kaplan voice called out, "Permission to join the bridge, sir."

"Aye," Miller answered.

The Exec came up to stand beside him, and asked, "May I take her out, sir? It would be good experience for me."

"Aye," the relieved Captain said. He liked Kaplan's nimble mind. They would get along well.

An hour later, with the docking crew still on deck, the Captain stood on the sail bridge, using the new night-vision binoculars to maneuver the boat next to a wooden pier on the north side of the harbor. Once a few lines were secured, he called for Lieutenant Kogel and his detail to report topside. When they reported, with sea-bags over their shoulders, he walked the dark line of faces, making out the correct sailors.

Each was handed a green, endorsed shore pass. "You are my Comrades. We have served proudly together," the Captain said quietly. "The war is lost, boys. You all have families and should not be sacrificed. These slips of paper should get you through our lines, but most likely not through the Allied lines. Your shore leave is good for 90 days. If the war is not over by then, report back to the Kiel shipyards… if it's still there. Good luck and God speed, my friends."

With only a sliver of moonlight in the sky, and without saying a word, each of the men shook the Captain's hand. Then they climbed a wooden ladder to the dock above. Miller looked after them with dewy eyes, watching as the silhouettes of his men disappeared into the night. Climbing the sail tower again, he ordered all lines released and used the intercom. "Engine room, all ahead dead slow. Maneuvering, steer for deep water. Navigator, plot the quickest course for the Faroe Islands." Clicking off the microphone, he lit a cigarette. *At least my friends are safe… for now.*

Skies over British Columbia, Canada

10 April 1964

The small compartment filled with a loud roar and quivered as the wheels of the DC7 slowly lifted off from Boeing Field in Seattle, Washington. Settled in a window seat, in the last row of the nearly vacant first-class cabin, Dutch Clarke was preoccupied with a gold necklace he held in his hands. His in-laws had given him the small Saint Jude medallion for Christmas. Jude was the patron saint for the sick and suffering, and offered hope for their struggles. They had given his wife Laura the same pendant three years before, when she was first diagnosed with cancer. He had buried her with it. Now he had his own medal. Somehow, the medallion comforted him and brought his beloved wife's spirit closer.

Glancing out the window, he watched the city beneath grow smaller, as the land soon turned to the waters of Puget Sound. It was a bright and promising day, and he looked forward to his short trip to visit Skip and Louise Patterson. His father-in-law had purchased the first-class airline tickets and sent them to him, insisting that Dutch come up in early April to spend some time sailing together. Dutch smiled. His wife's parents were a fine, loving family, and now he relished spending time with them and his long-forgotten sailboat.

Ring. The overhead 'no smoking' warning light went out. Looking back down at the medallion, Dutch found his mind chasing back to last Christmas. It had been a marvelous time with the entire family together for one last holiday at the family estate. Then, the day after New Year's Day, the banks had foreclosed and Dutch had moved out. Now that part of his life was behind him. His future would be what *he* made of it.

"Would you like some champagne, Mr. Clarke?"

Startled by the voice, Dutch looked up and found a young, attractive stewardess with an earnest face standing in the aisle beside his seat. She was dressed in a brightly colored provocative outfit, with black leggings and white patent leather boots. She wore way too much makeup, and her blond hairdo was piled high like a beehive.

"Yes, please," he answered.

"I was admiring that medallion in your hand. Is it a Saint Christopher medal?"

"No, Saint Jude," Dutch answered, and slipped the necklace back into his jacket pocket.

"Oh. I thought you might have a fear of flying."

"No, although this is the first time I've flown to Ketchikan on a DC7."

The stewardess smiled. "Western Airlines just started flying this route two months ago. They had to make many of the Alaskan runways longer. I'll get your wine, sir."

Everything had changed. Modern fashions were outrageous, large airliners flew to Ketchikan, his wife was dead, and the family business gone. *My God! What next?* His attempt at suicide, before

Christmas, had frightened him. He was determined not to feel sorry for himself again. But something else was haunting him. The voice of his dead Marine brother, Jack Malone, was in his head. There was something Dutch was supposed to do, but he didn't understand what. Frustrated, he tried to block the thought from his mind.

On New Year's Day, Dutch had said his final good goodbyes to Hank and Helen Clobber, his former household staff. Then he'd loaded up his old Ford pickup and moved to a cheap motel on the Jersey Shore. A few days later, his New York lawyer called and told him that the people from Atlantic Petroleum, the vultures that had bought the assets of his old business, were all in a dither. One of the hundreds of boxes of documents sent over to them had gone missing. It contained all of the geological field surveys Dutch had done in the last fifteen years. They had signed for the box, but it had gone missing. Could Dutch rewrite the missing reports? After some negotiations, a deal was made. Working with his personal field diaries and his secretary from Gold Coast Petroleum, they had painstakingly reconstructed all of the reports. On the final day of the three month project, Dutch had picked up twelve thousand dollars for his share of that work. Sweet revenge! He now carried half of that payment in his money belt.

As the attendant returned with his glass of champagne, Dutch lowered his tray table. She placed a crystal glass of the bubbly wine on it, along with a small dish of cashews. "Is your wife in Ketchikan?" she asked cheerfully.

"My wife?" Dutch retorted.

"I noticed your wedding ring and saw your name on your one-way ticket."

Shaking his head, Dutch replied sadly, "No, I'm a widower. But she was originally from Ketchikan. I'm going up to sail our boat down to the lower forty-eight."

"Sorry, sir. I didn't mean to pry. Sounds like a long and lonely trip."

"The ocean is a good place to think. I'm Dutch. What's your name?"

"Renee. I'll be serving lunch in just a bit. Call me if you need anything."

Dutch watched her long, shapely legs and swinging hips, as she returned to the forward galley. Was she flirting with him? That made him uncomfortable. He wanted nothing to do with this new generation; their values were too screwed up.

The meal was good, a warm Reuben sandwich served with chips and a cold beer. After the forward cabin was served, Renee helped out in coach. After lunch, Dutch watched the coastline of British Columbia slip by, while his mind wandered through his yesterdays.

Once they landed, Dutch was one of the first in line to deplane. While he waited for the door to be opened, Renee approached him with a small Western Airlines tote bag. "Dutch, I hope you enjoyed your flight," she said, with a perky lilt to her voice. "I've put some treats inside for your long sail home. Wish I was laying over in Ketchikan. We could have hooked up."

Dutch looked inside the bag and saw nearly a dozen small bottles of liquor, half a dozen splits of champagne and handfuls of little bags of nuts and pretzels. With a broad grin on his face, he answered, "How sweet, Renee. Thanks for the thought."

Her blue eyes came alive with a look that Dutch had only seen on his wife's face before. "Hope to see you again, on one of my future flights."

The door finally opened, revealing a gray, rainy day. Dutch put his hat on and, with a blush on his cheeks, turned and walked down the wet boarding stairs. She had flirted with him! But what the hell did 'hooked up' mean?

Inside the tiny airport, Dutch found his in-laws waiting. Louise gave him a big hug as she welcomed him. She was a Swedish gal, with drab blond hair and blue eyes that were as bright as a sunrise. Although she had put on a few pounds, the years had been good to her. Skip's handshake was still firm as a rock, but his jet-black hair was now peppered with a few strands of salt. He was a fireplug of a man, short and muscular. His mother had been a full-blooded Eskimo, his father a Frenchman. He had one hell of a temper.

After Dutch picked up his single suitcase at baggage claim, they got into Skip's old Dodge pickup and took the short ferry ride to town. It had been four years since his last visit to Ketchikan, but the little town hadn't changed much. Most of the roads were now paved, and there were even two traffic lights downtown. The marina looked a little bigger, with a few more colorful fishing boats pulling on their mooring lines. Warehouses and fish packers lined the shore, seaplanes came and went from the waterfront, and the rainy climate hadn't changed at all. It was good to be back.

They soon arrived at the Patterson's hill-top home. The house wasn't anything fancy, but to the family it was a warm and cozy place filled with loving memories. And its view of the little fishing village below was spectacular.

Louise showed Dutch to Laura's old bedroom, where they had always slept. The neat, clean room was still filled with knickknacks and reminders of their daughter.

"Oh, Dutch, I haven't changed this room very much. If that's a problem, I'll tidy up while you have a drink."

Dutch put his suitcase on the bed and turned to Louise. "No, it's not a problem," he answered, and removed the gold necklace from his pocket. "It's like the Saint Jude medal you gave me at Christmas. It makes me feel closer to her."

With misty eyes, Louise forced a smile. "Good. You freshen up and come into the kitchen. We want all the news."

With Skip mixing martinis, and Louise working at her stove, Dutch entered the kitchen and was greeted with the familiar smells of his mother-in-law's wonderful cooking. Soon the questions came rolling in like the surf, starting a conversation that lasted for hours. Dutch told them what he knew of their grandson Edward's experiences at Annapolis. He told them of leaving the Estate for the last time, and of his three-month project with Atlantic Petroleum. They talked of all things fishing; the past season, preparations for the upcoming season, and the price the fish packers were paying.

"There are those who say the cruise ships may start coming to Ketchikan," Louise said. "They would bring up tourists who would spend lots of money here."

Skip scoffed at the idea. "Ketchikan will always be just a fishing village."

"And you will always be the king of the salmon, thanks to Dutch and Laura."

Skip's face got serious. "That's true, woman. We owe them much."

Five years earlier, Dutch and Laura had loaned them a hundred thousand dollars to purchase three new sixty-foot fishing trawlers. Then, a few months later, out of love and generosity, they had forgiven the loan and signed all three boats over to Skip and Louise. The three new boats were now the best fishing fleet in town, and Skip was indeed the king of the salmon.

"You owe me nothing. You are family, fini. But I owe you." Reaching for his wallet, Dutch removed a hundred and ten dollars. Extending the money towards Skip, he continued, "When I was in Seattle, I cashed in my return airline ticket. Here's your refund."

Skip's jaw dropped, and Louise frowned across her stove to Dutch. "Are you staying on here boy?" Skip finally asked.

"That would be wonderful!" Louise added.

Dutch shook his head. "No, I'm sailing the *Pacific Lady* south, maybe to San Francisco or Long Beach. Some place warm."

Skip's expression turned angry. "You have some sort of a death wish? A lone sailor on a small boat, traveling almost a thousand miles on the open ocean is foolish."

Dutch put the money on the countertop. "If you recall, I sailed the entire family down to the Dean Channel, four years ago. We were fine."

Still fuming, Skip took a big drink from his martini glass. "You had Laura with you. She was one of the best damn sailors in all of Alaska. And it was the middle of summer. You're asking for trouble, Dutch."

"Oh, Dutch, please don't do this," Louise pleaded.

Dutch raised his hand. "Enough. Please. Let's just enjoy our time together."

And that's what they did. Louise served up Dutch's favorite meal: her delicious fish stew in a spicy red sauce, French bread and Swedish potato salad. After dinner, they played Monopoly, with a lot of friendly family banter. Not another word was mentioned about his plans.

When Dutch went off to bed, he spent a few moments walking around the room, touching and sniffing his wife's old curios: her hair brush, her perfume, her handkerchiefs. He felt comforted, holding those items in his hand. It was as if she was in the room with him.

With fond and loving memories, he soon found sleep in her bed, but it was a restless slumber. Skip and Louise's warnings played over and over again in his head. Then his Marine brother came for a visit, with words that soon became crystal clear: *The answers you seek can be found on the battlefields of the Pacific.* He didn't fully understand, but he believed Jack's words, even the next morning.

Dutch and Skip were on the docks by seven a.m. The weatherman had promised several days of sunshine, with moderate winds and tides. Skip had mapped out a trip to Humpback Island, sixty miles up the Inland Passage. His goal was to check the waters for any early arrivals of pink salmon.

Carrying supplies and foul-weather gear, the men came up to Skip's three trawlers moored next to each other at the outer dock. With a hint of sunlight on the wharf, the colorful boats seemed to shimmer in the warm morning light. The impressive steel trawlers were all of the same general design, and painted white, although each had a different color of trim. Their decks were filled with gear, and their diesel motors idled in preparation for a day of fishing.

Skip stopped to talk to his crews, while Dutch continued down the quay a little way to where his sailboat was moored. He paused next to her, and his mind filled with a flood of memories. The *Pacific Lady III* was a sleek-looking boat. Built in California, the CAL24 was one of the first sailboats made entirely of fiberglass. Her white hull was twenty-four-feet long and her beam was eight feet. Dutch stepped into her spacious cockpit, then loaded his bundles below in a small cabin made of teakwood. The boat could sleep three, with two forward in V-berths and one on the cabin settee, which had a fold-up table. Hidden beneath one cushion of the couch was a small toilet with a direct flush to sea. Beneath the other was a cubbyhole where he stored three sleeping bags and extra blankets. The tiny galley had an icebox, a two-burner alcohol stove, and a sink with a pump connected to 25 gallons of fresh water stored aboard. The small compartment was well lit by two windows on each side of the raised cabin roof. At the very aft of the boat was the tiller, with a ten horsepower gas outboard motor attached to the transom. The *Lady* wasn't fancy but she was easy to sail, and practical as a weekender.

Dutch's first duty was to put on a pot of coffee. As it brewed, he checked out the boat from stem to stern. Extra sails were aboard, the bilges were dry, the battery for the CB radio worked, the rigging was correctly fastened, and safety gear was stored aboard. Just as the coffee finished brewing, he checked the gas for the outboard motor. Then he started it. With the weather improving, Skip and Dutch shoved off, using the motor, at half-past seven.

Half an hour later, they maneuvered the boat to the wide, calm waters of the Inland Passage and raised the sails. The little sailboat heeled over, and they were soon riding a brisk breeze. With the boat under his heels, Dutch was excited to be at the tiller again. The sun soon darted out from behind some clouds. With it warming his face, the art of sailing came rushing back to him, like learning how to ride a bike again. There was something peaceful about the quietness and the rugged beauty of the passing landscape. It was as if he was sailing in God's palm.

"See, Skip? I told you she was a fine boat," he said with a smile, helm in hand.

Skip grinned at him, enjoying the ride. "The ocean is vast and stormy, the Inland Passage narrow and calm. This boat was built for waters like these."

Nine hours later, they dropped anchor in a little cove on the leeward side of Humpback Island. Skip stood on the bow of the boat, his binoculars searching three small tributaries that flowed into the bay. Pointing to the nearest stream, he yelled, "See that bear sow and her cubs? They're fishing. The pinks must be in."

Dutch craned his neck and watched a huge brown bear with two young cubs, lurking on boulders in the middle of the stream, not two hundred yards away. It was a vivid reminder of the beauty and dangers of the Alaskan wilderness.

Skip returned to the cockpit and handed Dutch the glasses, then went below. Dutch asked him through the hatch, "How much water do we have under the boat?"

Returning topside with a fishing pole in hand, Skip answered, "Sixty feet, with a sandy bottom. We'll be fine."

Within moments, Skip had a line with a bright lure in the water. "Thought you didn't much like pink salmon. Didn't you say they were only good for canning?" Dutch asked.

"Aye," Skip answered, holding his pole. "They're also really good crab bait."

In less than a minute, he had hooked a fish and reeled it in slowly, keeping his keen eyes on the fish while counting others in the water. "Not many yet. We're still a little early. Another week and this cove will be teeming with them."

He brought the fish aboard. At less than two pounds, it was small. "Grab my crab pot, fill the big tub half-full of bay water, and get a fire going under it. We'll have a crab feed tonight, and it's time for a beer."

With the sun low in the sky, the two men fished, crabbed, and drank for the next few hours. The results were two fat Dungeness crabs each, a loaf of garlic bread, and leftover potato salad. The conversation was as varied as the meal, and finally the talk turned to Dutch's future plans.

"I've lost everything," Dutch said, with the sun slipping over his shoulder. "No wife, no business, no money. All I have is Edward, my godson Jack Jr., and this boat. Somehow, I have to get back in the game and find something worthwhile to do."

Skip lit a cigarette and finished his third beer. "One thing you have to learn is not to worship money. That would be your ruin. Use money only as a tool. Then it will be your salvation."

Dutch forced a smile. "That's easy enough. I don't have much of either."

"You have more than you know. And, by the way, Louise and I love your family, and that includes you. But sailing this boat alone for near a thousand miles down the coast is crazy. It's too small, its beam is too narrow, and that ten horsepower outboard is too puny. Hell, the core of the fiberglass used to build her is just three-eighths inch plywood, and you'll be sailing in unpredictable weather. It's a suicide mission!"

Dutch lit a cigarette and replied firmly, "It's been done before."

"Yeah, but by better sailors than you, pal. Look, I'll make you a deal. I'll crew for you as far as the Columbia River, if you agree to have this boat surveyed at the Warrenton Boat Works. They built all three of my trawlers, and they're experts on all things that float on the ocean. I want you to hear their professional opinion, before you go sailing off into the sunset. Do we have an agreement?"

Dutch looked at his father-in-law in the waning evening light, and then flicked his cigarette overboard and extended his hand. "Aye, we have an agreement my friend. Thank you. I know I'm a pain in your butt, with salmon season coming on."

Skip smiled broadly. "Now two fools are on your suicide mission. Get me another beer, Dutch, before I change my mind."

Chapter Three

Hacienda Canario, Argentina

20 December 1944

A few miles south of the city of La Plata, were the rolling hills and rich soil of the Santiago River Delta. There, Señor Axel Garcia sat atop a large gray horse, surveying the forty acres of range and farm land he had recently purchased. Soon the lower half was to be cultivated for growing hops, while the upper half would be fenced for grazing the livestock. The hacienda had been purchased from an anxious woman whose husband was a political prisoner of the current government. She needed money for a bribe to the trial judge and the prosecutor. Once her husband was released, the couple would flee to Brazil. Argentina was a corrupt society but, because of that, Señor Garcia had been able to purchase the estate for a pittance.

He spurred his horse farther down the hill. The last few weeks had been filled with activity. With the help of Nicole López, the Scorpion, he had rented a small office/warehouse in La Plata and staffed it with a trustworthy German woman, Helga Hahn, as the office secretary. Phone lines had been installed, business cards and letterhead printed and a large sign erected out front that proclaimed 'South American Mining Company.' The ruse of the phony business was almost set.

What was next needed was an Argentine with deep roots in the mining business, so they had hired a sixty-year-old geologist named Bruno Vega. The gray-haired, skinny fellow called himself a geologist. Deep down, however, he was just a wrinkle-faced rock hound. Señor Vega had discovered copper, tin and iron mines all over South America but because of the current economy he hadn't worked for years. He relished the chance of making 'one more great discovery.' With him and his rock samples in the warehouse, the ruse was complete.

Axel had also met with the Vice Present of the Bank of Buenos Aires, to claim his numbered bank account. He was surprised to learn that the money the bank held was in US currency. The *Reichsführer* must have been playing it safe, to have used US funds for the original deposit.

Axel opened a business account and put twenty-five thousand dollars' worth of Argentine pesos into it. He did the same for his personal banking account.

While signing the papers for the accounts, Nicole had said, "You should include my name on those accounts. You never know what might happen."

She was a pushy broad, and Axel was embarrassed that she had said it in front of the banker. "Not now, woman," was his annoyed reply.

She glared back at him with a look that could kill.

In the course of these encounters, Axel's Spanish had improved as well. He now had confidence with his new language and was almost beginning to feel at home. He had received and sent three secret messages to his uncle, the *Reichsführer,* and was making progress with the diplomatic codes. But the news from Germany was not good. The Eastern Front was collapsing, and the Western offensive had yet to begin. Part of him desperately wanted to be in the fight, while another part was happy to be safe in his new homeland. The Fourth Reich now rested firmly on his shoulders.

With the sun low in the sky, Señor Garcia turned his horse for the hacienda. When he neared the compound, he paused for a moment. The setting was quite pleasing: the white stucco house was nestled in a small grove of shade trees, with a driveway that connected to a country road. It was a twenty-mile drive to the office, so Axel had bought himself a used 1938 blue Mercedes, which he kept in a large garage at the rear of the house. There was also a roomy wooden barn, a corral and other outbuildings in the backyard. All these structures needed paint and mending. The former owners had moved out a few years before, leaving the estate in disrepair. The main Spanish-style hacienda was spacious, with four bedrooms, three baths, and a good-sized kitchen connected to a covered veranda. Axel even had his own study, complete with a fireplace and red tile floors. Nicole had thought the property too ostentatious for a mere mining company owner. Her choices had been a few villas closer to town, but they were all so tiny and dingy that Axel had refused. He was not going to live like a peasant, so he bought the estate on the cheap, and renamed it Hacienda Canario. The Scorpion had been furious, but she still hired a middle-aged German couple as his household staff. The woman cooked and cleaned, while the husband tended the livestock and did basic maintenance. They lived out behind the house, in a small cottage of their own. Axel supposed that the office Fraulein and the couple were also spies for Nicole, but he didn't really care.

In the barn, Axel unsaddled the horse and gave it a rubdown. Then he led his mount into a stall and put the feed bag on. As he watched the horse eat, he reflected on his Bavarian youth. He had practically been born in a saddle. There was something majestic about horses, and he was pleased to be riding again, even if it was just an old gray mare.

Axel walked into his hacienda, which was as quiet as a tomb. It was Wednesday, and his staff had the day off. Moving to his study, he poured himself a whiskey and lit an American cigarette from a hidden pack in his desk. Turning on the desk lamp, he sat down and enjoyed the privacy of his vices. He would have to send another message to Germany soon. The codes for the Odessa operation had been approved. Germany called the men fleeing to Argentina 'canaries,' and the radiograms would read something like: *Condor, two canaries by sea, or one canary by air.* When they arrived in-country, they would call an unlisted phone number and simply say, 'Canary,' and give their location so that they could be picked up. Everything seemed to be in place, and he looked forward to having some of his SS brothers around him again.

The desk phone rang. It was the Scorpion, calling from the embassy. "I have news," she said with excitement in her voice. "The Fuehrer has launched his Western offensive. Our forces are on the move, and the Battle of the Ardennes has started. This has been confirmed by the Americans on the radio. They are calling it the Battle of the Bulge. How exciting is that? And I've been summoned to meet with Vice President Perón tomorrow. I'm sure he wishes to personally extend his congratulations to the Fuehrer."

"I wouldn't be too sure," Axel answered. "There has been tension between our two countries lately, so walk softly and call me after your meeting."

"What about our Western offensive? You don't sound excited."

"The *Reichsführer* briefed me on the battle plans before I left Berlin. We'll keep our fingers crossed and our ears open. I'll turn on Voice of America. Call me tomorrow."

Late the next afternoon, Nicole barged through the company's front door and marched straight into Axel's small, drab office, where he was speaking with his geologist.

Axel looked up from his desk with an angry glare. "I told you to phone me."

"What I have to say is not fit for the phone," she said, scowling back.

Axel excused his geologist, and Nicole took a seat, with fire in her eyes. She lit a cigarette and then told the story of her meeting.

"He flirted with me at first, as most men do. Then he told me that a German U-boat Captain, Jürgen Wattenberg had walked into the Argentinian embassy in Mexico City and asked for political asylum. He wanted to know what I knew of this man. Then he hinted that, for a sizable campaign contribution, he might consider the request. His wording was vague, and he had a funny smirk on his face."

"Had you heard of this Captain before?"

"No, so when I returned to the embassy, I did some checking. Captain Wattenberg and twenty other German POW's escaped from an Arizona prison camp, a few days ago. Most of the men have been recaptured. But Wattenberg must have made it to the Mexican border, then crossed and hitch-hiked to Mexico City. What do we do?"

Axel smiled broadly. "Maybe we have our first Odessa Canary. When will you see the Vice President again?"

"Tomorrow at eleven-thirty. He talked about taking me to lunch."

"Good. I'll pick you up at the embassy at eleven, and join you for your meeting. But first, I'll stop off at the bank."

"Won't that seem a little strange?"

"No. Just introduce me as Axel Garcia, a local miner of German descent. I'll do the rest."

The Vice President had a suite of offices in one of the many government buildings in downtown Buenos Aires. The capital edifices were large and impressive, with marble steps and Greek columns. Argentinian flags and large pictures of President Farrell and Vice President Perón were on display everywhere. In many ways, the complex of white buildings reminded Axel of Berlin before the war.

Nicole led them through the maze of offices until they reached the Vice President's suite. She checked in with the main secretary, who had them take a seat to wait. A few moments later, the massive double oak doors to the Vice President's office opened, and Juan Perón and a gorgeous young lady emerged. The Vice President noticed Nicole waiting, and they walked over to her.

"Miss López, how nice to see you again," he said. "I would like to introduce you to my fiancée, Eva Duarte. Eva, Miss López is with the German embassy."

The two ladies shook hands and exchanged an odd glance. They were both beautiful woman, and everyone in the office was staring at them. When Nicole introduced Axel as a local miner of German descent, the two men also shook hands, and Alex found Perón's grip firm and determined.

"Eva, was just leaving. I will walk her to the door and then we can meet," the Vice President said.

Moments later, they were seated in front of the Vice President in his massive ornate office, where soaring windows looked out at the Presidential Palace. Perón was a handsome man, tall, lean and trim as a boxer. His teeth were near perfect and bone white. His face was friendly, with a perpetual smile and probing blue eyes.

Nicole told him what she had learned about Captain Wattenberg, describing how he had walked over one hundred and thirty miles across a desert to make it to the border. "He is a brave man, and the German government hopes you will consider his asylum."

The Vice President turned his gaze to Axel. "So, what is this man to you, Señor Garcia?"

"Nothing really, sir, but I would consider sponsoring him."

"Señor Garcia is prominent in the local German community," Nicole inserted.

"Are you of German decent?" Perón asked.

"Yes, sir. My family immigrated here after the first war. I was born in northern Argentina, where my father worked as a miner. That's how I got into the business."

"So, both of you wish me to grant asylum to this man?" the Vice President asked.

"Yes, sir," Axel said quickly with an earnest face. He reached into his coat pocket and brought out a small brown envelope. "That reminds me, sir. I wanted to make a contribution to your upcoming campaign." He laid the envelope on the desk. "The mining business has been good to me, and I look forward to you becoming our next President."

The Vice President opened the envelope and looked inside. His expression showed that he was surprised by the contents. "Yankee one hundred dollar bills. Are you trying to bribe me?"

"No, sir. I only hope you will *consider* his asylum."

"Why gringo money?"

"The American dollar is fast becoming the international currency, and it is very portable."

The Vice President thought for a long moment, then grinned at Axel. "I approve your sponsorship, Señor, and will grant his asylum." He slid the envelope into one of his desk drawers. "Now, will you join Eva and me for lunch?"

The lunch was delightful. Eva captivated the table for almost two hours. The Vice President was relaxed and friendly, greeting his many admirers at the restaurant. The lunch chatter was light, and the food excellent.

On the drive back to the embassy, Nicole expressed her concerns. "You should trust my instincts, Colonel. I know these people better than you do. Offering a bribe to the Vice President was a foolish idea. He could have had us arrested on the spot."

Alex smiled at her. "I've seen men like him before. Taking your first bribe is hard, but after that they all come easy. Don't worry. Juan Perón has been in government a long time. He knows how to run a banana republic."

On Christmas day, Captain Wattenberg flew into Ezeiza Airport from Mexico City. Both Axel and Nicole were there to greet him. They whisked him away to the hacienda, where Canary Number 1 was taken under the wing of Argentine Odessa. It would take months of tutoring to prepare him to survive in his new environment. Along the way, he would be taught Spanish, the history of Argentina, and the culture of its people. Meanwhile, Axel was pleased to have another warrior under his roof, and they spent hours together, listening to the war news and talking all things German.

It was not the plan of Odessa to buy entry for their men. They would depend on the forged documents provided by the German Odessa. The case of Wattenberg, however, was quite different. He was one of only two U-boat Captains held in American captivity, and his escape made international news. The Americans even proclaimed that he had been recaptured, but obviously this was just Yankee propaganda. The twenty-five hundred dollars paid for his freedom had been worth the price. And Axel had made friends with the next President of Argentina, a relationship he would cultivate.

He didn't have to wait long. After the New Year, he and Nicole were invited to dinner at the private residence of Vice President Perón. Delighted, they promptly accepted. In the expectation that it would be a gala event, they both purchased the proper attire.

On the given evening, at the given time, they nervously stood before the imposing home of the Vice President in a rich neighborhood of Buenos Aires. Axel was dressed in a white Brazilian summer suit with dark Panama hat, although he secretly wished he was wearing his black SS uniform, much more impressive. Nicole was dressed in a revealing red summer evening outfit, with a large yellow flower tucked into her hair. Her makeup was impeccable, her high heels tall, and her shapely legs covered with silk stockings. Nicole was stunningly beautiful, and Axel had to keep reminding himself that she was the Scorpion and not to be flirted with.

A butler opened the front door, and the couple was shown into a parlor off the foyer. There they found Juan Perón reading a newspaper. He looked up from his armchair with an expression of surprise.

"Are we too early, Mr. Vice President?" Axel asked.

Getting to his feet, he extended his hand Axel. "I told my secretary this was to be a casual affair. Obviously she didn't listen." The two men shook hands. Then Perón gave Nicole a hug and continued, "Don't you look striking tonight, Miss López. You are a gorgeous senorita. Eva will be down in a moment. She is upstairs, freshening up."

"How many will there be?" Axel asked.

"Just the four of us," Perón answered, moving to a mahogany sidebar. "Let me mix us some drinks."

A few moments later, the parlor door opened and Eva entered wearing a white silk blouse and a yellow summer skirt. Her beauty filled the room as she greeted her guests. "Juan and I so enjoyed our lunch together that we wanted to get to know you better. I'm sorry you weren't informed it was casual. Please forgive us."

Perón handed the ladies champagne, and prepared whiskey sodas for the men. Then they walked out onto the veranda. The couples came to rest at a patio table and spent an hour, and another round of drinks, talking about the weather, world news and Argentinian politics. It was a friendly exchange, punctuated with much laughter. As the sun set, servants served a cold seafood dinner with local wines on the veranda. It was delicious and the conversation soon turned to the local theatrical scene. Eva had made a few movies and was planning on doing a play in the fall. She was a rising star, and Nicole seemed quite impressed.

After dinner, Perón invited Axel into his study for cigars and cognac, leaving the women on the patio to talk of Hollywood movies. The study was lavish, with floor-to-ceiling book shelves and a massive antique mahogany desk in front of three tall windows that reflected the rising moon. The Vice President went to a bar in one corner of the room and moved behind it.

Axel followed and took a bar stool facing him. A box of Cuban cigars appeared from behind the bar, and both men lit up. With blue smoke hanging in the air, two crystal snifters were filled with what remained of a bottle of Napoleon cognac.

Perón tipped his glass to Axel. "Here's to you, Señor Garcia. Thank you for the campaign contribution. Has your ward arrived yet?"

Axel swirled his glass. "Yes, sir. On Christmas day, thanks to you." He tipped his glass to his host and took a drink. "If need arises, I would sponsor more. All I ask is no Jews, no Gypsies, and no Bolsheviks."

The Vice President chuckled. "Who the hell are you really?"

"Just a German national with a love for my people," Axel answered, puffing on his cigar.

"Why don't I believe you?" Perón asked.

"Well, sir, given the recent news from the Western Front, Germany is in a struggle for her life. Many might need my help."

That started a lengthy discussion of the war. Perón proved quite knowledgeable, and offered many opinions on the likely outcome of World War II. At one point he held up the empty cognac bottle and asked, "Would you fetch me another from the bar in the parlor?"

Axel moved across the foyer to the open door of the parlor. The room was almost dark, with only a small light burning on the bar top. He found the right bottle and turned to leave. As he did so, he glanced out to the veranda, through the open French doors. What he saw froze him in his footsteps. Nicole and Eva, standing in the moonlight, were locked in a passionate embrace. It was an unexpected scene that made his blood boil. He walked to the open door and loudly cleared his throat. Instantly, the surprised pair parted. Eva turned her frightened face to him and sobbed, "Oh God, please don't tell Juan." Then she turned and ran into the night shadows.

Nicole walked towards him, clearly angry. "What's your problem?"

"Trust your instincts, my ass," Axel blurted.

"Down here, women kiss each other," she angrily replied.

Axel approached her, tempted to slap her face. "Not the fiancée of the next president of Argentina, you arrogant bitch!"

Faroe Islands, North Sea

15 March 1945

With the sun setting in the western sky, the U-3521 surfaced into rolling seas and moderate winds. Captain Miller and his navigator, Karl Fritsch, were first on the sail bridge. Both men used binoculars to check that the seas and skies were safe before calling up the lookouts. At dead slow speed the submarine pitched with the swells of the limitless green sea. The Faroe Islands were visible off the port bow, as the boat was only a few miles west of the islands. The windswept Danish archipelago was situated between the Norwegian Sea and the North Atlantic, only 200 miles north of Scotland. It was a dangerous place to be, due to the unforgiving weather and the ever-present British Navy.

"Get your position quickly, Karl. I don't want my ass hanging out here very long," Captain Miller said, with sunshine on his pale face.

Lieutenant Fritsch raised the sextant to his eye. "Where are we heading, sir?"

"South," the Skipper replied, and lifted the intercom receiver. "Maneuvering, make your course 210 degrees and increase speed to one third. Radar and Sonar, are we still clear?"

"Aye, sir," came both responses.

"I've got it, sir," Karl said, notebook in hand.

Miller nodded to him and shouted, "Lookouts below."

As the sailors slid down the open hatch, the Skipper said, "Plot us a course to Lisbon, Portugal."

"Well, that should be interesting. It will put us right in the middle of the Allied shipping lanes."

"Aye," the Captain replied with a grin. "We might not feel the sun again for a week."

After the lookouts and the Navigator slid down the hatch ladder, the Captain followed. Pausing on his way down, he secured the hatch from the sea, then slid down the rest of the way, landing on the conning-tower deck.

Turning to his crew, he ordered, "Chief, take her down to ten meters and start snorkeling. Once the batteries are fully charged, make your depth twenty meters."

"Aye, sir," the Chief replied.

Turning to Lieutenant Kaplan, the Captain continued. "Exec, you have the bridge. I'm going to get some sleep. Call me in six hours and I'll relieve you."

"Yes, sir," Kaplan replied.

Captain Miller had been on his feet for days and was almost punch drunk from the lack of sleep. But when he got into his bunk, he tossed and turned, his mind still swirling with worries about his crew, the mission, and the boat.

Three days before, after he'd dropped off his comrades near the Kiel shipyard, Major Schmidt had stormed into his compartment, his face suffused with anger.

"I saw what you did back there. Who gave you the right to release six of your crew?" he demanded.

"They are on a special detail, Major."

"You are a traitor, Captain, and I demand an official inquiry into your actions."

Miller glared at the SS Major for a long moment. "All of those sailors carried special passes signed by Commodore Krug. Their mission is none of your affair and we have not depleted this boats crew in any way, so remove yourself from my compartment."

"I will add to the inquiry that you have not provided me with proper officers' quarters, as called for in the regulations. You are forcing me to sleep with enlisted personnel. That is not acceptable!"

"He's *your* sergeant, Major. You brought him aboard."

"That makes no difference. It's still not right," Schmidt insisted.

Miller turned to the intercom and flipped the lever on. "Bridge, Captain here. Major Schmidt is demanding an official inquiry into my actions of releasing six crewmembers and requiring him to sleep with his sergeant. Log it, Exec." There was snickering on the other end of the line.

The Captain released the lever and turned back to Schmidt. "Now, you have two choices Major: get the hell out of my cabin or I'll pull over and drop you off. Which will it be?"

Fuming, the Major gripped his walking stick so hard that his hand turned red. Then he turned and limped out of the compartment.

Miller knew that the man would be a problem all the way to the Pacific. But they were experiencing a temporary reprieve, since the poor fellow became horribly seasick as soon as the boat entered the Baltic Sea.

When they arrived at the Kiel Lighthouse, a recognition signal was flashed; then the boat headed for deep water. In stormy seas, with a faint sunrise on the eastern horizon, U-3521 made her first dive.

The next three days would prove to be a shaky start. All the systems and operating procedures of the boat were foreign to his crew. On that first dive, the sub almost sank, due to the values being in the wrong position. It had taken quick action from Chief Huffman to stop the boat's rapid decent. On one surfacing run, the bubble of the boat was so far out of balance that the sub shot straight up like a cork. Then there were problems with the ventilation system, the snorkel device and the bilge pumps. But of all the new equipment, the radio, radar and sonar systems were the most challenging. His old crew had two radio and sonar operators, but none survived from the original U-3521 crew. Only Lieutenant Kaplan and Chief Huffman had any idea how to run the equipment. As a result, they used the manuals and spent three excruciating days teaching the crew that new technology.

Then there was the makeup of the crew itself. The engine room was short two mechanics, while the galley had two cooks. And his blended crew included two Ensigns, the last thing he needed. But they had completed the first leg of their mission. For that, he was pleased.

Sprawled out on his bunk, Captain Miller heard the low hum of the electric motors. It reminded him that, when the crew and the boat were in harmony, the U-3521 was indeed a magnificent fighting machine. As his eyelids grew heavy, his mind raced back to the glory days of the U-boats. Were those days gone forever?

The voyage to Lisbon would take seven to nine days, depending on weather conditions and possible interference from the Allies. Miller kept thinking about the old man's instructions: *This mission is defensive, not offensive*. He was to avoid any contact with the enemy. Still, his boat had to be prepared for every eventuality, and so the next day, he and his crew trained on the boat's offensive capabilities. The battle station alarm was sounded, and they surfaced many times, with battle crews scrambling topside to man and test-fire the twin anti-aircraft guns. Then they would crash dive and make mock torpedo runs.

At one point, Captain Miller ordered the torpedoes loaded into their tubes.

The Chief of the forward torpedo room came back on the intercom. "That might be a problem, Captain. You might want to come and see for yourself."

Moments later, he and Lieutenant Kaplan were standing in the forward torpedo room, gazing at a sight they couldn't believe. Everywhere in the room, colorful laundry hung in the air. Clothes dangled from the torpedoes in their racks and in front of the torpedo tubes themselves. Every lever and valve was draped with Japanese laundry. Moreover, there was a burnt odor in the room. As they moved farther into the compartment they found Commander Nomura wife, Choko, standing next to the cargo crates which were draped with a white table cloth. She was holding her child under one arm while swinging a meat cleaver with the other. The crew were just standing around with grins on their faces.

"What the hell goes on here Chief?" The Captain demanded.

"I tried to talk to her, sir, but she doesn't understand. She just keeps yelling at us in Japanese. She must think we are trying to steal her clothes. "

"What is that smell?" Lieutenant Kaplan asked.

"They have been cooking in here ever since we left Kiel," replied the Chief.

Miller didn't know whether to laugh or scream. "Where is her husband?"

"At his battle station in the engine room, sir," the Exec answered.

"Get him in here, Lieutenant. Explain to him – no more cooking, no more laundry. This is a torpedo room, not a laundry room." Turning to the Chief, he continued. "Once the washing has been removed, call me on the bridge. We will try this exercise again."

The practice drills went on all day. At first, the times were slow and clumsy, but improved as the day progressed. Even the torpedo room was brought back into action, and the men were soon loading and unloading the tubes.

That evening, there came a knock on the Captain's compartment door. When Miller opened it, he found Commander Nomura standing at attention in the passageway.

"Sir," the Commander said stiffly, "I've come to ask for your forgiveness for breaking the rules of your boat. I have brought a bottle of *sake* as my atonement. May we talk, sir?"

The Captain allowed him in, and showed him a seat next to his small desk. "It has been years since I last tasted *sake*," Miller said, reaching for two glasses. "Will you join me?"

The Commander opened the bottle and poured the rice wine into the glasses. "I'm concerned you will think poorly of us for our behavior." His German was flawless, and his white uniform impeccable, with two rows of colorful ribbons.

"Being a Navy man, I thought you would know better," Miller answered.

Nomura handed the Skipper a half-full glass. "This is the first submarine I've ever sailed on, sir, and the steamship that brought us to Germany was the first boat we had ever traveled on. My wife is very traditional. Cooking and cleanliness is very important to her. Unfortunately, I didn't think anything of it. You have our apologies, sir. "

Captain Miller was surprised by his confession. How could a decorated Japanese Commander be so inexperienced? He had much to learn of Naokuni Nomura and his enlightenment started that night. The Commander had been a logistical planner for the Imperial Navy for many years, before coming to Berlin as the Naval Attaché. In addition, he was the third cousin to Emperor Hirohito. That explained his rank, ribbons and rawness. But he was also a curious man who, with a second drink in hand, changed the conversation to the Type XXI U-boats. He asked many questions, and Miller gave him many vague answers. Attaché was really a code word for 'spy,' in Berlin, and while Captain Miller liked the man, he didn't trust him. With the bottle half gone, and Nomura a little tipsy, the two men said good night.

The next day, Captain Miller moved the two Ensigns from their tiny compartment to hammocks in the forward torpedo room, then moved the Nomura family into the cabin. It would be cramped quarters, but better than what they'd had. He also instructed the family to take their meals in the officer's wardroom. Then he made arrangements with the cooks that allowed Choko to prepare one traditional meal a day in the ship's galley. And if they were unhappy about the intrusion of a woman cook in their galley, Miller noted with satisfaction that they did not say so. There was much to be said for naval discipline.

At 0500 the next morning, Captain Miller was roused by the Exec. Sonar had multiple bogies on a zigzagging course. The skipper dressed and rushed to the control room. Hunched over the sonar man, he counted thirty or forty hits on the round green screen. The ships were traveling north-northeast and were twenty miles out. The U-3521 was heading due south at periscope depth. They were on a collision course.

"Are they pinging?" he asked the sonar man.

"Not yet, sir," was the reply.

"Radar, do you have anything in the sky?"

"No, sir."

"What time is sunrise?" he asked, turning to the Navigator.

"0634, sir."

Twisting to Chief Huffman, he continued, "Call general quarters and take the boat down to sixty meters. Maneuvering, the convoy is off our starboard bow. Once we have completed the dive, reduce speed to silent running. We'll let them come to us."

Looking down at his wristwatch, he moved to the navigator's station. Studying the map on the table, he was sure they had stumbled onto a large convoy heading for England. He had not seen this many targets in years, and his mouth watered.

"The crews are at their battle stations, sir," the Chief of the boat announced.

Captain Miller reached for the intercom lever and spoke into the microphone. "Torpedo room, load all six tubes and stand by."

Once they were at sixty meters, they waited and watched the clock. Miller paced the deck, stopping every few minutes at the sonar screen. Time drew out slowly, one tick at a time. He knew he had a decision to make.

At 0610, he turned to Huffman and said, “Take her up slowly, Chief, to periscope depth. Keep your bubble balanced. I don’t want to make any noise.”

The skipper moved to the periscope and placed his hand on the lever, waiting patiently as a crewmember called out the depth. The control room was like a coffin, with everyone holding their breath. A few bubbles could be heard rolling off the hull, as the sub moved ever so slowly to the surface.

At ten meters, Miller upped the periscope to his eye level. As the water washed away from the lens, he twisted the scope from one side to the other. He could not believe his view. They were right in the middle of the largest American convoy he had ever seen. In the dim morning light, he twisted the periscope 360 degrees. There were freighters, tankers, troopships and warships of all sizes. But the biggest target of them all was an aircraft carrier, sandwiched between two destroyers only a mile away. America’s might was on parade.

“Exec, hand me the recognition book,” Miller requested, lowering the periscope.

Thumbing through the pages, in the dim control room light, he stopped on one page with a large silhouette. Handing the book back to Kaplan, he raised the periscope and peered through the eyepiece again. “We have stumbled into the middle of a convoy that stretches from one horizon to the next,” he said to the room, slowly twisting the lens around. “And less than two miles off our port bow is the biggest target, an American Casablanca aircraft carrier. She is ten thousand tons, has a crew of nine hundred, and carries twenty-eight aircraft.”

Miller pulled his eyes away from periscope and stepped back. “Exec, please confirm.”

As Kaplan approached the periscope, the Captain continued. “Sonar, are they pinging yet?”

“Yes, sir,” was the sailor’s excited reply, “but their signal is weak.”

The Exec finished his time at the lens and stepped back. “Sighting confirmed, sir.”

Captain Miller approached the periscope and lowered it. Then he turned to Chief Huffman. "Take her down to hundred meters and rig for silent running. We'll let the convoy pass us by before we resume our course for Lisbon."

The control room crew let out a loud groan, and even in the dim red lights the Captain could see their faces, surprised and angry. He reached for the intercom microphone and told the entire boat what he had just seen, and what actions he had just ordered. Closing the message, he said, "It is with a heavy heart that I retreat from this battle, but my direct orders from Commodore Krug are to avoid direct contact with the enemy at all costs. That is all."

Turning to his Exec, he concluded, "Notify Sub-Command of the convoy's position. I'll be in my cabin."

As he moved through the boat, all the crew members sent resentful, sidelong glances his way. Miller felt their pain and hoped he would not regret his actions. In the passageway, Miller saw Sergeant Beck coming out of the galley. One side of his face was bruised and puffy.

"What the hell happened to you, Sergeant?" he asked.

"Just bumped into a bulkhead, sir," he answered, without making eye contact. Then he turned and scurried away. *How strange,* the Captain thought.

It had become the custom aboard to listen to Radio Berlin for an hour after each evening meal. That night, Miller gave instructions to the radio operator to include an hour of the BBC, as well. He had seen America's might firsthand, and he would ready his crew for the coming defeat.

Every U-boat skipper in the fleet knew of the bizarre port of Lisbon. When Portugal proclaimed neutrality in 1938, it interned all foreign vessels in the harbor, but the government allowed these ships to take on fuel, supplies and new personnel as needed. This started an economic tightrope between the Allies and Axis powers, and quickly turned the city into the center of the European black market. Soon, Lisbon was known as the harbor of hope and intrigue.

One of the ships to be interned was the *Wilhelm Russ*, a German-owned, aging passenger liner from the First World War. She had become one of the supply ships for the U-boats heading for the Mediterranean and beyond. Submarines from all nations were allowed into the port, but only under the cover of darkness. They had to be gone by the next morning. The Lisbon port officials looked the other way, in return for hefty bribes paid by interned Captains.

At 2100 hours on March 23, the U-3521 slipped into the Lisbon harbor. It soon located the *Wilhelm Russ*, anchored away from the waterfront and lit up like a Christmas tree. The sub maneuvered and was soon tied up on the seaward side of the liner, so it couldn't be seen from shore. As the boat prepared to take on fuel and supplies, Captain Miller and his Exec went aboard the mother ship to meet her Skipper.

They found Captain Higgins in his plush office just off the promenade deck. He was a huge, heavy-set man with beady black eyes and many chins. He wore a Captain's Merchant Marine uniform that was too small for his girth. Gesturing to a side table, he offered his guests schnapps, and they all took a seat. Higgins handed Miller a typed-out inventory of goods to be loaded aboard. It was the usual list of supplies, the bland fare of starches and sausages for the iron coffin's crew.

"No fresh fruit or meat?" Miller asked, sipping his drink.

"*Nein*, the government will only pay for those on the list," the fat man answered. "Fresh fruit and meat are considered luxuries, these days."

Captain Miller reached into his pocket, brought out a small slip of paper, and read the contents to Higgins. "Four full cases of oranges and apples, three dozen pineapples, one side of beef, a dressed-out hog, five cartons of fresh eggs, two cases of American cigarettes, a case of scotch whiskey and two bottles of Japanese *sake*." Miller handed the paper to the fat man. "Are these items available, sir?"

Higgins gazed down at the note and replied, with a smirk, "Yes, but too expensive for submariners. All these items could be found in the markets of Lisbon, but German money has no worth, these days."

The Skipper reached back into his pocket and brought out a small envelope. Opening it, he let the contents fall onto the table, five diamonds of various sizes. Higgins's jaw dropped, and Lieutenant Kaplan's expression froze.

The fat man moved to his desk and removed a jeweler's loupe from a drawer. Returning, he looked carefully at each diamond. "I could do this, but without the fresh meat. It's just too damned expensive," he said while examining the last stone.

Miller put his closed palm out in front of Higgins, then opened it slowly, revealing a large, bright-red ruby.

With sweat running down his forehead, the fat man snatched the stone and put the loupe to it. "Hmm" he mumbled. "Yes, yes, we can do this! For one more small diamond, I can also include hundred French postcards for the crew's amusement and a gross of condoms for their next port of call."

Miller grinned at the buffoon, "No, where we are going, neither would be very useful."

"Fine," he answered, "I'll send men ashore for your needs. We must hurry, though. Your boat must be gone by 0500."

As Captain Miller and his Exec hurried back to their submarine, Lieutenant Kaplan asked, "How did you do that, sir?"

Moving down the promenade deck, Miller grinned at his Exec. "When I was a boy, I wanted to be a magician. Knowing that we were coming here, I used a little sleight of hand, that day in the torpedo room," he said, then sobered. "I only wish that I could make this mission disappear as easily."

Queen Charlotte Sound, Canada

24 April 1963

With the sailboat heeled over in a brisk port tack breeze, Dutch and Skip entered Queen Charlotte Sound. The day was steel gray, with a threat of rain and manageable seas with long, deep swells. The men had waited ten days in Ketchikan for a weather forecast that promised a few days of winds out of the northwest and relatively calm seas. But it was spring time on the Inland Passage, and they knew that conditions could change in the blink of an eye.

Early that morning, Skip's wife, Louise, had seen them off at the dock. She had loaded the little sailboat with enough provisions for two weeks, more than enough food for the time Skip had predicted it would take to sail to the Columbia River. Then, standing on the quay, her eyes dewy, she had given Skip and Dutch instructions about staying safe. She was not happy that her husband had volunteered to sail south with Dutch but, being a fisherman's wife, she knew that the sea was calling, and there was nothing she could do. She hugged and kissed both men and said goodbye. Then she turned and walked away. "I'll be waiting," was all she had to say.

With his hands firmly on the tiller, Dutch twisted his head aft and watched Duke Island, the southern-most main island of Alaska, melt away in their wake. Just behind that outcropping was Annette Island, its tall gray-green peaks now looking small and unimposing. A few hours before, they had stopped at the Indian village of Metlakatla, the only town on the island. Almost twelve hundred Tsimshian Indians lived in the settlement. Skip, being a native himself, knew the local Chief and many of the villagers. It was always his custom to stop at the village for the Chief's blessing before navigating the open waters of the Dixon Entrance.

Dutch turned his head forward and surveyed the vast gray Pacific that sprawled out before them. They had fifty miles of open ocean to sail before reentering the protected Inland Passage again. He turned to Skip, who sat next to him in the open cockpit. "Those were nice people back at Metlakatla. Is that your tribe?"

"Nah," he replied. "My mother was a full blooded Haida Indian, my father French with a little Athabascan. I started stopping there thirty years ago. It's a native tradition of respect. But the funny thing is, today was the first time, in all those years, it wasn't raining. I think that's a good omen for our trip."

As those words rolled off his lips, a sudden squall blew through. Skip jumped to his feet, reefed the mainsail and eased the jib, then went below and put on his yellow foul-weather gear. Returning to the tiller, he relieved Dutch to do the same. With a wind chop on the water and curling seas, the *Pacific Lady III* sliced swiftly in a southwesterly direction. Five hours later, the boat approached Rose Point, and Skip tacked a southeasterly course. Now they had Graham Island on the starboard side, which offered some protection from the stormy seas.

The rains and squalls didn't stop all day. As night approached, the tired and wet crew searched for a protected cove on Banks Island. Using a chart and a bronze sighting compass, Skip soon piloted the boat inside a small inlet, where they dropped anchor in fifty feet of water.

With a kerosene lantern burning from the masthead, the men ate a hearty meal and crawled into their sleeping bags, knowing that sleep would come easy after their long day.

With brightening skies, the next morning, they returned to the Hecate Strait and continued sailing south. Along the way, Skip gave Dutch lessons on navigation. Using just a transistor radio and his pocket compass, he plotted their position all the way down the Inland Passage. He also taught him the native way of reading clouds. For thousands of years, the Alaskan Indians had been predicting the weather by the size, shape and color of different clouds. Each billow told the story of what the gods were planning.

After eleven days of sailing, they moored the *Pacific Lady III* at the transit dock in Port Angeles, Washington. When they got off the boat, they walked like drunken sailors until their shore legs returned. They spent the afternoon gassing up the two five-gallon tanks for the outboard motor, buying a few provisions, and enjoying a wonderful meal at a fancy dockside restaurant. They had traveled nearly nine hundred miles from Ketchikan and, for the most part, the winds and weather had been favorable. Now they faced over two hundred miles on the open Pacific.

Early the next morning, they ate breakfast at a dockside greasy spoon that was crowded with local fisherman. Skip asked a few of the captains about conditions in the Straits of Juan de Fuca, and what to expect once outside the entrance to the Pacific. Things looked dicey. The weather was changing, with winds out of the northeast, and a forecast of rain, and seas from three to five feet. They were also told which coastal harbors were best, if they needed to seek protection. The local fishermen were a fine lot, and full of helpful information.

They used the motor for the first few hours. Then, when they arrived at the middle of the straits, they raised the sails and tacked the *Lady* to a westerly direction. Two hours later, they were on the ocean, and sailed with the wind for another hour. Then they tacked the boat to a southerly course. By then, the seas were building and the rain pouring. As the swells increased and rolled across their bow, Dutch got his first taste of the mighty Pacific. At times, they rode the crest of the swells, and all they could see was an angry ocean boiling from point to point. They were but a tiny dot on a vast, stormy sea. Then they would fall into a trough, with towering waves that were almost higher than their mast. It was a miserable experience, with wet, bone-freezing winds all day. Dutch hadn't seen the seas so violent since the typhoon he had survived during the war. That simple thought sent a chill down his spine. What other memories of that horrible war had he forgotten?

With seas rushing out of the cockpit scuppers, and Skip manning the manual bilge pump, the boat inched down the coast under building dark clouds. During this time, Skip kept yelling that the Cal 24 was too damn small and had no business being on the open ocean. All Dutch could do was shake his yellow-hooded head in agreement.

Late in the afternoon, they approached the mouth of Grays Harbor and retreated inside the bay. Once across the bar, Dutch started the motor and turned the boat for a protected inlet on the north shore. There, they secured two anchors and took refuge from the rain in the cabin.

Wiping his face with a towel, Dutch said, "Don't think I've ever been so wet and cold."

Skip peeled off his yellow jacket and started drying his neck. "What did you think of the Pacific Ocean today?"

"To tell the truth, Skip, I was scared as hell out there," Dutch answered. "I had forgotten how unforgiving the sea could be."

With the sound of rain dancing off the roof, Skip replied, "Good! Keep a healthy respect for her. The Pacific can be a boiling bitch or as pleasing as a brothel. Her mood is always written in the clouds."

Skip was like that, a saying for almost everything. And after watching him handle the boat that day, Dutch thanked the Lord that he had come along. That night, they enjoyed a few shots of brandy and ate the last of the food Louise had packed. Again, sleep came easy.

Under clearing skies, they slipped out of Grays Harbor early the next morning. Turning south, they traveled the final forty miles to the mouth of the Columbia River. When they reached it, Skip laid off Point Adams and waited for slack tide. At 11:00 AM, they crossed the bar and, using the motor, they turned for the south shore. Just before noon, the *Pacific Lady III* tied up to a floating dock next to the Warrenton Boat Works. They had traveled a little over eleven hundred miles in thirteen long sailing days, and dry land never looked so good.

After they had been at the dock for few minutes, they were approached by a robust fellow with a friendly face. Skip recognized him right away, and stepped off the boat with an outstretched hand. As the two men shook, Dutch joined them dockside, and Skip introduced him to Ralph Higgins, owner of the Boat Works. He was a middle-aged man with a weathered face and salt-and-pepper hair. His grip was firm, and he had the hands of a working man.

"I've heard a lot about you, Dutch," Ralph said shaking his hand. "So, this is the boat Skip told me about." He walked the length of the craft, looking at her construction and rigging. Then, returning, he asked, "So, what are your concerns, Skip?"

"I'd like her taken out of the water and a complete survey done. Dutch wants to sail her south to warmer waters, but I don't think she's constructed good enough for the Pacific."

"Well, she made it this far," Dutch asserted with a hopeful smile.

"No problem," Ralph said. "We'll get her out of the water this afternoon. The inspection will take a couple of days, so I took the liberty of booking rooms for you guys at the Hotel Elliott in Astoria. It's cheap and clean. But first I want to show something you might find interesting."

The men moved to another dock, where the private boat slips were. At the very end of that quay, they came to a large moored sailboat that glistening in the sunlight. She had beautiful lines and was built of shiny white fiberglass, with a maroon waterline and rigging that looked brand new. On the aft transom, she even had a stainless-steel diving ladder. Dutch had never seen such a luxury sailboat before.

"This is the Voyager 45, built in Taiwan and distributed by East-West Yachts in Marina Del Rey. Isn't she a beaut?" Ralph said.

Perplexed, Dutch asked, “What’s she doing here?”

Ralph stepped onto the boat before he replied. “The distributor has been sailing her up and down the West Coast, doing boat shows. She did the Portland Show last weekend. That was her last, and now she’s for sale. Come on aboard. I’ll show you around.”

That started their tour of the Voyager 45, as fine a cruising sailboat as Dutch had ever seen. She slept six comfortably, with a hull that was forty-five feet long, and a beam of thirteen and half feet. The entire interior was handcrafted out of teak, right down to the cabin sole. The hull was built out of marine plywood, with a double coating of fiberglass. The forward compartment had a double V-berth, with a skylight. Just aft of it was an enclosed head, and, across from it, another stall with a full shower. The main salon was bright and spacious, with two settees, port and starboard, with a good-sized table. Aft of the salon was the galley, with a three-burner kerosene stove, double sinks and an electric refrigerator. Across from the galley was a nook, with a chart table and all of the controls for the boat. The master stateroom was tucked in under the cockpit, with a double berth, and it had both a skylight and two small portholes. On the other side of the companionway, leading up to the cockpit, was a smaller compartment with bunk beds and two portholes. There was plenty of storage, everywhere they looked. Under the main cabin floor, they found a 58 HP, 4-cylinder diesel engine, two large marine batteries, and a generator.

On deck, they walked the boat from stem to stern, looking at the rigging, the short teak bowsprit, the sail lockers and the general layout. The deck itself was made out of white nonskid fiberglass, with many strategically placed winches.

“Okay, I’ll bite,” Dutch finally said to Ralph. “What does this yacht cost?”

Ralph shrugged. “Let’s take her out first and see how she handles.”

A few minutes later, they motored out of the Warrenton boat basin and onto the Columbia River. With blue skies and a stiff easterly breeze, they turned the boat upriver. Standing at the wheel, Dutch could feel the power of the diesel engine working, and how the boat answered the helm. Once past Astoria, they turned with the wind and raised the sails, the Voyager 45 shot off like a skyrocket.

With a smile on his face and a warm breeze in his hair, Dutch yelled from the helm, "Alright, Ralph, what's the damn price?"

Mr. Higgins walked aft and stood next to Skip and Dutch at the wheel. "They're asking forty-nine thousand for her. But, being a dealer, I can sell her to you for only forty-seven and still make a little money. And I'll give you two thousand trade-in for your Cal 24."

Dutch whistled into the wind. "There was a time when I could have afforded a boat like this. But not now, sadly. I'll keep the Cal 24."

Skip hadn't said much since leaving the dock, but now he stood with a smirk on his face. "Dream a little, Dutch. If you *did* own her, what would you name her?"

Without hesitation he answered, "*The Laura*, of course."

A small tear appeared in one of Skip's eyes. "That's what I thought you'd say."

After they returned to the boat basin, Skip and Ralph went to the office, leaving Dutch aboard the Voyager 45 for one final walk-through. He was impressed. She was big and sturdy, and she sailed like a racer. But he also reminded himself that yachting was a game for rich men, something he no longer was.

Skip and Dutch borrowed the yard's pickup truck and drove to the Hotel Elliott in downtown Astoria. There, they checked in and then walked around town, looking at the quaint shops. Skip bought Louise a gift of a little porcelain figurine for her collection.

Later that evening, they met Mr. Higgins at the Thiel Brothers Restaurant for dinner. Ralph claimed it was the premier eatery in Astoria. When they walked into the fancy dining room, Ralph stopped and said hello to everyone he knew, which was most of the room. When they sat down at their table, he introduced Skip and Dutch to the couple next to them. The older man was Rolf Klep, with his wife, Alice. She had auburn hair, big brown eyes, and a pretty face. They were a friendly pair who had just retired to Astoria from New York. He was a marine artist and avid collector of nautical knickknacks.

That night, they had a wonderful steak and seafood dinner with all the trimmings and more than a few drinks. The banter between the two tables was lively, with talk of Astoria's colorful history, fishing and all things nautical. It turned out that Rolf Klep had a dream: he and his wife were planning on opening a Maritime Museum in the old Astoria City Hall in a few months. They were on the search for anything to do with the history of seafaring. Rolf handed his business card to Dutch and Skip, saying, "We'll take anything nautical that has a story to tell."

With a final round of drinks came the tab. Ralph paid for both tables. *No wonder he has so many friends here,* Dutch thought with fond amusement. It had been a memorable evening, one that he would not soon forget.

That night, as he and Skip walked back to their hotel, Dutch commented, "This is a nice little city, with good people. I hope Rolf and Alice's dreams comes true."

"You should give them your Cal 24," Skip answered. "It would make a wonderful exhibit with an interesting story."

"Maybe I will," Dutch replied, "after my story has played out."

Skip yawned. "I'm getting old, Dutch. Can't keep my eyes open anymore. But we can both sleep in tomorrow, so don't expect me early for breakfast."

The next morning, Dutch slept to near ten o'clock. Once he was finally dressed, he went down to the hotel lobby for a cup of coffee. As he walked past the front desk, the clerk stopped him and handed him an envelope. "It's from Skip Patterson, sir. He checked out, early this morning."

With a surprised look, Dutch moved to the side bar and poured himself some brew. Then he took a seat in one of the overstuffed arm chairs and opened the envelope. Inside, he found the key to the borrowed pickup and a handwritten message:

Sorry to leave in you the lurch. Western Airlines had a nine o'clock flight to Seattle, and from there I'll take the DC7 home. I'll be sleeping with my sweet bride tonight! Take the truck back when the boat is ready, and listen to what Ralph has to say. He *knows his stuff! Good luck, pal. It was fun being your crew, but I don't want to do it again soon!*

Stay safe, Skip

Dutch glared at the message for the longest while. He was disappointed at not having the chance to say goodbye and thank Skip for all that he had done. Getting up, Dutch walked across the street and had breakfast at a charming café. Then he drove to the Boat Works to see how things were going.

When he got to the dock, he looked down and found the *Pacific Lady III* still moored where he had left her. When he went inside the office, Mr. Higgins seemed surprised to see him so soon.

"Doesn't look like anything is happening to my boat yet," Dutch said calmly. "Did I misunderstand?"

"No. There's a lot happening, Dutch," Ralph said, getting to feet. "Let's walk down and I'll show you what I mean."

They moved down the gangway, past the Cal 24, then turned at the private dock slips and walked to the very end. There, moored in the sunlight, was the Voyager 45, with a painter lettering the transom of the boat. Using black letters with a gold outline, he was just finishing the writing: *The Laura*, Ketchikan, Alaska.

"What the hell is this?" Dutch mumbled, not believing his eyes.

"She's all yours, Dutch. Give the paint job time to dry and you can sail her away," Ralph answered with a proud grin on his face.

Dutch walked down the length of boat, and found *Laura* painted on both sides of the bow. Returning, he asked in bewilderment, "What goes on here, Mr. Higgins?"

"Simple, Dutch. Skip bought her for you. I told him about the Voyager 45 a few weeks ago. And he's giving the *Pacific Lady III* to the Maritime Museum. The boat reminds him of his daughter." Reaching into his pocket, Ralph handed him a piece of paper that simply read:

You're family Dutch, fini!
Love, Skip and Louise.

Chapter Four

Buenos Aires, Argentina
10 March 1945

With the muted sounds of a shower in the background, Nicole López sat on the corner of a ruffled bed, putting on her nylon stockings. When finished, she stood and straightened her blue summer skirt and buttoned her white silk blouse. With a smile like a Cheshire cat on her face she moved to the vanity, took a seat in front of a mirror, and started brushing her hair. The luxury suite of rooms, in a plush downtown hotel, was leased by the German Embassy for visiting dignitaries. She had commandeered the rooms for many weeks now. The suite made a fine love nest. Putting on her lipstick, she glared at her reflection; the hide-away was a perfect cover that no one would suspect.

From behind her, another face appeared in the reflection, wearing a white terrycloth bathrobe with a towel wrapped around her head. Eva smiled back at her in the mirror, and then placed a hand on her shoulder.

"This is a dangerous business," Eva whispered. "If Juan knew of this place, you would be dead and I would be in jail."

With a grin on her glossy red lips, the Scorpion replied, "We're safe here, sweetie. The Ambassador thinks I'm having an affair with an Argentine general. He is encouraging it, for the secrets I might learn."

"But I know no secrets," Eva replied.

Nicole stood and turned to her. "I do. Lots of secrets, enough for the both of us. I've got to go. We will leave as we always do. Same time, next week?"

Eva put one of her hands gently on the Scorpion's pretty face. "I wish I could say no, but I can't. Yes, same time, next week. But I will dream of you all weekend."

"How sweet," Nicole answered, giving her a hug. "Your scent will be with me all day."

It was just before noon when the Scorpion stepped out through the back door of the hotel and into the bright, warm sunlight. She glanced up and down the street with careful eyes, looking for any danger. The lane was parked with cars on both sides, but the sidewalks were almost empty. Satisfied, she turned to walk to the Embassy.

A burly, unshaven man in a dingy Kaiser Rambler, parked across the street, was pleased to have escaped her notice. Holding a camera with a long lens, he had taken a half dozen images of Nicole leaving, and now he waited for her to disappear before he drove to the front of the hotel, where he took another half dozen pictures of Eva departing. When he was done, he turned the Rambler for Hacienda Canario.

When the driver arrived at the villa he entered through the back door, with camera in hand, and walked to the den. Knocking on the closed door, he waited until he was instructed to enter. The room was bright, the window shutters open. Behind the desk, he found the Condor going through stacks of dispatches.

"Just like last week, Colonel. They arrived around nine thirty and left about noon. I've got them on film again. I'll develop it this afternoon," the burly driver said.

The Colonel looked up from his desk at the man. Hans Klein had been a Hamburg policeman before joining the SS in '42. He was a big fellow with broad shoulders, sandy hair and an ordinary face. Hans was the perfect detective, as he didn't stand out in a crowd. He had escaped from Italy after Mussolini was murdered, and he was a notorious SS sniper, wanted by the Allies.

"That woman is going to destroy our mission down here, damn her," the Condor answered angrily.

"If *we* know what's going on, sir, then you can bet the government knows as well," Hans answered solemnly.

"Yes, you are right. Something will have to done about the Scorpion soon. For now, however, get some lunch and then make those prints for the file," the Colonel answered.

The Condor had been busy for the past few weeks. There were now eight Canaries in country. He had purchased another safe house in the port city of Mar del Plata, and had moved U-boat Captain Wattenberg and three others into those quarters. At the Hacienda, there were now three new faces going through indoctrination. Once they were ready, he would buy another safe house, close to the waterfront in Buenos Aires, and move them there with Captain Klein in charge. The three villas would soon become the nucleus of his coming Fourth Reich.

The Colonel had not seen the Scorpion since the dinner party with Vice President Perón and his fiancée. They had had a terrible argument on their ride back to the hacienda. He had seen the two women kissing in the moonlight, and was mad as hell about it. He feared that the Vice President might find out, which could destroy his mission and be fatal to all involved. "I will go to the Ambassador and tell him of your immoral behavior," he had screamed at Nicole.

"Who the hell are you to preach morality, Colonel?" she had yelled back.

"In the camps we exterminate people like you," he had told her, and considered killing her right there in the car. But he hadn't. She still had a role to play, a purpose for her miserable life. Nevertheless, her time would soon come.

The sound of a knock at the front door roused him from his angry reverie. A few moments, later his housekeeper brought him a large manila envelope from the Embassy. He opened the manila packet and found a small wax-sealed envelope inside, dated 2.28.45. It was a fresh message from Reichsführer Hanke. Pondering whether the Scorpion had somehow managed to read the contents before it had been delivered to him, he examined the wax seal closely. It seemed secure, but there was no way to really know.

Breaking the seal, he removed the contents of the dispatch, which included a handwritten message with two small photographs. One picture was of a futuristic-looking submarine underway; the other was the same type of boat, moored in a harbor. Both images had the words 'Type XXI U-boat' stamped on the back.

The first part of the communiqué outlined the bad news from the home front: the Soviets had liberated Warsaw, and were now knocking on the gates of Berlin. On the Western Front, the Battle of the Ardennes had failed, and Allied victory was inevitable. When the time came, the Reichsführer was preparing for his own escape. He gave no indication of how this departure would come about, but he did warn that, with the coming collapse of the Third Reich, thousands of Canaries would be heading his way. "Keep your network secured and our men standing by."

The next part of the message was a revelation. The Reichsführer told of the mission and departure of two new types of wondrous U-boats and their secret cargos. He explained that both boats carried Japanese dignitaries and German scientists, and that the Japanese government had pledged to refuel and resupply the boats after the passengers arrived safely in the Pacific. The boats would then sail east towards Ecuador. On or about May 10, the two U-boats would rendezvous at Santa Cruz Island, part of the Galapagos group of islands, some 500 miles west of Ecuador. "You will have a supply ship waiting there, with six hundred tons[8] of diesel fuel and provisions for another month of sailing for a crew of hundred twenty. One boat, U-3521, has a cargo of fifty crates of SS gold. You will upload that cargo to your supply ship and return to Argentina via the Panama Canal, while both U-boats will sail for Mar del Plata, Argentina, via Cape Horn. You are to protect your cargo at all costs. See that it is deposited into the Bank of Buenos Aires and converted to American funds. Nephew, this money is the foundation of our Fourth Reich, so be vigilant."

The last part of his orders instructed him to present the two U-boats to the Argentine government, as a gift from the German people. "Tell Vice President Perón that these new types of wonder weapons will help Argentina reclaim the Falkland Islands from the British. You will find grid coordinates and contact frequencies below. Good hunting, Hanke."

The Condor folded up the message, placed it and the photos back into the envelope, and put it on his desk. When he had done so, he stared at the dispatch a good long while. *How the hell am I going to secure a supply ship with a trustworthy crew? I'm a soldier not a damn sailor!*

Scowling, he picked up the telephone and called Captain Wattenberg in Mar del Plata. He explained his needs and asked for the Captain's advice. Wattenberg agreed to do some checking on the waterfront for a merchant ship to lease, but warned that the major hurdle would be obtaining government permission to buy that much fuel and a sailing license for the ship. Due to the war, diesel fuel was being rationed all over South America. Regarding

[8] One Ton = 32 Gallons

the crew, he seemed confident that he could raise enough loyal German sailors.

When the call was over, the Colonel gathered up his dispatches and moved behind his desk, where he pulled back on a hinged oil painting of the River Delta, revealing a large wall safe. Working the combination, he opened the safe and deposited the papers inside. Once he had closed the safe and repositioned the painting, he moved to the glass veranda door and looked out onto the shade-covered terrace. There, in the shadows, his three new Canaries were taking instructions from the tutor he had hired.

As he watched them, he thought about his own family. How was the Reichsführer going to escape the grasp of the Allies? And his sister in Sweden, would she be safe?

Something had to be done about the Scorpion, soon. And the government red-tape for the freighter, how would he manage that?

The sound of his phone ringing startled him back to reality. Crossing to his desk, he picked it up.

"Señor Garcia," a female voice said, "this is the Vice President's office calling. Vice President Perón would like to meet with you tomorrow at ten. Would that be a problem, sir?"

"No, not at all," he replied. "Tell the Vice President it would be my pleasure."

"Hasta mañana," the voice answered back.

Taking his seat, the Colonel opened a desk drawer, took out an American cigarette, and lit it. As blue smoke filled the little room, he wondered why Perón had summoned him. Did he know of the affair between the Scorpion and his fiancée? No, if that was the case, he would have been called upon by secret police. Maybe he had more Canaries to bargain for. In any event, he would try to enlist the Vice President's help in securing a supply ship. Should he go to the bank for more bribe money?

At ten sharp the next morning, Señor Garcia was ushered into the Vice President's massive office. He found Juan Perón seated behind his desk, in front of a large Argentina wall flag, reading from a file folder. Perón stood as he came into the room and extended his hand. "Nice to see you again, Señor," he said as the two men shook hands. The Vice President motioned to a chair in front of his ornate desk and continued, "We have not seen each other since our dinner party. I do hope that Senorita López has fully recovered by now."

Axel took his seat and replied, "Yes, sir, fully. She just had a summer cold that evening. One of those inconveniences of the season."

The Vice President took his seat. "We will have to do that again soon. Eva is smitten with your Miss López. She talks of her often. She is such a stunning butterfly, and with such an interesting personality."

"Yes, that true," Axel replied, his mind racing. "It would be our pleasure sir. Is that what you wanted to see me about?"

"No," Perón answered, his expression quickly turning serious. "I have news that might affect our German nationals. Argentina will declare war on Nazi Germany on March 25. With our upcoming elections, we feel this is the prudent policy to follow. How do you believe the German community will react to such news?"

Axel shook his head. "Sadly, it is the right thing to do sir," he finally said. "The war is lost, and now the German people must look to their future. Argentina will benefit by being allied with the Americans."

The Vice President seemed stunned by his calm acceptance of the news. The two men talked further about the news and agreed that, in the future, Argentina would have much to gain by being a member of the Allies. "The world will soon be flooded with war surplus materials that we can use in our struggle to regain the Falkland Islands," Juan Perón said proudly, his bone-white teeth flashing.

His comment opened the door to Axel's problem. "I have an uncle, on my mother's side, back in Germany," he said carefully. "He tells me that two Type XXI submarines are sailing for Argentina as we speak." Axel reached into his pocket and pulled out one of the photos. Handing the picture across the desk to the Vice President, he continued, "These boats are to be given to the Argentine people from the German people."

Perón studied the image for a moment. "Tell me about this type of boat."

Axel shook his head. "My apologies, sir, but I have little knowledge of these boats. All I know is that they are called 'wonder boats,' back in Germany."

Perón slipped the picture into his desk drawer. "I'll see what our admirals have to say about this. Now, who is this uncle of yours?"

Axel told the story he had prepared about his uncle, 'General' Hanke, and his need for a supply ship with provisions and fuel so that the submarines could complete their voyage to Argentina. He assured Perón that his South American Mining Company would pay for all costs, but admitted that he needed help securing a sailing license and permission to buy six hundred tons of diesel fuel. Throughout his explanation, he spoke in vague terms and kept many of the details to himself.

During his plea, the Vice President listened carefully, while exercising his fingers together in deep thought. After Axel finished, he nodded his head slowly and grinned. "Yes, I like it. We declare war on the Nazis and, a few weeks later, two of their submarines surrender to us! Good election headlines. Where are you to assemble with these submarines?"

"Just west of Panama, sir," he lied to the Vice President. "The freighter will return via the Canal, while the subs will arrive at Mar del Plata, via Cape Horn. But it will require a license for the ship and written permission to buy the fuel. Can you help me, sir?"

Perón tapped his fingers on his desk, his probing gaze fixed on Axel. "Yes, I will help you, Señor. This will be excellent publicity for Argentina. *But,* my involvement must remain quiet. Do you understand?

Señor Garcia got to his feet, his hand extended. "Yes, sir, I do. I will be in your debt, sir."

As the two men shook hands, Perón answered, "Yes, you will be, Señor …and someday I may ask for your help with a problem."

Axel smiled at him. "It would be my pleasure, sir."

When the Colonel returned to the hacienda, he was surprised to find the Scorpion waiting for him in his den. Wearing a conservative business outfit, she was friendly as he walked into the room. "So nice to see you again, Colonel," she said with a warm smile. "I've come to apologize for that evening at the Vice

President's home. I promise it won't happen again, sir." Her demeanor seemed contrite, and Axel had to remind himself to hold back his anger.

Axel looked at her pretty face and thought, *She lies so well.* "What do you need, Nicole?" he finally asked.

"I know you received a dispatch from Germany yesterday. Was it of any importance, sir?"

The Colonel grinned at her as he took his seat behind the desk. "Yes, it was full of news and instructions, some of which are meant for you."

"What am I to do?" she asked, looking hopeful.

"You are to use your Embassy connections to buy six hundred tons of diesel fuel and thirty days of provisions for hundred twenty sailors. The Company will pay for these supplies, so the price must be rock bottom."

Nicole stood in front of his desk, looking confused. "Such purchases will require government approval, Colonel. How are the supplies to be used?"

Axel allowed himself a proud smile. "I've already secured government approval. And you will learn their use *if* and *when* you need to know. These provisions must be ready to ship out of Mar del Plata in thirty days. Do you understand?"

The Scorpion's green eyes glared back at him. "I don't like secrets, Colonel."

"Nor do I," Axel sternly replied.

Southern Latitudes

8 April 1945

Four days out of Lisbon, the boat approached the Cape Verde islands. There had been reports from Sub-Pack Command of a large Allied naval fleet in the mid-Atlantic, so Captain Miller and his Navigator had plotted a course on the leeward side of the islands. The weather had been hot, with humidity near 90%, and seas as calm as a corpse. As was their practice in the southern latitudes, the boat surfaced a half-hour before sunset, and all of the off-duty crew were allowed on deck to smoke and take short swims. Under the watchful eyes of the officers, the group of swimmers had until sunset to cool off in the ocean. It was a strange sight to behold: fifty lily-white, naked men laughing, splashing and diving off of the dead-in-the-water U-boat. On this evening, Captain Miller joined the men in the water and was enjoying his swim when he noticed Sergeant Beck using the rope ladder to pull himself back aboard the sub. In the waning light, his back looked beet-red and raw as meat. Miller swam in his direction and followed him up the ladder. By the time he got on deck, the Sergeant had disappeared down the aft hatch. Putting on his clothes, Miller climbed the sail bridge to relieve Lieutenant Kaplan for his swim.

As the Exec was about to leave, he asked, "Did you see Sergeant Beck when he was naked on the deck?"

"No, sir, I didn't notice him," Kaplan answered. "Was something wrong?"

"Not sure. You get your swim, Josef. I'll find out later."

Just as the last rays of sunlight bounced off the western sky, the U-3521 submerged and resumed her voyage south. At dinner that evening, Captain Miller asked Major Schmidt about the well-being of his Sergeant. "I don't know and don't care," was his rude answer. Schmidt was an annoying person, without a friend in the crew.

After finishing their meal, the officers stayed on in the wardroom to hear the radio news. Radio Berlin was piped throughout the boat for all to hear. The news itself was filled with patriotic music and Joseph Goebbels' voice reassuring the faithful that all was well. He talked of victories in the east and west, and new divisions on the march with wonder weapons. It was propaganda from start to finish. Right after Radio Berlin, the BBC came on. At that point, Major Schmidt got up and stormed out of the wardroom. As Captain Miller poured a second cup of chilled tea, he chuckled to himself. He knew that the BBC was also propaganda, but for some reason he believed the hated British more than Dr. Goebbels. The news from Europe was not good. The Allies were winning one victory after another. It was depressing to hear, and all the officers sat with long faces. Before the broadcast finished, the Captain excused himself and went to the control room for one final night check.

The Navigator, Karl Fritsch had the watch, and all systems seemed to be humming. As he read the daily logs at the chart table, he overheard the radio operator mumble loudly, "That makes no damn sense."

The Captain moved to the radio nook with the log book in hand. "What makes no sense, lad?" he asked the operator.

The freckle-faced sailor had headphones on, and sat before a large console filled with dials, buttons and meters, including the boat's Enigma machine, for coding and decoding all messages. It was the most complicated station on the boat.

The operator was surprised to see the Captain's face in his space. "Sorry, sir," he stammered, removing the headsets. "I shouldn't be talking out loud."

"What makes no sense?" he asked again.

The young operator shook his head. "When we arrived at Cape Verde, I was instructed to change to a new frequency for Sub-Pac South. Now they are telling me to change frequencies again, and provide them with our precise location and destination. Sub-Pac has never asked for that kind of information before. They usually only talk in grids and quadrants, sir."

The German Navy had divided all of the navigable waterways of the world into a two-letter alphabetical grid system; each grid covered roughly five hundred square miles. Within each grid was a 9x9 numerical quadrant. Those grids and quadrants allowed Command to keep track of the exact locations of their ships and submarines at any given time.

"Were your new instructions coded?" the Captain asked.

"Yes, sir. I decoded them myself."

Miller thought for a moment. "Alright, change frequencies and reply 'Proceeding to assigned grid for resupply.' Let's see how they answer that message."

"Yes, sir," the young operator said, turning back to his equipment.

The Captain placed the log book back on the chart table and turned to the watch officer. "Have Chief Huffman, Major Schmidt and Sergeant Beck join me in the Wardroom."

With two electric fans whirring, and his uniform dripping with sweat, Miller stood by the sideboard and waited for the men. The Chief was first to arrive, and he was directed to have a seat. Next from the passageway came Major Schmidt and his Sergeant. Miller confronted the two men just inside the compartment. "Major," he said making his expression friendly, "I've been admiring that walking stick of yours. May I see it?"

Schmidt looked surprised by his request. "You called us here to look at my cane?"

"Not really, but the Chief and I were just talking about it. May I see it?"

Reluctantly, the Major handed his stick to the Captain. Miller showed it to the Chief, pointing out the large silver skull on the top. Then, turning back to the two men, he said, "Sergeant Beck, remove your shirt please."

Beck's gray eyes filled with fear but he started unbuttoning his shirt.

"What the hell is the meaning of this?" Schmidt demanded.

"Hold your tongue, Major," the Captain angrily replied.

With the last button undone, Sergeant Beck slipped off his sweaty shirt, and the Captain had him turn his back to the room. There on his back were three red welts, six to eight inches long, with a rounded top and broken skin. The Skipper held the walking cane next to the welts so that everyone could compare the marks. Chief Huffman's mouth dropped open.

"I saw his back this evening while I was cooling off in ocean. He got out fast, as I imagine the saltwater made his sores hurt like hell," the Captain said.

"This is none of your affair," Schmidt shouted. "I can discipline my subordinates any way I wish."

"Not on *my* boat, you scurrilous bastard," he replied, glaring at the Major. Turning to the Chief, he continued, "You have an extra bunk in Chief quarters, put Sergeant Beck in it. And then lock the Major's walking stick in the firearms locker. He no longer needs it." Turning back to Schmidt, he concluded, "You're one sadistic prick, Major. If you cause any more trouble on my boat, I will load you, kicking and screaming, inside a torpedo tube and feed you to the fish. Do you understand me?"

Schmidt stood with fire in his eyes. "You're a traitor, Captain. You interfere with good discipline and allow the BBC to be broadcast on your ship. When we catch up with the U-3520, all of this will change. You will soon be hung for treason, and I will watch with joy!"

A grin chased over Miller's lips. "As always, Major, I will log your comments. Now get the hell out of my sight."

As Sergeant Beck carefully put his shirt back on, he said, "Thank you, Captain. Before the war, I was a damn good mechanic. Could you use me in your engine room?"

Chief Huffman stood with a smile. "You bet we can."

After the two men had gone, Miller stood in front of one of the fans, drying his shirt. He had lost his temper with the Major, something no captain should do. But, deep down, he knew something more permanent would have to be done soon.

The days and nights of the long voyage blended together as shades of gray. Twelve hours on and twelve hours off; the monotony would drive most men crazy. The boat traveled the daylight hours submerged, and would only surface for an occasional swim or in the middle of the night. Those few hours spent on the surface were used to recharge their batteries and pump fresh air though the boat's ventilation system. Captain Miller enjoyed the midnight runs, as the stars filled the sky with a clarity he had never seen before. He often stood alone in the sail bridge for hours, watching the sky and dreaming of better days. He called them his 'wake nights,' because of the long, white phosphorescent wake his boat made on the coal-black ocean.

As they moved farther south, the weather became more tolerable. Ever so slowly, they transitioned from the spring of the northern latitudes to the autumn of the southern latitudes.

A week out of Lisbon, with Cape Verde long gone astern, they received another strange message from Sub-Pac South. `'Advise as to your resupply grid.'`

This time, it was the Exec who brought the message to the Captain's attention. "The radio operator told me he spoke to you about these strange cables a few nights ago, sir."

Miller read the short dispatch. "The freckle-faced operator?" he asked.

"Yes, sir."

"I like that kid. He's suspicious about who he's talking to."

"I remember when we met with the Commodore in Kiel. He told us that he had already sent Sub-Pac all the grid numbers for our resupply. Why are they asking again now?"

Captain Miller stared at the message again. "You could be right, Josef. Send them this reply: `Coordinates available from Commodore Krug 7th Flotilla Kiel.`

"Yes, sir."

The next day, they responded by saying that Commodore Krug had been killed in an air raid, and that Sub-Pac South had not been advised as to the proper grid coordinates. If the boat wanted to be resupplied, it would have to send the grid and quadrant information, along with the date and time of arrival. The Captain and his Exec didn't trust the message and were still suspicious, but they had no way of proving their fears. After checking with the navigator, they replied: `Resupply GR5619, ETA 0900, 4.19. Advise as to description of supply ship.` This location was roughly two hundred miles south of Cape Town, and Miller fibbed about the last quadrant number by some twenty miles. They would lay in wait for the supply ship and approach with caution.

On the first night out of Lisbon, Captain Miller had invited Commander Nomura into his compartment and given him the two bottles of sake he had traded. Nomura seemed delighted with the gift, and the two men spent a relaxing evening sipping the wine and talking about the war. The Commander explained that his interest in German U-boats had begun when he had worked on a 'secret' submarine project back in Japan in '42. He called it the I-400 project. This new class of submarine was the brainchild of Admiral Yamamoto, the architect of Pearl Harbor. The I-400 subs were long range boats that could carry, of all things, three airplanes. Captain Miller had never heard of this type of submarine before, and was quite interested in learning more. But the Commanders replies had turned vague when the Captain started asking questions. His only other comment had been that he was in charge of support logistics for a planned future attack on the Panama Canal. Other than that, the Captain learned little more.

Now, with the boat only a few days from their resupply grid, the Captain was again curious about the I-400 boats, and invited the Commander in again. This time, he was supported by a bottle of schnapps and a map of the Pacific.

When the Commander arrived, Miller was surprised to see that the man now had a small, black pencil mustache on his upper lip. The dark, thin line looked out of place on his round face.

As the Captain poured him a small glass of schnapps, he asked, "How is your wife doing, cooking in our galley?"

Nomura took a seat in front of the Captain's desk. "Your cooks are helpful and polite with her. They allow her to cook two meals a day on their stoves. We appreciate it."

Miller handed him the glass and poured a like amount for himself. "Ah, that must be why I don't see you in the wardroom. You must be eating your meals in your quarters."

"No, sir," the Commander answered, taking a sip from his glass. "The cooks have provided us with a small table in the galley. My family takes its meals there."

"Your family is always welcome in the wardroom."

"Thank you, sir, but my wife is very shy and traditional. It would not be right for her to eat in a small room filled with male strangers."

The Captain opened the map book and placed it on his desk. "I pulled out my map of the Pacific and calculated the distance from Japan to the waters west of the Panama Canal. No submarine could travel that far without refueling."

The Commander swirled his glass with a grin. "You are correct, sir. The I-400 submarines would be sailing out of Rabaul, in New Guinea. Even then, they would need refueling for their return trip. That's where my section, support logistics, came in. We planned and built a refueling station, out in the middle of the Pacific."

Captain Miller freshened his drink with a nod of approval, and let the other man ramble on.

He learned much that evening. Admiral Yamamoto had ordered eighteen I-400 boats built, but when the Commander had departed for Berlin, only ten had been completed. The attack on the Panama Canal was originally planned for early 1944, but Commander Nomura had been reassigned to Berlin, and he had heard nothing more of the submarines or the attack.

"What of your refueling station? Was it ever completed?" the Captain asked.

"Yes, I was told that the engineers completed their work in late '43. They told the Imperial Navy that a thousand tons of diesel fuel and supplies were waiting on the island."

"Which island is that?" Miller asked, gesturing to the open map book.

The Commander shook his head. "No, I've said too much as it is, sir. All I can say about the island is that it's hidden in plain view, and only fit for desperate sailors."

The officers finished off half the bottle that night. The conversation ranged from war to peacetime dreams. Captain Miller didn't hear another word about the submarines or the island, but he was intrigued and determined to learn more.

A dozen days out of Lisbon, with fuel and supplies running low, the U-3521 approached its grid, submerged. The boat would lay in wait for their supplies. The time was 0600, and the Captain called the crew to their battle stations. The Navigator wanted to confirm their position by shooting some earlymorning stars. Both Radar and Sonar confirmed that the sea was empty, and Captain Miller agreed, but first he came to periscope depth and checked the area with his own eyes. The morning was still coal black, with an ocean of long, deep swells. The sky was clear and there was a slight southerly breeze. Miller slowly twisted the optical scope three-hundred-sixty degrees, confirming that the boat was safe. Lowering the periscope, he then ordered Chief Huffman to bring the boat to the surface.

He and the Navigator were the first on the sail bridge, followed by two lookouts. The morning air had a refreshing sharpness to it, and smelled sweet, as if land was nearby. A few minutes later, their work accomplished, the boat dove again to thirty meters. After some quick calculations, the Navigator confirmed their exact location on the map.

The Captain ordered the electric motors to dead slow speed and called for silent running. The boat was soon quiet as tomb; the only sound heard was that of the control room's whirling fans trying to keep the warm, stale air moving. Sunrise came and went at 0701, and the Captain paced the steel deck, waiting for the arrival of the supply ship.

Time drew out slowly, like the blade of a knife. At 0811 sonar picked up the faint sounds of a single-screw ship thirty miles out and moving slowly in their direction. It would take hours for the ship to arrive, so the Captain turned his boat in their direction and ordered the electric motors to half speed. As the U-3521 came to course, he ordered the forward torpedo room to load four tubes and stand by. "Are they pinging?" he asked the Sonar man.

"No, sir," was his reply.

"Take her up to periscope depth, Chief," he ordered, his khaki shirt damp with sweat.

An hour later, the ship came into view in his periscope. "What's the description we were given for the ship?" he asked, with his eye pressed to the optics of the viewfinder.

"6000-ton ship *Fidelity*, built 1921," his Exec answered. "She is a two-stacker with a white super structure, black hull and red waterline. She flies a Panamanian flag, sir."

"Everything is right," the Captain replied, "except that she is riding high in the water, and she has three funnels. Come take a look, Exec."

Lieutenant Kaplan confirmed the Captain's concerns. "Maybe she has been refitted, sir. Maybe we are the only boat she is resupplying."

"You might be right, Exec," Miller replied, taking over the periscope again. "But I don't feel like gambling with our lives."

The Captain maneuvered his boat into a position with the low morning sun at his stern, and with an angle of approach that would show the boat's smallest profile. Using the periscope, he marked the distance, direction and speed of the target. Then he lowered the tube and asked, "Any other targets?"

Radar and Sonar replied, "No, sir."

"The ship is still a couple of miles out. Exec, get your signaling torch and follow me up to the bridge. Chief, bring the boat up to deck awash and give me half power. Standby. We may have to dive fast."

The Captain and Lieutenant Kaplan waited on the conning tower deck as the boat slowly made its way to the surface. At five meters, only the teardrop sail bridge would be out of the water.

They would surprise the ship with a tiny, fast-moving profile out of the sun.

When the Chief called out five meters, the men opened the lower hatch and scurried up the ladder, where they opened the top hatch. They were on the sail bridge in a matter of seconds. Captain Miller plugged in the headset that hung around his neck, and lifted his binoculars to his eyes. The supply ship was off their port bow and just over a mile away. Lieutenant Kaplan stood next to the Captain and began flashing the monthly recognition signal.

"We've caught them off guard, Exec," the Captain shouted, with the glasses still to his eyes. "Send the signal again," he yelled over the thrashing diesel engines.

Still no answer.

Miller looked down and opened the water-proof cover to his bridge setup device. Checking the coordinates he had made with the periscope, he made a few corrections to his setup.

Still no signal from the ship.

He raised his binoculars again, just as small puffs of flame came from the ship's deck. Then large white puffs spouted from two of the deck guns. At the rear of the ship, he saw the Union Jack flying where the Panamanian flag had been.

Zap. Zap. The ocean in front of his boat came alive with tall splashes as .50mm bullets hit it.

Boom. Boom. The water on either side of the sail bridge erupted with large spouts of water.

"It's a damn British Q-boat[9], Josef," the Captain shouted. "Get below!" He flipped the switch for headset. "Chief, give me flank speed. Torpedo room, open outer doors. Fire one… fire two… fire three."

Boom. Boom. Two more near-misses drenched the sail bridge with water, knocking Miller to the deck. Quickly, he stood and yelled into the headset, "Fire four. Dive! Dive!" Slipping the headset off, he closed the cover to the setup device and quickly slid down the tube, closing the outer hatch just as .50 caliber bullets started ricocheting around the bridge.

As the drenched Captain propelled himself toward the conning tower deck, his Exec secured the final hatch after him.

---

[9] Merchant raider

Boom. Boom. Two more near-misses pursued the submerging boat as it sank into the turbulent waters. "How long to target?" the Captain asked.

"Eighteen seconds, sir," replied the Chief, stopwatch in hand.

He started counting down the seconds, but when he got to one, nothing happened. Three seconds later, still nothing. Then a distant, muffled explosion could be heard, followed seconds later by another explosion, much louder. The crew erupted with joy; the fourth torpedo had found its mark.

"I can hear the ship breaking up, sir," the Sonar operator shouted from his nook.

Captain Miller stopped the dive and brought the boat back to periscope depth. As he raised the viewing tube, he twisted his white cap backwards. Pressing his eye to the optics, he twisted the eye piece back and forth, changing the magnification. Then he removed his eye from the optics and, smiling, said to the darkened room, "Our boat is no longer a virgin, boys."

Approaching the Golden Gate Bridge

14 May 1963

With the Point Bonita Lighthouse off the port bow, Dutch furled his sails and started the engine. The weather was warm, with unlimited visibility and a hot swirling breeze out of the southeast. Savoring the low purr of the diesel motor, Dutch stood at the helm of his new sailboat, navigating the approach to San Francisco Bay. In his mind, he could see every reef and shoal, and he carefully kept to the center of the Bonita Channel. The high granite peaks of the shoreline, the rich golden sea grass, and the green scrub trees shimmered in the afternoon sun.

They had sailed for the last three days and nights, down the coast from the Columbia River. What professed to be his crew, a beatnik couple, had helped him furl the sails and then had taken their favorite places, seated on the bow with their legs dangling overboard, while smoking their funny cigarettes. They were an odd couple, as strange as a truthful politician.

After Skip's gift of *The Laura* and his hasty departure home, Dutch had spent three days tied up at the dock of the Warrenton Boat Works. He had passed the time wisely, first cleaning out his old Cal 24 boat of personal belongings. Skip had left behind his yellow foul-weather gear, his transistor radio and a bronze sighting compass. Dutch transferred those articles and the sleeping bags, blankets, tools and galley items to *The Laura*. Then he searched his new boat for more discoveries. In one of the drawers in the chart nook, he found all of the boat's manuals and a few maps.

Dutch read every page and studied every chart. He discovered that the boat had a small weather station, with a wind gauge on top of the mast. The VHF radio also had a directional finder. The boat's electrical system was both 110V for shore power and 12V for the interior and the night running lights. This power came off the batteries and the generator. Under one of the aft cockpit cushions, he found a small hibachi grill, with half a bag of briquettes and lighter fluid. Under another cushion were life-jackets, a canister inflatable raft, a flare gun and extra lines. Under another pillow, he found extra kerosene for the stove and more tools. In the galley, he uncovered some food stuffs, all the necessary utensils, and a half bottle of whiskey of a brand he had never heard of before: Yukon Jack. With the addition of a few more supplies, *The Laura* would be ready to sail.

Each morning, Dutch motored the boat onto the Columbia River and sailed her around. He had a burning question: could he sail her south, on the mighty Pacific, alone? After two days, he realized that he could, but it was a lot of work for a single sailor, so he decided to try and find a mate. That evening, he asked Ralph Higgins, the owner of Boat Works, for his advice. The very next morning, when he returned from his sail, Dutch found a couple waiting for him on the dock. After helping with the lines, they introduced themselves as Becky and Bobby, no last names.

"Are you married?" Dutch had asked.

The two smiled at each other, and Bobby answered, "Yes, in our own way."

They were a strange-looking pair, more Mutt & Jeff. Dutch guessed they were in their late twenties. She was short and dumpy, with a pretty face and long, straggly blond hair. He was tall and thin, with shoulder-length matted auburn hair. They wore dirty, ruffled clothes, and both needed a bath. They had heard Dutch was looking for a crew and they wanted to sign on. They were going to San Francisco for what they called an 'awakening.' Bobby claimed he had crewed for his father many times on the waters off Cape Cod. He knew how to man the helm, raise and furl sails, and work the winches. Becky said she was an expert cook and would keep the boat ship-shape.

Dutch hesitated at first, but then relented, with the stipulation that their only pay would be the trip to San Francisco. They agreed, and he invited them aboard and showed them around. On the tour, he emphasized the shower right next to the V berths where they would sleep.

"Where are you staying now?" Dutch asked, standing by the chart nook.

"The city park," Bobby replied. "We'll go break camp and bring our stuff down here."

Dutch checked the tides from a small booklet. "Slack tide is at eight A.M. tomorrow, so we'll leave the dock at seven. Be back here early this afternoon. I'll need help refueling, topping off the water tanks, and bringing supplies aboard."

That was the last Dutch saw of the couple until near six that evening. By then, he had done all the chores except the grocery shopping.

"Thought you would be here this afternoon," Dutch said irritably from the cockpit as they came aboard.

"Sorry," Becky answered, slipping off her grungy backpack. "We had some friends to see."

"Stow your gear below. You'll have to get to the market before it closes. I've made out a grocery list and included $40.00. You'll find it on the table. I'm going to say goodbye to Mr. Higgins. Be back in an hour."

As Dutch walked to the office, he worried that the couple might take the forty bucks and split. He had little trust in them. Dutch said his farewells to Mr. Higgins and gave him his sailing plan. The two men had a drink together and talked of the Bar conditions for the next morning. Then Dutch walked to the small town of Warrenton and bought two bottles of Yukon Jack.

With the sun low in the sky, he was back aboard by seven-thirty. He found the couple below, unloading the groceries. Surprised, he surveyed the items on the table.

"Where's the steaks, hamburger and bacon?" he asked.

"We don't eat meat," Bobby answered proudly. "We are both vegetarians."

Dutch shook his head in disbelief. "I see you got my cigarettes, but what are the two bags of Bull Durham for?"

"Oh, we don't use tobacco, but we need the rolling papers from the Bull Durham for our smokes," Becky answered.

"What kind of smokes?"

"Weed," Bobby replied.

Dutch's jaw dropped open. "You smoke dried weeds?"

Becky shook her head. "You know, pot. Mary Jane. Marijuana."

Dutch had heard of pot before, and he didn't like it. "Why ten boxes of Rice a Roni?" he asked.

"It was on sale for only 15 cents a box. It's good stuff," Bobby answered.

Dutch turned to the galley, opened one of the bottles of Yukon Jack, and poured himself a tall drink. The store was closed by now. What the hell else could he do? They had gotten a dozen eggs and some bread, even if it was wheat bread. And he found a half pound of bacon in the ice box.

"Where's my coffee?" Dutch demanded, noticing for the first time that Becky's legs were covered with stubble.

"We got tea. It's much better for us," she said with a smirk.

That was how the voyage started, and it was all downhill from there. Dutch laid out some rules: no smoking pot inside the cabin and, when on deck smoking it, keep downwind from him. He also told them to shower before leaving the dock the next morning. The cabin was already beginning to smell rancid.

Bobby was of some help crossing the Bar, the next morning. He got the working jib up without falling overboard, and even managed to raise the mainsail all on his own. With a fresh breeze from the northeast, the boat heeled over, and Dutch plotted a southwest course for deep water. That was when Becky lost her sea legs and went below. She was not seen on deck again until the next day.

Sailors get to know each other, working together. Bobby seemed quite intelligent, at first. He had graduated from a college called Reed, with a degree in Philosophy. His upper-class family lived in New England, where his father was a banker. Initially, Dutch was impressed. But then Bobby opened his mouth and started rambling on about 'Imperial America,' and America's corrupt political system. He seemed convinced that Socialism was the only answer.

"Make love, not war," he kept saying, or, "Down with the pigs and the baby-killing military!" He blamed America for all the world's faults, including dropping the 'bomb' on Japan during WWII. "The poor Japanese people were about to surrender, when the Americans dropped a second bomb that killed more children," he said with smirk.

At that point, Dutch had had enough. "Put a sock in it! I was there at the time, pal, and you don't know shit about what really happened. Trust me – I didn't go off to war for an imbecile like you. Grow up and shut up!"

That ended the boat's harmony for good. With all trust gone for his crew, Dutch manned the wheel day and night, and only took short 'cat naps' when Bobby was at the helm. The trip became one long, stressful, hungry voyage.

Turning the boat eastward, Dutch approached the underside of the iconic Golden Gate Bridge. He had seen this spectacular view once before, returning from the Pacific on a troopship in 1946. Laura had been waiting for him on the dock, that day. It had been the beginning of their life together.

Reaching for the transistor radio, he flipped it on. The cockpit soon filled with Peter, Paul and Mary singing *Blowin' in the Wind.* As the boat moved directly under the bridge, it was an awesome sight, something he had never expected to see again...

Oh, how he missed his wife.

Once inside the Bay, he turned the boat north and raised the sails again. Heeled over, they made good time up to Sausalito, where they furled the sails and motored into Pelican Yacht Harbor. They moored at the transit dock, where Dutch secured all lines while his crew gathered up their things. Soon they were standing on dock with their backpacks on.

"Do you have carfare to town?" Dutch asked from the deck.

"Nah, we don't need it. We'll hitch to the City," Bobby replied, clearly anxious to leave.

"Mr. Clarke," Becky said earnestly, "you should come with us. You're so uptight! We could teach you how to tune in and drop out."

Dutch smiled at the couple. "Thanks, but no thanks," he said. "See ya around."

Then he watched them walk down the dock and up the ramp and out of his life for good. Halleluiah! He hated this new generation. Dutch went below and opened all the skylights for fresh air. That was when he noticed that there were still five boxes of Rice-a-Roni in the pantry. Shaking his head he thought, *That brand will always remind me of that beatnik couple.*

When Dutch got off the boat, he walked to the Harbormaster's Office, paid his moorage fee, and made a collect call to Skip and Louise in Ketchikan. Skip was out fishing, of course, but Louise was delighted and relieved to hear from him. Dutch gave her the Harbormaster's phone number and told her he was going to stay in Sausalito for a few days. Then he thanked her and Skip for the wonderful gift of the boat. "It's like having Laura close to me again," he said, his voice cracking. He heard Louise sniffle on the other end, and they said a fond goodbye.

Dutch walked to town, where he found a quaint little market and bought some *real* groceries and three bottles of local wine. Returning to the boat, he spent the warm afternoon washing, polishing and cleaning the boat, inside and out. It wasn't a chore; it was a labor of love. He coiled every line and neatly tucked away all the canvas. When he was finished, *The Laura* looked just like she had on the day he had first seen her at the Warrenton docks.

With the sun low in the sky, and shadows lengthening, Dutch fired up the hibachi on the aft deck and dropped a foiled potato into the coals. Then he poured himself a tall drink of Yukon Jack, turned on the radio, and sat in the cockpit, reading a newspaper and watching the grill. It was a perfect evening, and many of the other boats around him were doing the same. The little boat basin soon filled with all the different sounds of the radios and on the docks, people taking their evening strolls. At the given time, Dutch put a giant chuck steak on his grill and opened a bottle of red wine. As the meat cooked, its savory aroma mixed with the music adding to the charm of the evening.

When Dutch rose to turn the steak, he noticed a man standing on the wharf, staring at his boat. He slowly walked towards Dutch and glanced at him.

"Wow, your boat looks like it just came off a showroom floor," he said with friendly smile.

"You'd be right," Dutch answered, flipping the meat. "Got her only last week."

"Where are you from?" the stranger asked.

"Sailed her down from the Columbia River."

"Where are you going?" he asked, his expression earnest.

Dutch picked up his wine glass and took a sip. "Lots of questions."

The stranger looked sheepish. "Sorry. I walk these docks two or three times a week, fantasizing about where the boats have been and where they're going. Didn't mean to be a pest."

The stranger was a trim, well-dressed, good-looking chap dressed in a sport coat, slacks and polished wingtips. His curly hair was a sandy blonde, trimmed high and neatly combed. His face was narrow, with soft features and twinkling brown eyes. For some reason, he looked vaguely familiar to Dutch.

"No problem. I think I'll sail south, and then maybe to Hawaii."

"I envy you, sir," he replied.

Dutch narrowed his gaze. He *had* seen this man before, but where? "Are you from around here?" he asked.

"No, moved here after the war. Born and raised in San Diego."

"What theater?" Dutch asked.

"I was a carrier pilot in the Pacific."

Slowly, Dutch smiled from ear to ear. Now he recognized this guy. "Your name is Doug…Doug Asbow, if I remember right. I talked to you right after you had been shot down over Mindanao Bay. I always wondered whether you survived the Kempeitai[10]."

The man looked dumbfounded. "Wow!" he stammered. "You're that poor, emaciated POW that gave me the advice that saved my life!" He moved closer to the boat and extended his hand. "Sir, I always wanted to thank you."

---

[10] Japanese Secret Police

The two men shook hands, and Dutch invited him aboard. In the next few hours, they shared a meal and two bottles of wine while they reminisced about their time in Japanese captivity. Both had suffered greatly, and both still had problems with lingering malaria and recurring nightmares of the war. But they also had pride, and would not portray themselves as victims.

Doug told stories of the POW camps on Mindanao Island, in the Philippines, speaking of the cruel and brutal treatment he had received from the Japs, and the number of his mates that had been killed. At one point, he said, "The only letter I ever received in that hell-hole was from my wife's attorney, suing me for a divorce. Go figure." He went on to explain that when he got back home, his wife was long gone. He kicked around for a while, jumping from one two-bit job to the next. Five years later, he had taken his current job, selling life insurance. "I hate the job, but it's good money," he said, pouring another glass of wine. When he started making money, his former wife reemerged demanding alimony. "She sits on her ass all day doing nothing, while I give her forty percent of my pay. Now she's after me for more!"

Doug's stories were interesting, sad, and at times, depressing. Unfortunately, his story about his wife was all too common. Many a 'Dear John' letter was gleeful delivered by the Japs to their prisoners, as they loved watching the misery those letters brought to the POWs.

With a half-moon shimmering on the bay, the two men parted company, with another handshake. As Doug stepped to the wharf, he said, "We who have seen war will never stop seeing it."

Dutch nodded his agreement and replied softly, from the cockpit, "You want to go sailing, tomorrow afternoon?"

"What time?"

"Three, if that's okay."

Doug smiled, his white teeth flashing in the overhead light. "I'll be here at two."

"Wear some deck shoes, and bring a light jacket," Dutch replied.

Doug waved a hand in the air as he turned and walked away. Dutch watch him turn up the ramp and disappear into the night. He liked the guy; they were kindred spirits, from the same generation.

Dutch was roused from his berth at nine AM, the next morning, by a loud knocking on the main hatch cover to the cabin. When he opened the doorway, he found a young man standing in the sunshine in the cockpit. "There is a phone call for you, Mr. Clarke, at the Harbormaster's Office. It's some lady from NBC," he said with excitement in his voice.

"I'll be right there. I've got to get dressed," he replied.

Minutes later, as he rushed to the office, he wondered what the hell NBC could want with him, and decided it was probably a wrong number.

Picking up the phone on the office counter, he said into the receiver, "Dutch Clarke here." He had to repeat it twice before an operator came on and replied, "I'll connect you with Miss Meede's office."

Now Dutch was sure it was a wrong number; he had never heard of such a person.

On the second ring, a lady's voice came on. "Dutch? Is that you?"

"Yes," he answered.

There was a long pause. "You don't know who I am, do you?"

"No. Sorry, ma'am," he replied.

The lady chuckled. "Dutch, this is Maggie. You worked with me and Colonel Ford at OWI[11] during the war."

Dutch's jaw dropped. Now he could place the sweet voice on the other end of the line. "My God, Maggie, I never expected to hear from you. How did you find me? The last I heard, you had just gone to work for NBC."

"That was fifteen years ago, Dutch. Now I'm the Network Programming Manager. At your wedding, Skip gave me his business card. I've kept it all these years. So when I needed to find you, I called Ketchikan and talked to Louise. She gave me this phone number. I understand you're in Sausalito."

"That's right. But why do you need me? Is Colonel Ford okay?"

"He's fine, Dutch. He's Executive Vice President of the network now. We have a new project we're working on and we

[11] Office of War Information

need your help. Do you have a few minutes? I'll tell you the details."

That started a twenty-minute conversation that opened up new prospects for Dutch. The network was producing a miniseries about WWII, tentatively titled 'Witness to Yesterday.' They were hiring military experts from all the theaters of the war. The men and women involved would do on-camera interviews, help write the storyline, and select the right film footage and photos from material provided by the National Archives. General Omar Bradley, Admiral James King, and many other top-ranking military people had signed on to bear witness. Maggie was asking Dutch to join the group as an expert on Marine battles in the Pacific, the POW camps, and the early occupation of Japan. "The contract would be for five to six weeks at $200 a day, with a $55 a day per diem," she said.

"You can count me in, Maggie," Dutch replied enthusiastically. "But I was just a lowly Captain, and my uniform is back in New Jersey."

Maggie sighed. "According to Admiral King, you were a Lieutenant Colonel, and your unit liberated more POWs in Japan than any another, and that's how you will be portrayed. Don't' worry about the uniform. That's why we have a Wardrobe Department. I'll send a car to pick you up at eight AM on Monday the 19th. What hotel would you like to stay at?"

Dutch put his hand over the receiver and asked a lady behind the counter, "What's the best marina in Long Beach?"

"Alamitos Bay Marina," she answered quickly.

Dutch removed his hand and told Maggie where he would be.

"You're staying at one of the hotels at the Marina?"

"No, my sailboat will be moored there. That's where I live now."

"This I've got to see. Can't wait, Dutch. See you Monday!"

Dutch and Doug spent the afternoon on San Francisco Bay. They motored out of the harbor for a few miles, and then Dutch showed Doug how to hoist both the jib and mainsail, and how to adjust the sheets with halyard tension. They talked about sail control, and how to get the most efficiency from whatever the wind had to offer.

Soon, they were tacking back and forth across the bay in a warm, brisk wind out of the southeast. Doug was a fast learner and a born sailor. He never asked the same question twice, and was as neat and tidy as a Catholic priest on Easter morning. Being a former pilot, he had no fear, knew navigation, and coped well with the ever-changing tide and weather conditions. Dutch also noticed that he treated the boat just like his own.

When they reached the south bay, they turned the boat and heeled her over into a brisk wind. At that point, Dutch turned the helm over to Doug. "Take over, pal. Plot us a course for the north shore. I'm going below for some champagne. We'll have a little celebration."

Dutch returned with two plastic water glasses half full of wine. Handing one to Doug, he told him about the phone call he had received that morning, and about the 'Witness to Yesterday' project. He told him all the details, including the pay, and the men drank to Dutch's new prospect.

Dutch concluded by saying, "I talked to Maggie about your story and the POW camps you were in. She would love to have the point of view from a downed flier. You'd probably only get a week's work, but do you think you could get the time off?"

With his hands firmly on the stainless-steel wheel, and his sandy hair flapping in the wind, Doug flashed one of his toothy smiles. "Funny you should ask. When I went to the office, this morning, my secretary told me there was a man who wanted to see me. She warned me that she knew the man, and said he was a Process Server. He probably had papers from my wife. She's trying to bleed me for more money. I'm done with her greedy ways, Dutch. It's time for me to disappear and start over again. So yes, I'd love to join you, and thanks for asking. When do we leave?"

Dutch finished his wine and put a hand on Doug's shoulder. "We'll sail Friday morning with the tide, and should be in Long Beach by Saturday afternoon. Are you sure? Seems like you're giving up a good-paying career."

"I'll be aboard. You can count on it!"

Chapter Five

Freighter Hercules, Mar del Plata Harbor

26 April 1945

Colonel Kolb had driven from La Plata early that morning with fresh dispatches, grid coordinates and radio frequencies. "Not much new information about our submarines. They are coming from Rabaul, New Guinea," he said to Captain Wattenberg on the bridge of the old freighter. "You have only a couple of weeks to reach the rendezvous point. Will you make it on time?"

"Yes, sir. We will be underway within the hour, and Captain Martin has assured me that we will be at Santa Cruz Island on the morning of the tenth of May."

"I don't like having this Captain Martin in command. You should have been allowed to be the skipper," the Colonel answered, scowling.

The *Hercules* was a six-thousand-ton freighter, owned by a Brazilian company. Senor Garcia and his South American Mining Company had leased the ship for sixty days. The terms of the lease required full payment of ten thousand dollars, a sailing license, insurance, and the services of Captain Martin and his chief engineer, as the owner's representatives. All other expenses, crew, fuel, and cargo costs were also paid by the Mining Company. The Colonel had over twenty thousand dollars invested in the resupply of the two submarines, and continually fussed over the details of the mission.

"The crew is all with us, sir," Captain Wattenberg replied. "They can be trusted to a man. We will return with your cargo safe. You can count on that."

"I trust you, Captain. It's the others who might get greedy, with tons of gold aboard. Stay alert, and monitor my radio frequency each evening. I want to follow your progress daily."

Some moments later, the departure whistle blew as the ship's motors started vibrating the decks. The two men shook hands at the rail, and the Colonel exited down the gangway. The morning dew was still on the docks as he paused by his car to watch the rusty *Hercules* lumber out into the harbor and begin its voyage north.

The old ship wasn't pretty, but she was right for the job. For over twenty years, the *Hercules* had been an inter-island, inter-country coastal freighter. The aft hull was a series of tanks which contained, that morning, six hundred tons of diesel fuel and four thousand gallons of fresh water. The forward hull was half refrigerated and half dry storage. It contained enough provisions to supply one hundred and twenty sailors for the next thirty days. The fuel alone had cost nearly three thousand dollars, and that didn't include the operating fuel for the ship. The mission was a big gamble, and the Condor was determined to protect his investment at all cost.

Opening the back door of his Mercedes, he slipped into the rear seat and ordered the driver to the Mining Office in La Plata. As the car pulled away, he removed a thermos from the seat pouch and poured himself a cup of hot coffee.

The driver, SS Corporal Kurt Hirsch, was one of half a dozen new Canaries who had arrived a few weeks before. He had worked as a clerk/bookkeeper at one of the camps in occupied Poland. After Poland fell to the Russians, Kurt had escaped through Switzerland to Lisbon. He was also a skilled typist and talented counterfeiter. The Colonel liked the kid, who spoke fairly fluent Spanish and was smart as a whip. Now the Condor had a real bookkeeper and forger in his ever-growing network, as well as six safe houses scattered around the port cities of Mar del Plata and Buenos Aires.

Much to the chagrin of the Scorpion, he had promoted U-boat Captain Jürgen Wattenberg as his second-in-command and Captain

Hans Klein, the former policeman, as the enforcer of the network. The enterprise was getting so big that he had written a manifesto detailing the rules of the Argentine Odessa. Every member had signed a pledge, agreeing with the terms of the program. Behind his hacienda, he had even built a fifty-foot antenna that was connected to a ham radio setup inside his office. The Condor was ready for the flood of SS brothers who would flow into Argentina after the end of the war.

When he got to the office, his secretary gave him his messages. Nicole had called and needed to talk to him. A realtor had phoned with a new listing for a small apartment building just outside of La Plata, and Vice President Perón's office had called, inviting Senor Garcia to have lunch with the Vice President the next day.

Handing the messages back to his secretary, he said, "Call Nicole. Tell her the ship departed on time. Have the realtor send over more details on his listing, and call the Vice President's office and confirm lunch for tomorrow. Where is Vega?"

Taking back the messages, she replied with a smile, "He's in the warehouse, getting ready for another scavenger hunt."

Bruno Vega, the company's geologist, was a likable man who took long trips into the Argentine back-country in search of another great mineral discovery. Bruno knew the Condor only as Señor Axel Garcia, the owner of the South American Mining Company.

He found his geologist loading up his old Ford pickup with tools and camping equipment. "Where are you off to this time?" Senor Garcia asked.

A large smile creased Bruno's weathered face. "I'm going west. I had a revelation the other night. It was just one word – copper."

"I thought Chile had a corner on the copper market."

Vega placed an armload of tools in the back of the truck, walked to the cab, and removed a tattered map and placed it on the hood of the pickup. "Let me show you, Señor."

Axel hovered over his shoulder, watching as Vega placed a wrinkled finger on the paper. "Argentina has copper mines here, around the western town of Mendoza, but I believe that here, a few hundred miles south of the city, close to the border with Chile, there may also be rich deposits."

"Why copper?" Axel asked.

Bruno said proudly, "That was the revelation, sir. When this war is over, the world will have to be rebuilt. And what materials will be needed the most?"

"Wood and nails," Axel answered.

Vega shook his head with a smile. "No, sir. The world has lots of timber and iron. It's copper. Every one of those new buildings will require electrical wiring, wiring with copper. Copper could soon be more valuable than gold."

Axel grinned at the old man's enthusiasm. Putting a hand on Vega's shoulder, he asked, "Who owns the land out there?"

"Mostly the government, although there are some private sections around the Río Colorado area. It is a beautiful place, but out in the middle of nowhere."

"Well, Bruno, I wish you the best of digging. I will keep my fingers crossed. Maybe someday you will make us both rich men."

Axel helped the old man finish packing up his pickup, then they said goodbye and watched as the oil-burning truck rattled down the road in a cloud of white smoke. He liked the old geologist, who was the perfect front man for his company. Maybe Vega would even find something, someday.

That afternoon, when he returned to his hacienda, he found Nicole waiting for him in his study. She was in a surly mood, pacing the floor, smoking one cigarette after another.

"Colonel, I don't appreciate you not calling me back," she said as he entered the room. "Are you having me followed?"

The Condor placed his briefcase on his desk and took a seat. "No. Why would I do such a thing? I've been too busy getting the ship prepared."

"I've seen the same man, watching me from a distance, for the last few weeks now. He looks much like your Captain Klein."

"You must be seeing things, Nicole. The Captain has been working on the *Hercules* for the past few weeks. Now he's out to sea."

The Scorpion stared directly at the Colonel. "Very well. Maybe I *am* just seeing things. Do you know what happened today?"

"Yes, the German Embassy closed. Why the long face? We knew this was coming."

Nicole stopped pacing and replied sadly, "Tomorrow, all my German coworkers will board a Swiss ship and be returned to Germany. What will they find back home? Only death and destruction, I imagine. You could have saved some of them for our network."

"The Odessa is only for our SS brothers. If you're sad about your Embassy friends, you should go along with them."

"You can't get rid of me that easily," she said, scowling. "With my job at the Embassy gone, I can now devote full time to our network. What will my pay be?"

"Pay? No one gets paid to be in the Odessa. You will find a job, just like everyone else."

"You pay a monthly wage to your secretary, and to that phony geologist. Why not to me? It was I who got your Odessa up and running. I know all your secrets, your safe houses, your sham businesses, and your illegal radio antenna. You need me, Colonel, more than I need you."

"A little blackmail, Nicole? I'm surprised," the Condor answered calmly, opening his brief-case. "That reminds me, the deed for our last property came in the mail today. Take a look at who owns the villa." He opened the envelope and handed the deed to her. "And you should know I have a license for the radio tower, signed by the Vice Present himself."

With a blank expression, she read the document. When she came to the last line, her mouth dropped open. It was a spot-on copy of her signature, using her German name, Nicole Lang. "How did you do this?"

With great pleasure, the Colonel said, "You might be quite surprised at the other bank records and Odessa documents that link you directly to the network. There will be no blackmail, Nicole. No threats. You are in this with us, up to your pretty neck. If the network goes down, then you go down," the Colonel concluded. Then, to drive the point home, he added, "Do you know the Grand Hotel in downtown Buenos Aires? It turns out that the German

Embassy kept a suite of rooms there. With the Embassy closing, I was able to pick up the lease. It's a perfect place for our men to unwind. I'm sending three Canaries there this weekend. They will need some *Frauleins* for Saturday night." The Colonel reached back into his case and brought out another envelope and handed it to Nicole. "This should more than cover the cost. And remember, no street walkers, no Jews, no Gypsies. Use only professionals who know their trade."

Nicole was speechless, red-faced. She had lost her job, and now her love nest, and the Condor was refusing to pay her. Glaring at him, she mashed out her cigarette in his ashtray. "Shall I get you a whore, as well, or do you only prefer boys?"

With a smirk, the Colonel answered, "Not necessary. The housekeeper's daughter and I have been seeing each other for over a month now. I'm surprised you didn't know that. I thought you were the security officer."

"I will not pimp for the Odessa. That's just not right."

He smiled. "It's up to you. See to it, or board that ship tomorrow and return to Germany."

When the Scorpion departed, her mood had gone from foul to frightful. She slammed all the doors, and spun her car wheels all the way up the driveway. The Condor lit one of her cigarette butts, not sure whether she would stay or go. He hoped it would be the latter.

Later that evening, he poured himself a drink and turned on Voice of America. He could not believe the news: Adolf Hitler had killed himself by gunshot, and his girlfriend, Eva Braun, had died by taking cyanide. There was much speculation about who would replace the Führer, and what his death would mean for the outcome of the war. The Colonel felt frozen in place. A part of him could not believe it, while another part rejoiced at this news of the Führer. The man had killed his father, and now he was dead as well. Few people in the world would mourn the passing of Adolf Hitler. Then came more bad news: German forces in Italy had surrendered, on the same day as his suicide.

He changed the station to Radio Berlin. With somber music in the background, Dr. Goebbels, the arch liar, spoke of a great man being killed with his troops while defending the Fatherland. There was no mention of the surrender in Italy. Lies, lies, and more lies. Goebbels said that Admiral Karl Doenitz would assume command of the Third Reich, but the Colonel doubted that, as well. Only an SS brother like General Hanke would be worthy of that command.

Angrily, he turned off the broadcast and turned on his ham radio set. He would need to tell Captain Wattenberg the news.

Late the next morning, Corporal Hirsch drove the Colonel to Buenos Aires and then to the address of the restaurant his secretary had written out. From the street in the theater district, the Jolie Bistro was a bizarre-looking place. The run-down, three-story brownstone had garbage cans littering the front entrance, and a black wrought-iron gate as a door. Only the faded front awning confirmed the name and address of the Bistro. The Corporal dropped the Colonel off at the curb, then parked across the street in the shade of a deserted building.

Once inside, the Colonel found a sign for the Bistro, with an arrow pointing to a dark stairwell. As he carefully moved down the narrow treads, his nostrils were struck with a strong smell of whiskey and stale tobacco. At the bottom of the stairs, he was confronted by a large, dim room with a long standup bar on its rear wall. The sides of the room were filled with red vinyl booths, with candles burning on the table tops. The center of the room offered a small dance floor, with a scattering of chairs and round tables. Only a handful of patrons occupied the tables.

The Colonel wondered whether he had come to the wrong restaurant. The last time they had met for lunch, it was at a fancy, brightly lit hotel, in a room full of admirers, not a dark and dingy bistro.

He turned back toward the stairs, then hesitated as he heard his name called out from the darkness. “Señor Garcia, over here.”

Moving in the direction of the voice, he found the Vice President seated in a large booth next to the bar. He was alone, and had a drink in his hands. “Have a seat, Señor. We will get you a drink.”

As Axel slid onto the bench on the other side of the booth, his eyes began to adjust. In the candle light, he could now make out Juan Perón’s face. It wore a friendly expression, and the two men shook hands. "I thought I had the wrong place, Mr. Vice President. I have not heard of the Jolie Bistro before."

"It is a sentimental favorite of mine, a place full of actors, bohemians and dreamers," Juan said. "I met Eva here, a few years back. These days, we often come here after the theater."

A waiter appeared and took their drink orders. Juan requested a second whiskey sour, while Axel ordered only a beer.

"I'm surprised you're not drinking something stronger, Señor, after the recent news from Germany."

"Not many people will mourn the death of Adolf Hitler, and neither will I."

The two men talked of the war news and all of the speculation that had sprung up around it. The Vice President was pleased that German nationals had not complained loudly when Argentina declared war on Germany. "You were right when you advised me that the war was lost, and that the German people must look to their future."

The waiter brought their drinks, and the two men toasted the suicide of Hitler. It was a morbid thing to do, but the world was in a dark mood.

"So, how is your resupply mission coming? Your picture of the new submarine has my Admirals drooling."

Axel smiled proudly. "The resupply ship departed Mar del Plata yesterday morning, sir. I talked to them late last night on the radio. No problems so far."

"Good. Do you think the German crew of the submarine would help train our sailors?"

"Don't know, sir," Axel replied. "I'm sure some of the men will want to stay in Argentina. Others may want to join your navy, or find their way home. It's up to them – and, of course, up to you, sir."

The men ordered sandwiches and another round of drinks as they talked further of the future and the outcome of the war. When the food came, it was remarkably good. As it turned out, the Jolie Bistro was the best German deli in all of Argentina.

After the meal, the Vice President's mood changed. His smile became a frown, and his eyes turned to fire. "I had a more sinister reason for having lunch here today. I have a problem, Señor Garcia, and you may be able to help."

"Of course, Mr. Vice President. What is it?"

Juan slowly looked around the dark room, then reached into his suit's breast pocket and pulled out a small manila envelope. Opening it, he slid two black-and-white pictures into the candlelight.

Axel looked closely at the dim images. One was of two girls dancing together on the bistro dance floor. The other showed the same two girls kissing, under the stairwell. The girls, he saw with a sinking heart, were Nicole and Eva. His mind began to race, and his heart skipped a beat. So, the Vice President knew.

"Where did you get these pictures sir?"

"Anonymously in the mail," Juan said, quickly scooping up the pictures and placing them back in the envelope. "This is a Catholic country, Señor. Unlike Germany, it is very traditional. If these pictures got out, I would never be elected President. Your girlfriend is putting my future in jeopardy. This I cannot allow."

"She is not my girlfriend, sir," Axel pleaded. "I met her at the Embassy and had no idea of her deviant proclivities."

"For many reasons, my fingerprints cannot be on the solution to this problem. I'm taking Eva to Washington, D.C., next week, after which we will spend another week in New York City, attending the theaters. If Nicole is gone by the time we return, by whatever means, I will be in your debt. Will you help me, Señor?"

"Count on it, sir," Axel quickly replied, with the sweet taste of revenge on his lips.

On the Indian Ocean

13 April 1945

With the diesel motors churning, Captain Miller hunched over the chart table in the darkened control room, reading the entries in the log book. It was near midnight, and Lieutenant Kaplan, his Exec, had the bridge. The forward and aft deck hatches were open, and the boat's ventilation system was humming, pulling in fresh air while blowing the stale, noxious fumes out through the stern vents. This was a nightly exercise to which the crew had grown accustomed.

After sinking the British Qship, the U-3521 had changed course to the northwest and reestablished contact with Sub-Pac

South, using the old frequency. They advised Command that the British had compromised the Enigma machine, and reported the sinking of the freighter. With fuel and food running low, they also requested immediate resupply. The next day, they were given new grid coordinates for a rendezvous with the South African freighter *Brutus*, fifty miles southeast of Madagascar.

The following morning, at the given time, grid and quadrants, the resupply ship came into view. Cautiously, with two forward tubes loaded and with the sonar and radar operators glued to their machines, the boat surfaced. Moments later, with gunners manning the anti-aircraft weapons, the recognition signal was flashed and immediately responded to correctly by the freighter.

As soon as they had maneuvered the U-3521 into position, the actual resupply began. It took only a few hours to complete. During that time, Captain Miller was able to trade his last diamond for forty gallons of ice cream. He also learned from the freighter captain that the U-3520 had been resupplied by the *Brutus* only a week before. With any luck, the two boats would join up before they reached the Bay of Bengal.

The Captain closed the log book. They were now three days out from Madagascar, and had another week of travel before their next resupply. Turning to the radio nook, he asked the freckle-faced operator whether he had made contact with the U-3520 boat.

The young man shook his head. "Not yet, sir, but I'll keep trying."

Turning from the nook, Captain Miller checked the barometer and humidity gauges. The pressure had fallen a bit, and the humidity was finally nearing eighty per cent. The ventilation system was doing its job. Moving to the coning tower ladder, he shouted up the hatch tube; "coming up, Exec."

It was absolutely magnificent, topside. The stars and a near-full moon contrasted with the coal-black sky and sea with such brightness that the Skipper could almost count the rivets in the steel plates.

"The barometer has fallen some. It's still monsoon season out here, so we'll have to keep an eye on the weather," Miller said, lighting a cigarette with his back to the wind.

"Couldn't you sleep, sir?" Lieutenant Kaplan replied.

"No. Too damned hot, below. I'll relieve you, Exec. Check the batteries and let me know when they are fully charged."

After the Lieutenant had descended the hatch, the voice of Commander Nomura shouted up, "Permission to come to the bridge for a cigarette?"

"Aye," Miller replied.

When the Commander reached the bridge, the Captain was surprised to see him wearing a red silk kimono. "Never saw you out of uniform before," he said to Nomura.

"Too hot for sleep or clothes. The silk is cooling, like a fan."

The two men talked for a while of the moon, the stars, and the white phosphorescent wake of the boat. There were even flying fish leaping from the sea, their silvery bodies shimmering in the moonlight. Everything in nature had a special meaning to the Japanese, and Nomura told several fables. Then the banter turned personal. The Commander and his family were excited to be so close to the Pacific and home. "I'm afraid, when we set foot on Japanese soil again, it will not be the same as when we departed," Nomura said.

"When we last talked, you spoke about your refueling station, in the Pacific. What did your engineers have to do to prepare the island?" Miller asked nonchalantly.

Turning away from the wind, the Commander lit a cigarette. Then he turned back and said, "A sea cavern had to be enlarged so that a submarine could fit inside. Then a dock was chiseled out of the stone, and mooring nets were made. Finally, they blasted fuel and storage hollows into the sides of the mountain. It was a big undertaking. It took a battalion of engineers over three months to complete the work. It was a grand scheme."

"Did you ever visit the island?"

The Commander shook his head. "No, I only saw pictures. The Admiralty named the island Haiku. It was the perfect name for a deserted tropical wasteland."

"What does 'Haiku' mean in Japanese?"

"A Haiku is a three-line poem about a fleeting moment of nature. This island was only a fleeting moment of creation."

"So, where is this island?"

The Commander smiled broadly. "That I cannot tell you, sir. It is no more than a rock needle in a haystack of islands." He took a drag on his cigarette. "Where will you go, after Rabaul?"

So, Nomura had turned tight-lipped again. The Captain didn't mind. He had already learned much, that evening. "East across the Pacific, and then around the horn to Argentina."

The bridge intercom buzzed.

The Captain opened the water-tight cover and flipped the switch. "Bridge."

"The batteries are fully charged, sir," the Exec announced.

"Very well. Prepare the boat to dive. I'll secure the bridge."

The next evening, when they surfaced again, they were greeted by an angry sea. A stiff headwind was blowing out of the northeast, with curling waves and swells six to eight feet tall. It wasn't raining yet, but the skies were filled with ominous clouds. The temperature had dropped to just below the century mark, with humidity near the same. It was still hot and sticky, but the stormy seas were too dangerous for swimming.

With the boat's bow into the wind, the aft and bridge hatches were opened for fresh air. The bow hatch remained closed, as the forward deck was awash in the stormy seas. Behind the protective bridge tower, safety lines were rigged, and the crew was allowed on deck in small groups, to smoke and to gaze at the vastness of the Indian Ocean.

With the last muted colors of the setting sun fading in the western sky, it started to rain, not gently or lightly, but with the gusto of the monsoon season. The decks were quickly cleared, the hatches closed, and the boat descended again into the quiet waters to a depth of sixty meters.

That night at dinner, Major Schmidt was missing from the wardroom. The next morning, he was absent from breakfast, as well. Captain Miller dispatched Oliver, the officer's steward, to find the Major and check on him.

A few minutes later, he returned alone. "He is not in the aft engine room, sir, and his hammock does not appear to have been slept in," the Greek lad reported.

"No one can go missing, like a fart in the wind, on a submarine," the Captain said, reaching for the intercom to alert the crew and ordered a complete search of the boat.

Hours later, they had still found nothing. Miller called Lieutenant Kaplan and Chief Huffman to his cabin, and ordered an official inquiry into Schmidt's disappearance. Every locker, bilge, torpedo tube and cubby hole would be searched again, and all crewmembers would be interviewed, to establish the last time the Major had been seen. Being swept overboard from a fast-moving submarine in stormy seas was a clear and present danger for everyone. There was no other way for anyone to go missing.

That afternoon, the answer to the puzzle began to take shape. The previous night, the boat had not surfaced at midnight, due to the still raging storm. If the Major had fallen overboard, it had to have been at sunset, the previous evening. No crewmember had seen him, after the boat submerged, but one of the cooks recalled watching him climb cautiously up the aft hatch ladder, just before it started to rain. "It was a strange sight, with his gimpy leg and all," the cook reported.

But that was it. After all the interviews, they could find no crewmember who had actually seen him on deck.

Captain Miller hadn't much liked the Major, and he wouldn't mourn his loss. He simply logged the conclusion of the official inquiry: Schmidt's disappearance was attributed to his being swept overboard during stormy seas on the evening of 15 April 1945.

As the Captain closed the logbook, his was interrupted by his Exec.

"We've made contact with the U-3520 boat, sir. Here is their decoded message."

Miller opened the slip of paper: `One day out from Monsoon supply sub. Approaching Java Sea. Four days to destination. Minor problems plague the boat. Commander Herbert Wiener, U-3520.`

"What's a 'Monsoon Sub?" Kaplan asked.

"U-boats that operate in the Pacific and Indian Oceans are all called Monsoon Subs. They are a special breed of submariners, so far away from the Fatherland," Miller answered as he wrote out his reply.

"How big is this Monsoon fleet, sir?"

"About forty boats," the Captain answered, handing back his reply and the logbook. It was a simple response: `Two days from milk cow[12]. Sailing Java Sea approach as well. See you at destination ETA: 04.21. All is well. Captain Hans Miller, U-3521.`

"Have the radio operators establish a regular contact time with our sister ship. If they are having problems, they might need our help."

"Yes, sir," Lieutenant Kaplan answered.

After his Exec left the compartment, the Captain stood and stretched his legs. He was pleased with the inquiry, and delighted they had finally made contact with their sister ship.

There came a knock on his door.

Opening it, he found Sergeant Beck standing in the companionway, his face long and sullen, with dark circles under his gray eyes.

"May I talk to you, sir?"

"Yes. Come in, Sergeant, and close the door."

As Beck entered the cabin, Miller sat once again behind his small desk. "And what can I do for you?" he asked, looking up at the Sergeant.

"I've come to turn myself in, sir," the man answered, standing at attention, with his eyes straight forward.

"For what, might I ask?"

"For the death of Major Schmidt, sir. I killed him, last night on the aft deck," he answered, his sad gaze drifting downward to the Captain.

"I just finished the official inquiry. Why are you coming forward now?"

The Sergeant's tense body loosened, and he shook his head. "Can't live with myself, sir. What I did was cowardly. I am not fit to wear this uniform."

"Let me be the judge of that. Stand at ease and tell me what happened."

Beck parted his legs and placed both hands behind his back. Then, staring straight forward, he told his story. The previous

---

[12] Supply Sub

evening, the Major had confronted Beck in the noisy engine room. Yelling at him for moving into the chief's quarters, Schmidt said he had deserted his post, and screamed that a hangman would be waiting for him in Argentina.

The Sergeant had heard these ramblings before, so he simply turned away from the angry Major and moved to the aft hatch, where he climbed the ladder for a smoke. Topside, he found the stormy deck deserted. Holding on to one of the safety lines, he got his cigarette lit just as the bow of the boat crashed through a deep swell, sending a spray of sea water over the top of the conning tower, and drenching him.

Throwing the wet cigarette overboard, the Sergeant turned to leave. That was when he noticed the Major's head clearing the aft hatch. Beck was frozen in place, holding on to the safety line, not believing his eyes. It started to rain just as Schmidt reached the deck and got to his feet. He staggered forward, yelling more obscenities. When he was a few yards from the tower, he lost his footing on the wet deck and started to roll overboard. With one hand, he got a grip on a vent hole, but his legs were dangling overboard. With his other hand, he reached for help.

The Sergeant moved down the safety line toward him, but couldn't quite reach him. He stretched his arms as far as he could, but he and Schmidt were still inches apart. Then the bow hit another deep swell, and the Major was bucked off the boat and thrown into the ocean.

With tear-filled eyes, Sergeant Beck concluded by saying, "I will never forget the panic on his face as he was tossed into the sea. I should have let go of my line and saved him. For this, I am guilty of his death."

The Captain asked a few more questions, then brought out a bottle of scotch and poured a small measure into two glasses.

Handing one to the Sergeant, he said, "Let us drink to Major Schmidt. We both played a small role in his demise. I confiscated his walking stick, while you might not have gone topside last night. But that is all that either of us has done wrong," the Captain said, and drank his whiskey in one gulp.

Beck hesitated. "So you're not reporting me, sir?"

"No," the Captain answered firmly. "There will be no hangman waiting in Argentina. You are more valuable to us in our engine room. Keep your story to yourself. I will not be making any changes to my official inquiry."

The Sergeant's face filled with relief, and he drank his whiskey in a single gulp as well.

At mid-morning, two days later, the boat reached its assigned grid for resupply. Using the boat's sonar system and hydrophones, they finally made contact with the Monsoon boat two hundred miles northeast of Sri Lanka. After some maneuvering, the two boats came to the surface at the same time, less than half a mile apart.

When Captain Miller reached the bridge, he was greeted by calm seas and crystal-clear skies. Gazing off his starboard, he could not believe the size of the milk cow. The U-490 was a Type XIV submarine that could be used both for troop transport and resupply. She could carry over four hundred tons of fuel, extra torpedoes, and food-stuffs for many months at sea. Her home port was Singapore, and she had been on station since early1943.

With both boats on full alert, the two subs came along side of each other, and the U-3521 took on twenty tons of fuel, fresh water, and provisions for another two weeks of travel. As this was carried out, the two captains stood on their respective bridges, shouting tidbits of information to one another. Miller learned that the Americans had long since bypassed Rabaul and had established a naval blockade of the harbor. He was cautioned about his approach. He was also told that the Java Sea might have American submarines lurking by many of the islands, waiting for prey. Miller asked whether the U-490 had resupplied the U-3520 boat, and was told that they had, three days before. As was the custom, the two Captains also exchanged bottles of liquor.

Just before parting company, the other Skipper shouted, "You're going to love our bread. We are famous for it. And the Singapore pork sausage is quite good." He hesitated. "I've been out here for over two years now. When do you think the war will end?"

Captain Miller tipped his white cap to the other Captain. "For all I know, sir, it may be over by now, and we just haven't been told. Stay safe, sir."

With every sailor pitching in, resupply took less than two hours. It would, however, take days to figure out what they had actually taken aboard, as the labels on all of the crates and boxes were written in Chinese.

With the sun high, the U-3521 submerged and turned southeast, making its way through the deeper waters of the Indian Ocean. Early the next morning, they turned northeast and passed Jakarta on the starboard side; here they entered the shallow waters of the Java Sea. The chart that the Commodore had given them was dated 1908, so Miller didn't put a lot of faith in his map. Instead, he consulted with his Navigator and changed the cruising schedule. The boat would remain on the surface during the night and only travel submerged in the daylight hours.

After entering the Java Sea, they began to feel the effects of the tropical breezes. The temperature dropped a few degrees, and the humidity dropped, as well. Late that first afternoon, they made contact with the U-3520 and were given instructions on the proper course for New Guinea. Commander Wiener was currently off Rabaul and would run the blockade early the next morning. The next evening, when they made contact with him again, he was moored safely inside the Rabaul Harbor. All had gone as planned.

Two days later, the U-3521 also ran the American blockade and entered Blanche Bay. Once inside the bay, Miller signaled ashore and waited, submerged, for a Japanese Minesweeper to lead the way into the harbor.

It was early evening by the time U-3521 moored next to its sister ship, under a large camouflage net in the Japanese shipyard. The lines had barely been secured when Commander Nomura, his wife Choko, and their baby appeared on deck, ready to leave. Captain Miller couldn't blame them; they had been thirty-five days at sea.

As they said their farewells by the gangway, the Commander handed the Captain a small, intricately folded slip of paper. "We Japanese love riddles, so I give you one, as our parting gift. Thank you for all kindness of your boat. Please read it after our departure."

Bowing, the Captain extended his hand to Nomura. "Thank you, sir. You and your family were a delight to have aboard."

As the two men shook hands, a group of Japanese officers appeared from across the gangway, led by an Admiral. When they confronted the Commander on deck, they all bowed deeply to him, including the Admiral.

That isn't right, Captain Miller thought, and only later discovered that Commander Nomura was of the Royal House of Japan, and third in line to be the next Emperor.

Alamitos Bay Marina, Long Beach

20 May 1963

With waters gently lapping against the hull, the little travel clock next to Dutch's berth emitted its annoying buzzer. Twisting in bed, he fumbled with the timepiece and finally managed to turn off the alarm.

It was a bright sunny morning, and his compartment was filled with harsh light spilling in from the skylight and portholes. Dutch slipped out of his bunk, wearing only skivvies, and opened a storage drawer under his berth. He removed a towel, a clean pair of underwear, and his shaving kit. Opening the louvered doors to the main saloon, he paused in the galley long enough to light a fire under the coffee pot.

The harbor was just coming alive; in the distance, he heard a few dogs barking, mixed in with music. The Long Beach marina was packed with hundreds of boats of all sizes and shapes. The moorage basin was a small community of boat lovers within the sprawling area of the greater limits of Los Angles.

Turning from the stove, Dutch walked the length of the saloon and entered the forward head, where he took care of business, then shaved in the small basin next to the toilet. When finished, he moved across the passageway and took a shower in the tiny stall. Drying himself in the companionway, he pounded on the louvered doors to Doug's compartment and yelled, "Assholes and elbows. We have to go to work today."

Doug's sleepy voice rang out from the other side of the door. "What time is it?"

Dutch slipped on a clean pair of skivvies. "It's after eight. The coffee's on and I'm going to dry my hair in the sun, so move it!"

"Drop dead!" Doug yelled back, clearly not a morning person.

Just after nine, the guys were picked up just outside the marina main gate by a Lincoln Town Car sent by NBC. The gray-haired limo driver, Max, gave each man a personalized folder that outlined the production schedule and details for the 'Witness to Yesterday' project. "I'll be your driver while you're working with the network. If you want to go anywhere, see anything, or need anything, just call me. It's almost an hour's drive to the Burbank studios, so sit back and relax."

Sliding into the luxurious backseat, the men found fresh coffee and donuts waiting. While drinking the hot brew and munching on the sweets, they read the thick folder and watched the palm trees speed by. When Doug finished his folder, he closed it and read the front cover: 'Welcome, LTJG Doug Asbow.' Then he noticed Dutch's front cover: 'Welcome Lt. Col. Dutch Clarke.'

"What the hell! You never told me you were some damn Colonel."

Dutch closed his folder and poured himself more coffee. "It got complicated at the end of the war. When Admiral King sent me to Japan, at the beginning of the occupation, he promoted me to the temporary rank of Lieutenant Colonel. A year later, when I mustered out, it was only as a Captain. No big deal."

Doug grinned at his friend. "Yeah, sure pal. I think I'm in for a lot of surprises with you, Dutch."

The NBC Burbank studios were an extensive compound of buildings and sound stages, with lots of Hollywood glitter. The complex reminded Dutch of the back lot of Paramount Studios, where he had worked for a time during the war.

The driver dropped the men off at studio headquarters. Inside, they checked in with a receptionist, who directed them to the offices of Ms. Meede. As they walked the busy executive corridors, Dutch felt a twang of nervousness roll through his body. Eighteen years had passed since he last saw Maggie. He remembered her as a beautiful woman with a charming personality. Had she not been ten years older than Dutch, he would have fallen for her. He straightened his sports jacket and collar as they came to her office. Inside, they checked in with a front desk secretary and were immediately shown into Ms. Meede's plush executive suite.

She was on the phone as they entered the office. Maggie glanced up at Dutch with a big smile, inviting them in with a swipe of her finger.

Dutch couldn't believe his eyes; she looked just like he remembered her. She had that special look, more handsome than beautiful. Her figure was still trim and full and her clothes, as always, were elegant. The only real difference he could see was a streak of gray mixed in with her auburn hair.

Hanging up the phone, she got up, moved to Dutch, and gave him a big hug. "Oh, Dutch," she murmured, "I was so sorry to learn of Laura's death. She was a very special woman."

As they parted, Dutch kissed her on the cheek. "Thank you, Maggie. I miss her desperately." Then he pulled back with a broad smile and continued, "You haven't changed one damn bit, lady!"

Dutch introduced Doug, and they talked for a few minutes about the old days and OWI. Doug listened patiently, clearly smitten with Maggie's beauty as well. As they headed farther down memory lane, her office intercom came on. "Ms. Meede, you're needed in the theater."

Maggie's hazel eyes twinkled. "Okay, boys, they need us in the theater. Everyone should be there by now. We can continue this later, Dutch, when you take me sailing."

The ground-floor auditorium held about three hundred seats, nearly all of which were full when they walked in. Maggie excused herself and went backstage as an usher showed Doug and Dutch to a pair of seats in an area reserved for the program witnesses. As Dutch took his place, he glanced around the theater and spotted Admiral King seated next to General Bradley. The Admiral nodded, and Dutch nodded back. Other than that, all the other faces were strangers. He guessed there were about a hundred witnesses seated in the reserved section. Then the lights dimmed, and the program started.

Many of the NBC executives were on stage, supported by their staff of producers, writers and directors. Maggie did the introductions then turned the program over to the show's executive producer who outlined his vision for the 'Witness to Yesterday' project. The six-part miniseries would air in 1965, the twentieth anniversary of the end of World War II.

The assembled observers were from all different disciplines. There were professors and intellectuals, who were experts on the world conditions that had led to the war. There were statesmen and diplomats, who would explain the failed diplomacy of the time and the Generals, Admirals and politicians, who had developed the final winning strategies. Then would come the front-line stories from the sailors, airmen and soldiers, of both the victors and the vanquished. The final episode would deal with the occupation of Italy, Germany and Japan. That would include stories about the horrible POW and concentration camps, and war-crime trials of the defeated countries.

The National Archives had sent over enough film footage for a dozen mini-series, along with thousands of still photos. All these materials would have to be reviewed and selections made for the final program. Scripts would have to be written, interviews filmed, music scored, and new graphics prepared. This would be accomplished by small working groups of the observers and NBC staff. The 'Witness to Yesterday' project was a major undertaking by the network, and it was being organized like a detailed battle plan. The executive producer ended his presentation with three simple words: "Informative, entertaining, enlightening."

The witnesses spent the rest of the morning filling out administrative paperwork. Then they walked to a back-lot soundstage, where they enjoyed a catered lunch. The group's mood was good as they mingled with each other, drinking fine wines and munching on fresh seafood. Dutch got a chance to speak with Admiral King, whom he had not seen since his uncle's funeral. By the end of the war, Admiral James King was the highest-ranking officer in the Pacific, reporting directly to the President. Unbeknownst to Dutch, Admiral King and Dutch's Uncle Roy had been boyhood friends, which had resulted in the Admiral acting as Dutch's 'Rabbi[13]' during the war. They enjoyed a pleasant exchange of memories, and agreed to get together for dinner before the project was over.

[13] High-ranking officer who watch's out for subordinates

At that first lunch, Dutch met many new faces, one of which belonged to a Professor Eric Jacobs. He was a strange little guy with a nervous twitch in his right eye, and looked much like a mad scientist. The Professor was in charge of German studies at UCLA. He had escaped Germany just before the Nazi's came to power, and had given counsel to the American Government on German Culture. Dutch took a liking to him right away. Then there was an older Japanese Navy Captain who claimed he had commanded a top-secret submarine that could carry airplanes during the war. Dutch had only a vague recollection of such a type of a submarine and he wondered about the truth of the man's claims. All told, the observers were an interesting group, and the next few weeks were filled with brain-storming and fascinating war stories.

After lunch, those who would be interviewed had a fitting at the Wardrobe Department, after which Doug and Dutch were split up and taken to their assigned work areas. There they met the other members of their respective teams. Dutch's production group included a line producer, a lady writer, a film editor, and two research assistants. His observer team included two enlisted mud Marines, who had seen action in most of the major Marine battles in the Pacific, as well as a full Colonel, who had commanded the Marines on Guadalcanal. There were also two retired navy nurses, one of whom had been stationed on Guam and the other aboard the *USS Relief*. Her name was Nancy, and she had served on the hospital ship on which Dutch had been transported to Hawaii in April 1945. "You were just skin and bones at the time," she said. "I remember you because you had a condom around your neck that no one could touch." Her words brought back a flood of dark memories to Dutch, and he made a concerted effort to refocus his attention to the activity around him. It helped that, right from the first, he liked his team. Each observer would offer a unique perspective in telling the story of the Marines in the Pacific during the war.

At four-thirty, Doug and Dutch met up again in the front of the headquarters building and were soon picked up by Max. As they slipped into the back seat, Max slid open the glass divider and handed Dutch an envelope. "It's a note from Miss Meede, sir. If you want to send an answer back, I'll see that she gets it."

Dutch took the envelope and opened it. It was just a single line: *When do we go sailing? Can Colonel Ford join us? Maggie.*

As the car pulled away, Dutch wrote out his reply, on the back of her note. *How about a week from Saturday at noon? Dock 14-slip 21, Alamitos Bay Marina. Of course Colonel Ford can join us. We'll sail to Catalina for a fine meal and a sunset cruise back. Can't wait... Dutch.*

Placing the note back in its envelope, he handed it to Max. "Do you know Miss Meede?"

"Everyone at the network knows her, sir," Max answered, looking at Dutch in the rear view mirror. "She's the glue that holds the peacock together. Would you guys like to stop for a drink?"

"Not tonight," Dutch said. "What time is call tomorrow?"

"Nine, so I'll pick you at eight. How about some female company?"

Doug spoke up from the back seat, with a grin on his face. "Thanks, but no need. We've got a whole damn Marina full of babes that live in their bikinis."

Max, smiled back in the mirror. "I envy you guys."

It didn't take long for Dutch to realize that having Doug aboard was like having a chick magnet around. Each night, with his striking good looks and trusting personality, Doug managed to welcome one or more of the local babes for cocktails and the occasional barbecue. On many early mornings, Dutch could hear one of Doug's 'lady friends' quietly scampering off the boat just before sunrise. They were all young, their bodies shapely as they lounged around in the most revealing bikinis Dutch had ever seen. And they all were as shallow as a mud puddle. He didn't mind having the eye-candy aboard, but his interest stopped there. He wanted nothing to do with the younger generation.

At the end of the first week, with a half-moon in the sky, and a warm breeze in their hair, the new mates sat in the open cockpit of the sailboat, enjoying a late nightcap. Doug had a few more days of production work, and then his portion of the program would be done.

"What are you going to do while I'm at work?" Dutch asked.

Without hesitation, Doug replied, "I'm going to renew my diving certificate."

"Wow, I didn't know you dove. When did you learn that?"

Doug took a sip of his brandy. "In San Diego, when I was a kid. I learned to surf, too. I always wanted to be a part of the 'endless summer' bunch."

Watching the moon shimmer on the water, Dutch turned serious. "What do you think about your work at the network? Are you glad you came along?"

Doug poured himself some more nectar, took another sip, and replied, "It rekindled too many damn memories that I've tried to forget. Guess I just can't figure out why I survived, while so many others didn't."

"That's why I was going to Hawaii," Dutch answered.

"Other than pretty girls, what's in Hawaii?"

"Navy records. I'd like to know where and when the hell ship[14] I was on went down, and where, and when I was rescued, weeks later. That might fill in some of my questions of *why*."

Doug flashed his friend one of his toothy smiles. "Well, it's your boat, and you're the skipper. Let's go there. I always wanted to see Hawaii as a civilian."

The following Saturday, Doug and Dutch welcomed Maggie and Colonel Ford aboard. It was grand to see them both again, without the distractions of the network. With a pair of stylish sunglasses on, Maggie stepped aboard wearing a pair of tan cargo shorts that revealed her muscular dancer's legs, and an elegant yellow silk blouse. She looked like she had just stepped out of a movie magazine. Dutch remembered Colonel Ford as a short fireplug of a man with salt-and-pepper hair and a personality that commanded respect. Now, at sixty-eight years old, the salt had displaced the pepper, and the fireplug had put on a few pounds, but his forceful personality remained undimmed. He was a combat hero from World War One, and had been a Lieutenant Colonel in charge of a Marine detachment of the Hollywood OWI during World War Two.

---

[14] Japanese POW ship

Dutch proudly gave the couple a short tour of the boat, then poured some iced tea and took everyone topside, where they came to rest in the comfort of the cockpit. With the engine started, Doug cast off the lines, and Dutch slowly backed out from the boat slip. It was tight quarters in the marina, but Dutch skillfully turned the boat and put her in forward gear. For the next few minutes, he maneuvered her around several obstacles while pointing out all the different types of boats in the moorage. Once in the harbor, Dutch increased speed and headed for the breakwater.

"Wouldn't want to be drunk, trying to getting in and out of that maze of a marina," Colonel Ford commented, grinning.

"I love the name of your boat, Dutch," Maggie added. "Where did you learn to sail?"

Standing tall at the stainless-steel wheel, Dutch smiled at his old friends. "Laura and her father taught me. And being drunk out on the ocean is really a poor idea. So, Colonel, are you still hobnobbing with the Hollywood elite?"

"Not so much anymore," he replied with a long face. "They see television as a threat to the movie industry, so they treat me like some kind of a leper. No more Brown Derby and no more polo games with the rich and famous. I'm just an old has-been, looking for a green pasture."

Maggie squealed with laughter. "He's pulling your leg, Dutch. The old movie moguls stand in line to have a few words with the Colonel. They both fear and respect him."

Once past the breakwater, Dutch aimed the boat west towards Santa Catalina Island. A few miles later, he turned the boat into a warm breeze and headed northwest. With Doug refreshing the iced teas, and serving appetizers from time to time, the conversation continued for the next few hours. Doug was a receptive audience for their stories about the old days at OWI and how the Navy hated Dutch for raiding some of their personnel for the Marines. Maggie talked about her 'boys' and how they went off on a secret missions, some never to be seen again.

With Catalina not far in their wake, Dutch turned the boat into the wind and Doug hoisted the sails. With the welcome quiet of sailing, the boat heeled over 20 degrees and took off like a rocket. The bow sliced through the water, kicking up a cool white spray, and everyone moved to the high side of the cockpit.

It was a perfect day to sail, and Dutch asked Maggie to join him at the helm. Standing behind her, he placed his hands over hers as she gripped the wheel and fondly whispered instructions in her ear. Soon, she was sailing the boat. With her face alight with excitement, she turned to Dutch and said, with a giggle, "This is better than dancing."

Everyone aboard enjoyed a marvelous run down to Avalon Bay on the southeast shore of Catalina Island. Dropping anchor, Dutch called on the radio for a water taxi, and they all went ashore for dinner.

A few hours later, with Doug at the helm, they departed Catalina and turned the boat for Long Beach. They had enjoyed a wonderful Italian meal on the island, with two bottles of excellent Chianti that Maggie had selected. In response to their questions during the dinner, Doug finally got a chance to talk a little about himself. He told them of his experiences as a POW during the war, and both Maggie and the Colonel seemed quite impressed with him. The Colonel had paid for the meal and purchased another bottle of Chianti for the sail home. Now, with only the jib raised, the boat slowly sailed for the mainland with the sunset in their wake. It was spectacular, filling the water with rich colors and striking reflections.

"Where are you boys going after the project is over?" the Colonel asked, opening the third bottle of wine.

Without hesitation, Dutch replied, "Hawaii and then maybe visit some old battle fields."

"Why?" Maggie asked. "What's out there, Dutch?"

Doug turned from the wheel. "Maybe some answers to the question *why*. Both Dutch and I don't understand *why* we made it, when so many others didn't."

The Colonel took a sip of wine. "*Why* is the age-old question of all warriors. I experienced it myself, after the First War. *Why* had I lived?"

Maggie grabbed on to Dutch, who was seated next her. "Are you sure you want to go? We could get you guys a job with the network. A damn good job, right, Colonel?"

Colonel Ford nodded, but said, "I don't think these guys are looking for work, Maggie. They're seeking something else, something I can understand. Still, if they're going to the Pacific, why not arm them with some cameras?"

"Cameras?" Dutch exclaimed. "What for?"

"The producer of the 'Witness to Yesterday' project has been complaining that he doesn't have very much cut-away footage," the Colonel answered. "So you guys could shoot some. You know, show what the battle fields look like, twenty years later. Rusty war relics, sunken ships, the white sandy beaches of the islands…that kind of stuff. NBC would loan you all the equipment, and buy all the film. What you shoot, you own, but we'd have first right of refusal on all the footage you bring back. If we use any, we'd pay you the standard going rate for stock footage."

"How much is that, sir?" Doug asked.

The Colonel replied, "Fifty bucks a second."

"Wow," Doug said, his mind clearly working overtime. "That's… Wow."

With the third bottle of Chianti almost empty, Dutch took the helm and started the engine while Doug lowered the jib. With a sky full of stars, he guided his sailboat back into the Long Beach harbor and through the maze of the marina. As Doug secured the boat, Dutch walked his guests to the front gate. It had been a wonderful day on the water, and the three friends said their good-byes under the harsh parking lot lights.

As Dutch pulled away from an embrace with Maggie, he asked, "Does the Colonel always make decisions so fast?"

She smiled. "Yes. Always. He's still in command."

Shaking the Colonel's outstretched hand, Dutch said, "Thank you, sir. We won't let you down."

"We have a deal then," the Colonel replied, with a firm handshake. "I'll send over the equipment next week."

On Thursday of the following week, when Dutch returned from work, he found Doug in the cabin, stacking cases and boxes on the salon table.

"What the hell is all this?" Dutch asked of his mate.

Doug handed him a typewritten letter on NBC stationery, from Colonel Ford. It outlined, in detail, all the equipment he had sent. The largest aluminum box was a complete outfit for an Arriflex motion picture camera with a zoom lens. Another large case held the underwater housing for the film camera, along with a battery-powered light strip that could be used underwater. There was also a long fiber case that contained a tripod. The smallest aluminum case held a Nikon Nikonos V 35MM underwater camera, assorted lens and two different types of light meters. The cardboard boxes were filled with raw film of all formats and speeds. There were sixty-two items typed out on the inventory list. Colonel Ford's closing paragraph said it all: 'Don't think we missed anything. Hope you guys scuba. Good shooting!'

Both Dutch and Doug were overwhelmed by the amount of equipment, and by its weight. Together, they began the slow process of moving all the gear into the storage bins under the port-side settee.

"What do you figure this equipment is worth?" Doug asked, lifting the largest aluminum case.

Placing boxes of film into an upper storage bin, Dutch replied, "Twenty grand, I'll bet. We've got a lot work to do on our way to Hawaii. I don't scuba dive and you're no photographer. This should be very interesting."

Doug flashed his friend a broad smile, "Well, at least we're NBC correspondents now. The ladies will like that."

Two weeks later, Dutch finished up with the network project. They conducted his interview on the morning of his last day. His uniform from the Wardrobe Department fit him perfectly, and they even had all of his battle ribbons correctly displayed on his left breast. The interview was easy; a line producer asked questions off-camera, and Dutch answered them on camera.

After the filming, he joined his group for a farewell lunch. Afterward he filled out a few more administrative papers, then went to the accounting department to pick up his pay. Doug had been paid for seven days, while Dutch was paid for nineteen days, which came to $3,800 before taxes. His per diem was an additional $1,045 tax-free.

That afternoon, Max drove him to a local bank, where he cashed the checks. Returning to the limo, he climbed into the back seat and began stuffing the big bills into his money belt. With all that cash in hand, he felt a little rich again. Thank God for Maggie and the Colonel. When the limo reached the marina, Dutch tipped Max a hundred dollar bill, and they said their farewells.

As Dutch walked towards the main gate, a man got out of an old, beat-up, pre-war Aero Willys convertible and approached him.

"Pardon me. Do you have a boat in this marina?" he asked. The man was fat and wore a lightweight, wrinkled trench coat. He was clean-shaven, with beady eyes and no chin. His shoes were dirty and his hair unkempt.

"Yes," Dutch answered, approaching the gate.

"I'm looking for a guy. Maybe you've seen him around," he said, and handed Dutch a small black-and-white photo.

Dutch looked at the picture. It was of Doug, dressed in a business suit and tie, looking every bit like the insurance man he once had been. "Why are you looking for this man?" Dutch asked.

"I'm a private detective from Frisco. He was last seen on some sailboat from Alaska in Sausalito. Do you know him?"

"That doesn't tell me *why* you're looking for him."

"I work for the Marin County courts, and I have some papers for him," the fat man answered.

Dutch handed back the picture, and turned to unlock the gate. "Sorry. I can't help."

"Well then, I'll just walk down with you and take a look around."

With the gate partly open, Dutch froze. "No you won't. You're not my guest." He pointed down the parking lot. "The Harbor Master's Office is down the block. They might give you a pass, but I won't."

The fat detective glared at Dutch. "You don't keep a very friendly moorage, do you?"

Dutch walked through the gate and closed it after himself. "Get lost, gumshoe."

Rushing to the boat, Dutch found a sunbathing Doug in the cockpit, drinking iced tea with one of his lady friends while the radio blasted out the Beach Boys.

Dutch hurried aboard. "Did you get the boat fueled up?" he demanded.

"No," Doug answered. "I don't feel comfortable, moving her alone."

"Well, we're going to move her now. We'll take on what fuel we need and get out of Dodge."

"What are you in such a fuss about?" Doug demanded, sipping his tea.

"There's a fat flat-foot up in the parking lot, flashing your picture around and asking questions. Your wife must have sent him."

"Your wife?" the lady yelled. "You told me you were divorced."

Doug turned to her with an earnest face. "Honest, I thought I was when I got home from the war. Then she reappeared, telling me there *was* no divorce, and demanding money."

The girl got to her feet, picked up her towel and suntan lotion, and departed in a huff.

"Thanks pal," Doug said, watching her sway down the dock.

With Doug hiding below deck, Dutch maneuvered the boat to the fuel dock and took on the diesel he needed. As he was paying the attendant, he noticed the flat-foot coming down the ramp from the Harbor Master's Office. Handing the kid his gate key, Dutch said, "Tell the office we're checking out."

Seconds later, with the engine humming, the boat pulled away from the fuel dock, while the fat detective fumed at the end of pier. Doug came topside and looked back at him. Raising his middle finger, he yelled, "Drop dead, gumshoe."

Chapter Six

Hacienda Canario, Argentina

21 May 1945

Señor Garcia sat atop his horse, surveying the work that had been done on his property. The lower portion of land had been tilled, in preparation for the spring planting of hops, and the upper pasture was completely fenced. All he needed now were a few head of cattle and couple of additional horses to make his dream of becoming a gaucho a reality.

He spurred his mount towards the barn. The last few weeks had been miserable. First had come Hitler's suicide, then the total surrender of Germany, and last evening he had ordered Captain Wattenberg back to port. The *Hercules* had spent ten days waiting in vain. The freighter had arrived at Santa Cruz Island on time and sent out numerous radio calls for the submarines, but no response had come back. It was as if the ocean had swallowed up both boats in a single gulp. Now the Colonel had nothing: no gold for his Odessa, no U-boats to present to Vice President Perón, and he hadn't even taken care of the Scorpion as he had promised. All seemed lost.

Inside the barn, he fed his horse and brushed him down. He always thought better on top of a mount, but tonight had been different; he couldn't shake the feeling of despair. In the waning light, he walked to the hacienda and noticed a light glowing from the housekeeper's cottage. They were snug in their home, while he felt lost on his own property.

Entering the house, he fumbled for the light switch, reminding himself that all of the Canaries were gone, except for Corporal Hirsch, his driver. Still, he was confident that the villa would soon fill again with a fresh batch of SS Brothers.

As he reached his den and turned on the desk lamp, he heard the front door bell ring. It rang twice more as he hurried to the entry. "Alright, alright," he yelled, turning the porch light on.

Opening the door, he was stunned to find Bruno Vega, his geologist, standing on the stoop, carrying an armful of rocks. The man's hair was matted, his face filthy and his clothes looked like rags.

"I must speak with you, Señor," Vega said with great excitement. "This cannot wait until morning."

Axel showed him into his den, where Vega dumped the stones onto the desk. As the cloud of dust dissipated, he said, "I told you I had a vision, and here it is."

Axel stood dumbfounded, looking at the pile of rocks. Most were the size of a fist, while others were three times as big. "What the hell is this?" he demanded.

The old man picked up one of the stones and pointed to it. "See the green color of the stone? And here, the pure copper veins. These are rich beyond my wildest dreams, Señor."

Axel picked up a rock and looked at it closely under the glow from the desk lamp. It looked mostly volcanic, with a greenish coloration, and small lines that looked like pure gold in the light. It was heavy, rough and flaky. "Is it of commercial grade?" he asked, holding back his own excitement.

"I will get them assayed tomorrow," Bruno assured him, his weathered face confident. "But, from my years of experience, I say yes. I have half of a truckload outside." Reaching inside his rag of a shirt, he pulled out the tattered map and spread it on top of the pile of rocks. "Let me show you where I found these."

The two men talked for well over an hour, as Bruno explained his travels. He had searched a large area in the southern province of Neuquén, and had been lucky in stumbling across a mostly deserted valley in the volcanic foothills of the Andes. His sample rocks had come from all across that valley, and each rock had a grease pencil number that corresponded with his map, to show where the samples had been found.

On his return trip, Vega had stopped off in the capital city to look up the owners of the land in question. For the most part, it was owned by the Central Government, but three parcels were owned by private landowners. Vega thought those parcels could be purchased, for the right price.

"Have you told anyone of your discovery?" Axel asked his mind reeling.

"No, Señor. Only you."

"I'll wake my driver and we will go to the office and help you unload. Leave the map here. I wish to study it tonight."

"Sí, Señor," the old man answered, puffed up with pride.

In the warehouse, the men unloaded the samples, placing them in cardboard boxes with the correct corresponding number written on the sides. When they finished, Axel gave the old man money for gas and groceries. "Tell no one of your discovery. We will take the samples to the Assayer tomorrow morning, so be here early. And, Bruno, get a good night's sleep. You deserve it, sir."

Corporal Hirsch and Axel watched as the old man's oil-burning pickup pulled out of the warehouse. Once he was gone, the Colonel said, "We will follow him home – but at a discreet distance. He doesn't need to know."

Axel had been to Bruno Vega's home only once before. It was a rundown villa, high up in the foothills that surrounded the city of La Plata. He remembered the drive up to the hacienda as long and dangerous, with many blind curves, a good twenty-minute drive from the city.

With the pickup's red taillight some distance ahead of them, the Corporal asked from the front seat, "Why are we following the old man, Colonel?"

"I want to make sure he gets home safely – and doesn't stop along the way to blab about his discovery."

Axel's mind was still awhirl with his good fortune. Only hours before, he'd had the sinking feeling that all was lost. Now he had the copper to hang his hat on. If he could secure mineral rights on the Government land and buy up the other three parcels, his money worries would be over, and Vice President Perón would be pleased with the news of a major copper discovery. This would enrich the Government's coffers, and more than make up for his lost submarines. For all of that to work, however, the secret of the discovery had to be kept.

When the pickup turned off the paved road and headed up the gravel driveway, he had the Corporal stop his car. "Let's give the old fellow time to reach his hacienda. Then we will follow. It's a treacherous drive, so stay alert."

As they waited, the Colonel climbed out of the backseat and went to the trunk. There, he removed a small flashlight and pliers from a toolbox. On his return, he said, "All right, let's creep up the hill."

They used only the parking lights, and it was after midnight by the time they reached the hilltop. The car stopped when the hacienda was only a few hundred yards away.

There were no lights to be seen. In the starlight, they could just make out the front of the villa, where Bruno had parked his old pickup. The Colonel got out of the car and joined his driver in the front seat. All was quiet, not even a barking dog. The night was cool but clear, and stars filled the sky.

"Now what, sir?" the Corporal asked. "Should we turn around and go back down?"

"No," he answered firmly, handing the pliers and flashlight to his driver. "Go to his truck and loosen the brake lines to the rear wheels."

Even inside the dark Mercedes, the Colonel could see the surprised look on the Corporal's face. "Why, sir?" he whispered. "What has the old guy done to us?"

"Nothing at all, but he's a Jew. I won't share the riches of this copper find with non-Aryans. He has to be eliminated."

The Corporal slowly shook his head. "Sir, the old fool just made us rich. It doesn't seem right."

"This is not a request, Corporal Hirsch, this is an order," the Colonel answered angrily.

Still shaking his head, the Corporal opened his door and quickly exited.

The Colonel watched as he approached the pickup and slid under the rear of the truck. With the flashlight blinking on and off, it only took a few minutes. Then he returned to the Mercedes. "Done, sir. Should we turn and go back down the hill, now?"

The Colonel didn't like the tone of his voice. "Yes, Corporal. You have done your duty."

The next morning, Axel was at the warehouse early, looking through the rock samples and studying Bruno's old map. As he worked at writing out a packing list for the Assayer, he heard his secretary rush through the front office door for a ringing phone. She wasn't on the telephone for long before Axel heard sobbing, and then silence.

A few moments later, with an empty coffee pot in hand, she entered the warehouse for its sink. Her eyes were red, her face long. "Oh! Señor Garcia. I didn't know you were here. Did you hear the phone ring, just now? That was the police. Bruno Vega is dead!"

Axel was prepared with a look of sad surprise. "How can that be? I helped him unload these rock samples, late last night. How did he die?"

Shaking her head she replied, "Some sort of accident, coming down from his hacienda. His truck plunged over a cliff and caught fire. So sad. I liked the old gentleman very much."

"So did I," Axel answered, forcing a sober tone. "Well, we will have to find another geologist, so get some feelers out. Oh, and have my driver pull my car around. I'm going to take Bruno's samples to the Assayer. Then we'll be out of town until late Thursday night. I'll be back in the office on Friday morning."

His secretary just stood there for the longest moment, holding the empty coffee pot, as if the cold practicality of his comments had shocked her. "Yes, sir," was her only reply.

After dropping off the ten boxes of ore samples at the Assayer office, Corporal Hirsch turned the Mercedes toward the southern province of Neuquén. It would be a thirteen hour journey across the heartland of Argentina to reach the capital city. With the Colonel quiet in the back seat, studying Bruno's old map, the car sped across some of the richest land in all of South America. They passed hayfields and farms, one after another, and ranches filled with working gauchos and cattle. Colorful towns, villages, and produce stands were sprinkled here and there alongside the road. This was the underbelly of the country, the pulse of the Argentine people.

The Colonel hardly noticed the fence posts go by, consumed as he was, with plotting how best to gain control of the mineral rights for the lands of Bruno's discovery.

It was near midnight by the time they reached the capital city. It was easy to find their hotel; at five stories, it was the tallest building in town. The Colonel took a two-room suite on the top floor, while securing a sleeping room with a shared bath on the ground floor for his driver.

They spent the next morning in the Hall of Records, retrieving all of the information and necessary forms to secure the mineral rights to the lands in question. That afternoon, they drove across the province until, in the shadows of the snow-clad Andes Mountains, they found the little valley of Bruno's disclosure. They spent hours walking the property, taking pictures of the area.

With all of the proper paperwork in the Colonel's briefcase, they headed back to La Plata early the next morning. During the entire trip, the two men hardly exchanged a dozen friendly words. If Corporal Hirsch was still brooding about his role in the old man's death, the Condor couldn't be bothered to notice, intent as he was on his plotting and planning.

They arrived at the mining offices just at dusk. The Colonel had the Corporal drop him off at the front door, telling him to wait while he ran into the office to see if the Assayer's report had yet been delivered.

He found it waiting on his desk, and quickly read it in the waning light. The Assayer had written out how much copper could be produced from how many tons of ore. All ten sample areas looked promising, and he had used words like 'of commercial grade' and 'a major discovery.' At the end of the summary, the Assayer predicted that the find could be worth millions of dollars.

Delighted with the news, the Condor stuffed the report into his satchel.

It was dark by the time they drove along the hacienda driveway. The villa was as black as the sky, reminding the Colonel that it was Thursday; his household staff had the day off. He used the car headlights to illuminate the entry while he unlocked the front door and flipped the porch light on.

"Take the car around back," he snapped at his driver.

Inside, he crossed the entry and turned down the hall to his office. When he approached his den, however, he noticed a sliver of light glowing at the bottom of the closed door, and he could smell cigarette smoke.

Reaching for the latch, he pushed the door open and stepped into the room.

His desk lamp was on, and his tall leather desk chair had its back to the room. Behind the desk, he saw that the hinged painting was pulled away from the wall, and the safe open.

As he took another step, the chair swiveled around, revealing the Scorpion, dressed in her formal black and white SS uniform. She had her Captains SS hat on, with its highly polished silver Totenkopf[15] reflecting the lamplight, the desk was covered with papers and files from the safe.

In her right hand, she held a Luger pistol.

"So you are back, Condor. How nice to see you again," she said sarcastically.

"What the hell are you doing here? And why is my wall safe open?"

A grin chased across her pretty face. "I could not resist its contents. You did have me followed, you little scoundrel."

"I never shared those pictures with Perón, but he knows. He told me so."

"Yes, I know," she said. "I sent him the pictures from the bistro."

"You what? Why? You could get us all killed."

She shook her head slowly, her green eyes glowing. "The negatives are my life insurance policy. If anything happens to me, every newspaper in the country will get prints of those pictures, along with the story of the Argentine Odessa." With her left hand, she lit another cigarette. Blue smoke hung over her hat like a cloud. "But that is your problem, Colonel. You didn't trust my instincts. When it comes to blackmail, no one plays the game better than me."

The room went quiet as the Condor glanced around, noting that the ham radio dials were lit up. "You don't have the guts to

[15] Death's head symbol

kill me," he said. "Without my bank account numbers, the Odessa is dead."

Nicole chuckled. "I knew those bank account numbers two days after our first meeting with your banker. I let him have his way with me, while I secretly took a few indiscreet pictures. The next day, when he was given the choice of me sharing the pictures with his wife or making me a full partner on the account… well, you can guess the outcome." She puffed on her cigarette. "And as to having the guts, do you recall me telling you about my good-for-nothing father who was killed by a political rival? That rival was me, at twelve years old. He had put his filthy hands on me for the last time. I shot him dead, and my mother helped me bury him before we returned to Germany. So, you see, I have no problem with killing."

"I never touched you!" the Colonel angrily replied.

"You were wise. Had you tried, I would have killed you."

Behind the Condor, the door to the study opened.

He twisted around and saw Corporal Hirsch entering the room, also dressed in his SS uniform. He was carrying a Luger pistol in his right hand. "Any problems here?" Hirsch asked.

"Yes," the Colonel answered. "Point that weapon at Nicole. She has threatened to kill me. That is an order."

The Corporal lifted his pistol towards the Scorpion, and then slowly changed its direction to aim directly at the Colonel. "All the copper information is in his briefcase. I know exactly what has to be done."

"Relieve him of it," Nicole answered.

The Corporal moved forward and took the satchel from the Condor's hand.

As he did, the Colonel glared at him. "I'm surprised at you, Hirsch. I thought you were a loyal Brother."

The Corporal grinned, moving away. "I'm done with doing your killings, sir. No more 'drive me here, drive me there.' And no more sleeping in dumpy rooms at fancy hotels. I prefer what Captain López has to offer."

"The Corporal has many hidden talents," Nicole added with a sly look, "some of which might surprise you, Condor."

The Colonel shook his head slowly and raised his hands, palms up. "Why all the uniforms? Are we going on parade?" he finally asked with withering sarcasm.

The Scorpion put her cigarette out in the ashtray. "No. I'm relieving you of the command of the Argentine Odessa."

"Captain Wattenberg may well have different ideas."

"I've already talked to him. He wants no part of the FBI waiting for him on the docks. He is still a wanted felon in America, you know. He accepts my command, as does Captain Klein." Her face turned to stone, and her grip on the Luger tightened. "You are hereby relieved, Condor."

Bang.

The Colonel heard the shot, feeling his leg buckle, he started to collapse, but managed to brace himself against the back of a chair. "You arrogant bitch," he moaned.

"I will be the queen of the Fourth Reich," the Scorpion answered with a manic grin.

Bang, bang, bang. Three more hot bullets riddled the Condor's chest. He fell backwards and crashed to the floor, with a dead blank stare looking upward.

As the stench of the gunpowder cleared, the Scorpion lit another cigarette. "Strip him of his identification. Take him to the docks, weigh him down, and dump him in the bay. Then hurry back. I'll put some champagne on ice, and we will share it in the Colonel's bed.

The Corporal smiled at Captain López, "Yes, ma'am. I do love a woman in uniform."

SS Colonel Rolf Kolb had but a fleeting heartbeat for his ATONEMENT.

Rabaul, New Guinea

30 April 1945

After the departure of the Japanese brass, Commander Herbert Wiener of the U-3520 came aboard and introduced himself to Captain Miller. As a full Commander, Wiener outranked Miller and, at thirty-five, he was one of the oldest living submarine Captains in the fleet. His reputation had preceded him, and Captain Miller welcomed him with respect, escorting him below to the wardroom to share some schnapps.

Over their drinks, the two Captains talked of their passage from Germany. Commander Wiener's boat had suffered from sea seepage during the entire voyage. While the Type XXI submarines were rated for a maximum depth of two hundred and forty meters, his boat would start leaking seawater at a mere sixty meters. These new types of submarines had been built by joining together a number of watertight compartments, and those components were then bolted together, using a rubber gasket between each watertight section. That was where they leaked the most, as the workmanship at the joints was unreliable. But what could a skipper expect? When the war first started, all of their submarines were built by skilled German workers. Now, those same workers were either dead or in the military, and the boats were built with forced laborers, under inadequate German supervision.

Captain Miller's boat had experienced the same problems, in only eighty meters of water. Huffman, the Chief of his boat, had come up with several fixes that minimized the problem, but Captain Miller still would not go any deeper than one hundred meters.

"I'll send my Chief over to your boat, sir. Perhaps he can show your Chief how to carry out the same fixes."

"Good idea. You heard that Hitler is dead?" Wiener asked matter-of-factly.

"No, sir! Our low-band radio went out a few days ago."

"Yes, he killed himself. We heard it last night on the BBC," Wiener said, expressionless. "They say Admiral Doenitz is now in command. I'll send my radio operator over. He might be able to help fix your radio."

Captain Miller was dumbfounded by the news. "Thank you, sir. Admiral Doenitz is a good man."

"Yes. But I don't want to linger here in port very long. I don't trust the Japs. When I asked for fuel and supplies, this morning, they gave me the run-around. How much fuel do you have in your tanks?"

Miller flipped the intercom on and put that question to Chief Huffman. The reply came quickly: roughly forty-four tons.

Commander Wiener scratched his weathered face and drained his glass of schnapps. "My boat has a little over thirty-five tons. We will need another fifty or sixty tons per boat to get to our next destination. After chow, let's walk over to the Admiral's headquarters and see what they have to say tonight."

After the Commander departed, Captain Miller returned to his compartment and removed, from his pocket, the intricately folded slip of yellow paper given to him by Commander Nomura. After carefully opening it, he read the riddle written in German; *100 miles northeast of where the Bounty boys hide, you will find Haiku Island.* He grinned at himself and flipped on the intercom. "This is the Captain. Anyone know what the words 'Bounty boys' might mean?"

His Exec came back to him. "It's from an old British seafaring book about the mutiny of the ship 'Bounty', sir."

"And where did the 'Bounty boys' hide?" the Captain asked.

There was a long pause. Then Josef replied, "Sorry, sir. I read the book years ago and I can't remember."

The voice of the freckle-faced radio operator came on. "Pitcairn Island, sir. The boys burned the ship 'Bounty' and the British never found them. Some descendants still live there today."

"Very good," Miller answered with a smile. "Thanks for the help. Captain out."

He opened his chart book and flipped through pages until he came to the map of the Society Islands, some thirty-five hundred miles away. Soon he located the Tahitian Islands, then searched the surrounding waters. It took some time, but finally, thirteen hundred miles, ESE, of Tahiti, he found a small dot on the map called Pitcairn. Northeast of that island, there were a few other tiny dots with no names. Now, he knew it all. But could he believe the story the Commander had told?

With dusk approaching, and with the sweet smell of jasmine in the air, the two Captains walked to the Admiral's headquarters. Once inside, they were informed that the Admiral was unavailable and were told to return the next day. Commander Wiener didn't appreciate being put off again, and began to argue with the Japanese officer at the front desk. Neither man understood the other, and the disagreement became a shouting match. As this was happening, Captain Miller moved to a window and noticed Commander Naokuni exiting the building through a side door.

Miller rushed out of the headquarters and sprinted around the corner, where he found the Commander just getting into the back seat of a staff car. He yelled to him, and waved his hands as he rushed forward.

"Commander, we need to talk," he said approaching the car.

From the darkening shadows of the back seat, the Commander's face appeared in the open car window. "Sorry, Captain. I must get to the airport."

"It's a matter of honor, sir. Your honor."

Naokuni scowled. "Very well," he said, stepping out of the car. "What is this all about?"

"I was told that you and Von Ribbentrop[16] came to terms for this mission. Is that true, sir?"

"Yes. Why do you ask?"

"Well, sir, as part of that agreement, you gave your word that the Japanese Government would resupply and refuel our boats after we reached Japanese soil. Well, we are here now, and the Admiral is giving us the run-around. That's not right, sir. It's not honorable."

The Commander glared at Miller, clearly offended by the implication that he wasn't honorable. "Very well. We will go and talk to the Admiral." Naokuni turned to his driver and rattled off a string of Japanese words.

The driver turned off the engine.

With the Commander leading the way, they walked back through the front office, where they found Wiener still arguing with the front-desk officer. Miller turned to him and said, "Follow us, sir."

They walked down a hall and passed, unchallenged, into the Admiral's plush rear office, where Naokuni picked up the phone and rattled off more Japanese words. When he hung up the receiver, Captain Miller introduced Commander Wiener to him. The two men shook hands and bowed to each other.

Commander Naokuni turned on the Admiral's desk lamp. "We will have some sake while we wait. The Admiral is on his way."

---

[16] Hitler's Minister of Foreign Affairs

Not long afterwards, the Admiral and his Adjutant came into the office. The three Japanese officers exchanged some heated words. The conversation lasted only a few minutes before Naokuni turned to the Captains and said, in German, "The problem stems from the naval blockade. Because of it, we are short of fuel and supplies on the base. And, with Hitler being dead, the Admiral doesn't want to waste his provisions on the lost cause of the Germans."

Captain Miller nodded his head gravely. "I can understand that, but you and Von Ribbentrop are still alive. It is your agreement to honor, sir."

Naokuni glared at the two Captains for the longest moment. Then, visibly fuming, he turned back to the Japanese officers and spoke to them with great animation.

That started an hour-long negotiation between the Germans and the Japanese, with Naokuni providing the translations. It soon became apparent that the biggest sticking point was the diesel fuel. The Admiral offered only twenty-five tons, while the Germans required over a hundred. In the end, they compromised on fifty-five tons. The balance of the discussion concerned bags of dry goods, cooking oil, canned goods, and fresh produce. The Captains even negotiated four cases of Japanese sake. The provisions they finally secured were meager but adequate, at least, for another few weeks at sea.

Once the talks were over, the five men bowed to each other, and Commander Naokuni hurried back to his car for the airport.

With a sky full of stars, and a cooling tropical breeze on their faces, the two Captains walked back to their boats. "We don't have enough fuel to cross the Pacific," Wiener said. "But there is enough to get us to Singapore."

"And then what, sir?" Miller asked. "The war in Europe is lost, and the Japs are only hanging on by a thread. We could be marooned in China for years."

"You're right, Captain, but it's over nine thousand miles to the Galápagos Islands. Bluntly put, we can't get there from here."

"Maybe we can, sir. We could load all of the fuel from both boats into just one, and leave the other boat behind, although many of the crew would have to stay, as well. Or…we could gamble on something Commander Naokuni told me."

"And what is that?"

The two men stopped to have a smoke, and Captain Miller divulged the secret of Haiku Island. In the end, although both men questioned the validity of the story, they had to agree that it was a better option than Singapore. And there was the chance that they could find some merchant ships to raid out in the Pacific.

The next morning, a Japanese barge came alongside and started pumping diesel fuel. The U-3520 would get thirty tons, while Captain Miller's boat took on only twenty-five tons. As the refueling proceeded, the docks gradually filled with trucks and trailers carrying food provisions. The decks of both boats soon became a beehive of activity.

In the midst of it, an SS Colonel came aboard the U-3521 and demanded to see Major Schmidt. He stated that his name was Colonel Friedrich Reinhart, and that he was in command of the SS contingent on the boats.

Captain Miller, informed of his demands, went topside to meet the Colonel. Standing on the aft deck, the two men saluted each other and then shook hands. Reinhart was young, with blonde hair and blue eyes. Captain Miller explained the death of Major Schmidt and the official inquiry he had ordered. "Schmidt's disappearance," he told the Colonel, "was attributed to his being swept overboard during stormy seas on the evening of 15 April 1945."

Reinhart listened carefully to the official findings, then demanded to see Sergeant Beck. Captain Miller took the visitor below to the wardroom and called in his Exec, with the log book, along with Sergeant Beck. The Colonel interviewed the Sergeant and read the findings in the book. Within the hour, he seemed satisfied with the inquiry, only expressing his personal grief for the death of the Major. "He was a good officer. I looked forward to us being together in Argentina."

After the Colonel returned to his own boat, Captain Miller closed the book again on Major Schmidt. *Reinhart seems like a reasonable man*, he thought, *even for an SS officer*.

Late that afternoon, both crews were mustered on the forward decks of their boats, wearing clean uniforms, with white porcelain coffee mugs in hand. Each Captain gave a rousing pep talk to the assembled crews. Wiener talked about the Fatherland, and the families left behind. He thanked the men for their service, and prayed for calm seas for the next leg of their journey. Miller took a different approach, speaking of the historic voyage that had brought both boats to the Pacific.

After the speeches, the young Ensigns walked among the ranks, pouring sake into all of the coffee mugs. Then, with Japanese sailors watching dockside, both German crews began to sing an upbeat Bavarian drinking song. Their rhythmic voices filled the air and drifted down the length of the waterfront. When the song was finished, the crews raised their mugs high over their heads and stomped their feet on the deck for a few seconds, then stopped and drank the Japanese wine in a single gulp.

Captain Miller watched the spectacle and thought, *We Germans may be defeated, but we still have the spirit to survive.* Then the Chiefs blew their whistles, and the crews reported below, preparing to get underway.

With the sun low in the sky, they departed the shipyard and followed the minesweeper through the mine fields. Once the boats were safely in Blanche Bay, they submerged and waited for nightfall. A few hours later, both boats slipped past the blockading ships and headed for the Solomon Sea. With crossed fingers, and fuel tanks below half-full, the Captains prayed they would make it across the Pacific.

With Commander Wiener's boat twenty miles in front of the U-3521, the Captains stayed submerged all night and all of the next day. When Miller surfaced, late on the evening of May third, he found the island of Bougainville twenty miles off his port beam. It was a beautiful night, with a cool breeze, so he released the off-duty crew for an hour's worth of swimming.

During that hour, his boat made radio contact with Wiener's boat, which was now fifty miles in front of them. Captain Miller cut the swimming time short. Once the crew was secured, he stayed on the surface, increasing his speed as they headed for the Coral Sea.

Two days later, they were well past the Solomon Islands, expecting soon to find the Fiji Islands off their starboard quarter. That was when they received the last contact with U3520. It was a short, garbled message that made little sense. It mentioned radio problems and confirmed the rendezvous point, which was thirty miles east of Pitcairn Island. Other than that, they could not even decipher the boat's current position. Captain Miller sent a response, but it was never acknowledged. The U-3520 seemed to have disappeared.

That evening, while having dinner, the Captain told all of the officers about the muddled message from their sister boat. "Due to fuel supplies, we will wait only 24 hours at the rendezvous point. Then we will proceed and attempt to find Haiku Island."

The faces of the men in the wardroom were filled with concern. "And what if we fail to find this mythical gas station, sir?" Navigator Karl Fritsch asked.

"I think we will succeed," Miller answered. "I have a fairly good idea of where it's located."

Lieutenant Kaplan spoke up next. "What if we get there and there's no fuel on the island, sir?"

Captain Miller raised his eyebrows. "If I have calculated right, we should have enough fuel to make it back to Tahiti, where we can surrender to the French."

Now all the faces were long. "The 'frogs' hate us sir. They will beat the shit out of us," one of the young Ensigns exclaimed, his face clouded with anger.

"I know," Miller replied, lighting a cigarette. "But there are no POW camps out here. They will have to send us back to Europe."

"Or there's always Devil's Island in French Guiana, sir," his Exec reminded him grimly.

They arrived off the southern coast of Tahiti late in the evening of May eighth. When the boat surfaced, they found themselves in the middle of a raging tropical storm. With gale-force winds blowing, the swells were twelve to fourteen feet tall. They had traveled for the last seventy hours underwater, and the boat's batteries desperately needed recharging. Since snorkeling in these heavy seas was out of the question, Captain Miller rode the storm on the surface for the next several hours. Being aboard a submarine while surfaced during a violent storm was like riding a bucking bronco, and half of the seasoned crew was soon seasick. As soon as Miller's Exec told him that the batteries were fully charged, he submerged the boat to the quieter waters of fifty meters, and turned east for the rendezvous point.

Early the next morning, they arrived, thirty miles east of Pitcairn Island. Before surfacing, they came to periscope depth and checked the weather. Miller was surprised to find calm seas, with no hint of a wind. When they surfaced, he and his Exec rushed to the sail bridge and found the ocean littered with storm debris. There were parts of trees, coconut husks and other vegetation floating all around the boat. When they looked straight up, they saw a small patch of blue sky; otherwise, from horizon to horizon, there was nothing but black, ominous clouds.

The Captain reached for the intercom quickly. "Chief, give me dead slow speed. The sea is covered with storm rubbish. We have surfaced in the middle of the eye of a hurricane." Almost instantly, the boat stopped in the water.

"This isn't good," Miller told his Exec. "If we hit a floating log, or if any of that vegetation fouls our propeller, we're in trouble."

Flipping the lever again, he said, "Chief, prepare to dive the boat very slowly to sixty meters. We'll wait out the storm underwater, and hope for the arrival of the U-3520 boat."

"Aye, sir," the Chief replied.

The diving horn blew, and the lookouts and his Exec descended below, but the Captain hesitated for a moment. Looking astern, he saw a tiny dot on the horizon: Pitcairn Island. He wondered how many descendants of the 'Bounty boys' still lived there.

Causing any submarine to dive is really quite simple. Sea water is allowed to flow into large saddle tanks on both sides of the boat. As the weight of that water increases, the boat descends. The depth of the dive is controlled by turning 'on' and 'off' a series of valves that allow the flow of the sea water. To surface the boat, seawater is pumped back into the ocean until the submarine has regained sufficient buoyancy. Captain Miller had submerged and surfaced thousands of times in his career. It was as commonplace to him as eating.

Standing in the control room, he watched the depth gauge slowly move downward. "Sonar, what's the depth of the water?" he asked.

"Hundred and fifty meters, sir," came the reply.

"And what does the bottom look like?"

"A few reefs and rocks, but mostly sand, sir."

At fifty meters, the Chief shouted to the sailors controlling the values, "Close the intake."

The boat's decent slowed a little, then increased again. The gauge soon was past sixty meters.

The Chief moved to the intake station and took over the controls for the four valves. Working the levers and reading the instruments, the Chief said calmly, "Valves one through three are all closed, sir. Valve four is still half open and taking on water. The forward, port side intake valve must be fouled with some debris, sir."

As the port tank grew heavier than the starboard side, the entire boat begin to list. "Start the port side pumps," the Chief ordered. Then, reaching for the intercom, he talked to the forward torpedo room. "Get your men searching for a manual shut-off lever for the port-side intake valve."

"Can the pumps keep up with the intake water?" Captain Miller asked, watching the depth gauge.

"No, sir," the Chief replied. "But they can slow the total intake."

A few minutes later, as the boat descended past the hundred meter mark, the list was almost twenty percent to the port. "Flood some water into the starboard-side tank, Chief, to correct this list," Miller said calmly.

"Aye, sir."

As time dragged on, reports of sea seepage in the watertight compartments begin to fill the intercom. "I've turned the bilge pumps on, sir. If that leakage gets to our batteries, we're cooked," the Chief said with concern now in his voice.

As the entire crew worked frantically to regain control of their boat, they had no way of knowing, that the day before, Germany had surrendered to the Allies. The war in Europe was over!

As the boat passed one hundred and thirty meters, the forward torpedo room called to report that they had found the manual intake valve, but that it was frozen open.

Chief Huffman went forward abruptly to help them close the lever.

At one hundred and forty meters, Captain Miller flipped on the intercom. "Prepare to impact the bottom."

With a heavy thud, that rattled the boat from bow to stern, their iron coffin hit the ocean floor, and all the lights went out.

Captain Hans Miller now faced his time of ATONEMENT under a shroud of five hundred feet of water.

Fifty Miles WSW of Long Beach

19June 1963

The cockpit of any sailboat is like a living room. While the cabin can provide protection, sustenance and a place to sleep, the cockpit is where you go for comradeship and conversation. Doug stood at the wheel with a warm evening breeze in his hair, watching the sunset just off the port bow. "What the hell are you doing down there, Dutch?" he yelled down the companionway hatch.

"Be right there," came the muffled answer from below.

The boat was under full sails, six hours out of Long Beach. Dutch had been below for almost an hour, and Doug had thought of some questions that needed answers.

With coffee mug in hand, his mate finally came topside and took a cushioned seat next to the helm. "Been plotting our course to Hawaii, and I cooked up some beans and franks for dinner. They're on the stove when you get hungry."

Doug put his back to the wind and a lit cigarette, then turned and pointed towards the bow. "Look how vast this damn ocean is. How are we going to find Hawaii?"

Dutch smiled at his friend. "Ah, so you've been thinking about navigation. Good. We'll stay on this course for the next three or four days, then we'll turn more south than west. By then, I hope to have a Honolulu radio station we can hone in on."

"How long do you think it will take us to get there?" Doug asked in the fading light.

"As a straight line, it's 2,200 nautical miles[17] to Hawaii. But we'll be on more of a curved course, so we will have to travel 2,700 nautical miles. With any luck, we'll manage it in sixteen days."

"How do we stand our watches?"

"Six on, six off. I'll take graveyard, starting tonight at midnight." He looked around. "Turn on our running lights. It's getting dark, and I don't want some big ship to run us down."

Doug flipped a switch on the helm column, and the lights came on. The masthead had a dim white light, with red and green hull lights, port and starboard. There was also a small light inside the compass dome. If needed, there was another switch for a harsh white light behind the cockpit.

Dutch stood. "Go below and get something to eat. I'll relieve you. What's your wife's name?"

In the last rays of the setting sun, Doug's expression turned to surprise. "Trudy. Why do you ask?"

"You've got a problem pal," Dutch said, taking the wheel. "She and that flatfoot will dog you the rest of your life if you don't do something."

Doug paused at the hatch cover and looked back at his friend. "Screw her!"

Sailing across the vast Pacific on a small sailboat can be a humbling experience. There are no road markers or signs. Other than seeing a few distant ships, the mates were totally alone. Living aboard the boat soon fell into a routine that only changed with the weather and sea conditions. Dutch ran the generator each morning, recharging the two batteries that had been used the day before to run the icebox and running lights. He also kept a daily log, where he wrote down the boat's estimated position, weather conditions, fuel consumption and fresh water usage. Each evening, after dark, he would turn on the radio and search for Hawaiian radio stations. On the third night out, he connected with a weak signal from Hilo, on the Big Island of Hawaii. Using the boat's directional finder, he was able to hone in on the station and confirm his general location on the navigational chart.

---

[17] 1 NM = 1.1508 statute mile

Doug's time away from the helm was spent keeping the boat ship-shape. He was even more finicky than Dutch when it came to keeping *The Laura* clean and neat. The upper deck was washed with soapy seawater, brushed and hosed down every day. All lines were curled and carefully stowed, and the rails were cleaned and polished. He kept the inside of the cabin spotless, as well, except for his forward V-berth, which looked like a pig sty.

The weather, currents and winds were with the boat for the first couple of days. On the morning of the third day, they approached the center of the high pressure system that was always parked off the California coast during the summer months. There, the winds died out and the sea became as smooth as a lake. Doug took that opportunity to give Dutch his first scuba lesson. They spent a couple of hours in the water with just fins and masks, swimming under the boat and checking out everything below the water line. Then Doug put on his breathing apparatus and showed his friend how the equipment worked. At the end of the lesson, Doug dove deep under the boat with spear-gun in hand, looking for fresh fish for dinner. A few minutes later, he returned to the surface empty-handed and climbed back into the boat, using the swim ladder on the stern.

"Saw a few sharks, but I didn't like how they looked at me," he said, removing his air tank. "Damn, that water is warm and clear."

Dutch grinned at his friend as he folded up the ladder. Then, standing by the wheel, he fired up the engine. "We've got plenty of beans & franks, although, I was looking forward to fresh lobster."

That night, before his graveyard watch, Dutch joined Doug in the cockpit. Only the jib was rigged, waiting for wind conditions to improve. Over the low hum of the engine, the two mates talked about what they hoped to find in the Navy records.

"Admiral King was kind enough to write me a letter of introduction. Maybe it will open a few doors on our quest," Dutch said, drinking coffee from a mug.

"Can't do any better than that," Doug replied from the wheel. "Do you think they'll really open all the records for us?"

Dutch chuckled. "Nah, the Navy is very protective of its own. What were you flying when you got shot down?"

"Dauntless SBD[18] off the aircraft carrier *USS Sargent Bay*. I got hit after my first bombing run over Davao Bay. The anti-aircraft fire was fierce, and we were strafed in our fuselage when I pulled up. It killed Henry, my rear gunner. The bullets only missed the back of my head by inches. Why he got hit and I didn't, I'll never know. Anyhow, my plane went down like a rock, straight into the bay. I no more than got out of the cockpit and the damn thing sank. Don't think I was in the water any more than a few minutes before the Nips had me. You know the rest."

"Was your carrier a baby flattop?"

"Yeah, a CVE[19]. It was brand new, fresh from a Kaiser Shipyard."

"Where did you take your advanced flight training?"

Doug frowned. "Astoria, Oregon."

"I've been there. I like that little town."

"All it did was rain, and the locals were as backward as a caboose."

Dutch noticed anger in his voice. *Doug's pretty opinionated*, he reflected. "So, what do you hope the Navy will tell us?"

"I want to know what happened to my ship, and to the other pilots in my flight. I think I was the only one hit, that day, but it's mostly just a blank memory to me, now. There's got to be more to the story."

Dutch stood and approached the wheel. "I'll take over, pal. Write all your that information down. We can give it to the Navy, if they need more time for research."

"Have you written yours out?"

"Yep, I'm on the beam."

Early the next morning, just before Dutch got off the night watch, the winds began to pick up. By mid-morning, they were under full sail again, making good time. Dutch figured they had lost a full day by having to use the engine, and they'd burned about ten gallons of fuel. He hoped for clear sailing, the rest of the way.

As they inched closer to the islands, tropical storms and rain squalls built up on the western horizon and then slowly drifted

---

[18] Douglas Aircraft dive bomber

[19] The type of a smaller aircraft carrier

their way. The first good-sized storm hit the boat at about the halfway point of their passage. Late one afternoon, the winds kicked up and the seas turned dicey, with five-to-six-foot swells. Soon, the boat was deluged with one rain squall after another. The mates put on their yellow foul-weather gear, lowered the mainsail, and reefed the forward jib. This allowed the boat to answer the helm better as they turned diagonal to the wind. The Voyager 45, surprisingly took the storm in stride, and cut through the sea like a warm blade through butter.

When Dutch stood his watch at midnight, the sea conditions were still miserable and building, so he put on a lifejacket and tied his waist-rope to the boats railings, port and starboard. Being hog-tied to the boat assured him that no sneaker wave could throw him overboard. Then he turned on the small bow headlight that had been installed back at the Warrenton Boat Works. Skip had warned him many times about sailing in a storm at night. There were too many floating obstacles, reefs and shoals that he needed to see in the water.

About two A.M., Doug poked his head up through the cabin hatch and yelled over the wind, "Can't sleep in that damn forward berth in this storm. Been bucked out of bed three times."

Dutch looked at his friend in the dim cabin light. "Try one of the bunks in the aft cabin. They're off the wind. When we get to Honolulu, we'll buy some lee cloths to strap ourselves into our bunks. Get me a cup of coffee, pal, and a dry towel. I feel like a drowned rat."

A few hours later, the storm blew itself out. Just before sunrise, the skies cleared for a brilliant new day. Their first big storm had been a learning lesson about surviving whatever Mother Nature might have to offer.

On the sixteenth day, the Big Island of Hawaii came into view. Dutch's navigation had been off by only a few miles. The mates soon found a small protected cove on the north shore of the Big Island and dropped anchor. There, Doug gave Dutch his second diving lesson, and they snorkeled all around the inlet. It was an amazing experience, and that night they enjoyed fresh fish for dinner, along with a few drinks of whiskey.

The next day, they turned the boat into the channel that separated Maui from Hawaii, and sailed due west for about thirty miles before turning north for the island of Oahu. It was late in the afternoon of July seventh that they moored the boat in the Waikiki Marina, inside of the Ala Wai Boat Harbor. The sailing gods had been good to them, and the friends celebrated with an expensive meal at one of new, tall hotels that had sprouted up along the shoreline. After dinner they walked to a market, bought a few provisions and the local newspaper. Then, back at the boat, they enjoyed themselves by catching up on the news and talking about future plans.

Doug handed Dutch the front section of the local paper and pointed out a small story on Page Three. "Read this."

The headline said, 'Cannibal Tribes Discovered on New Guinea'

"I understand there are lots of Cannibals out here in the islands," Doug said, looking concerned. "Do you have any firepower aboard for protection?"

"Nope, only our flare gun and my Marine-issue side arm," Dutch answered.

"Well, if we're sailing out there, we'd better buy some. We need a shotgun and a rifle, with extra ammunition."

Dutch chuckled at his friend. "I've had some first-hand experience with Cannibals, so all right, we'll arm *The Laura*."

Doug looked stunned. "Tell me about it."

That started another evening of swooping stories about the POW camps. It was constant subject of conversation, as both men had been so severely scarred by their captivity.

Early the next morning, the mates got up, showered and shaved with fresh water. What a luxury! Then they dressed in their best street clothes, walked to the marina main gate, and hailed a cab for the Fleet headquarters on Ford Island. As they drove downtown, Dutch was amazed by the growth of Honolulu and all the tall new buildings that had sprouted up to awaken this once-sleepy island town. He also took note that there were no longer guards checking traffic as they drove onto the Pearl Harbor Naval Station. *The world is at peace*, he thought as they pulled up to the headquarters.

Once inside the building lobby, they found hordes of busy people, both in and out of uniform. Making their way to the reception desk, Dutch confronted a young Navy Yeoman.

"Can you please direct us to Navy records?" he asked.

"Do you have an appointment? If not, state your business," he replied nonchalantly.

Dutch quickly recalled the old Navy shuffle. "We don't have an appointment," he answered, reaching inside his breast pocket for his letter. "But I do have a letter of introduction from Admiral James King." He handed the young man the paper.

The Yeoman glanced at it. "Sorry, sir. I don't know the man. He's not in our chain of command and I can't help you," he said, handing back the letter.

Dutch chuckled to himself. *The Navy hasn't changed at all.* Pointing to the letter, he raised his voice. "You don't know Admiral James King, Yeoman? See those five stars on his letterhead? Admiral King is the man who helped win the Pacific War. Now, sonny, direct me to someone who *does* know something!"

Just as Dutch had hoped, a passing officer in a full Commander's uniform stopped dead in his tracks when he heard the loud commotion, and turned back to the reception desk. "May I see that letter?" he asked.

Dutch handed him the short note.

10 June 1963

To whom it my concern,

Please extend to Lt. Col. Dutch Clarke all military courtesy in his quest for information concerning the details, plans and results of actions, taken in the Pacific theater of operations during WWII. This information may be used in the production of a documentary film being produced by the NBC Television Network to celebrate the twentieth anniversary of the end of World War II.

Lt. Col. Clarke, along with other former military personnel, are assisting the

network in the production of the 'Witness to Yesterday' project.
Sincerely,
Admiral James King

The Commander, keeping the letter, scolded the Yeoman. "I'll take care of these men. Son, you'd better bone up on your Navy history if you want to succeed out here." Then, turning to the mates, he continued, "Follow me, fellows. I know who you should see."

They walked with the Commander to an elevator and took the car to the top floor. Then the three walked down a long corridor to an office with a door that proclaimed: *Commanding Admiral, Seventh Fleet*. Inside the office, the Commander talked with the woman at the front desk, and the three were soon taken into the Admiral's impressive office.

"I rescued these men in the lobby, sir. They have a letter of introduction written by Admiral James King, and I thought you might like to meet them," the Commander said, handing over the letter.

The Admiral read the note with a broad smile on his face. "Which one of you is Clarke?" he asked.

Dutch came to attention and replied, "I am, sir. Dutch Clarke, US Marines. And my friend here is Lieutenant JG Doug Asbow. He was a Navy flyer, we were both POWs during the war."

The Admiral got to his feet and extended his hand across the ornate desk. The men all shook hands. "I'm Admiral Thomas Moorer, and the Commander here is Bill Hitch, Fleet Public Information Officer. I served on Jimmy's staff in '45. He's a fine officer and a great leader. How can I help you?"

Dutch explained their needs at Navy Records, the Admiral instructed Commander Hitch to take them there personally and introduce them to the commanding officer. "Anything else?" he asked.

That was when Dutch dropped the bomb shell. "Yes, sir. We would like permission to dive on the Battleship Arizona. We would also like to photograph the new memorial. We saw it this morning when we drove in. It's a beautiful monument, sir."

Both officers' faces looked stunned by the request. Dutch had read somewhere that the Navy never allowed diving on the sunken ship. They considered it to be a sacred resting place for over a thousand who had lost their lives aboard.

"That's something we just don't do," Commander Hitch began, in a somber voice.

But the Admiral interrupted. "Except maybe in this case, Bill. A celebration of the twentieth anniversary of the end of the War might be the perfect time for Americans to see the new memorial and the tomb of our dead sailors." He nodded slowly and said, "Yes, I'll allow this. When, Dutch?"

"How about tomorrow, sir?" Dutch answered, excited.

Doug shook his head. "Wait, Dutch! We've got to get your diving certificate, and organize all of that film equipment. How about this coming Saturday, Admiral?"

The officers agreed, and Commander Hitch was given detailed instructions on what paperwork would be needed. As the men left the Admiral's office, he said, "Bill, don't forget to alert the Shore Patrol. I don't want these boys spending their weekend in our brig."

Commander Hitch walked the men over to Navy Records and provided the introductions, then said goodbye. He was a fine officer, and the mates knew they had been lucky to have his intervention.

The Commanding officer personally saw to their records needs and instructed them to return on Friday for photostats of the information they might find.

On the cab ride back to the marina, they stopped off at a war surplus store and bought an M1 carbine and a pump-action 12G shotgun. While they were there, Dutch discovered a near-new portable Smith-Corona typewriter, which he bought for keeping his journal and daily logs. Then, with the firearms tucked away in leather pouches, the men returned to the cab, where Doug told the driver to take them to the best diving instructor on the island.

"When you asked the Admiral about diving on the Arizona, I about passed out. I had no idea you wanted to do that. Geez, Dutch, give a guy some warning."

"I didn't know myself, until we drove in this morning and I saw the new memorial. This could be some great footage for the program."

"Yep, and at fifty bucks a second, it'll be a real money-maker."

Dutch frowned. "No pal, it's not about the money. The Admiral was right. This is the perfect time for Americans to see the new memorial and the tomb for our dead heroes." Dutch never revealed his true motivation for wanting to photographic the memorial. That was his secret alone.

The dive shop wasn't far from their marina. Dutch paid off the cab and they went inside and met the owner, a bronzed young man named Pete Smith. He and his wife taught diving and surfing to locals and to the tourists on Waikiki Beach.

Pete had been a Navy Frogman during the Korean War. When he learned that the guys had official permission to dive on the Battleship Arizona on Saturday, he got so excited that he offered his instruction for free, if he could join the dive. "I'll have you fully certified by then," he promised Dutch. They agreed, pleased that they would have a professional coming along.

The next few days sped by like a whirlwind, taken up by diving instructions with Pete in the mornings and equipment testing and filming with Doug in the afternoons. They found a local film lab that developed their footage overnight, and Dutch was quite pleased with the early results. The mates even dove in the marina waters, testing the underwater housings for the cameras. For Dutch, returning to film work was like riding a bike – it just came naturally.

By late Thursday morning, Dutch had earned his diving certificate and purchased a complete scuba outfit from Pete, who talked Dutch into also buying a used, rubberized dive suit. "There are lots of sea creatures that sting out here, and the suit will give you some protection," he insisted. The tab for the equipment wasn't cheap, but Dutch gladly paid it, grateful for all of the free instruction he had received.

With his arms loaded with the new outfit, Dutch departed from the shop with Doug "See you at the boat at 0800 on Saturday," he called to Pete. "This should be a dive to remember."

That afternoon, Doug and Dutch returned to Pearl Harbor and shot footage of the new USS Arizona Memorial. Their first setup was from the shores of Ford Island, looking out across the harbor. The white monument was a sleek-looking, open-air structure that straddled the space above the sunken battleship. It was beautifully designed, and well suited to serve as a sacred tribute to all who had lost their lives on that horrible day, December 7, 1941. The weather was nearly perfect, with puffy white clouds in the background that contrasted nicely against the dark blue sky. With only a slight tropical breeze, the American flag flapped lazily on top of the structure as crowds moved around inside the monument. Dutch was pleased with what he saw in his viewfinder, and excited to take the short boat trip out to the memorial.

Their second setup was from the dock of the monument, with the green hills of Oahu in the background. He and Doug shot footage of people arriving on Navy shuttle boats and walking up the gangway to the memorial.

Their final setup was inside the open-air structure. As Doug set the camera up on the tripod, Dutch walked around, looking at all of the exhibits that told the awful tale of that day of infamy. At the closed-off end of the monument, he found a marble shrine that contained the names of all of the gallant men who went down with the ship. His keen eyes quickly found the name he was looking for: Lieutenant JG Ralph Earl Person. Going down on one knee in front of the panel, Dutch pressed his fingertips gently to Person's etched name. Then, lowering his head, and with tears in his closed eyes, he said a silent prayer. When he had finished, he stood and kissed the fingertips that had touched the name.

"Did you know the Lieutenant?" one of the Navy guides asked.

Dutch wiped away his tears. "I introduced myself to the Lieutenant, and told him I had married his widow and raised his son. I told Ralph about his fine boy, and how he's now in his second year at Annapolis."

The Navy guide shook his head sadly. "I hear these tragic stories all the time, sir. Step over here. I want to show you something."

Dutch joined the sailor at one of the open-air windows and looked down on the sunken ship. "See that oil still rising from the wreckage? We call that the 'black tears' of all the men entombed aboard. He is thanking you, sir, for your words of love."

Late that afternoon, they returned to the boat and lugged all their equipment into the main cabin again. As Doug went topside, Dutch went to work, unloading the four-hundred-foot reel of film[20] that he had loaded that morning. Afterwards, he did the same with the 35mm camera Doug had used. The exposed film would be taken to the lab the next day.

As he worked below, he could hear Doug topside, washing down and mopping the deck. Then there were muffled voices. A few moments later, Doug pounded on the deck with his mop handle and called out, "Hey, Skipper, you've got two young ladies admiring your boat. Come up and meet them."

Dutch shook his head. *Here we go again*, he thought as he moved up the companionway.

Topside, he found Doug leaning on his mop handle, a huge smile on his face as he talked with two attractive young women on the dock. The first, was short with long blond hair and overstated makeup, dressed in a colorful bikini and a see-though kaftan. The other was a redhead with short hair, wearing a sleeveless yellow blouse and black shorts. Both had pretty faces, shapely bodies, and leather sandals on their feet.

The redhead smiled at Dutch. "We just told your friend, here, that your boat was the best of the bunch. Are you guys sailing back to the mainland?"

"No," Dutch replied. "More than likely, we'll head south to the Marshall Islands, then on to the Philippines."

"Why?" the blond asked with a surprised look. "What's out there?"

Before Dutch could answer, Doug replied, "We're NBC correspondents, so we go where they send us."

The redhead frowned at Doug, who was still leaning on his mop. "Sure you are. Well, boys, you're going the wrong way. We're trying to hitch a ride back to the States. Sorry if we interrupted your important work."

---

[20] About twelve minutes of footage

There was just bit a of a New York accent in her sarcastic voice. "No problem," Dutch said with a grin. "Good luck to you, ladies. Hope you find a ride home."

The two girls turned and started walking away. After a couple of strides, the redhead turned back to the boat and said, staring right at Dutch, "Good luck to you, too, Skipper."

As Dutch watched them walk farther down the dock, he was surprised by the look the redhead had flashed him, and the fact that he'd felt it, deep inside.

"We should have asked them aboard for a drink," Doug said, still watching them.

Dutch moved towards the hatch. "No, you're thinking with the wrong part of your body again, pal. We came out here for answers, not bimbos."

Returning to the cabin, he opened the bottle of Yukon Jack. He hadn't had a feeling like that for almost three years. *Maybe I'm not as dead inside as I thought*, he mused, and poured himself a stiff drink.

Chapter Seven

USS Arizona Memorial

It was ten in the morning by the time *The Laura* motored into Pearl Harbor and dropped anchor one hundred yards off the Memorial. It was another perfect day in paradise, with gentle breezes and clear blue skies. As the three divers prepared their equipment, Pete Smith, the diving instructor, was about to put out the red diving buoy when a navy launch approached. Aboard were two Shore Patrolmen and Commander Hitch standing in the bow.

As the boat came alongside, Dutch called out, "Commander! Surprised to see you again, sir. Are you diving with us?"

"No," he answered, with a single sheet of paper in his hand. While the two sailors held their skiff to the sailboat rails, he continued, "The Admiral and I wrote out some do's and don'ts for your dive. We would like to see the results of your work when you're done, so I've put my phone number at the bottom of the sheet. Please give me a call when you're ready." He handed the paper across to Dutch. "Read these and let me know if you have any questions."

They were simple rules. The Navy considered the sunken hulk of the Battleship *Arizona* to be a sacred resting place for the 1,102 Sailors and Marines entombed aboard. Therefore, the divers could not come to rest on any part of the ship, nor touch anything, peer into windows or open hatches. The tomb was not to be disturbed in any way. They could swim or float by the ship from above or alongside, but they could not stop with any part of their bodies touching the *Arizona*.

"I don't see any problems, sir," Dutch said, handing the rules to Doug and Pete. "The film will be ready Monday afternoon. I'll phone you to confirm, and give you the address of the lab."

"We didn't think there would be any problems, Dutch," Commander Hitch replied with a proud smile. "Get your buoy out and we'll stand off to keep the area clear of other boats. Have a safe dive, guys."

As he put on his scuba equipment, Dutch was as nervous as a bridegroom. The day before, the Navy hadn't been very helpful.

Both Doug and he had been disappointed with the photo-stats they had received from Navy Records. All that Doug learned was the day after he got shot down, his CVE was ordered to the Philippine Sea, where they transferred all their aircraft and pilots to a big fleet aircraft carrier. Then his ship steamed home for more pilots and planes. The only other record he got was the official report on him being shot down in the skies over Davao Bay. Dutch had been a little more fortunate and had received seven battle reports from warships and subs operating near the Philippines during the first week of March, 1945. One report, from the sub *USS Trigger*, described the sinking of a Japanese destroyer and the probable sinking of a freighter four hundred miles north-east of Mindanao. It had all the right details: time, location and date. He was confident this was the battle in which he had escaped his Hell-Ship. But that was it. They had no records of PBY[21] rescues in and around Guam two weeks later. "If you want that information," the Commanding Officer had told them, "you'll have to visit Naval Records on Guam. They're photo-statting all their records, but that project won't be completed until next year."

Back on the boat that night, Doug and he had mused on the lack information. Finally, they had decided to sail for Guam and then Mindanao, where they had both been held captive. The only problem with their plan was that Guam was four thousand miles away! That would be a long thirty-day sail, with only one rest stop along the way, at Wake Island. They had spent a sleepless night, worrying about such a long and dangerous passage.

But the challenge for today was diving around the *Arizona.* As he slipped on his heavy breathing tank, fins and mask, Pete checked his equipment. Doug was first into the water, and then Dutch went down the ladder. Pete handed the hefty tripod to Doug, and the bulky film camera in its water-proof housing to Dutch. Then Pete joined them, with two still cameras in hand. "We dive slow and deliberate," he said calmly. "I'll turn on your air valves, and you do the same for me."

When everyone was ready, the three men slowly descended into the depths of Pearl Harbor. Dutch's mind ran like a racehorse as he went down. "*I'm an oilman, not a damn photographer*," he

---

[21] Catalina flying boat.

thought. "*Don't descend faster than your bulbs rise. Keep your wits about you, you fool.*" Then a sand shark swam by, and he snapped back to reality. What he saw through his mask was spectacularly beautiful, a whole new world. And the imposing gray hulk of the *Arizona*, while tragic, was like a looming, ghostly image, both frightening and marvelous.

When the divers reached the shallow, sandy bottom, they found fish everywhere and clumps of seagrass blowing to the rhythm of the currents. It was almost hypnotizing. Using hand signals, Dutch had Doug set up the tripod close to the ship's bow. Then he fastened and leveled the camera on top. Finally, after taking a light-meter reading, he stood and stared out at the wreckage, giving it a momentary hand salute. This was the tomb of his brothers, and the resting place of Laura's husband. He prayed his work would be worthy of their memory.

So resolved he began filming in the bright and shadows of the reflecting sunlight on the coral green waters. He did all the basic shots: slow zooms, tilts and pans. While he filmed, Doug and Pete used their still cameras, doing the same. They moved the tripod twice more, to the stern and then to the beam. In each new location, he repeated his filming techniques. Once done, he removed the film camera from the sticks and swam, handholding it, down the entire length of the battleship from a low position. Then he slowly swam back from a high viewpoint. By the time he reached the bow again, he was out of film. Using hand signals, he told his diving partners he was going up to reload. They signaled the same need for their own cameras.

Pete was first on the surface and climbed the aft ladder. Doug was next with the heavy tripod, which he handed up to the boat. Dutch was the last on top, and handed the camera to Doug. Then, climbing up the ladder, he heard applause. Standing in the cockpit, the men took their masks off and turned in the direction of the clapping.

Across the water, on the Memorial, a large crowd of people were watching the divers. The men smiled and waved back their appreciation, then set about reloading their cameras. A few moments later, they were ready to dive again.

"We all have about twenty minutes of air, so keep any eye on the time," Pete said, and rolled back into the water.

On the second dive, they didn't bring the tripod, and Dutch had increased the camera's speed to twice the normal setting. That change would allow him to shoot slow-motion footage as he swam the length of both sides of the battleship. This new setting would also consume twice as much film as the normal speed. It was a gamble of film usage versus visual effect.

His first swim down the port side of the Arizona was from a high vantage point. As he floated down the ship, he kept his eyes concentrated on his viewfinder. On the starboard side swim back, he changed his angle and held the camera out in from of him. That way he could point the wide-angle lens to different areas of the ship. It was a jaw-dropping experience to watch the twisted wreckage, mangled decks and colorful tropical fish slowly pass by his camera lens.

Twenty minutes later, the men were back on the sailboat, with proud smiles all around. This had been, indeed, the dive of a lifetime, and the men couldn't stop talking about it. Waving to the crowds still watching from the Memorial, they unloaded their cameras and stowed the equipment below. Then, snatching up their diving buoy, they weighed anchor and did a final bow for the folks across the water.

As the sailboat motored past the Navy launch, Doug shouted to Commander Hitch, "See you on Monday, sir. We got some great footage."

The Commander smiled and saluted back.

Dutch stood at the wheel on the way to the marina, while Doug and Pete sat in the cockpit, still yacking about the dive. He had shot two four-hundred-foot reels of 16mm film, while they had shot two rolls each of slide film. They talked about the colors, and the quality of the underwater light, and worried openly about their exposure control.

Changing the subject, Doug looked up to Dutch and said, "Saw you saluting the ship. Didn't know your wife had been married before, or that you had a stepson."

Dutch smiled at his friend. "Don't have a stepson. I call him son. I'm the only father he's ever known. He's a fine young man and will make a great officer."

"You and your wife never had any children together?" Pete asked.

"No. God knows, we tried. The doctors think it was the malaria that caused the problem. They kept telling us that time could heal all things, but it never worked."

Doug shook his head sadly. "Same with me. That damned malaria made me sterile. Guess we all came back from that lousy war with scars."

"Yep," Dutch answered, maneuvering the boat around another craft. "But we're still alive. Not like those poor brave bastards back on the *Arizona*, God bless their souls."

As Doug secured the boat in their slip, Pete came up from the cabin with his equipment. Handing his two rolls of film to Dutch, he asked, "Will you take my film to the lab? And can I come with you guys on Monday?"

"Absolutely. We'll pick you up at your shop, Monday afternoon. And thanks, Pete, for introducing me to that beautiful world down under."

After a quick lunch, Dutch and Doug hailed a cab and took all their film to the lab. On their way back, they had the cab stop off at a Marine chandlery, where Dutch bought two navigational charts for their sail to Guam, and two more maps for their passage to Mindanao. He also got lee cloths for all the berths, more teak oil, and four five-gallon containers. The two metal cans would be used for extra diesel fuel, and the two blue plastic containers for extra water. As they shopped around the store, Dutch noticed a thick book with a cover that proclaimed, *Divers Guide to the Pacific Islands*. Thumbing through the pages, he found maps, pictures and text about hundreds of different islands scattered around the Pacific. He snatched the book up, without a second thought.

When they returned to the boat, Dutch and Doug filled the new cans with fuel and water, respectively, and secured them under the cockpit seats. Then they installed the lee cloths on all the berths. It was late afternoon by the time the mates decided to go out to dinner to celebrate their dive. "We owe it to ourselves," Doug said. "After all, we made some money today."

It was near dark by the time they left the boat, dressed in street clothes, and headed for Waikiki. They had heard the music and gaiety many times since arriving at the marina, and now they looked forward to experiencing the local flavors.

They didn't have to go far before finding a Polynesian eatery called Bob's Bamboo Room. It was a typical restaurant for Waikiki: wicker walls and open windows, with palm trees and tiki torches out front. Inside, Don Ho sang Hawaiian music from a Wurlitzer, while Mai Tai's flowed like a river. It was a noisy joint, but clean, so the mates pulled up a couple of rattan chairs to a cane table. They started out with a rumaki appetizer and Piña Coladas, and then ordered steaks. When the food came, they found the ribeye's smothered with a savory teriyaki sauce, with fresh pineapple spears and fried rice. Over the food, they relived their morning dive, and toasted each other. After dinner, both friends changed their drink orders to rum and Coke, and watched the tourists come and go.

Soon, the jukebox was turned off, and a live band started playing more modern music. Then people started dancing. Once Doug saw that, he was out of his chair and on the dance floor with a pretty Hawaiian gal. Dutch watched them dance, nursing his drink. He was envious of Doug, and how the ladies liked his style. *One thing for sure, he doesn't waste any time*, Dutch thought, swirling his drink. Then he felt a tap on his shoulder. Looking up, he saw that the redheaded gal who had stopped by the boat was standing next to his table. She wore a smile and a short, colorful muumuu around her trim figure.

"Want to dance, Skipper?" she asked with a friendly face.

Dutch was stunned by her presence. "Didn't expect to see you again," he stammered. "Where's your friend?"

"She's walking with a gentleman friend on the beach. I'm going to rescue her in few minutes, so let's dance. It's a good Twist song."

To his own surprise, Dutch found himself getting to his feet. He hated the dance crazes of this younger generation, and hated their music, as well. He had never tried twisting before. *What the hell am I doing?* he thought as they stepped onto the dance floor.

"Just let the music move you," the redhead whispered in his ear. Then she started dancing, twisting her hips and arms to the rhythm of the music. Her movements were as graceful as a swan, and Dutch tried to follow along. There was something special about her, but Dutch couldn't put his finger on it. Instead, he kept thinking, *This is a silly dance…no one touches*. Fortunately, a few minutes later, the music stopped and they left the dance floor.

"Will you join me for a drink?" Dutch asked as they returned to his table.

"What time is it?" she asked.

Dutch looked at his watch. "It's early. Just ten o'clock."

She shook her head. "Sorry, I can't stay. I promised Heidi I'd rescue her at ten. Maybe another time." She turned and started to walk away.

"What's your name?" Dutch called out.

She stopped and turned around. "Lois Berg. See you around, Skipper." Then she flashed him another one of her looks, and Dutch felt that knot in his stomach again.

The next morning, over a late breakfast, the friends read in the newspaper about an approaching summer storm. It was scheduled to hit Oahu on Sunday afternoon. "Opportunity is knocking," Dutch said with a grin. "We'll take the boat out and get some cut-away footage of the dark storm clouds over Oahu. It could symbolize the coming of war in 1941."

They spent most of the afternoon out on the choppy waters, filming Diamond Head and the mountains surrounding Honolulu. It was good stuff, and they returned to the marina with another reel of film. As they pulled back into their boat slip, they spotted the redhead and her friend, Heidi, waiting on the dock. They both were dressed in shorts and floral tank tops.

"Thought you guys might have shipped out for good," Lois said with a smile, as Dutch turned off the engine. "We came bearing gifts. Can we come aboard?"

"I think you'd better. It's going to rain," Dutch answered as he stepped off the boat and secure the aft line. He helped both girls aboard. "Let's go below. We're about to be drenched."

They had no more than gotten into the cabin when the tropical squall hit the docks. Over the sounds of the downpour, Dutch showed the ladies around the boat, while Doug secured the movie camera and stowed it away. When they returned to the main salon, Lois reached into her handbag and handed Dutch a book.

"You told us you were off for the Marshall Islands, and we thought you might need some extra reading material. It's a used copy of *Mutiny on the Bounty*."

"And my gift is shirts," Heidi beamed. As she pulled two garish Hawaiian shirts from her pink poodle bag. "You boys need to start looking like the natives."

The guys were amazed by the gifts. "Very nice," Doug said, taking one of the shirts.

"Yes, very nice, but why the interest?" Dutch retorted.

"We need to get off this island," Lois said, with a hopeful expression. "And we were thinking about signing on with your boat."

Dutch smiled broadly while shaking his head. "I don't think so ladies. This isn't a pleasure cruise, or some type of a love boat. We have a long, dangerous voyage ahead, and the last thing we need is two more mouths to feed. Sorry, but it's not going to happen."

Still with an encouraged look, Lois replied. "Hear us out, Skipper. Maybe we can change your mind. We would make good mates."

"Yes, let's hear them out," Doug eagerly responded.

"Alright, but first understand this. My name is not Skipper, it's Dutch Clarke, and my mate here is Doug Asbow. Our plans have changed. We are sailing Wednesday morning for Guam, not the Marshall Islands. Now tell us your story."

If Lois wondered *Why Guam,* she didn't ask. Instead, she explained that she'd been born in '33, and came over from Germany when she was just two years old. She was raised by her maternal uncle in New York City, where she attended private schools. After high school graduation, she'd gone to Boston College, then came west and earned a master's degree in sociology from UCSB. For three summers, during her college days, she had crewed aboard a sailboat taking tourists on sight-seeing cruises around Boston Harbor. In June, after graduation from UCSB, on a lark, she had signed on as ship's cook with a large, fancy yacht out of Long Beach. The owner of the cruiser was a rich businessman who was taking four of his cronies to Hawaii for the fishing. Lois had met Heidi aboard the yacht, where she had signed on as a bartender and waitress. They were the only women aboard. Everything went well for the first few days, but then the men started wanting more than just food and booze from the girls. That was when things had turned ugly.

"When we reached Honolulu, the captain ordered us off his ship and refused to pay our wages. We've been marooned here for four weeks now. We both got part-time jobs, but at a dollar an hour, we can't afford to live out here. The fact is, Dutch, we're dead broke."

"Why didn't you wire home for money?" Doug asked.

"My pride, I suppose. They had already done so much. I couldn't ask for more," Lois answered, looking determined.

She was one smart cookie for a thirty-year-old, and she knew her way around sailboats. Certainly, Lois had some talents the mates could use. But then there was Heidi. She was born in '40 in Bakersfield, California, where her parents owned an almond farm. Heidi was pretty, but as naïve as a preacher. Her only claim to fame was that she had been the Almond Queen for Kern County in '60, after which she had gone off to bartending school. Dutch knew right off that she would be just an extra mouth to feed.

When they finished telling their story, Lois asked, "Well, Dutch, did we change your mind?"

"I'll think on it," Dutch replied with a frown. "You girls come back, late tomorrow afternoon, and I'll give you my decision."

"Let's have Heidi mix us some drinks," Doug said with an enthusiastic smile.

"No," Dutch replied firmly. "I've got letters to write. We can have a drink together tomorrow, after we return from the lab."

That evening, while Dutch sat in front of his Smith-Corona, pecking out letters, Doug bent his ear about the girls. He thought it was a great idea to have an extra person at the helm.

"And what would Heidi contribute?" Dutch asked.

To that question, Doug was quite silent.

The next afternoon, wearing their loud Hawaiian shirts, they hailed a cab and picked up Pete at his dive shop. When they arrived at the lab, they found the Admiral and Commander Hitch waiting in one of the projection rooms. Soon the lights dimmed and the projector flickered on. The screen filled with the scorched and rusty hulk of the *Arizona*, strands of seaweed hanging from its rails and dancing in the currents. Just as a rainbow-hued fish swam by, the camera moved in on the forward deck guns, askew in their mounts and crusted with barnacles. The iconic old battleship had never looked so proud.

For any photographer, viewing their own raw footage was a nerve-racking experience, even without an audience. Dutch had worried all weekend about his shot selection and exposure control. But it soon became clear that the photography gods had been with them. What they saw on the screen was outstanding. The camera work was slow and deliberate, the colors vivid, and the shot selection and exposure were near perfect. Even the Admiral applauded after watching the film. Dutch puffed himself up a little, proud as hell of what he had just watched on the screen. As the lights came back on, both the Admiral and Pete asked for duplicate copies of the film. Dutch explained his deal with NBC, and how they had 'right of first refusal' for all his footage. Then he showed them the letter he had written to Ms. Meede, requesting that copies of the Hawaiian footage be given to both Pete and the Admiral, as a gesture of thanks for all their help.

"These copies can't be used commercially until after the airing of the 'Witness to Yesterday' program," Dutch told them, but they seemed happy with his explanation, and accepted his terms.

As the Navy got up to leave, the Admiral asked, "Is there anything else we can do for you, Dutch?"

"Yes, sir, if you would. We are sailing for Wake Island. Will you contact the base commander and let him know we're coming?"

"No problem," the Admiral replied, shaking hands with Dutch.

After the officers were gone, the guys and the lab manager went over the still pictures and did some paperwork. Dutch gave him the letter to Maggie, to include with the shipment of the film back to NBC. An hour later, they were finished and on their way back to the marina.

On the ride back, Doug told Pete about the two gals who had volunteered to become crew members.

"One knows her way around sailboats," Doug said with a grin, "while the other chick can mix drinks. They are both awesome eye-candy."

"Just what we need," Dutch inserted with sarcasm, glaring at his mate.

Pete shook his head with a far-away look. "Wish it was me coming along, guys, but my wife would kill me. Besides, you'll have more fun with the ladies than you would with me."

"See?" Doug said. "Even Pete thinks we should take them along. How about it, Dutch?"

When they arrived back at the boat, they found the two girls, in cutoffs and blouses, seated in the cockpit.

"Hope you don't mind that we came aboard to wait," Lois said.

"Not at all," Dutch replied, unlocking the hatch cover and sliding it back. He then opened the twin louvered cabin doors from the inside.

"Come below, ladies," Dutch invited. "I have something to show you."

The girls took a seat behind the table on the starboard settee, while Dutch reached into his nook and brought out two navigational charts. He unfolded the maps on the table and put them side by side. As Doug slid onto the couch next to Heidi, Dutch said, "I want to show you where we are going." He took his finger and pointed to the Hawaiian Islands. "Here's where we are." Then he moved his pointer finger slowly across the lengths of both maps before dropping it on a small island. "And here is our next destination, Guam. That island is thirty-eight hundred miles away. That's a passage, if we're lucky, of just under a month. If we get in trouble out there, our only hope is here, Wake Island. It will be our only rest stop, and it's about halfway between here and Guam. Many a ship has perished trying this passage. We could hit bad weather, someone could get sick and need a doctor, or we could lose the wind and drift aimlessly for weeks. Worse yet, we could run out of fuel, food and water. All sorts of calamities could happen to us." Dutch paused and stared somberly, directly at the gals. "Think over what I've just said, while I make us some drinks."

The girls looked bewildered as they gazed down at the maps. Dutch moved to the galley and reached for some plastic glasses. He was proud of himself; the first part of his plan was working. He hoped the ladies would soon be scared off the voyage.

Reaching for some ice cubes, he asked, "Heidi, what would you like to drink?"

"Wine spritzer," was her quick answer. Doug wanted his usual. Then Lois slid out from behind the table and crossed over to the galley. "What are you drinking, Dutch?"

"Yukon Jack. It's a whiskey. What the hell is a wine spritzer?"

Lois smiled, her green eyes glowing. "White wine and club soda."

"We don't have any club soda."

"Just pour the wine over the rocks with splash of water. She won't know the difference. I'll join you in some whiskey."

Moments later, Lois handed both drinks to the table and returned for hers. Dutch poured one finger of Yukon Jack into her glass, and two fingers' worth for his glass. Lois frowned at him. Then she picked up the bottle and added one more finger to her glass.

She stared right at him. "I'm no lady, Dutch. I'm a redhead filled with determination and a fiery temper. The Lord gave me a body suited for pleasure and a mind full of dreams. If you treat me with respect, I'll repay you tenfold."

She raised her glass and tipped it to Dutch, and then she took a drink. "Good stuff," she said with a smile, and returned to the table.

Dutch just stood there for a minute, watching her. He was beginning to see her in a different light; she had courage, spunk and honesty, rare qualities for her generation. Then Doug started explaining the boat's assignment for NBC, and how the mates would be filming the old Pacific battlefields. As he talked, Dutch slipped into his stateroom and retrieved from the closet the firearms they had purchased at the surplus store, and his handgun, which he kept under his berth. After checking that they were all still unloaded, he returned to the main salon and put the guns down on the maps.

"Now *why,* you might ask, would we need all these guns, if we're just sailing around the Pacific? Well, that's a good question. It's because many of the islands we might stop at could have cannibals," Dutch said, keeping his expression serious.

"Wow," Heidi answered, big-eyed. "A 12-gauge Winchester plumb-action and a .30 caliber M1 carbine. Those are fine weapons."

Dutch was surprised by her awareness. "You know about guns?"

"Yep. My uncle came back from Korea with an M1. It didn't have a firing pin, though. My brother and I played with it growing up. And Dad took me bird hunting all the time. In fact, my 'talent' for the Miss Almond Pageant was skeet shooting."

Dutch pointed to his pistol. "And this?"

"That's easy. Colt 45, Navy issue. Never shot one before, but Dad told me they have a hell of a kick."

Dutch shook his head slowly. "You're full of surprises, Heidi. Now let me tell you about the weather out there..."

He talked gloom and doom for another few minutes, and finished up by telling them that it would be the first of next year when – and *if* – the boat reached home again.

"I hope you can see how dangerous our voyage will be, and reconsider your request to join us," Dutch concluded with his most somber look.

Doug glared at him. "Geez, Dutch, you've got *me* scared as hell! You're the best damn preacher of pestilences I've ever heard. Makes me want to jump ship before it sinks," Doug said sarcastically. He turned his face to the girls. "Listen ladies, is it going to be a long, dangerous trip? YES. Is it going to be the adventure of a lifetime? YES. Do you girls still want to come along?"

Lois turned to her friend. "What do you think, Heidi?"

"That's why I signed on with the yacht," she replied. "I wanted to have an adventure. This is better yet."

Lois nodded. "I agree. If we don't sign on, we'll regret it for the rest of our lives."

"Wait a minute," Dutch objected as his plan slipped away. "Did I try to scare you a little? Maybe. But if that's not going work, then I'll try honesty. Lois, you know your way around sailboats and the galley. Those are skills we could use. Heidi, unfortunately, your only skill is bartending, and we don't drink while we are underway. So I'll pay for your airfare home."

Without even thinking, Lois quickly said, "No. When we got marooned out here, we promised to stick together. We're a pair. I'll teach Heidi her way around the galley, and she'll keep the coffee hot and plentiful. She also knows about guns, and she can stand guard on the boat when you guys are diving or going ashore. Don't shortchange her, Dutch."

"And," Heidi inserted proudly, "I have another skill. I gave my father and brother haircuts while I was growing up. And you guys look like you need some help in that department."

"Come on, Dutch. We both could use a trim," Doug added with a hopeful smile.

Dutch swirled his glass, staring into it, lost in thought. "Alright," he finally said. "But there are three conditions. First, this is not a pleasure boat. There will be no onboard romances. Second, Doug you'll have to move into the bunk berths so the girls can have the forward compartment. And, finally, I'll draft some 'ship's articles' tonight, and tomorrow everyone will sign them. Do we all agree?"

"No problem," Doug answered. "The V-berth has better storage for the girls."

Dutch looked over at the gals; they both had wide grins and nodding heads. They were, indeed, about to start the adventure of a lifetime.

Before the girls departed that evening, Dutch gave each of them twenty dollars and instructed them to use the money for buying any personal items they might need on the voyage. "Where we are going, there are no grocery stores," he told them. Lois hesitated at first about taking the money. Her pride seemed to be in the way, so Dutch reminded her that they were now part of his crew, and that he was their Skipper. Reluctantly, she finally took the money.

That night, as Dutch typed out the ship's articles, Doug asked, "Are you pleased the girls are coming along?"

Dutch chuckled, "Yes. We're a civilized crew now. We even have our own barber aboard."

Passage to Wake

The next morning, the mates took a cab to the largest supermarket on the island, where they purchased two shopping carts of food. The tab came to just over a hundred and twenty dollars. When they returned to the marina, the cab driver helped the guys make two trips down to the boat. Dutch tipped him five dollars, and then they set about storing all the supplies in the cabin. When they finished, there wasn't any spare storage space left.

As Doug moved from the forward compartment to the bunks, Dutch motored over to the fuel dock and filled up the diesel tank. Returning to the boat slip, he secured the fresh water hose connection and electric power for one more night. Then he walked to the Harbor Master's office and paid their tab.

Back on the boat, he counted out the remaining money in his belt. The stopover in Honolulu had drained his purse by almost six hundred dollars. And now he had two more mouths to feed.

When the girls came aboard in the afternoon, the guys helped them get squared away, and Dutch gave the ladies a detailed guided tour of the sailboat. He first stressed the importance of conserving the fresh water. "We only have two hundred gallons of water. That's our lifeline. Once underway, the toilet and shower will only pump seawater. But the galley sink is connected directly to our fresh water, so use it wisely. It's only for cooking and drinking." He showed them how to operate the hand-pump sea toilet, how to light and use the gas stove, and how the refrigerator worked. He took them into his small nook and explained all the different equipment. He even opened up the sole floor and showed them the engine and the generator compartments.

After that, they went topside, where he showed them where the life jackets were stowed, and how to inflate the rubber life raft. Each gal stood at the helm, and he explained all the levers, switches and gauges. He concluded by giving them a safety pep talk. "Your life is worth more than this boat, but this boat is our only lifeline. Treat it with respect, and it will reward you. And if you get into trouble, shout out."

Going below again, he passed out carbon copies of the ship's articles. The first part of the document was simple: who, what, where, when and why. The last section spelled out the money part. "Ship's articles have been used by sailors for hundreds of years," Dutch explained. "It's all about shares. Any money we make from this voyage will be shared in this way: I get twenty-five percent, the boat gets twenty-five percent, Doug gets twenty-five percent, Lois gets twelve and half percent and Heidi the same. Any questions?"

"What money?" Lois asked.

Doug explained their deal with NBC, and told them about the price that would be paid for the stock footage.

"Why does the boat get twenty-five percent?" Heidi asked, looking confused.

"Because the boat provides all the food and fuel for the voyage. It provides the means to make the money. As it is now, I'm lending the boat that money, and it will pay me back from its share. It's the way the old whaling ships worked."

"How much do you think we might make?" Heidi asked.

Dutch smiled at her. "If we're lucky, we'll share five or six thousand dollars."

The girls beamed at each other. "Wow," Lois said. "We signed on with the right whaling ship. Let's make our mark and be on our way."

Everyone agreed with good cheer, and they all signed at the bottom of the articles.

Later that afternoon, Lois took charge of the galley and cooked a bon voyage feast. Her spaghetti dinner had all the trimmings: garlic bread, green salad, and couple of bottles of red wine. It was a marvelous meal, with flavors and smells that would linger for days. At the table, Dutch said the blessing, holding his wine glass high. "We pray for fair winds and will fear not the storms or the calm."

At the crack of dawn the next morning, everyone took their last fresh-water shower and had a hardy breakfast. The boat was underway and out of the harbor while the sun still low in the sky. With calm winds, Dutch motored due south for almost an hour, then as the breeze freshened he turned the boat due west and stopped the engine. Taking his pocket-sighting compass in hand, he checked the coordinates of Diamond Head to the north and the island of Molokai to the west. Then he went below and checked his sightings on his chart. With the boat's general position plotted, he figured out what the heading should be.

"Let's hoist the sails," he shouted as he returned to the helm.

Both Doug and Lois were topside quickly. Dutch watched carefully as Lois cranked up the heavy mainsail. Her face was full of determination, and her muscles glistened in the morning sunlight. Within a few seconds, in a brisk breeze, both sails were set, and the boat was underway, heeled over nearly 15 degrees. Lois proved herself that very first morning. She knew her way around the deck, and was as strong as an ox.

As the *Laura* sliced through the water, the bow slapped the seas, sending loud crashing noises down the length of the hull. Dutch turned the helm west-southwest to 265 degrees, ecstatic to be sailing again on the open ocean.

When Doug and Lois joined him in the cockpit, he pointed to the compass and said, "This is our course for the next week or so. Once we make radio contact with Wake, we can make any necessary corrections."

In the open companionway hatch, Heidi showed her concerned face. "Do I need my life jacket?" she asked in a frightened voice. "The boat is leaning badly. Are we sinking?"

Lois and Doug laughed. "No, Heidi, we're just underway," Dutch called from the helm with a grin.

The crew soon fell into the typical routine of a sailboat. Lois took the helm from eight in morning until four in the afternoon. Doug had the afternoon-to-midnight watch, and Dutch stood the first dog watch, midnight to eight. After each watch, there was extra duty for all the crew. Heidi helped Doug keep the deck scrubbed, while Lois worked in the galley, making simple but tasty meals. Dutch kept the logbook and watched over the navigation.

The farther the boat sailed from Hawaii, the hotter it got. Without the cooling tropical breezes, it was soon over ninety degrees on deck. Everyone aboard dressed down as far as they could. The men wore shorts, deck shoes, and their loud Hawaiian shirts, while the ladies lived mostly in their bikinis.

On the second morning, Heidi set up the nook chair on the top deck, in the shade of the mainsail. Then, with the warm wind in her blond hair, she set about giving Doug a haircut. Lois had the helm, while Dutch stood next to her, watching Heidi work. She wrapped a white towel around Doug's neck and, clad only in her bikini, started moving her shapely figure while cutting and trimming. All the while, Doug just sat there, watching her every move with a lecherous gleam in his eyes. When she finished, she snapped the towel free of the hair and turned aft to the wheel.

"It's your turn, Dutch," she said, smiling, with towel in hand.

As he moved towards the main deck, Lois quietly said, "Enjoy."

Dutch found himself surprised by Heidi's skills. She had a gentle touch, and used her scissors and comb with great skill. She even talked incessantly, like a real barber. Her banter was mostly about herself and how she almost became a hairdresser. "I would have taken up cosmetology, but the bookwork looked so hard. So I took up bartending instead. We only use one book, Old Mr. Boston's Bartending Guide."

When Heidi finished with his haircut, she bent low in front of him, and removed his towel. As she did, she said, in a soft, persuasive voice, "I give really good close shaves, and I have all the right tools…if you're ever interested."

Uncomfortable at her boldness, Dutch stood slowly and looked at her with a red face. "Thanks for the trim," he said meekly.

With his face still flushed, he moved to the cockpit and asked Lois, "Are all the girls in your generation that forward?"

"Don't know. Never met all the girls in my generation. Did you enjoy the view?"

He answered with a shy grin. "First time I ever had a haircut by a barber in a bikini. I could get used to this."

"I'm pretty good with scissors and a comb, myself," she replied.

Dutch raised the palm of one hand. "Whoa, you'll make me blush again. I'm going to bed."

"Sweet dreams," she answered with a grin.

Dutch didn't mind his midnight watches. The weather was cooler, and he trusted himself while underway at night. He had keen eyes and above-normal night vision. He also loved the visitors that infrequently stopped by: dolphins, flying fish, and the occasional whale. There was something about the solitude of being under the stars that he relished.

The quiet nights also gave him time to reflect on family, friends, and what the future might hold. Before leaving Hawaii, he had sent letters to his son and godson at Annapolis, to Skip and Louise in Ketchikan, and a lengthy note to Maggie. Everything seemed right, but he was still worried. He wasn't sure having the girls aboard was a good idea. They were too much of a distraction, too much of a temptation. The memory of Laura was still heavy on his soul, and he wouldn't let her go. He would never forget or replace her.

After Lois relieved Dutch on the fourth morning, he went below to make entries in his daily logs. While he made the notes, he noticed a problem. The boat had already used almost twenty-five gallons of water. That was impossible; the crew could not have drunk or cooked with that much water in such a short time. As he scratched his head, he heard the shower running and watched more water disappear in the gauge. Getting to his feet, his ire up, he swiftly moved forward and pulled open the shower door.

Inside, Heidi let out a scream, her hair full of shampoo. In the hot fog, he saw the intake lever, behind her, open to the freshwater tank. Reaching in quickly, he moved the lever to seawater.

"What the hell are you doing?" she yelled as the saltwater flowed.

"Get your damn clothes on, Miss Beauty Queen. You and I are going to have a talk," he yelled back angrily.

He paced the cabin, waiting for her to reappear. As soon as she did, he lit into her. "I told you about our limited supply of water. Why the hell are you using our drinking water to wash your damn hair?"

Heidi's hazel eyes quickly filled with tears, her hair still wet and sticking to her face. "The seawater takes away my sheen," she sobbed. "I only used a little."

Dutch looked her, about to explode. "I couldn't care less about your damn hair. This isn't a beauty pageant, and no one is watching. You owe the boat ten gallons of water. And if you ever do that again, I'll throw you to the sharks. Do you understand, Miss Almond Queen?"

She rubbed her tears away and answered meekly, "Yes. But how do I repay the boat?"

Dutch forced a smile. "I'll let you know when the time comes."

As luck would have it, at the crack of dawn the next morning, the time came. Nimbus clouds had stacked up on the western horizon overnight. Using his binoculars, Dutch could see rain squalls heading their way. Tying off the helm, he removed the two blue plastic containers from under the cockpit seats. Then, keeping one eye on the boat and the other on his task, he moved both containers to the deck and located the freshwater intake cap. Removing the plug carefully, he placed a large, white-plastic funnel in the hole and drained both containers of water. After screwing the cap back in place, he returned to the cockpit and strapped both empty cans to the aft railing. Then he went below and retrieved two foul weather jackets and his yellow rain hat. Leaving one jacket behind, he returned to the cockpit and untied the helm. Now, keeping his eyes on the weather, all he had to do was wait.

Soon, the sky clouded over and the winds pick up from the approaching squalls. When he heard Lois below in the galley, preparing the morning coffee, he tied off the helm again and shouted down the hatch, "Lois, get Heidi out of bed and up here. I need her help." Then he went on deck and trimmed both sails.

When he returned to the helm, he found Lois at the cabin hatch. "She's getting dressed. Why do you need her?"

Dutch slipped on his jacket. "She has a job to do. Have her wear that extra jacket on the table."

Lois glared at him. "She is afraid of you, Dutch. She thinks you're going to throw her overboard."

He grinned back at her. "Tell her it's time to repay the boat. She'll understand. No one is going overboard."

When it rains in the tropics, it rains. Just as Heidi came up the companionway with her yellow jacket on, the downpour started. She had a frightened look on her face, so Dutch greeted her with a big smile. He pointed to the two blue containers strapped to the railing and showed her how to use the funnel to catch the rain.

"Fill both of them up and you're square with the boat," he shouted over the noise of the deluge.

With rain running down both sides of her pretty face, she went to work. Dutch watched her carefully as she funneled the first blue can. She looked like a drown rat, and he felt a little sorry for her. Taking off his hat, he placed it on her head. She nodded her thanks, with an approving grin.

Within the half-hour, both containers were full. As Dutch secured the last one under the seat, he shouted to Heidi, "Now get below and get dried off. All is forgiven."

The squalls blew through by late afternoon, and the weather improved to cloudy skies. Late that night, before his watch at the wheel, Dutch made radio contact for the first time with Wake Island. After Dutch reported the boat's general position, the operator gave him the frequency for the navigational beacon on the island. With that number, he was able to hone in on the island and replot his course. He would do the same each night until the boat arrived safely at the island.

After pouring himself another cup of coffee, he went topside. "Made contact with Wake, and we have a new course. Let's make it 270 degrees, due west."

Doug turned the boat slightly. "Never knew you had such a temper, pal," he said, his face visible in the glow of the running lights. "She wasn't happy, out in the rain, filling your cans."

Dutch took over the wheel. "Not my cans. *Her* cans. She wasted it, she could fix it. That's the Marine way. If you screw up, there are always consequences. Bet she'll never do that again."

"She's never been on a sailboat before. Cut her some slack, pal." Standing next to the helm, Doug put his back to the wind and lit a cigarette. "I have just one question," he said quietly. "Are those tits for real?"

Dutch chuckled. "Hell, I don't know. I was looking at the intake lever, not at her bosoms."

Doug took a seat next to the wheel and drank a few sips of Dutch's coffee. "Yeah, sure, pal. You didn't see a thing. Say, how about those haircuts? She can trim my hair anytime."

Dutch shook his head. "There you go again, thinking with the wrong part of your body. I'm not sure I made the right decision about these ladies. They're a real distraction. Our mission is before us, not under us."

Standing up, Doug moved towards the cabin door. "Not much you can do about it, now," he observed, taking a puff from his cigarette.

"We could buy them airfare home, on Guam."

Flipping his smoke overboard, Doug shook his head. "I sure hope not, Dutch. I can still taste that spaghetti dinner Lois made. It was a hell of a lot better than your beans and franks. And Heidi is a delight to be around. Don't be a bully. Let the ladies be ladies. Goodnight, pal."

Doug's words stayed with Dutch for the rest of the night. What he'd said was true. Lois's meals were great, and he had been a bully. That night at the wheel proved to be long and dark. He knew another decision would have to be made, once they arrived on Guam. And he had been angry, rudely angry. He hadn't been that mad since the night he almost shot himself. Why now, and why at her?

While he stared out at the coal-black night sky, he felt the presence of his wife again. She gave him loving encouragement, and thanked him for his tribute to her dead husband at the Arizona Memorial. "The work you do is more important than you know," her spirit whispered in his ear. "Trust in yourself and your crew. Never fear. I'll always have my hand on your shoulder."

Then, in the night sky, he saw the images of his mates in the prison camps. He saw their faces, felt their agony, heard their cries for mercy. It was a gruesome sight, and he shook away the ghostly nightmare by recalling a rhyme he had once read.

God moves in a mysterious way, His wonders to perform.

He plants his footsteps in the sea, and rides upon the storm.

Another rhyme came to him, which he changed for his dark night sky:

I must go down to the seas again, to the lonely sea and the sky,
and all I ask is for a sailboat and a star to steer her by

Other than that one day of rain squalls, and another of calm winds, the weather stayed with the boat all the way to their destination. On the morning of the sixteenth day out of Honolulu, the boat approached Wake Island from the southwest. The island didn't look like much, just a low, level strip of land with white, sandy beaches and a green crown of scrub and tall palm trees, surrounded by the vast emerald ocean. This isolated postage stamp of land's closest neighbor was the Marshall Islands, some six hundred miles to the southeast.

With the sails furled and the motor started, Lois skillfully maneuvered the boat around a few coral reefs and into the channel entrance that lead to the interior lagoon. Half an hour later, the boat was secured at a dock next to an airport runway.

Wake Island had been occupied by the Japanese in December of '41. It was the site of two bloody invasion attempts by the Nips, who held onto the island through the end of the war. Now it was a US territory, administered by the Navy, with the primary mission of being a refueling stop for aircraft and ships traversing the Pacific.

The crew spent the first day at the dock, taking on fuel, water and what few fresh provisions were available on the island. On the second day, thanks to a radio message from the Fleet Admiral, the Navy loaned them a pickup, and the guys went out to film whatever war relics they could find. Lois tagged along, as she wanted to watch the boys work, and explore the remote coral atoll.

During the excursion, they found many old cement bunkers and pill boxes dotting the shoreline. In the shallow jungle, they stumbled across a Nip artillery piece with weeds hanging off the gun and white orchids growing out of its barrel. Down on the beach they found an old American tank, stuck in the sand and rusting in the surf. As the guys worked, Lois asked questions, and the mates did their best to explain their photographic techniques. In the end, Dutch was pleased with the 'cut-away' footage they filmed that day.

On their last night in port, they had dinner with the base commander at the 'O' Club. The crew dressed up, as best they could, and Dutch even allowed Heidi to give him a shave. While she worked, with a straight razor in hand, she commented on his courage because of their spat about the water.

The girls proved to be a smash hit with all of the young officers at the club. There were fewer than two hundred men on the island, and Heidi and Lois were the only women on Wake. With a long line of handsome young men waiting for a turn, the girls could have danced all night. While they partied, Dutch and Doug had a long talk with the base commander. He was a fountain of information and explained, in great detail, what to expect on their passage through the Mariana Islands and on to Guam.

Mariana Islands

The boat cast off just after dawn, the next morning. At the wheel, Dutch motored out into the lagoon channel and a few minutes later crossed into the Pacific. Once beyond the reefs, he turned due south and checked the time. It was a stunning morning, with the sun still low in sky and the coral-green waters glistening. He stayed on that course for almost an hour, watching Wake Island slowly disappear into the sea.

At eight, Doug relieved him at the wheel. "Stay on this course for another hour while I go plot us a new heading," Dutch told his mate.

When he went below, he found Lois in the galley, cleaning up from her Spam and eggs breakfast, while Heidi watched with coffee in hand.

"Did you girls have fun last night?" he asked brightly.

Both ladies beamed. "They were nice boys," Lois answered, "so lonely, and so far from home."

"And those white uniforms! Boy, did they look handsome," Heidi added.

Dutch poured himself more coffee. "Yes, young men in uniforms. A tragedy and a triumph. God bless them all. I hope they never have to go war."

He moved into his nook and spread out his charts. The Mariana Islands were an arc-shaped archipelago made up of the summits of fifteen volcanic mountains in the western Pacific. With names like Guam, Saipan, and Tinian, they were well known to the soldiers who had fought and died on those desolate strips of land. Using just a ruler, pencil, calipers, and his pocket compass, he went to work plotting the new course.

When finished, he moved to the companionway hatch and yelled up to Doug, "Stay on this course until nine, then turn the boat west-southwest to 250 degrees. Lois and I will set the sails, and we'll be on our way." Returning to the galley, he heard the shower running, and found Lois standing in his nook, staring down at the charts.

"Will you show me where we're going?" she asked.

"Sure," he answered, reaching for the maps. "Let's move to the table."

They both slipped onto the settee, and sat next to each other while Dutch spread out the large charts. He pointed to Wake Island on one map and Guam on the other. In between those points, he had drawn a curved course. "Guam is fifteen hundred miles away, as the crow flies. But we're not crows, so we'll have to sail almost sixteen hundred miles," he said to Lois, watching her green eyes. He went on to explain how the winds and currents played into his course selection. He concluded with a brief history about the Marianas Islands during the war.

"Why aren't we stopping at some of those islands along the way?" she asked, pointing at a line of islands on the map.

He had considered a stopover on Saipan for more war footage, but the island was over four hundred miles out of his way, so he had decided that the Navy records on Guam were more important.

"Summer is the stormy season out here, and those islands are like storm magnets," Dutch explained to her. "Our best bet is to avoid all the islands until we get to Guam."

"Isn't Guam an island?"

"Yes, a big one, almost two hundred square miles. But it's the most southern island in the Marianas, where the weather is better."

A strange look came across her face, and she shook her head slightly. "I don't understand you," she finally said.

"What don't you understand?"

"You have a head for navigation, and the eyes for film making. The gossip around the marina in Honolulu was that you were a rich oilman. Where did you learn film-making and navigation?"

Dutch chuckled. "I was an oilman once, and rich, too, but then my uncle died and my wife got sick."

"Your wife! I thought so. Bet her name is Laura. Where is she now?"

"Laura died two years after my uncle, and that's when I lost it all. But now my life is richer for me being poorer."

Lois looked at him with concern. "Sorry, Dutch. I didn't realize you were a widower. How did it happen?"

He glared. "It's a long story."

She swiped her hand down one of the maps, and smiled. "And we have a long way to go. You and I really haven't had much time together. You're at the helm when I'm sleeping, and I'm at the helm when you sleep. I want to learn more about you, and your family, and all those hidden talents."

The thought of sharing that much personal information with Lois was out of the question. Dutch was relieved when Doug turned the boat, shut off the motor, and yelled, "Let's get the sails up!"

Beginning that morning, the crew made some changes to their routine. To begin with, they swapped watches. Doug had the morning watch, and Lois took over the swing shift, while Dutch remained at his midnight watch. He was reluctant about agreeing to the changes, and concerned about Lois's ability to sail at night, and so that first evening out, he planned to join her in the cockpit.

With the sunset fast approaching, he grabbed a bottle of Coke from the icebox and climbed up the companionway stairs. Once on deck, he found Lois clad in the same tan shorts and yellow sleeveless blouse she had worn on that first day they met. With the glow of low sun on her golden-brown face, wind rustling through her red hair, and her green eyes covered by sunglasses, she looked marvelous.

"Can I get you a Coke?" Dutch asked.

"No, but I'll take a sip of yours," she answered.

He handed the bottle to her. "No bikini tonight?"

She smiled, took a drink, and handed the Coke back. "No, I thought it might cool down after dark. But it hasn't yet. It's been hot as hell up here all afternoon."

Taking a seat next to the wheel, Dutch replied, "Same below. But once the sun is in bed, it will cool down fifteen or twenty degrees. That's why I like my midnight watch. It's cool and quiet. By the way, yellow is your color."

Lois turned towards Dutch and peered at him over the rim of her sunglasses. "Thanks I never thought you noticed me."

He chuckled. "With your carrot hair and that tanned figure, I'd have to be blind or dead not to notice."

Lois took her sunglasses off and slipped them into the pocket of her shorts. "Did you come up here to check on me or to give me compliments?"

Dutch stood up and approached the helm. "A little of both, maybe. Sunset is a great time to see what tomorrow's weather will be. It's all about reading the clouds on the horizon. It's the way the Native Alaskans do it."

He removed the field glasses from the helm hook and placed them to his eyes. Panning the skyline, he found some puffy clouds just to the right of the sinking sun, and others on the far left. Removing the binoculars from his eyes, he handed them to Lois.

"Just to the right of the sunset, see those puffy white clouds? They are ote-lagh[22] clouds. Out here, they predict another sunny day. But on the far left of sun you can see some snass[23] clouds building. They can produce storms and rain squalls."

Lois removed the glasses from her eyes and handed them back to Dutch. Then, in the last vestiges of sunlight, she switched on the running lights. "How did you learn those Indian cloud names?"

With the hot deck starting to cool, and a moon about to rise, Dutch told her how he had learned to sail with his native-born father-in-law. "Skip told me that the Indians have been predicting weather from the clouds for thousands of years," he said proudly.

That conversation, and others about sailing, rambled on for hours. At midnight, Dutch took over the helm. An hour later, Lois excused herself for bed and moved to the companionway. Halfway down stairs, she paused and looked back at Dutch, where he stood at the wheel.

With the dim cabin light on her face, she asked, "Have you read *Mutiny on the Bounty* yet?"

"I started it a few days ago. Not sure I'm into it yet," he called back.

"Too bad," she answered. "It's all about people like us – sea scavengers searching for adventure, profit and justice."

"Then I must be Captain Bligh."

---

[22] Chinook word for sun or cumulus clouds

[23] Chinook word for rain or stratus clouds

She shook her head with a smile. “No, you’re more the Fletcher Christian type. Good night, Dutch. I enjoyed our time together.”

Chapter Eight

Guam

In the early morning hours of August 25 1963, Rota Island appeared off their starboard bow. A few hours later, the cliffs of Guam came into view off the port bow. From there, they sailed into the Philippine Sea and changed their course to south-southwest. During the next few hours, as they sailed with Guam off the port beam, Dutch reminded himself that he'd been to the island before, although he couldn't remember a thing about it, other than the Navy hospital where his life had been saved.

The United States territory of Guam is the largest island in Micronesia and was the only U.S. held island in the region, before World War II. The island was captured by the Japanese in December of '41, just hours after the attack on Pearl Harbor, and was occupied for two and a half years. During the occupation, the people of Guam were subjected to all kinds of atrocities, including forced labor, torture, beheadings and rape, and they were required to adopt the Japanese culture. Guam was subjected to fierce fighting when U.S. troops recaptured the island in July of '44. The battle for the remote and dangerous Mariana Islands was some of the bloodiest of the war.

On Guam, Dutch's cab stopped at the main gate. A Marine Corporal approached the car and looked through the open window.

"State your business sir," he said with authority.

Dutch reached into his wallet and handed the Corporal his old Marine ID card as he replied, "Navy Records."

The young Marine bent down and looked in the rear seat. Dutch was dressed in a blue button-down shirt with tan slacks. Next to him, Heidi was wearing a long black skirt and a white silk blouse. Despite her plain outfit, the Corporal goggled at her for a long moment.

"She's with me," Dutch said. "Can you give us directions?"

The young man handed back his ID and stood up. "Yes, sir." He gave the driver instructions and waved the taxi through.

Dutch sat back in his seat, with a grin on his face. He was surprised his twenty-year-old ID card had done the trick. His plan must be working. When it came to the Marines, the Navy always liked to say no, so he had invited Heidi to join him as a distraction.

After completing a voyage from Hawaii that covered over four thousand miles, the boat had arrived late the day before at the capital city of Agana. This small, charming seaside town was both the commercial district and the seat of government for Guam.

Earlier, Dutch had hailed a cab for the four mile drive to the Naval Air Station, while Doug and Lois did some local grocery shopping. Now the cab pulled up to a long row of Quonset huts and stopped in front of one that had a sign reading Navy Records. Dutch paid the driver, and he sped away.

"What do I do again?" Heidi asked before they entered the building.

"Nothing. Just be yourself," Dutch answered.

"But I'm dressed in my waitress uniform. No one will notice me."

Dutch grinned at her and opened the front door.

Inside, they found a Yeoman and a Navy Lieutenant working at desks behind a long wooden counter. When the officer looked up and saw them, he got right to his feet. *Here comes trouble*, Dutch thought, looking at the approaching young man. But he was wrong. The Lieutenant couldn't have been more helpful. After learning of Dutch's needs, he escorted him to a seat in front of a Photostat machine, and showed him how to use it.

All of the records for March 1945 had already been photographed and reduced down to a dozen reels of film. Soon Dutch was spinning though all the archives. When he found a record of interest, he pushed a button and a Photostat was made that he could buy at ten cents a copy. It was an amazingly modern way of managing reams of documents.

While Dutch worked at the machine, Heidi and the Lieutenant sat at his desk, enjoying coffee and talking of home. An hour later, Dutch was finished, and paid his thirty cents for the records. To Dutch's astonishment, the Lieutenant even called a cab for them. Had the Navy changed that much?

Back on the boat, Heidi got out of her uniform as fast as she could, while Dutch made a bee-line for his nook. Unfolding his charts, he looked carefully at the stats he had taken. One was the Rescue Report, made by PBY ZH151, on March 28, 1945. It gave the general location of the rescue as two hundred miles southwest of Guam. He scratched his head. That didn't seem right. Back in '45, a nurse at the hospital had told him he was rescued three hundred miles east of Guam.

He grinned and shook his head. Back then, he had been severely sedated and had probably heard the nurse incorrectly. For now, he would trust the pilot's report. He marked the rescue point on his map. Then, reaching for the Action Reports he had been given back at Pearl, he found the one from the submarine *USS Trigger*. It listed the attack position as four hundred miles northeast of Mindanao. He marked that point on his map. Then, taking his ruler, he drew a straight line between the two points. The raft had drifted almost five hundred miles in nineteen days! But, search as he might, he couldn't find any islands on the map that were close to their course. How could that be? He remembered the island he called Gibraltar as big, with four small atolls protecting its eastern slopes. The only islands he could find, even close to their drift, were the Yap Islands, some five hundred miles southwest of Guam. That would be their next destination.

Just before noon, Doug and Lois returned from their shopping trip. Dutch helped them stow the four bags of groceries in the galley.

"How did it go with the Navy?" Doug asked as they worked.

"Surprisingly well, I got everything I needed. We can shove off tomorrow. "

"Maybe not," Doug replied. "On our way to the market, we found a boat shop that makes small skiffs out of balsa cored fiberglass that can hang off the back transoms of sailboats. One of those would be a perfect diving platform, and good way of getting on and off the islands. You should take a look."

"Good idea. After lunch, let's go see."

"And there's more," Lois added. "We might want to rent a car and drive to the other side of the island. At the market, a handsome Lieutenant told us that there are lots war relics over there."

Dutch smiled at his mates. "All right. That's why we came out here."

Early that afternoon, Doug and Dutch walked to the nearby boat shop. The Guamanian owner made three different models of lightweight dinghies for sailboats. Dutch liked the smallest design. It was only eleven feet long, with a beam of four feet. The boat could seat three people – four, if necessary – on three seats, fore and aft. The skiff was designed to rest horizontally on teak cleats fastened on the transom of the sailboat. It came with a pair of seven-foot oars, a tiny lead bell anchor, a small survival kit and a canvas tarp, all stowed under the aft seat.

The man wanted two hundred and fifty dollars for the boat, but that included installing the teak cleats and fastening the dingy to the aft rails, using bungee cords. He also promised to do the work first thing the next morning. The mates liked the man; he was a proud craftsman, with arms covered in Marine tattoos. "I design all of my boats for Pacific Island conditions. They are a wise investment."

Dutch agreed and paid off the builder, saying, "Semper Fi, brother."

The owner was surprised they were brothers, and they yacked about the Marines for a while. When Dutch told him about their NBC assignment, he gave them some tips on where to find old war relics. "But don't forget Liberation Park. It's five miles north, on the west shore of the island. There is a completely restored M4 Sherman tank up there. It overlooks the cliffs of Guam, and it's really a sight to see," he said with pride.

After leaving the boat shop, the guys walked to the local Avis dealer and rented a station wagon. Returning to the marina, they loaded the car with their film equipment, and put the ladies in the backseat. Then they drove across the island and turned up the east shore.

The roads were surprisingly good. They stopped a few times, crafting photos of monuments, memorials and a few burnt-out Japanese cement pillboxes. It was all fairly mundane stuff, as the beaches had long ago been cleared of battle scars.

Late in the afternoon, they came to Andersen Airbase, on the northeast corner of the island. There, they turned and headed for the western shores. That part of the island was hilly and arid, with only occasional farms and ranches dotting the landscape.

A few miles after turning south for the capital, they came upon Liberation Park. When they pulled off the road and walked up to the restored Sherman tank, Dutch knew that this one stop would make their day.

Nestled in a grove of tall palm trees, the tank rested on a thin concrete pad overlooking the cliffs of Guam, facing due west. The Sherman's dark-brown paint looked fresh, emphasizing its sleek lines and menacing shape. The gun turret even had an American white star stenciled on the sides of its steel plates. The tank glistened in the warm light, with vivid colors reflecting from the sinking sun.

As the light faded, they set up the camera, framing the tank with some palm trees. Dutch shot all the basics: slow pans, tilts and zooms. Then they moved the sticks and shot a forced perspective from the side of the tank, with a slow zoom down the length of the gun barrel and out to the setting sun. Although Dutch wasn't shooting an old war relic, what he saw in his viewfinder was an iconic image that shouted, *America Standing Guard*. By the time they finished, Dutch was entirely pleased that they had spent the extra day on Guam.

By the time they returned to the dock, it was dark. With a cooling breeze, under the marina lights, they lugged the film gear back down to the boat. Afterward, Doug returned to shore, parked and locked the car, while Dutch unloaded the cameras and made notes of what they had photographed that day.

As he worked, Lois was busy in the galley, preparing dinner, while Heidi watched with a glass of wine in hand. When Dutch finished, he stowed away the gear and reached into his nook for the small pamphlet, which he placed on the counter next to the stove.

"I picked this up this morning, on our way to Navy Records. Thought you girls might like to read it," he told them with a sober face.

Lois glanced at the brochure. It had the logo of Pan American World Airways across the front. "Why?" she asked looking up at Dutch.

"Pan Am has two flights a day to Hawaii, with connections to the Mainland. You ladies have spent a month of monotony on this boat, and I thought you might want to reconsider my offer to fly you home."

Lois frowned at him, shaking her head. "Are you telling us our work isn't satisfactory?"

"No," Dutch quickly replied. "But this might be the last airport with direct connections home. I thought you'd be bored with sailing, by now."

Lois glared at him. "You can't get rid of us that easily," she retorted.

Just then Doug came down the steps. "What smells so good?" he asked with a bright smile.

"Lasagna," Heidi answered. "But Dutch wants to send us packing."

"What?" Doug shouted, entering the galley.

Dutch shook his head and raised the palm of one hand. "Alright, I've made my offer. My conscious is clear. You gals are more than welcome to stay aboard."

Lois picked up the brochure and held it up, staring at Dutch. Then she dropped it into the garbage sack and smiled. "This stove top lasagna will be ready in a half hour. Let's have a cocktail."

Early the next morning, the boat builder and his son carried the new skiff down to the *Laura* and went to work installing it. While this was happening, Dutch returned the station wagon and walked back to the marina. By the time he got to the dock, the builder and his son had finished, and were looking at their work.

"Hope you don't mind the logo I put on your transom," the Guamanian asked as Dutch approached.

Dutch looked out at the white fiberglass skiff that rested across the aft of the sailboat, and noticed a US Marine sticker on its small transom. Smiling, he answered, "Not at all. What do you call these kinds of boats?"

"Cleat-boats," the son said proudly.

The Guamanian shook hands with Dutch. "See you around, brother."

After they stopped at the fuel dock the boat cleared the harbor, with the sun still low in the sky. With Lois at the helm, they motored the boat north, into the wind for an hour. Then they turned west with the wind, and set sail.

Two hours later, Dutch corrected the course to due south, keeping the shores of Guam off his port beam. Once Mt. Lamlam, the tallest mountain on the island, was off his beam, he turned to his final course, southwest. Dutch had planned this heading carefully, as he was determined to visit the place where he had been rescued almost twenty years before.

That first bright morning out, while he was sitting in his nook working on his daily logs, Doug came below for more coffee.

"Never got a chance to see the records you got from the Navy," he said from the galley. "Can I read them?"

Dutch opened a drawer, pulled out the stats, and handed them to Doug. "A one-page Rescue Report and a two-page Hospital Admittance Form. I was lucky to be alive."

Doug took the reports and joined the girls in the cockpit.

Dutch remained in his nook, making a few more notes. Then he put on his sunglasses, grabbed his coffee, and went topside, as well.

"My God, Dutch," Lois said from her seat as he stepped on deck. "You only weighed a hundred and ten pounds when you were rescued. Did you read all the diseases the doctors thought you had? Half of them, I've never even heard of before."

He took a seat next to her. "I bet Doug's Admittance Report would look the same. Those Nips loved to watch us die in the camps."

Doug shook his head from the helm. "I wasn't as bad as you, pal. You *were* near death."

Dutch stared into his coffee mug. "After our hell-ship was attacked, five of us poor bastards spent nineteen days in an open Jap raft, with death hanging on our elbows. Starved and dehydrated, we drifted almost five hundred miles. Lady Death visited us many times during the journey. We lost three souls, and rolled their bodies overboard with a silent prayer. On the very morning of my rescue, the Angel of Death had kissed me on my lips. But for some reason, I eluded her call. Why I lived while so many others didn't, I'll never know." When he looked up, everyone was staring him. "Sorry. Didn't mean to get maudlin. Let's change the subject."

Heidi wiped a tear away. "Why were the Japs so nasty?"

"I was taught not to use disparaging terms for people. Why do you guys talk that way about the Japanese?" Lois added.

Dutch and Doug looked at each other and shook their heads. "Let us tell you a few facts about the *Japanese,"* Doug replied with a frown, "since Dutch and I both have some first-hand experience..."

Just before his watch that night, Dutch plotted the boat's position, using the radio directional finder. When he was done, he calculated that they were one hundred and sixty miles southwest of Guam. They were making a fast passage.

Before he went topside for his watch, he placed the book *Mutiny on the Bounty* next to the stove and poured himself some coffee. When he climbed the stairs, he found Lois at the wheel, her hair ruffled by the warm breeze.

"Finished the book. It was great. I put it by your stove."

"Thanks," she answered with a smile. "I knew you'd like it."

Dutch relieved her at the wheel. "Sorry if Doug and I bent your ear this morning about the Japanese. We have some strong opinions on that subject."

She shook her head as she moved away from the wheel. "You guys have some real demons, Dutch. But who can blame you? I've got another book for you to read. I'll give it to you tomorrow."

"We all have demons," Dutch answered. "What's the title?"

"*Moby Dick* by Melville" she replied, moving towards the hatch. "It's another tall-ship tale." She paused at the stairs and looked back. "I learned a lot today. School never taught us much about the Pacific war, other than we dropped *the bomb* and killed tens of thousands of innocent people. It was good to hear the other side. Good night, Dutch."

That first night out of Guam proved to be long and lonely. Even with a sky full of stars and a new moon rising, Dutch felt trapped in the inner spaces of his mind. He had studied his charts all day, looking for an island with the shape and size of Gibraltar, but had found nothing. Now he questioned whether the island had only been a mirage conjured by his dying imagination. It was a silly notion to try and find Gibraltar again, not worth the effort.

Time at the wheel dragged on like the endless sea, and the night crept ever closer to him. His mind started to fill with nightmares of the past again, and he prayed for solace. Then he felt his wife's hand on his shoulder, and all his anxiety drained away like dirty bathwater.

At first light the next morning, with a red glow in the eastern sky, he tied off the helm and eased the mainsail. With only the jib set, the boat instantly slowed to a crawl, and the heel corrected itself. Dutch moved to the bow and looked out across the sea. *This is the place where I was rescued,* he thought. But the ocean looked the same in all directions; there was nothing unusual about this place.

What had he expected? He hung his head and closed his eyes. The visit to Guam had brought back long-forgotten monsters. Those dark memories would once again have to be shoved to the back of his mind. He would stop dwelling on the past, and get on with living.

When he set the mainsail again, the boat heeled over, and Dutch changed the course to south-southwest.

Yap

Late in the afternoon of the fifth day, the boat approached the small raised island of Rumung, the northern most point of the Yap Islands. According to the *Divers Guide to the Pacific Islands,* the Yap group was roughly eighteen miles long and six miles wide. The capital of Colonia was on the largest southern island of Yap. All of the four main islands in the group were surrounded by a common coral reef; they all had tall green crowns of vegetation, and toothpaste-white beaches. The book described the waters as 'pristine' and filled with all types of sea life, including large rock lobsters.

With the sun low, Dutch decided to find a route through the reef, and anchor in the tranquil waters beyond. Here they could snorkel for some lobsters. After checking the charts, the sails were lowered and the motor started. With Lois in the nook, calling out water depth, and Doug at the bow, watching the approaching mirror-clear waters, Dutch turned the sailboat for the entrance to the lagoon. Ever so slowly, with small white breakers on both sides of the boat, the *Laura* found the entry and was soon anchored in thirty feet of turquoise water.

With only two snorkels, masks and spear guns aboard, the crew would dive in pairs. After the skiff was removed from its cleats and secured to the diving platform, Dutch and Lois were first in the new dinghy. They rowed the boat for the shallows and set their small anchor in ten feet of water. Once over the side, they swam next to each other, looking at the depths. It was if they were diving inside a tropical aquarium. Colorful reefs and fish were everywhere; it was like watching the changing spectrum of a rainbow. The ocean floor, alternately rocky and sandy, had clumps of sea grass that danced in the currents. *How*, Dutch thought, *can the underwater be so beautiful and peaceful, while the top of the ocean is so hostile?* Diving below the surface, the two of them were soon hovering over a bottom of clams, crabs and rock lobsters. They were swimming in a magnificent Garden of Eden that few people had ever seen.

Half an hour later, they rowed back to the *Laura,* with their catch in the bottom of the boat. As they approached, Dutch held up two fat, greenish lobsters and shouted, "We've got our dinner. Now it's your turn."

"We caught a nice sea bass, too," Lois added, rowing.

With smiles and good cheer all around, Doug and Heidi suited up and were soon in the skiff, rowing for the shallows. Not long after, they returned with two more lobsters.

Handing their catch up from skiff, Doug asked, "How long before dinner? We want to go to the beach."

From the galley below, Lois called out, "About an hour."

"Good," Doug answered with a grin. "We'll be back for chow."

"And bring back a coconut, if you find one!" Lois added.

Dutch looked down at the small bobbing skiff. "Hey, Doug, keep in mind that the book says there's a native village on this island. Stay close to the beach, where we can see you."

Doug looked up at his mate with a frown. "Yes, Father. I'll drive safely."

That evening, they enjoyed a succulent lobster feed, with wild rice, fresh coconut, bread sticks and two good bottles of Riesling. The table chatter was almost as bright as the sunburn across Doug's back. Heidi and he kept looking at each other, giggling. Dutch suspected more than lobsters had been taken from the lagoon that afternoon. Now, Dutch understood why Doug had lobbied so hard for the dinghy.

Early the next morning, they motored back across the reef and turned south-southwest, keeping the lush humpback islands off their starboard beam.

Four hours later, they arrived at the capital town of Colonia.

Thanks to the Versailles Treaty, the Japanese Empire was given the Yap islands at the end of the First World War. During the Second World War, the Japanese built a major communications center and airfield on the island. The garrison that protected Yap held over five thousand men. As the war progressed, however, the islands were bypassed by American forces as part of their island-hopping strategy. Following the war, Yap came under the control of the United States as part of the Trust Territory of the Pacific Islands.

The waterfront of Colonia was small and mostly deserted, with a few wood-framed warehouses built upon planks on log pilings. The main pier, stretching out from the palm-treed shore into the harbor, was over one hundred feet long, with an open-air shelter at the very end. As Doug maneuvered the boat for docking, Dutch noticed a large American flag flying in the breeze above the thatched roof of the cabana. He glanced up to his tall mast and eyed the smaller flag flapping in the halyards. He chuckled in amazement. *We've sailed almost eight thousand miles, and we're still under the protection of Old Glory, amazing!*

The boat was no more than secured when they were approached by a burly white fellow, smoking a cigar, and wearing a straw hat, a Hawaiian shirt and baggy walking shorts. He carried a clipboard in one hand, and had a ukulele slung around his shoulder.

"Aloha! Welcome to Yap," he called brightly from the pier. "I'm Mr. Hale Long from the Port Authority. Which of you is the Captain?"

Dutch stepped up and off the boat, and walked towards the man. "I am, sir. Have we docked at the wrong place?"

"No, you're fine," Mr. Long replied, looking up at the sailboat's flag. "Is everyone aboard an American?"

"Yes, sir. Would you like to see our passports?"

"Not necessary," Mr. Long answered, puffing on his cigar. "What brings you to Yap?"

Dutch explained their assignment with NBC and what he had learned back at Pearl about old war relics on the island. "Could you direct us to a guide that I could hire to see these old relics?"

Under the brim of his reed hat, Mr. Long smiled. "I'm also the official guide for visiting dignitaries," he answered proudly.

"You're a man who wears many hats," Dutch replied with a grin. "Can we go this afternoon? What would be your fee?"

As it turned out, in addition to his other titles, Mr. Long was the assistant to the local Governor, who was vacationing back on the Mainland. He was also the Harbor Master. Dutch introduced his crew to Mr. Long, who bowed low to the ladies, with a sweeping gesture of his reed hat. Dutch paid him fifteen dollars for his guide services and a five-dollar moorage fee for one night.

"Why the ukulele?" Dutch asked as they finished up.

Mr. Long took the instrument from his shoulder and strummed it a few times. "I play each evening at the Yap Hotel. You should come and hear me tonight."

Early that afternoon, Mr. Long returned to the pier, driving an old army Jeep. With a warm and friendly smile, he passed out gifts for all four of them: reed hats, made by the local woman out of palm leaves. "These Yap hats will keep the hot sun off your faces and will help you blend in with the natives," he said as everyone squeezed aboard the Jeep.

Mr. Long drove them through Colonia, pointing out places of interest, including the Yap Hotel. The capital was a quaint little town, filled with many bamboo shops, restaurants and bars. Outside of town, he turned south and started telling them about the local culture. Under the blazing sun, he talked non-stop until they came to the tiny Yap airport. There they turned onto the concrete tarmac and drove down the middle of a long runway with weeds growing out of the cement. "This was a Japanese Navy Airfield during the war. They flew bombers out of here, and two of their derelict planes still remain."

Stopping at the end of the field, they got out of the Jeep and walked around. There was one bomber parked next to an old wooden hanger, and another collapsed in the tall grass just off the edge of the runway.

Doug recognized the aircraft right away. "Wow. Mitsubishi G4's. We called these planes Betty. They're the long-range bombers that wreaked havoc all over the Pacific."

Both planes were in sorry shape. Dutch got the gear out, and the guys went to work. They filmed the plane in grass first. It was damaged with bullets holes in the tail section and one wing was missing.

"Why do you think the Japs left these two planes behind?" Dutch asked as he worked.

"That's easy," Doug replied. "These planes were cannibalized for parts. They were a long way from Japan."

They were able to get inside the second plane. Knocking down all the spider webs, they moved up the narrow fuselage. There was a funny, stale smell in the aircraft, but the interior was in surprisingly good shape.

"The Nip pilots called these planes 'cigars' due to the round shape," Doug commented as he slipped by the navigators cramped nook.

The cockpit was riddled with dozens of bullet holes, and they found some of the instruments missing. Dutch looked around the cramped space and spotted a small Japanese flag. It was a tattered insignia, mounted on a short bamboo stick. Taking the flag in his hand, he stuck the stick into a seam in the plane's instrument panel and slid the pilot's side window open. As the small, torn flag flapped in the breeze, Dutch filmed a close-up of it, then zoomed out to reveal the bullet-scarred cockpit. He repeated the shot twice more, varying the speed of his zoom, hoping to use the footage to symbolize the demise of the Japanese Empire.

They worked a few more setups inside the plane, and then filmed a few more exteriors. When they were done, they packed up the gear in the shade of the old hanger, and Mr. Long drove back up the runway.

"Is the airport used anymore?" Doug asked from the backseat.

"Yes, we have two flights a day," Mr. Long replied as they approached the small terminal, "a morning flight to Guam, and an afternoon flight to Mindanao. Those flights and the inter-island freighters are our only contact with the outside world."

Their guide then turned north on a coastal road, and the crew enjoyed the spectacular vistas of the white beaches and the coral green reefs. They stopped a few times to film the seascapes. It was as if the images had come straight out of a travel brochure.

Soon, they arrived at the picturesque village of Kanif. It was a place of large reed huts, tall palm trees, and friendly natives who lived off the land and sea. Mr. Long even introduced the crew to the local chief, a big, strange-looking man who wore an old black bowler, a floral sarong, and fish bones dangling from his ears.

Mr. Long talked to him in his native language with great animation. The men seemed to argue for a while, with the chief shaking his head. At one point, Mr. Long held the palms of his hands up, then reached into his baggy shorts and brought out a pint of rum. He uncorked the bottle and offered the chief a drink. The chief's stony expression brightened as he took a swig of rum. Mr. Long did the same, after which he handed the bottle back to the chief, and both men nodded. With a smile, Mr. Long explained to Dutch that they had just been given permission to film in the chief's jungle.

With a villager hacking a trail for them with a machete, the crew spent the next few hours trudging through a steamy tropical forest of Mangrove swamps and tall reeds. The jungle smelled of rotting vegetation, and the miserable path was slow going.

Soon they came to the first relic: a Grumman Wildcat stuck high up in a Mangrove tree. The wings had been sheared off and rainforest vines had wrapped themselves around the fuselage. From the ground, they saw that the cockpit hatch was open, and they could make out the American star under the obscuring foliage.

"What do you think happened to the pilot?" Heidi asked, craning her neck and peering up.

"He bailed out over water, if he was lucky," Doug answered. "If he was unlucky, the Nips got him, and he's buried here on the island."

The guys filmed the aircraft from the ground, and then climbed up the tree. It was a slow, difficult, dangerous ascent, but soon they were above the Wildcat, looking down on it. Half an hour later they were done and climbed back down, sweat rolling off their faces.

They shot two other setups that afternoon: a Mitsubishi bomber's tail section, covered with vines, and the fuselage of a Jap Zero[24] lying on the forest floor. By the time they were done, everyone was exhausted and dripping with sweat. The march back seemed to take an eternity. When they finally arrived at the village, the four of them could hardly wait to cool off with a dip in the ocean.

As Mr. Long drove them back across the island, traveling on a long, hot jungle road, Dutch noticed two native men wearing hats, dressed in white shirts and long black pants, walking alongside the deserted way.

"Who the hell are they?" he asked as the Jeep passed them.

Their guide smiled. "Mormons, doing missionary work."

When he'd recovered from his surprise, Dutch replied, "Well, Mr. Long, we sure got our fifteen dollars' worth of guide services today. You're a man of many Yap hats."

Mr. Long grinned back. "Thanks. I'm a jack of all trades and a master of some, like music. Will you come and hear me play tonight at the hotel?"

Dutch turned to his mates in the backseat; they all had bright smiles and nodding heads.

Early the next morning, with a throbbing headache, Dutch filled the boat with fuel and topped off the water tank. Then they motored out of port, with the sun still low in the eastern sky. The night before they had enjoyed an evening at the Yap Hotel, drinking rum, dancing with strangers, and listening to the talented ukulele of Mr. Long. The man was indeed an island character, right out of the pages of *Robinson Crusoe*.

Once they were beyond the reefs, they set the sails, tacking to a new course of west-southwest. Their next major stop was Mindanao, seven hundred and fifty miles away, where they hoped to film both of the prison camps in which the guys had been held during the war.

---

[24] Mitsubishi A6M Zero

With the boat heeled over, Doug took the helm, and the mates filled the cockpit, with mugs of morning coffee in their hands.

"What will you remember the most from the Yap Islands?" Dutch asked.

"Drinking too much rum," Doug answered from the wheel.

Lois looked up from her coffee, with the trade winds rearranging her auburn hair. "That lagoon we snorkeled in."

"Yes, that lagoon was a blast. I'll never forget it," Heidi agreed.

Dutch frowned. "For me, it was that Wildcat perched in the Mangrove tree, or those two Nip bombers."

Lois shook her head. "There you go again, thinking only about yesterday, while we're talking about having fun."

"I agree with the girls," Doug asserted, with an unusually serious face. "I'll never forget that lagoon, because that's where Heidi and I found each other. We are now officially an item."

Dutch's jaw dropped, and he took a slow sip of his coffee while glancing over to Lois. She wore a stunned expression, as well. He looked up at his mate at the wheel. "Sorry, but I have no idea what 'item' means. Have you told her everything?"

"Do you mean about his wife back on the Mainland?" Heidi answered. "Yes, I know. When we get Stateside, we'll take care of that problem."

"The point is Dutch, Heidi and I would like to bunk together. But you're the Skipper, so what do you think?"

Dutch stood, moved to the cabin hatch, and looked back at his crew. "I told you all, back in Honolulu," he said angrily. "This isn't a pleasure boat. But now it looks like lust has stepped aboard. I want nothing to do with your sleeping arrangements. You three can work that out. I'm off to bed. My head's still pounding."

In his cabin, Dutch undressed, still fuming. He crawled into his berth and stacked both pillows behind his head. The skylight above was ajar, and he could hear his crew's conversation in the cockpit.

"I think he took it pretty well," Heidi said in a hopeful voice.

"Maybe," Lois added more cautiously. "Why does he always just focus on the assignment?"

"He was seething," Doug answered firmly. "Once a Marine, always a Marine. In Dutch's world, there's only room for duty, honor and country. I feel like I let him down."

Dutch rolled over in his bunk, rearranged the pillows, and closed his eyes. He *was* disappointed in his crew. But what the hell could he do about it now? After all, he wasn't Captain Bligh. Things might have been easier, if he were.

Mindanao

Late that evening, after pouring himself a mug of fresh coffee, Dutch climbed the stairs to the cockpit, to relieve Lois.

"What did the weather look like at sunset?" he asked, checking his course.

Lois took a seat next to him. "Some dark buildup in the west, with a few puffy clouds in the southwest. You slept almost all day. Are you feeling alright?"

Dutch drank some coffee and lit a cigarette. "I'm fine. The heat of Yap must have gotten to me. Where are you sleeping now?"

"Can I have one of your smokes? I'm sleeping in the bunk berths. The forward compartment is a better place for Heidi and Doug."

Dutch lit another cigarette and handed it to her. "Didn't know you were a smoking gal."

Lois took a puff and coughed a little. "There's a lot you don't know about me, like I only smoke at night, when I'm trying to relax. So, what do you think about Doug and Heidi?"

"Guess it's none of my affair. I just hope their relationship won't harm our mission."

"Where does this self-discipline and mission stuff come from, Dutch?" she asked mildly. "The Marines?"

He looked down at her in the moonlight and saw honest curiosity. "No. When I was growing up, the toughest Sergeant I ever had was a black lady named Hazel. She had rules for everything and little clichés for all, 'If a job's worth doing, it's worth doing right.' She was one tough cookie."

"Who was she to you?"

"She was my nanny," Dutch replied warmly.

With the boat heeled over in a warm breeze, they started a conversation about their childhoods that lasted into the early morning hours. It was by far the longest personal exchange Dutch had had in years. When Lois finally departed the cockpit, around two in the morning, he was sorry to see her go. For some reason, that night, he had opened up to Lois, hopefully laying the foundation of a lasting friendship.

Late in the morning on their third day out of Yap, Dutch snug in his berth, woke to rain dripping onto his face from his partly open skylight.

Reaching up, he secured the hatch.

A clap of thunder rolled overhead, just as the bow crashed through an ocean swell. With the weather changing, he quickly got out of bed. But when his feet hit the deck, he got dizzy and had to hold himself upright. He didn't feel so good. Another lightning flash rolled overhead, followed by thunder. He didn't have time to be sick, so he shook it off and put on his clothes.

Outside his door, he stood on the companionway stairs and poked his head above the hatch. Doug was at the helm in the pouring rain.

"Do you want your rain jacket and hat?" Dutch called out over the downpour.

"Just the hat," Doug answered. "It's still too damn hot for the slicker."

Dutch opened the locker next to the stairs and took out both rain hats. Putting one on his own head, he took the other out for Doug. Handing the hat to him, Dutch shouted, "The wind is still out of the northwest, so maybe this is just a passing squall."

Doug pointed towards the bow. "Look at those clouds out there. They're as black as my wife's heart, and the swells have doubled in size in less than an hour. I think we're in for it."

Dutch looked out through the gloom and saw black, angry clouds stacked up like so much cord wood on the western horizon. He nodded his head. "You're right. Hold her steady in the wind while I get the storm jib up and reef the mainsail."

Manning a wet deck in a storm was always a potentially dicey move, but setting the smaller storm jib would give the boat more maneuverability if the weather deteriorated further.

By the time Dutch was done, the waves had built to nearly five feet, with a wind chop blowing atop the curling seas. "I'm going below to check on the weather. Hit the horn if you need any help. Sure you don't want that jacket?"

Doug smiled at him through the huge raindrops. "Yes, please. I'm feeling like a drowned rat."

Dutch went below, got both jackets, put one on and returned to the cockpit with the other. "Lois has all our dry towels set out on the table. She's on her way up to relieve you, and I'll relieve her in two hours."

"Got it," Doug yelled back over the pounding rain. "Hope we'll be out of this soon."

Below deck again, Dutch took off his rain jacket and hat, grabbed a towel from the table, and turned for his stateroom.

"Do you want something to eat before I go up?" Lois asked from the galley.

"No, thanks. Not hungry. Where's Heidi?"

"She went back to bed. She's a little seasick."

With water dripping from his clothes, Dutch was leaving a puddle where he stood. "Get her out of that forward compartment. It's a miserable place to be during a storm. I'm going to dry off."

Inside his stateroom, he stripped naked and dried himself. As he put dry underwear on, he felt nauseous and clammy, but he had no time to be sick. The boat was in danger.

Taking his wet duds to the galley sink, he wrung the water out and returned to his cabin to hang them up to dry. Then he moved to his nook to try to learn more about the approaching storm. The barometer had fallen ten isobars since his morning readings. He flipped on the radio and started scanning the frequencies for weather news.

"Dutch, I'm going topside to relieve Doug," Lois said, standing next to the nook with her rain gear on. "Heidi's lying down in my berth, so she should be okay."

Just then, the boat crashed through a large wave that made the hull quiver from stem to stern.

"Tie yourself into the cockpit like I showed you, and hit the horn if you get into trouble. I'll relieve you in two hours."

But Lois just stood there, looking at him. "Are you alright, Dutch? Are we in trouble?"

Dutch forced a smile. "We're not in trouble. It's just a storm. See you in a couple of hours." He returned to his radio and continued searching for a weather frequency.

A few minutes later, he found a Marine weather station out of Mindanao. The signal was weak, but he caught the English translation of the forecast, which told him what to expect. Turning off the radio, he looked up and spotted Doug in the cabin, taking off his rain gear.

"There's a typhoon off the northeast coast of Mindanao, heading our way. I'm going topside to lower the mainsail. Then we'll turn and run south with the wind. In five or six hours, we might escape the worst of the storm."

"I'll come up and help," Doug answered.

"No, you stay below and get dried off. I'll take over the helm until we're out of this. It's my boat and my responsibility. Heidi is in Lois's bed, for now. She's a little green around the gills," Dutch added slipping into Doug's gear. "You might want to check on her now and then."

With the seas still building, Dutch lowered the mainsail and secured it to the boom. Immediately the boat's speed decreased and the heel corrected itself. Now the boat bobbed at the mercy of the tall swells. Quickly, he returned to the helm and had Lois turn the wheel with the wind. When the small jib filled with the strong north-easterly gale, the boat picked up some speed again.

"You go below. I'll take over," Dutch shouted over the weather.

From under her yellow hat, she frowned at him. "I'm fine. I can handle this."

Dutch moved behind the wheel and said into her ear, "We have a typhoon bearing down on us. It's going to get real snotty up here. I'm taking over until the weather improves."

Lois untied her safety ropes and relinquished the wheel to him. Then she tied the lines around his waist.

"I don't like it, but I'll do it," she said. "You're the Skipper. Doug or I can relieve you anytime. Just hit the horn." With that, she moved to the companion way, opened the hatch, and disappeared down the steps, closing the cover.

The stormy deck was all Dutch's.

A flash of lightning rolled across the sky, followed quickly by an ear-splitting crack of thunder. The swells had deepened to over ten feet, and the ocean curled all around his boat. There was nothing he could do now except run with the wind.

A cold chill raced through his body, and he felt clammy again. He had a fever and a headache, and he feared the worst: his nemesis, malaria.

He hadn't had an attack in five years. "Why now? Why here?" he yelled angrily at the wind. Shaking his head, he knew he would have to ignore his concerns.

With a loud crash, a sneaker wave rolled across the bow. The boat quivered and twisted from the force and the weight, flooding seawater all the way back to the cockpit. The deck scuppers filled, and the sole of the cockpit drained quickly, but Dutch tasted fear as he looked around and spotted more towering waves, some as high as his mast. He turned the wheel, correcting his course with the swirling winds. Keeping his eyes glued on the waves, he helped the boat dodge in and out of a few troughs of white caps, then ride with the wind to the top of the tall swells.

With the howling winds and colliding seas, it was a deafening experience on deck, but finally the rain stopped, as abruptly as it had started and patches of blue sky appeared between the distant dark clouds. Still, the winds were increasing, pushing the seas ever higher. The cockpit got drenched many times by tall sneaker waves, sometimes forcing Dutch to his knees behind the helm.

He battled the wind and the sea for the next few hours. As night approached, the winds abated some, and the swells slackened. Off the starboard quarter, he could see the dark shapes of threatening storm clouds moving away in his wake. The worst was over, but the swells were still eight to ten feet. Dutch removed his yellow jacket and let the wind dry his sweaty body. He was dizzy again and had had enough, so he sounded the horn.

Doug was on deck in a matter of seconds, dressed in his gear.

Dutch untied himself and mumbled, "Take over. I'm going below. The worst is over. Stay on this heading until morning. Then I'll replot our course."

Doug got behind the wheel and tied the safety lines to his waist. "You alright, pal? You look like shit."

Dutch moved towards the hatch. "Just a touch of malaria. I'll be fine in the morning."

When he got below, he found Lois making coffee while Heidi read a book at the table. Both looked at him, wide eyed. "You were out there for almost six hours," Lois snapped. "Why didn't you call us earlier?"

"I'm going to bed. We can talk about it tomorrow."

Lois moved to him and put her hand on his forehead. "You're burning up. Why didn't you call us?"

Dutch turned for his cabin in a daze, and stumbled. Lois rushed to his side, taking hold of him. "Heidi, give me a hand," she yelled.

The two gals helped him into his stateroom and stripped him down to his underwear. Then they helped him into bed. "I'll be alright. Leave me alone," he said, but he couldn't keep his voice from slurring. As his head hit the pillow, he closed his eyes, and the world slid away.

Lying in bed, Dutch blinked. It was dark all around him. Then his eyes focused on a dim glow. The skylight above his head was open, and a cool breeze was washing over his face. The boat was heeled over, and he heard the gentle slap of the sea against the bow.

A single bed sheet covered his body. When he lifted it up and looked at himself, he found that he was dressed in just his skivvies, and his arms were covered with small white blotches. A single nightlight burned in the cabin. Next to it, Lois was slumped over in the nook chair, sleeping. Why was she there? What day was it?

Dutch looked at his watch, but it took a few seconds for his eyes to adjust. Six in the morning…but what morning? He needed the head, and he was thirsty. Quietly, he slipped out of bed. He was a little wobbly at first, but he managed to open his cabin door and step out into the companionway.

The boat was as quiet as tomb. Once he was finished in the toilet, he returned to the galley and gulped down a glass of water. Then he reached into the icebox and grabbed a Coke, opening it, he climbed up the stairs to the cockpit.

In the predawn light, he found Doug seated on a cushion behind the helm. The wheel was tied off, and Doug's head hung low in slumber.

Once on deck, Dutch turned and checked on the progress and condition of his boat. All seemed fine. Turning back astern, he moved to the helm and cleared his throat loudly. Almost instantly, Doug's head snapped up and he blinked his eyes a few times. Shaking his head, he said, "Gee, Dutch, didn't expect to see you! Sorry. I was resting my eyes."

He started to stand but Dutch stopped him. "Don't get up. I'll join you."

Doug dropped back down on his cushion. "I'm pleased you're back from the dead."

"How long have I been out?"

"Three days, counting today. You had us all scared shitless, pal. That was one hell of an attack of malaria. I checked your kit for quinine pills, but didn't find any. Luckily, I had some from six years ago. They must have worked."

Dutch looked at his friend in the warm glow of the morning sky. "Thanks, pal, for being there for me."

Doug lit a cigarette and shook his head again. "Don't thank me. It was Lois who saved your bacon."

"What do you mean?"

"She's been caring for you from that first moment you went to bed. When you barfed, she cleaned you up. When you were cold, she piled on the blankets and crawled into bed next to you to share her body heat. When you had hot flashes, she washed you down with wet cloths. She fed you broth and got you to the head twice a day. She's a hell of a nurse."

"I don't remember any of it. Now I'm embarrassed. What are all these white blotches on my arms?"

"She put some kind of lotion on all your mosquito bites. You had them all over your legs and arms, probably from the Yap jungles."

"Didn't you get bit out there?"

"I had a few, but not like yours. They must love your blood."

"Have you been working the helm twenty-four hours a day?"

No, Heidi took the day shifts and I took the nights. We're on course, and we should be in Mindanao in a couple of days."

"Heidi?"

"Yep. She's a good sailor, pal."

Just then, from the wake, they heard the loud howling of a black-footed Albatross hovering over the boat.

"That a good sign," Doug added, watching the birds. "Now we can get back to normal again."

Lois's head popped up above the open hatch. "What the hell are you doing out there, Dutch?" she barked.

He got up and moved to the cabin entry. "I'm fine. Thanks for saving my life, lady."

She blushed. "You'd do the same for me. Are you hungry?"

"Starved."

"I saved two fresh eggs for you. I'll get them fried up with Spam and toast. Nice to have you back, Skipper."

Dutch knew he had been a very lucky man, and that he owed his crew a lot. Doug had taken command and plotted the correct new course after the storm. He had even made daily entries in the log book. Heidi had stepped up when she was needed most, and now the boat had another helmsman. And then there was Lois. He was both indebted to her and embarrassed about her. The last person to nurse him through a bout of malaria had been his wife, Laura.

The old seafarers believed that the Albatross were the long-forgotten souls of shipwrecked sailors. Maybe they'd come that morning for Dutch's soul but, thanks to his crew, they hadn't gotten it.

Two days later, the boat entered Davao Bay and motored north for their approach to Mindanao. The rugged garden island was the second largest and southern most major island of the Philippines, and Davao City was the largest city on Mindanao. In 1941, Davao had been among the earliest to be taken by the Japanese, and the city was immediately fortified as a bastion of defense. It was subjected to extensive bombing by the Allied Forces before the Americans finally landed on Leyte in October of 1944. The Battle of Davao, towards the end of World War II, was one of longest and bloodiest battles during the Philippine Liberation, and it had brought tremendous destruction to the city.

On the radio Dutch, made contact with the Davao Harbor-master, and received instructions on where to find a transit dock. It was near dark by the time they reached the marina and tied up at a pier.

That evening, the mates walked the hot, humid streets of the city, and were surprised at the smells and the squalor. With tall new buildings and noisy traffic, Davao was no longer the sleepy little bayside town Dutch remembered.

After the simplicity and isolation of the Yap islands, it was a culture shock to be in the Philippines again. Soon, they found a fancy hotel restaurant where they sampled some local cuisine. Their waiter, an older Filipino named Louie, spoke near-perfect English and turned out to be a fountain of information. The city now had a population of almost a million people, he told them, and most of its war scars had been erased by time. The old POW camp, where Dutch had been held, had been converted into a federal maximum-security prison.

"They don't allow visitors inside the walls. There are a nasty bunch of criminals over there," Louie told them. Dutch asked if the train still ran to the northern city of Butuan, where Doug had been held prisoner. The old man told them it still did, but explained that that city, as well, had been scrubbed of any reminders of the Japanese. "If you're interested in film of the occupation, you should see Mr. Franco Ramos, over at the new television station. He took a lot of footage during the war. I know he has some of the old prison camp."

"What other old war relics might we still find here?" Doug asked.

"After the war, the government wiped Mindanao clean of all reminders of the Japanese. We don't even have a museum about the occupation."

As far as their assignment was concerned, the mates were disappointed by what they learned. The Filipinos wanted to forget the war and move on. And who could blame them, after what they had suffered?

As it turned out, that night's food was good, but the information was even better, so Dutch tipped Louie five dollars and thanked him for the help.

Back at the boat, the crew sat in the cockpit, sharing a nightcap while they talked about what to do next.

"Do you want to take the train to Butuan?" Dutch asked Doug.

"No" he answered. "If the Filipinos can forget that damn war, it's time for me to do the same. But, since we're here, I would like to dive the bay and see if I can find my old plane."

"Alright, we'll go see Mr. Ramos in the morning. Maybe we can buy some of his footage. Then, in the afternoon, we'll see what the bay has to offer."

Early the next morning, the guys took a taxi to the local television station, while the girls went shopping for supplies. Dutch had given them a hundred dollars and instructed them to buy another three weeks' worth of provisions.

The station was in one of the new high-rise buildings close to the city center. Once inside the office, Dutch and Doug introduced themselves to the receptionist as NBC correspondents who wished to see Mr. Ramos on network business. That must have done the trick because, after only a short wait, they were ushered into Ramos' small, cramped office.

Mr. Ramos was a young looking Filipino with dark brown eyes and a friendly smile. His hand shake was firm, and the mates were invited to take a seat in front of his cluttered desk. They told him about the 'Witness to Yesterday' project, and about their interest in buying old footage of the Japanese occupation. At first, he seemed aloof to the proposal, but once he learned that both men had been prisoners on the island during the war, he warmed right up.

"I was just a teenager with an old Bell & Howell camera, during the war," he told them. "If the Nips had caught me filming, they would have confiscated my camera, so I didn't shoot a lot of film. Then, in December of '44, the Commandant of the local POW camp hired me to film the prisoners building a rail line, up in the jungle."

"Would that Commandant be Colonel Hisachi?" Dutch asked.

"Yes. Did you know him?"

"Yes, I knew the prick. I was held in his camp, and I slaved on that damn railroad."

Franco went on to explain that, two weeks after filming up in the jungle, Colonel Hisachi had brought him back to film the prisoners receiving Red Cross parcels for Christmas. “The Colonel agreed to send me some money to get the film processed, but he never did, so I kept the film.”

Using a 16mm film viewer with hand cranked reels, Dutch and Doug watched four fifty-foot spools of footage – two from the rail line and two more from inside the camp. The camera work was a little shaky, but the subject material was starkly vivid and true. Dutch didn’t see himself on the film, but he did recognize a few faces from his past.

By the end of the meeting, he had purchased the U.S. rights to the film for twenty dollars a reel. Franco was so proud to have his work associated with NBC that he released the camera originals to them.

As they were leaving, Dutch told Franco that they would be sailing next to Peleliu, in search of old war relics to film.

“I was there last year,” he told them. “Not much remains of the war. If you’re looking for old relics, sail to Rabaul. The waters there are filled with sunken hulks, and the beaches are littered with war junk.”

Mr. Franco Ramos alone made their stopover in Mindanao well worth their while.

The waters of Davao Bay were warm and clear, but not as pristine as the Yap islands. It was hot and humid, that early afternoon, as they motored slowly out into the bay. Doug stood at the bow, trying to remember his plane’s approach. Once the boat was half a mile offshore from the town, he yelled, “This is the place. I can feel it.”

The guys put on their wet suits and snorkel outfits, and slipped into the water from the swimming platform. Doug took the portside of the boat and started searching, while Dutch did the same on the starboard side. The bottom of the bay was littered with all kinds of junk, from bicycle wheels to old iceboxes, and even a few automobiles, but no planes.

They moved the boat three times and searched for well over an hour before Dutch spotted what looked like an American plane resting upright in forty feet of water. He dove down to it and found both canopies open and the fuselage riddled with bullet holes. The aircraft was covered with muck, but its profile looked like a dive bomber. Dutch marked the wreckage with an orange compressed-air diving buoy and returned to the sailboat.

They moved the boat to the buoy and put on their scuba gear.

Dutch picked up the watertight camera and attached the light bar to it. "It's a little murky down there. I'll use the light, if necessary. How will you know if it's your plane?" he asked Doug as they moved to the swim platform.

"That's easy. In all excitement, I left my Saint Christopher medal hanging from the instrument panel. With any luck, it'll still be there."

Once they were in the water, Lois handed down the camera. "If the medallion is still there, let me film you finding it," Dutch said, and pulled down his mask.

After turning on each other's air tanks, they dove for the bottom of the bay.

Twenty minutes later, they returned to boat, beaming. They had found the medallion, still dangling from the panel. It was all crusted over with mud, and Doug had cleaned it off in full view of the camera lens. Finding the medal and cleaning the mud off of the instrument panel made for great footage. Doug had even sat in the cockpit again, and recovered his old map pouch from beside his seat. Using the light bar had been bulky work for Dutch, but it proved to be the best option in those murky waters.

In the course of the afternoon, they were able to film two other relics, as well: a Nip plane upside down on the bottom and a badly damaged Japanese freighter lying on its side. All good footage. Then, with their air tanks almost empty, and two more rolls of film exposed, they returned to the marina.

That night after dinner, Dutch sat at the table and packed up all their exposed film from Wake, Guam, Yap and Mindanao. They had nine four-hundred-foot reels, as well as the four fifty-foot spools he had purchased from Mr. Ramos. Before sealing the package, he inserted a typed letter for Maggie, and his hand-written description of the footage he was enclosing.

"I'm going to run this out the airport. Would anyone like to come along?" he asked his mates.

"What time are we leaving tomorrow?" Doug replied.

"0800, after we fuel up."

"Heidi and I want to go to town and walk around. Odds are we'll never be here again. And we might spend the night at that hotel we were at last night. Would that be okay, Skipper?

"It's none of my affair," Dutch answered with a frown. "Just be back before we cast off."

"I'll go with you, Dutch," Lois said from the galley, and smiled.

At the airport, they had to wait at the Pan Am counter for a freight agent. While they did, Lois pointed at a stack of flight brochures. "Are you still disappointed that Heidi and I didn't fly back to the States?"

Dutch saw *that* look in her green eyes again, and knew he had to be careful with his words. "I owe you, lady. You saved my life. I'm very pleased you stayed the course."

Lois grabbed one of his arms and pulled him close. Looking into his eyes, she whispered, "You said a lot of things while you were delirious with that fever, and it made me realize I can't compete with a ghost. But that doesn't mean you can't buy me a drink and tell me how wonderful I am."

Chapter Nine

Duke of York Island

At the crack of dawn, September 23, 1963, Dutch's eyes suddenly opened. He felt the boat gently rocking, and listened to the lapping water against the hull. All seemed right. Comfortable in his bed, he turned his head to the compartment and watched the brass storm lantern swivel to the rhythm of the swells. He had to remind himself of where he was, and what day it was.

The 2,200-mile sail from Mindanao had taken thirteen days, with just one stop over for fuel and provisions in the Admiralty Islands. The journey, while long, had been mostly uneventful. During the passage, he had filmed his crew sailing the boat. He got footage of Heidi cutting hair, Lois cooking in her galley, and Doug working in the navigation nook. One evening, the whole crew had taken turns at the wheel, with the glow of the low sun on their faces. He had also used the dinghy as a shooting platform, to get footage of *The Laura* underway with full sails, near sunset. The time it took to film his mates helped break up the monotony of the long, hot days.

Dutch slipped out of his berth and pulled on his tan shorts. He almost didn't recognize himself in the closet mirror. His body was a dark bronze, and the few strands of gray hair at his temples were almost pure white, making him look distinguished. But he also found wrinkles around his eyes which made him look older. Island living was catching up with him. He longed for the colder October weather of the Northern Latitudes. With a frown, he closed the closet door, slipped out of his cabin, and quietly climbed the stairs.

Once on deck, he felt a refreshing breeze on his face, and looked up to a breathtaking crimson sky above the boat. In the tropics, the cool, beautiful mornings were a gift from Mother Nature, the reward for surviving her hot midday sun.

Dutch turned aft and saw the mountains and clouds of Rabaul, some twenty miles across the St. George Channel. They had spent three productive days on that island.

Rabaul was an island of New Britain, and before the war it had been controlled by the Australians. Captured by the Japanese in

’42, it quickly became the main base of Japanese military and naval activity in the South Pacific. In the summer of ’43, U.S. Forces in the Pacific launched a series of amphibious assaults aimed at encircling the Japanese on the island. General MacArthur led the Allied advance across Papua New Guinea, while Admiral William “Bull” Halsey led a simultaneous northward advance in the Solomon Islands. The two-pronged campaign was able to neutralize Rabaul by March of ’44, effectively cutting it off from the rest of Japan’s islands in the Pacific. When Japan surrendered in August of ’45, there were still 70,000 troops on the island. In the years since, the quaint little villages population had dwindled to fewer than 1,500 residents, mostly Australians and various indigenous people.

Mr. Ramos had been right; the island soon proved to be a treasure trove of old war relics. On the first two days, Dutch and the others trudged the mountains and jungles that surrounded the old town. They found concrete shore batteries that still contained old, rusty artillery pieces aimed toward the sea. Around the outskirts of the town, they also found clusters of anti-aircraft cannons, still pointing skyward. Up in the steamy hot jungles, they filmed the wreckage of planes of all descriptions and sizes, including two American B25 Mitchell bombers. Dutch even located the old jailhouse where he had first been interrogated by the Japanese after his capture. The iron cells looked larger than he remembered.

On the third day, they explored the teal-green waters of the main harbor, where they found several sunken hulks, including a Japanese destroyer, two minesweepers, and three freighters. By the time they finished their explorations, Dutch had exposed nine reels of film on the island.

They had departed New Britain early the previous evening, sailing across the channel for the Duke of York Islands. There, in the shallows, they had been told they could find three Japanese tanks resting in a straight line on the bottom of the sea. That was something Dutch had to see, so they had anchored overnight in the pristine waters of a cove, off the leeward shore of the main island.

Dutch moved quietly to the bow, not wanting to disturb his mates, and straddled the short teak anchor prow to stare out at the lush jungle of the island. The crowns of green vegetation, combined with the narrow beaches and inland mountains, reminded him of Yap. However, they didn't have to cross a reef, and the mountains were taller. Back in town, he had been told there were coconut plantations on the islands now. Gazing at the jungle, he heard birds squabbling and, in the far distance, roosters crowing.

He lit a cigarette, thinking about going ashore. When they filmed up in the jungles of Rabaul, he had strapped on his side arm, and dressed in long pants with a long-sleeved shirt. He would have to do the same here, as he wanted to avoid another bout of Malaria.

Where to next? he thought. Before answering that question, he had to figure a few things out. They were running low on two important items: money and unexposed film. There were only eight rolls of raw stock remaining. But the money was his biggest worry. Yesterday, after fueling up and buying provisions on Rabaul, he had counted less than eight hundred dollars remaining in his money belt. That might be just enough for the eleven-thousand-mile passage home. Was it time to quit?

But he shook his head. *No.* Just a two-day sail away was the town of Kavieng, on the island of New Ireland. It was there that his best friend, Jack Malone, had been beheaded by the Japanese. Jack was the reason for his pilgrimage back to the Pacific, even though the thought of returning to Camp Ireland pulled his mind back to that horrible time and place.

The next thing he knew, Lois was on the deck.

"What are you doing up here so early?" she asked approaching. "I brought you some coffee."

She handed the mug to Dutch and sat next him, with her feet dangling over the bow. "Thanks," he replied. "Just enjoying the jungle serenade."

Lois gazed out at the island, with the warm morning light glistening off her auburn hair and raspberry lips. "Are you thinking about the war again?"

Dutch took a sip of coffee. "I was just thinking about where we would go next. There's a small town, a few hundred miles north, where I was held captive. That will be our next destination."

Lois frowned at him. "See? You *were* thinking about that damn war again. We have to learn to forgive, if we want to live."

"Has the whole damn world forgotten the war, except me?" he demanded.

"I don't know, Dutch." She got to her feet. "I've got to get breakfast started. I'll tell you this, though – when you were sick, I noticed you have a nice hard body for a man fortyish. Someday, we should compare pecs."

Dutch rolled his eyes and looked up, blushing. "Why is your generation so forward?"

She smiled at him. "Because your generation is too damn timid. Times have changed, Dutch. The Russians have the *bomb* now, and you're still looking for a girl with virtue." She shook her head. "Sorry, my friend. I can't help you there. But breakfast will be ready in half an hour. That I can help you with."

After breakfast, Dutch loaded the cameras with film while Doug got out the snorkeling gear. Soon after, they loaded everything aboard the dinghy, and Doug rowed across the cove to where they had been told to look for the tanks. The water beneath them was as clear as a mirror, so it didn't take much time for them to locate the dive sight.

"How in the hell did these tanks end up out here?" Doug asked, putting on his fins.

Dutch checked his camera settings. "The Aussie that told me about them said that most likely they slipped off the wet deck of a Nip barge during a storm."

Doug stood with his gear on, and pointed at the water. "But look how straight they landed, in less than twenty feet of water. It's if they were driven out here."

Dutch stood next to him. "Yep, Mother Nature is poking fun at us. There's no other rhyme or reason for this."

They spent a half hour diving on the tanks. All three were of the same model and had the same markings. It made for weird footage, with all the colorful fish swimming in and around the gray hulks parked in a straight line on the bottom of the ocean. Dutch liked what he saw in his lens, the more bizarre the better.

As they rowed back to the sailboat, Dutch said, "It's getting late in the season, and we're running low on film. After one more stop at Kavieng, I'm thinking about heading home. What do you think?"

"That's fine with me, pal. Which way would we go?"

"Out here, the prevailing winter winds are mostly out of the west, so Fiji, Tahiti, Galapagos and up the west coast, about eleven thousand miles."

"That's a long haul, so let's get started. Always did want to see Tahiti."

"So you don't want to go ashore on this island?"

Doug's expression soured. "No. If you've seen one jungle, you've seen them all. Let's get the wind in our sails."

Within the hour, the boat weighed anchor, and Doug motored out of the cove and turned northwest in the channel. They hoisted the sails into a fresh southwest breeze. Once the canvas was set, the boat heeled over, with New Ireland ten miles off the starboard beam. As Dutch and Lois returned to the cockpit, Heidi appeared topside with glasses and a pitcher of fresh sun tea.

As she poured the drinks, she asked, "Why are all the big islands out here named for Englishmen, like Duke of York Island?"

"It's not British," Dutch replied. "Long ago, these islands were called German New Guinea. The Krauts had great influence out here. After the Kaiser lost the first war, thanks to the Versailles Treaty, the Australians and New Zealanders took over the islands."

"Why would Germany want these remote, desolate places?" Lois asked.

"Coal," Doug answered from the wheel. "In the old days, Germany had coaling stations all over the Pacific for their steamships."

"That's back when Germany ruled the seas," Dutch added. "And their colonies were rich with rubber plantations."

Lois frowned, "How do you guys know all of this?"

Dutch smirked at her. "It's called history, lady, and that I can help you with."

She grinned back at him. "Smart ass."

Early the next morning, Dyaul Island appeared off the starboard bow. Two hours later, Dutch changed course to due north. Soon they approached a labyrinth of small islands that separated the northern tip of New Ireland from the southern shores of New Hanover. The area was noted on his chart as notorious for reefs and shallow shoals, so they lowered the sails and started the motor. With Doug on the prow, watching the turquoise waters, and Lois below in the nook, calling out depths, Dutch slowly maneuvered the boat through the maze of tiny islands. A few hours later, the waters of Balgai Bay came into view, and Doug took the wheel. By early afternoon, the boat was moored at a pier in the deep harbor, next to the town of Kavieng.

The sprawling village was the capital of the province of New Ireland and was the largest town on the island, with a population of over ten thousand people. In the early days of World War II, the town had come under attack from the Japanese. Because of the constant aerial bombardment, vast numbers of Australian and New Zealand civilians were evacuated. In January of '42, the Japanese invaded and occupied the island. Over the next few years, almost all of the white people who had remained on the island were brutally killed by the Japs. By the time the Allies retook the town in '45, Kavieng had been almost completely destroyed. This hell-hole was the first POW camp to which Dutch and his mate, Jack Malone, had been sent.

After securing the boat to a log-and-plank pier, the guys dressed in shirts and shorts, with their Yap hats on, and went ashore to find the Harbor Master.

When Dutch set foot at the end of the wharf, he couldn't believe his eyes. He remembered Kavieng's waterfront as filled with buildings and commerce. Now he was greeted with vacant lots, burnt-out rubble foundations, and only a handful of businesses. It was as if half of the town had been flattened. There were a few wood-frame structures still standing, and on the shore next to the piers, there were two newer stone warehouses with corrugated metal roofs. The main street had a few cars and trucks parked alongside, and the buildings that remained looked freshly painted and well-maintained, but the only structure that Dutch recognized was the old Kavieng Hotel.

Turning to Doug, he said, "This place doesn't look right. Let's go over to the hotel and get some information and a beer."

A block down the street, they came to the four-story wood-frame hotel that faced the harbor. Entering through the front door, they found an empty lobby, but next to it were a pair of glass doors, etched with the word *PUB*. Pushing them open, the guys entered a smoky room, and were greeted with curious stares from a half-dozen patrons. The room was long and narrow, with tables and bentwood chairs in front of a standup bar at the rear. Its decor seemed to be African safari, with whirling ceiling fans and thatched walls covered with mounted animal heads and old black and white photographs.

The mates moved towards the back bar. As they approached, the barkeep looked up from the counter and said loudly, "Strangers in town."

The patrons snickered at his obvious comment.

The bartender was a burly man with reddish gray hair, and hairy arms as thick as legs. He reminded Dutch of Popeye. All that was missing was his can of spinach.

"Looking for the Harbor Master," Dutch said.

A grin chased across the man's weathered face as he turned to the room and called out, "We've got Yanks here, boys." Turning back to Dutch, he replied, "Don't have no Harbor Master. I do have empty rooms upstairs, if you're lookin' for a place to stay."

He had a heavy Kiwi accent and a friendly smile. Hanging on the back bar wall was a large stuffed boar's head. Below it was a wooden sign that read 'Boar's Head Pub.'

"Sorry, sir," Dutch replied with a pleasant smile. "We just came in on a sailboat, and I moored her to the long pier. Is that permissible?"

"Reckon so, mate," the burly fellow replied. "Where'd ya get them fancy hats?"

"Yap Island," Doug replied with pride.

The barkeep glared at the reed hats. "What brings you blokes to our little slice of paradise?"

Dutch turned his head to scan the room, knowing full well that everyone was listening, then looked back. "Be pleased to tell you, sir, over a cold beer."

One of the patrons yelled out, "Gus, put their pints on my tab. It's nice to hear a Yank again."

The barkeep poured the beers and put the mugs in front of the guys. "I'd be Gus Savage out of New Zealand. I own the joint. Who would you be?"

Dutch extended his hand, and introduced Doug and himself. Then, taking a sip of his brew, he said, "Always had a soft spot for the name Gus."

"Why's that?" the barkeeper asked.

"Once had a dog named Gus. Best damn hound I ever had."

The room chuckled loudly, and one customer yelled, "I told you, Gus, you got a face like a bulldog."

These guys were a nice bunch, and they seemed to love Americans. Soon everyone was crowded around the bar, listening as Dutch told his story. He explained that he had been to Kavieng once before, as a guest of the Japanese. "It was back in '44, and one of my best mates is buried up behind the camp. So we came to pay our respects."

Just the mention of the Japanese brought out sour faces. Over their beers, Dutch and Doug learned the disturbing truth. Just before the end of the war, the Japs had burnt down the POW camp and robbed the prisoner cemetery of all of its bodies. The remains were barged out to sea, where they were dumped overboard. They did the same with a civilian internment camp a few miles away. Their goal was to erase any evidence of camps on the island.

As Dutch listened to this news, he stood speechless, with damp eyes and a sad face. "May all those yellow bastards rot in hell."

"Not one of those bloody Nips ever stood trial for their war crimes," one angry man added.

An older man told the tale of how the Nips had tried to burn down the town on the day of the surrender. The locals had saved what they could, while the Japs escaped into the jungles. "Almost all those devils were killed or captured when the Yanks liberated us a week later," he added.

Gus had listened to all the war talk with a frown. "We're slowly rebuilding the bloody town. But we've got a long ways to go, so let's talk about the future, not the past."

Doug nodded his head, while pulling out a ten dollar bill and ordering another round of beers for the house. As their faces brightened, he then told them about the NBC assignment that brought them to islands. The locals talked at length about the different war relics that could still be found in the jungles and out in the sea. They also told Dutch and Doug about one small island, just outside the harbor, where they could find the remains of a Japanese bomber resting upright at the bottom of twenty feet of water.

"Not far from the bomber, you'll also find a Nip Zero, also resting upright," another man eagerly added.

"The fact is, our waters are filled with war relics," Gus said. "We hope someday the waters will help bring us tourism. We need all the help we can get."

Most of the men in the bar were local farmers. They were mainly mango and pineapple growers, although one man had a rubber plantation, and another bloke owned a nearby sheep station. Most of the guys were Kiwis, with a sprinkling of Aussies. These were men with calluses on their hands, and friendly faces, one and all. Dutch and Doug, enjoying their fellowship, lost all track of time. Just as Dutch finally looked at his watch, the barroom doors opened, and in walked Lois and Heidi, dressed in their Yap hats, short-shorts and blouses.

Their sudden appearance silenced the room. With beers in their hands and jaws dropped, the patrons stared at the ladies, who walked towards the back bar. As they approached, Dutch heard a few whistles and cat calls.

"Where the hell have you guys been?" Lois demanded, with fury in her voice. "It's getting dark, and we're hungry."

"Uh-oh, the Missus is here," one bloke shouted.

The room laughed, and a red-faced Dutch raised a hand and answered, "Not wives. These ladies are the rest of my crew."

"Can I join your crew?" another patron yelled.

Dutch introduced the girls to their new friends, and someone bought the house another round. The gals soon felt the hospitality of the room, and a good time was had by all. An hour later, Gus's wife cooked up a mutton dinner in the small hotel dining room for the crew. As the pub customers filtered out of the bar for home, many of them stopped by the table to say goodbye. It was an evening of sharing many stories and making new friends.

Early the next morning, Dutch heard Lois in the galley, and rolled out of bed. Getting dressed in his long pants and cuffed shirt, he exited his compartment.

"You're up early again," Lois said, looking up from her stove in surprise. "The coffee isn't ready yet."

"I'm going for a walk."

"Why the long pants and sleeves?"

"I'm going out to my old POW camp site. Don't want any more bug bites."

"Do you want me to come along?"

"No," Dutch quickly answered. "This is something *I* have to do. I'll be back in a couple of hours, and we'll shove off."

Dutch slipped off the boat and walked to the end of the pier in the damp, cool morning air. Instinctively, he turned to the right and headed out of town.

Only a few blocks down the road, where the pavement gave way to gravel, he turned off for the camp. As he walked, his mind filled with horrible memories of this place, and of the distorted faces of his long-forgotten mates. Yesterday, he had been reminded of the brutality and inhumanity of the Japs. His heart filled with hate, and his mind with anger. How could such evil people live on this earth? And then there was his best friend, Jack Malone. It was because of him that Dutch had made this pilgrimage. *It is here that I must seek his forgiveness,* he thought. Dutch's sin had been his zeal to join the war, while Jack's sin had been his anger, which had caused his death. Now both needed forgiveness.

Two miles out of town, he came to the shade tree that had once stood in front of Colonel Hisachi's headquarters. He remembered it well, but walking over to where the building had been, he found nothing. Turning to where the camp itself had stood, he found only a grassy parcel of land. Long gone were the barbed-wire fences and the guard towers. Even the Nip barracks were gone. There was no evidence that Camp Ireland had ever existed.

Moving to where the main gate once stood, Dutch entered the old compound grounds, which were now nothing more than scrub brush and weeds. Walking across the open land, he felt the hot morning sun on his back, and heard the low chatter of bugs in the grass. Climbing the slight rise at the back of the camp, he soon stood on the old site of the prisoner cemetery. He visualized where Jack had been buried, and moved to that general area. Dutch guessed where Jack's grave had once been, and found a scrub bush growing atop the old plot.

Dutch dropped to one knee and reached under his shirt, removing Jack's old dog-tag chain. He slipped it onto the thorny bush in front of him, and bowed his head.

"I have news, my old friend. You have a son. His name is Jack, Jr. He's a fine boy, and I'm proud to be his Godfather. He and my son are fast friends. In fact, they're attending Annapolis now, and they'll make fine officers."

With a bead of sweat rolling off his face, Dutch paused, then reached out and held Jack's dog tag in his palm. "I had no right to convince you to become a Marine. If you'd stayed in the Navy, you'd still be alive." His eyes welled up, and tears mixed with his sweat. "Please forgive me, my old friend. My regret is that I wronged you."

Dutch began to pray, with strong words that just came to him, "If you forgive my sins, our heavenly Father will forgive yours. But if you do not forgive me, then our Father will not forgive yours. God bless you, my friend."

Dutch slowly stood, removed the dog-tag from the bush, and came to attention, giving Jack a slow hand salute. As he did, he felt Laura's hand on his shoulder, and heard her voice in his ear: *Forgive the Japanese, as well, and atonement will be yours. God loves all.*

Dutch dropped back to his knee, bowing his head. "God help me, I also forgive the Japanese. Their sins and lawless acts I will remember no more."

It was still early morning when the boat motored out of the Kavieng Harbor and turned south-southwest into the wind. The small island that the pub patrons had told them about was just five miles south of the main harbor. Reaching it, they easily found and photographed the two Japanese plane relics, then set sail north with the wind. As the boat heeled over and sliced across the turquoise waters, Dutch stood in the cockpit, looking astern, watching Kavieng slip away off their starboard quarter.

"Lois told me you went to your old camp this morning. How did it go?" Doug asked from the wheel.

"Just like the Kiwis told us, there was nothing. Like a mystical bird, Camp Ireland sprouted wings and flew away," Dutch answered, without turning to Doug. "I think the bloody Kiwis are right. It's time to think about the future, not the past."

"So what's our plan, pal?"

Dutch turned to him and said with confidence, "Fiji. It's about two thousand miles southeast of here. With any luck, we can make the passage in less than two weeks. I'll go below and plot us a course."

As he moved to the cabin hatch, Doug replied, "So we're going home?"

"Yep," Dutch answered, and slipped down the passageway.

New Ireland is a dog-leg-shaped archipelago, the most easterly province of New Guinea. The island curved over two hundred miles from its most northern point towards the southern island of Bougainville. Dutch plotted his deep-water course, keeping New Ireland twenty miles off the starboard beam, and corrected that heading as needed, down the eastern coastline. Once they entered the Solomon Sea, he would change course again.

As was his habit, Dutch used the radio directional finder to plot their rough position, late that evening. When he went topside for his watch, he found a refreshing cool breeze on his face, and the sky full of bright stars.

"How were the clouds at sunset?" he asked.

"Clear from horizon to horizon," Lois answered brightly from the wheel.

"I put *Moby Dick* on your bunk. Finished it this afternoon," he replied.

"What did you think?"

"I remember it from high school, although I never finished it. But now I seem to understand it better. The language was a hard read."

"Melville's like that. Doug tells me we're going home. Is that right?"

"Yes. It's late in the season and we're running low on film. The assignment is over."

Dutch took a seat next to her and lit two cigarettes. Handing one to Lois he added, "It's time to confront the future."

Lois smiled at his words. "How did it go at the camp, this morning?"

"I made my peace."

"With whom?"

Dutch took a drag of his cigarette and exhaled it into the breeze. "With myself, for my past sins."

"What kind of sins could you possibility have? You're such a Boy Scout!"

Dutch stood and moved to the wheel. "That's all in the past. Let's talk about the future."

As Lois relinquished the helm, she quickly turned to Dutch and kissed him on the cheek. "Welcome home, my friend. There's a whole new world waiting for you."

"Thank you," Dutch replied shyly. "Do you have any Mickey Spillane or Jack London books in your library?"

"No Spillane, thank God. But I do have *Peyton Place*. It's a tangled love story set in New England. Would you like to read it?"

Dutch smiled at her as she took her seat next to the helm. "A love story is too much of a leap for me. Where did you get all these books?"

Lois flipped her cigarette overboard. "Remember that twenty dollars you gave us, back in Honolulu? I spent it at a used bookstore. And yes, I have a Jack London book. I remembered you talked about him once."

"Which book?"

"Another sailing story with a twist. *The Sea-Wolf.* Have you read it?"

"I don't think so. But then, it was back in my boarding school days that I read his stuff."

"Poor little rich boy, had to read Jack London novels when he was away at school," Lois said sarcastically as she got to her feet. Moving towards the cabin hatch, she stopped and turned back to him. "I'll leave the book on your berth. It's a good read. By the way, Jack London doesn't write *stuff*, he writes damn good novels. Good night, Dutch."

Dutch grinned from the wheel as she disappeared down the hatch. Lois had taken him to the woodshed again! She was one smart lady.

Late the next day, the tallest mountain on New Ireland, Mount Taron, appeared off their starboard bow, and Dutch changed the boat's course to south-southeast for the Solomon Islands. A few days later, they were sailing down the long chain of volcanic islands on a cobalt blue ocean. During the Second World War, the Solomons saw fierce fighting between the United States and the Empire of Japan. Dutch knew full well that the islands were noted for their tropical inlets and huge lagoons, and for an ocean floor littered with dozens of sunken warships. The *Diving Guide* mentioned over a dozen spectacular sites on the islands. Dutch was tempted to go ashore, but he also knew that the jungles were infested with mosquitos, and it was rumored that some of the natives were cannibals. At least, that was what he told himself. At heart, however, he knew that the biggest reason for not stopping was that he had tired of filming war relics. He wanted to move on.

On the sixth day out, with the Solomon Islands off their starboard beam, Dutch worked in the nook, typing out a list of all the setups they had photographed. When he was done, he climbed the stairs to the cockpit, with the list in hand. It was still cool on deck and everyone was seated around the helm, enjoying their morning coffee.

Taking a seat next to Louis, Dutch told the crew, "I figured out how many setups we photographed during the voyage – forty-seven different war relics and fourteen sea and landscapes. We shot almost a hundred and twenty minutes worth of film. That should be more than enough cut-away footage for NBC."

"How many seconds is that?" Doug asked from the wheel, with a shoe-string chin strap holding on his Yap hat.

Dutch smiled at his friend. "Are we thinking about money now?"

Lois grabbed on to one of his arms. "What do you think, Dutch? How much could we make?"

"Well, if they use just two percent of our footage, that's over seven thousand dollar's worth," he replied.

Heidi's eyes got big. "How much would I get?"

Dutch thought a moment and then stood. "Almost nine hundred dollars."

All the crews faces brightened.

"Not a bad deal," Lois said. "A trip to the South Pacific, and money to boot. We knew you guys were special, back in Honolulu."

"Of course you did," Doug said proudly from the wheel. "We're NBC correspondents."

Dutch smiled at his crew. "Doug, I'm going to bed. When you find Guadalcanal off your starboard beam, change course to due east. That's where we'll enter the Coral Sea. Good night, mates."

As Dutch crawled into bed, he overheard his crew's conversation in the cockpit. It was all about money and the adventures of the voyage. He grinned, settling his head on the pillow; it was a joy to hear the excitement in their voices.

Sandalwood Island

Six beastly hot days later, the boat approached the Fiji Islands. Dutch was the first to notice the distant dots on the horizon. Taking the binoculars in hand, he moved to the bow to watch their approach. As he scanned across the teal-green waters, Lois joined him.

"Are there just two islands in the group?"

Without removing the binoculars from his eyes, Dutch replied, "No, Fiji is made up of over three hundred islands, half of which are uninhabited. Those two big dots on the horizon are the main islands. "

Dutch removed the glasses from his eyes and handed them to Lois.

As she gazed across the water, Dutch continued, "The island on the left is Sandalwood, and on the right is Viti Levu. According to the *Diver's Guide*, the big island has a budding tourist trade, while Sandalwood is a working island. The book said it's noted for its sugarcane plantations, waterfalls and pristine inlets filled with sea life. That's where we'll anchor tonight."

Lois lowered the binoculars with a big grin. "Yes! Waterfalls! Fresh, pure water. I can finally wash the salt residue off my body."

Dutch smiled at her. "You're easy to please."

"More than you know," she answered with a smirk. "Can we be the first to go ashore?"

That afternoon, the boat dropped anchor in the clear waters of Wainunu Bay, on the leeward side of Sandalwood Island. When Dutch finished securing the boat and looked across the water, he found immaculate, uninhabited silver-sand beaches for as far as he could see. Above them was the rich vegetation of a thick jungle of trees, crowned off with cloud-capped Mt. Thurston, which stood over three thousand feet tall. Dutch just stood at the bow for the longest moment, taking in the breathtaking seascape.

When he returned to the cockpit, he found Doug getting out the snorkeling gear. "How much water do we have under the boat, Skipper?"

Dutch moved to the stern and unfastened the dinghy. "Thirty feet. Lois wants to go ashore for a fresh-water shower, so you and Heidi can dive for our dinner, while we're gone. We'll be back in an hour. Then you can go ashore and do the same."

Doug grinned at his mate. "Don't do anything I wouldn't do."

Dutch frowned at his friend's old cliché as he went below. In his cabin, he slipped on his blue, long-sleeved button-down shirt and put his knife on his belt. Then he covered his bare legs with suntan lotion and put his shore shoes on. Grabbing his Yap hat, he went topside again.

Lois was already in the skiff, waiting. She wore a white halter top and navy blue shorts, with a see-through kaftan, and she carried a large beach bag. "Let's get going," she called.

As Dutch rowed towards the beach, he noticed that her bag was overflowing. "What's in the wicker, lady? Are you setting up housekeeping?"

"No," Lois answered. "I brought two large beach towels, so we can dry off, some soap, shampoo, and a bottle of cold white wine."

"I'll take my shower after you," Dutch replied, pulling the oars.

She smirked. "Dutch, we can take a shower together out here. There's nobody watching. You scrub my back and I'll scrub yours."

Dutch shook his head with a grin. "I don't think so. I'll keep a watch."

As they got close to shore, Dutch noticed small creek beds that flowed out of the mountainous vegetation and drained across the beach into the surf. He aimed at one of the biggest and pulled to shore. There they dragged the dinghy out of the water and secured it with the bell anchor to the beach.

Walking up the rocky creek bed, they entered into the jungles of the tall mountain. Once within the shade of the tall palm trees, with the cool waters of the creek on their feet, the temperature dropped off to a comfortable level.

They heard it before they saw it: the gentle rushing of waters, mixed with the chirping of the birds. Around the next bend of the creek, a rocky cliff waterfall came into view. It was like a sun-drenched oasis in the middle of the thick overgrown jungle. A wide plume of water flowed off a bluff of volcanic stones, some fifteen feet above a shallow pond. On both sides of the falls, long vines of wild flowers grew out of the rock crevices, with all the surrounding boulders covered with a thick moss. The entire cove smelled sweetly of gardenias. At the very base of the wide waterfall was a large, flat stone resting at a slight angle, half in and half out of the lagoon. This lush, green sanctuary, with its misty rainbows and sparkling waters, was as tranquil as a summer breeze.

Lois beamed as she moved to the small sandy beach next to the lagoon. She spread out the two beach towels and reached for her soaps. "Let's give it a try," she said, grinning at Dutch.

"You go ahead," he replied. "I'll check the perimeter."

Lois scowled at him and moved across the rocky bottom to the plume of water, where she slowly backed into the flow. "My God, Dutch, this is heaven. Come join me!"

Dutch smiled at her, then turned and moved into the jungle. But the invitation to join her kept ringing in his ears. Why this temptation now? He stopped in his tracks, thought a moment, then turned back for the lagoon.

Stopping at the beach towels, he took off his Yap Hat, belt and knife, then marched into the pool of water. Soon, he stood before her. "I'll scrub your back."

She gave him one of her looks and handed him the soap. "I'm easy to please," she said, turning her back to Dutch.

He gently rubbed her shoulders with the bar of soap, letting the cool, refreshing water flow over their sun-tanned bodies. It was the touch he had craved for thousands of miles. She turned back to him, staring into his eyes, then untied her halter top and let it drop into the water. For an instant, he felt frozen in place, his gaze fixed on her breasts.

"I'm touchable," she whispered.

Feeling like a fool, Dutch just stood there, gawking.

Lois reached up, placing one hand on the side of his face, and kissed him on the lips. "I'm the real deal… here and now."

Her kiss seemed to wake him, and he pulled her back for another.

When they parted from their embrace, Lois started unbuttoning his wet shirt. "Glad we tried that kiss again. It's better when we both do it."

"This is impossible," Dutch whispered, staring into her green eyes.

Lois put two fingers on his lips. "Don't break the spell. We've both waited too long."

In the afterglow of love making, they sat naked on the towels, drinking wine and brushing each other's hair in the sunlight. It had been a dream-like encounter.

With brush in hand, and Dutch's back to her, Lois said, "Look at this lagoon, our own little garden of love. I will never forget this slice of paradise."

With the flush of love still clear in his mind, Dutch replied, "Aye, you've awakened emotions and desires in me that I thought were long gone."

She kissed the back of his neck. "You've done the same for me."

By the time they rowed back to the boat, reality began setting in. Dutch knew that their relationship would complicate what remained of their passage.

"Was I a good lover?" Lois asked shyly.

Dutch smiled at her question. "You're asking the wrong person. You're only the third woman I've ever been with, so my experience is limited. But I'd say yes," he replied, pulling the oars. "No need to tell Doug and Heidi, though. This is our secret."

Lois's expression turned serious. "I'll take what you have to offer, Dutch, but I will not lie about what happened. We made love – good, compassionate love – and I hope this is only the beginning."

As the skiff approached the sailboat, Dutch paused at the oars. "Let's concentrate on getting home. We still have ten thousand miles to go. We can't take our passion aboard the boat. It wouldn't be right."

She frowned. "You just don't want Doug and Heidi to see you as a hypocrite. I don't like it, but I understand it. We *will* find more time for us, before this voyage is over."

What have I started? Dutch wondered, but the ocean offered no reply.

Back on the *Laura,* Doug and Heidi were waiting. Once the boat was secured, they traded places, eager to go ashore.

"I put our catch in your sink, Lois – a fat soldier fish and a rock lobster," Doug said, getting into the dinghy. "There were lots of blue shrimp swimming around under the boat, but I had no way of catching them."

"I've got a small net stowed below. I'll give it a try," Dutch replied as they departed.

"Dinner will be ready in a couple of hours," Lois added from cockpit. "Thc waterfalls are marvelous!"

Dutch snorkeled while Lois cleaned the catch and started dinner. When he returned to the galley, he added another soldier fish and four pounds of blue prawns to the menu.

"What are you making?" he asked, watching Lois at her stove.

She smiled at him. "Fish stew in a marinara sauce. Why don't you clean your catch and help me garlic the bread?"

Twenty minutes later, everything was done, with the potatoes simmering in the broth. It smelled wonderful.

Lois removed her apron and turned to Dutch, who was making drinks. "It still has another hour to cook. Should we take our drinks into your compartment and explore some more?"

Dutch was determined not to bring his lust aboard the *Laura*. Handing Lois her drink, he replied, “I don’t think so. They might return anytime.”

Lois put both of her hands on his face and pulled him close, then gave him a kiss. “We would hear them coming. And your bed will be more comfortable than that flat rock,” she whispered.

Like a drunken sailor, he found that her kiss and touch melted away his resolve like an ice cube in hell. He pulled her back and embraced her again with passion.

The loud report of a shotgun echoed across the water.

“What the hell was that?” Dutch blurted, breaking away.

Lois just stood there with a startled look on her face. “I don’t know.”

Dutch turned and raced up the companionway to stand in the cockpit, looking out across the water, he snatched the binoculars from the helm and put them to his eyes. At first, he couldn’t believe what he saw. Just off the shoreline, almost a mile away, Doug, butt-ass naked, was frantically rowing the dinghy towards the sailboat. In the aft seat was Heidi, wearing nothing but an expression of stark terror. A small outrigger was a few hundred yards behind them, containing two natives rowing in hot pursuit.

Lowering the binoculars, Dutch handed them to Lois as she came on deck.

“Doug and Heidi have their asses hanging out,” he said with a grim chuckle. “I’m getting the rifle.”

He raced to his cabin and grabbed the M1 carbine. Back on deck, he loaded the weapon and slid the safety on. “What’s happening now?” he asked Lois.

“One of the rowers has stopped and is standing in the bow with a shotgun,” she replied, the binoculars still pressed to her eyes.

Dutch slipped off the safety and fired the carbine over their heads.

Bang!

The report echoed across the water. The surprised pursuer sat down and resumed paddling, without firing his shotgun.

A few long moments later, Lois helped secure the skiff to the aft of the sailboat, and Doug and Heidi rushed aboard. As Heidi streaked, naked, for the cabin hatch, Dutch looked away with a grin on his face.

Doug approached the companionway. "Those guys scared the shit out of us, Dutch. I think they're cannibals, so be careful."

Standing on the deck, with the carbine still in hand, Dutch smiled as his mate disappeared down the hatch.

Soon, the native outrigger came within earshot. "What seems to be the problem, boys?" Dutch shouted, with a smile.

Both muscular natives were dark brown, with wide, fleshy noses, thick lips and dressed in floral shirts and colorful sarongs. "Your mates were poking around our gold claim. We had to chase them off," the first broad-shouldered, scar-faced guy said, with a British accent.

"Gold? I had no idea there was gold on Fiji," Dutch replied.

"There are mines all over the mountain, and we protect our claims."

"Sorry if they intruded, boys. They only went to ashore to shower in your waterfalls."

The scar-faced Fijian snickered. "Yeah, we found them naked in our gold pond." He reached into his boat and lifted up a bundle of clothes, wrapped in a towel. "In their haste to leave, they forgot their duds. Can I toss them up to you, Captain?"

"Sure. Listen fellows, they meant no harm," Dutch answered, resting the rifle on the deck.

As the first guy tossed the bundle aboard, the second fellow asked from the canoe, "What smells so good, mate?"

"Fish stew with garlic bread," Dutch answered. "Would you like to join us?"

Both Fijians flashed their white teeth in broad smiles. "Bloody nice of you," the first native replied. "We're famished."

With the sun low in the sky, the natives came aboard and took cushions in the cockpit. While everyone waited for the stew to finish cooking, Heidi cautiously mixed drinks for their husky guests. As they tasted their drinks, they explained that gold mining was the third largest industry on the islands. "Only tourism and sugarcane are bigger," one of them said. They must have loved the Yukon Jack, as they downed two more drinks as they talked about the different gold operations on the island. Over the meal, Dutch learned that Fiji had no airports with direct flights to the United States. The closest International airport was on Tahiti, which was their next stop. He also found out that the largest port on Sandalwood Island was the town of Savusavu, some dozen miles due east from where they were anchored. There, they could buy fuel and supplies.

Their Fijian guests were hard-working chaps, who ate every morsel of bread and finished every spoonful of stew. With twilight fast approaching, they got to their feet and headed for their boat, thanking the crew for the delicious meal. At the rail, the scar-faced fellow reached into his sarong and handed Dutch a small glass vial with a cork in it. "It is our custom to repay generosity with a gift. Here's the color we panned this morning. It's only few grams, but its Fiji gold, so keep it as a memory of us."

Dutch held the bottle up to the last vestiges of the sunset, and found half a dozen small pebbles inside, all of which glittered with color. He extended his hand to the Fijian. "Thanks for the gift, mate. We will always remember your visit."

As they paddled away, Dutch turned back to the cockpit and tossed the small bottle to Doug. "Here's the most gold we'll ever see," he smiled. "Cannibals indeed. Now tell us what the hell really happen on the island."

Early the next morning, they sailed due east for the historic little village of Savusavu. They moored at the village marina, and the girls went into town for supplies. While they were gone, the guys did some overdue boat maintenance and topped off the water and fuel tanks. Then they walked up to the marine store, where they purchased a navigational chart of French Polynesia and more lamp oil for the four onboard storm lanterns.

It was early afternoon by the time the *Laura* cleared the harbor and motored south. An hour later, the boat turned south-southeast with the wind, and the sails were set.

Late in the afternoon, with the third largest Fijian Island, Taveuni, off their port beam, Dutch corrected their course to due east. Tahiti was now off their bow, a little more than two thousand miles away. Standing at the aft rail, feeling a few scattered drops of rain, he watched through the binoculars as Fiji melted away in their wake.

"Penny for your thoughts," Lois said from the wheel.

Dutch lowered the glasses and hung them back on the helm. "With its cooling trade winds and colorful people, Fiji reminded me of *Mutiny on the Bounty*. Someday, I hope to see these islands again."

Alone with Dutch in the cockpit, Lois asked, "And what about our little garden? Would you like to visit that again?"

Dutch hesitated. "Sure. Someday."

Lois gave him a shy look. "My garden is always open for another visit. Just give me a nod."

Dutch shook his head and moved to the hatch, "We can't bring our lust aboard. It's just not right. I'm going below. See you at the watch change."

Late that night, when he returned to the helm, he found a surly Lois waiting. "At sunset, I noticed a few rain squalls off our port bow. Maybe a good downpour will soften your rude mood."

"What mood?" Dutch replied approaching the wheel.

Lois glared at him. "When you left the deck this afternoon," she said in an angry voice. "You talked to me like I was a Honolulu whore. 'We can't bring our *lust* aboard. It's just not right,'" she mocked. "How dare you, Dutch? I don't deserve that!"

Standing next to her at the wheel, he replied, "I didn't mean it that way. You're no slut. You're one smart lady. I just don't want to complicate our voyage."

Lois moved away from the wheel. "So you're apologizing to me?"

"Yes. I never meant to offend you."

She smiled at him in the starlight, then reached over and kissed him on the cheek. "Good, I'll take your lame apology under advisement. Now light me a cigarette and tell me about your first woman."

Dutch tied off the helm and put his back to the wind to light two cigarettes, then handed one to Lois. "What woman?"

You said I was only your third. Who was the first?"

"Oh, that. It doesn't matter." He frowned, untying the helm. "It was just a one-night stand, many years ago."

"How, where, and who?"

Dutch puffed on his cigarette, not wanting to answer, but it was clear that Lois was going to keep insisting. "It was just before

I shipped out for overseas, he finally explained. "I was young and dumb, and this washed-up Hollywood starlet seduced me on a train. It wasn't a big deal."

Lois was all ears, with a grin on her face. "What was she wearing, and how did she seduce you?"

Dutch shook his head. "No. Only cads *take and tell.* I wouldn't do that to her, or you."

Lois took a drag from her cigarette, then stood and flicked her smoke overboard. "Good answer. Just when I thought you were going to be just like all the other guys, your chivalry steps in and proves me wrong."

"Duty, honor, country," Dutch answered with a proud smile.

Lois moved quickly to the cabin hatch, then looked back at him. "Our secret is safe with me. I'll grab your rain gear, on my way to bed. Good night, Dutch."

Swaying Palms

It takes a special kind of sailor to live and thrive on a small sailboat. The boat becomes an island onto itself, with nowhere to hide. During the long, monotonous months of the passage, each crewmember seemed to gravitate to a special place on the boat where they could find solace, read, or just wonder at the passing beauty. For Heidi, it was the point of the bow, where she could dangle her feet overboard and watch the boat slice through the crystal-clear sea. For Lois, it was sitting Indian-style in the shade of the mainmast, reading a book. Doug's place was in the nook, with the headset on, listening to whatever music he could find on the radio. Dutch had his place, as well: straddling the beam rails and watching the islands slip by.

The Pacific was vast, lonely and unforgiving, but while traveling from Fiji to Tahiti they sailed through a maze of lavish islands. Most were small and uninhabited, some only specks of coral with white beaches and a few coconut palms swaying gracefully in the breeze. The majority of the larger islands had just a single volcanic mountain, while others were more mountainous, with numerous cloud-capped peaks. Each island they passed, large or small, seemed to have its own personality. It was if Mother Nature were still working on her canvas, not yet sure of her final composition.

During the journey, they passed a number of local villages on the shores of the larger islands. Some were so close that they could make out the huts and see the children playing in the surf. A few times, they sailed past natives fishing from their canoes, using large, round nets that they threw into the sea. Most of the fisherman waved at the passing sailboat, while others proudly held up their catch. These were hard-working Polynesians, living off the land and the sea. The sailboat moved through the middle of their culture, an amazing place to be.

The weather had changed from hot and humid to mild and comfortable, with daily rain squalls. Only an artist's brush could capture the changing view. The colors were more muted, the lines less sharp, the palette inclined to more shades of gray. This was the South Pacific at its very best.

Early on the morning of October 22nd Tahiti came into view, with the island of Moorea off the port quarter. Tahiti, with its hundred and twenty scattered islands, was the economic, cultural and political center of French Polynesia. On the northwestern coast of the main island was the city of Papeete, the administrative capital of the region. It was there that they secured the sailboat to a transit dock, some hours later.

In the Tahitian language, Papeete meant "water from a basket." It was the largest city they had visited since Mindanao. The streets were wide, the buildings tall, and the harbor filled with commerce. Tahiti was a small jewel in the endless teal-green ocean.

When Dutch walked to the Harbor Master's Office to pay his moorage fee, he noticed posters on a bulletin board, promoting 'barefoot' sailing excursions to Moorea and back for thirty dollars per person. When he asked about it, the Harbor Master explained that there were a few sailboats that specialized in such day charters. "The tourists seem to love the adventure of sailing the islands. Most days, the boats are sold out."

When Dutch returned to the *Laura*, he finished typing a letter for Maggie. He thought about asking her for money, but pride held him back. When it was finished, he packed the letter and hand written shot sheet into a package for NBC. Then he and Doug hailed a cab and went to the airport, while Lois and Heidi went to town to buy provisions.

As they waited for a freight agent at the airport, Dutch picked up a flight schedule, and was surprised to find that Douglas DC-8 jet service was available for all Pan Am International flights. A flight to LA, via Honolulu, that once had taken eighteen hours was now only twelve hours. But the cost for the new service was outrageous: two hundred and forty dollars a seat. The freight costs had also skyrocketed, so Dutch sent the film back to NBC 'freight collect.'

On the ride back to the marina, Doug asked, "How much raw film do we still have?"

"Three rolls of 16mm and six rolls of black & white film. I figured we'll shoot that up when we get to the Galapagos Islands."

"We're going to the Galapagos? How far are they?"

"Four thousand one hundred miles, then up the west coast for home."

Doug smiled. "We're almost there. Dutch, could we stay a few extras days here in Tahiti? More than likely, I'll never be out here again."

Dutch looked at his mate's earnest face. "My heart says yes but my head says no," he said with honest regret. "Hurricane season is upon us, and I hope to miss it."

Back at the boat, Doug helped the girls stow away the groceries, while Dutch topped off the fuel and water tanks. Later in the afternoon, everyone walked to town to do a little exploring.

The weather was warm and humid, with occasional showers. The waterfront of Papeete seemed prosperous, with hotels, storefronts and restaurants around every corner. Lois soon found a used bookstore and dragged Dutch inside. There she bought him his next book, *To Kill a Mockingbird* by Harper Lee. "You're going to love this book, Dutch," she said with confidence. "It's all about injustice."

While they were busy, Doug and Heidi went into one of the beach-front hotels and inquired about getting a room for the night. But when the two couples met up again at a sidewalk café, Doug was furious. "Do you know what a room costs in this town? Sixty dollars! That's twice what we paid on Mindanao."

Dutch shrugged. "Your berth on the boat is cheaper."

While at the cafe, the crew sampled a local Tahitian beer called Hinano. It was served cold, and proved to be quite refreshing. As they continued to walk around they found, of all things, a pizza parlor, there in the middle of the tropics. They happily devoured two large pizzas and more Tahitian beer. The patrons of the restaurant were a mix of New Zealanders, Australians, and a few Yanks. Everyone had a marvelous time, chatting about the islands, the black-sand beaches, and the local beer, while eating pizza that tasted like Italy.

It was almost dark by the time they returned to the boat. As everyone came aboard, Dutch invited them into the cabin for a crew meeting. While Heidi poured nightcaps, Dutch brought out his chart for French Polynesia and spread it out on the table.

"We'll cast off in the morning. But before we leave, we have a few problems to talk about." Using his finger, he pointed to Tahiti on the map. "Here's where we are now." Moving his finger way off the map in a north-easterly direction, he continued, "Way up here is Los Angeles, six thousand miles away as the crow flies. If the winds and currents were with us, we could be home in a month or six weeks. But on this course, once we get to the Northern Latitudes, the winds and currents will be against us all the way home, almost doubling our travel time."

Heidi passed around the drinks. Dutch had everyones attention, as they all stared at the map.

"So," he continued, "when we leave here tomorrow, we'll set a course due east, with the winds, for about fifteen hundred miles. Once we have Pitcairn Island off our starboard bow, we'll change that course to northeast and sail for the Galapagos Islands, off the coast of Ecuador." Dutch took a sip of his whiskey.

"Is that the same Pitcairn Island from *Munity on the Bounty*?" Lois asked.

"Yes, and we can stop there if we have to, but if we don't have to, we won't. We'll just keep moving. Once we're on the west coast of South American, we'll have the winds and currents with us, all the way up the coast to Los Angeles."

"Didn't you say something about the hurricane season out there?" Doug asked.

"Yes. That's another problem. I'm hoping we'll beat the weather home."

"We could winter here in Tahiti," Heidi suggested, with a hopeful look on her face.

Dutch smiled at her. "Which brings me to our last problem – we're almost out of money. I've got enough to get us home, but we'll be eating beans and rice for most of the voyage. We'll have to take a page from the Polynesians and learn to live off the land."

The crew seemed stunned by Dutch's words. They sat silently, with long faces, startled by the blunt truth.

"I've got a few extra dollars, if the boat needs it," Doug finally said.

"Me, too," Lois added.

"I've got a twenty-dollar bill pinned inside one of my bras, for emergencies. My father gave it to me when I left home," Heidi said sheepishly.

Doug turned to her, his face a picture of surprise. "I never saw any twenty dollar bill in your bra."

Heidi grinned, "You're always looking in the wrong places."

Dutch stared at his generous mates, and then raised his glass. "Here's to my crew and to home. We'll make it just fine."

Twelve days later, after a stormy passage of heavy rains and mild temperatures, the *Laura* approached the eastern-most waters of French Polynesia.

In the early afternoon, Doug yelled down the open cabin hatch, "We've got an island off our starboard bow."

Dutch put on his rain jacket and went topside, where he used the binoculars to try to identify the distant land. It was a murky view, as the island was shrouded in dark clouds and fast-moving rain squalls. He studied it for a long moment.

"That's Pitcairn Island, right where I thought it would be," he finally told Doug, lowering the binoculars. "Once it's off our beam, turn northeast to forty-five degrees."

"We're not stopping?" Doug replied.

"No. Too damn wet, and the book says there's not much worth seeing on the island."

"Lois will be disappointed. She wanted to visit the Bounty boys," Doug answered from the wheel.

Dutch moved to the hatch and looked back at him. "I'll tell her. We've got to keep moving. This weather is turning snotty."

The next afternoon, Dutch was just waking when he heard Heidi call down the cabin hatch, "Doug, we've got another island off our bow."

He slipped out of bed, put on his deck shoes and shorts, and went topside.

When he got on deck, he was greeted with a sunny warm day. Doug was already standing on the bow with the binoculars to his eyes.

Dutch joined him. "What do you see?" he asked of his mate.

"Not much. The island is big, with high rocky cliffs, thick vegetation and one small mountain on the northwest corner." Doug lowered the glasses and gave them to him.

Dutch looked across the water. The island was about five miles away, and had a craggy shoreline, devoid of much color. "That's Henderson Island," he finally said, removing the binoculars from his eyes. "The diving book just says it's arid, sterile and uninhabited. On the northwest shore, there's a place called Frigate Cove. That's where the diving is best. Let's see if we can catch some dinner there."

An hour later, the boat dropped anchor in the cove, where tall island bluffs gave way to numerous large sea caves that were carved deep into the sides of the cliffs. Above those crags was the only mountain on Henderson Island.

As the men got out their snorkeling gear, Lois stood at the aft rail, looking over to the rocky caverns. "Lobsters love dark places," she said, turning to the guys in the cockpit. "Look just inside those caves. That should be your best bet."

Dutch smiled at her as he picked up his spear gun. Then, with his fins in hand, he moved down to the swim platform and slipped into the sea. As he put on his fins underwater, he shouted up to her, "A lobster dinner sounds mighty good to me about now. We'll bring back something."

With the sun low in the sky, Doug joined him, and they swam for the shoreline. When they were fifty yards from the cliffs, they started snorkeling towards the largest cavern in the bluffs. The water was clear, the ocean floor was covered with rocks of all sizes and a few clumps of sea grass swaying in the currents. But they saw no fish, nor any signs of sea life.

When they got close to the big cavern, they noticed the sea floor was covered with much smaller rocks that seemed to flow out of the deep-water opening of the cave.

Still no signs of life.

Once inside the cavern, the ocean floor fell into deep shadow, and Dutch signaled Doug he was going to look up. When he did so, it took a few seconds for the water to clear from his mask. Blinking his eyes a few times, he could not believe what was before him. With only sunlight reflecting underwater, they were in a large, dark cave.

A murky, cigar-shaped ship was docked to a rocky ledge.

The boat stood tall above the water's edge, and looked to be over two hundred feet long. Dutch tapped Doug on the shoulder with his thumb up.

Doug lifted his head slowly from the water. Removing his snorkeling mask, he looked around and asked, in a near-whisper, "What the hell is this place?"

Treading water next to him, Dutch answered, "Looks like some kind of submarine."

Doug's eyes were big as he stared at the hulk some fifty yards away. "Have we stumbled onto some secret submarine base?"

"No, look at the deck plates. They're covered with rust. This tub has been here a long time."

"I've never seen a submarine that looks like... Let's get the hell out of here."

Dutch smiled at his mate in the shimmering water. Then he yelled, at the top of lungs, "Hello! Anyone here?"

Only his echo answered back.

Chapter Ten

Discovery

Lois stood at her stove, cooking pancakes and spam, as Dutch and Doug prepared to return to the cavern. With the light fading the night before, they had swam back to the sailboat without any fish for dinner, but with a thrilling tale of finding a submarine in a sea cave. The crew had spent the evening speculating on their discovery and wondering what other surprises Henderson Island might hold.

"Doug and I will row over with the camera gear," Dutch told his mates, wearing long pants, with his pistol and knife on his belt. "Once we know the cavern is safe, we'll come and get you, Lois. Heidi, I brought out the shotgun. You stand guard in the cockpit. If you see another boat approaching, fire it off. We will hear you and return as fast as we can."

Lois served up the grub with many questions. Everyone was a little nervous about the guys returning to the dark, dingy cave, as they had no idea what they might find. Was their discovery real, or only a mirage?

After breakfast, the guys loaded the dinghy, including the only two flashlights aboard, and two of the storm lanterns for additional light. Then, under a clear morning sky, they rowed back across Frigate Cove for the sea cave.

As they approached the shore's cliffs, Dutch studied the caverns opening. Its height was tall, a good eighty feet, and the opening at the waterline was roughly sixty feet. He also noticed that the shape of the opening looked to be handcrafted, not the work of Mother Nature.

A few moments later, they rowed across the jaws of the opening. The light inside the cavity seemed brighter now, with the sun in the eastern sky. The grotto was deep and tall, with volcanic walls that glistened in the reflected underwater light. The fissure was as quiet as a tomb. The only sounds they heard were from their own oars and the lapping waters against the skiff.

As thcy approached the dingy gray submarine, Doug stopped rowing and stood in the boat, with his still camera at his eye. When he finished taking pictures, Dutch did the same with his movie camera on the tripod. The interior light was dim, the exposure wide open – not the best for shooting color film, but this was a scene he could not pass up.

The dinghy rowed alongside the aft of the sub until they found a way to board. Doug was first up the rusty hull plates, using hand and footholds in small vents on the sides of the hull. Dutch followed after. Both mates had flashlights in hand. They moved across the beam of the boat and pointed their lights at the rocky dock that held the sub in place.

On the right end of the pier were stacks of fuel barrels that turned out to be empty. At the other end was the dark opening of what looked like another cave. Resting on the center of the wharf was a wooden boarding platform that had been pulled away from the submarine. Beaming their lights on the stone dock ledge, they found three iron anchor holds secured deep inside the rocks. Those cleats were connected to the submarine by thick rope lines, with enough slack to allow the boat to move with the tides. Between the stone ledge and the hull was a double-heavy rope cargo net that prevented the boat from rubbing against the rocky pier.

"This moorage was well planned," Dutch said, shining his flashlight down the length of the boat. "This sub has been here a long time."

On the deck, they found the aft hatch and tried to open it.

It wouldn't budge.

They moved up the boat and walked carefully alongside the tear-drop conning tower, looking for another entry point. There was a flush door on the tower, with no dog-ears to open it. The submarine was long, narrow and sleek, with few protrusions on the deck. Forward of the tall conning tower, they found the bow hatch and tried to open it. It, too, was rusted shut.

Doug found iron ladder treads on the tower, and scurried up it. Once inside the sail-bridge, he flashed his light around the boat's rusty plates. He disappeared from view for a moment, then stood and looked down at Dutch, still on the bow. "There's another hatch up here. It was covered with a tin cloth. I think we can open it."

Dutch joined his mate in the tower, and soon they were able to pull open the hatch cover. As the stale air from inside the sub escaped, they both turned away. "What the hell is that smell?" Doug asked, holding his nose.

"I don't know. Rotting food? Mold? Maybe dead bodies," Dutch answered, pointing his light down the hatch tube. He could see the deck below, and the iron steps of a ladder inside a tube. Without the flashlight, it looked like the depths of hell. But it had to be explored. "Just keep your light on the tube while I crawl down," he said.

Doug shook his head. "We don't know what the hell is down there, pal. This could be a plague ship, with its dead crew below."

"Maybe, but it's a risk I'm willing to take. Just keep your light on me. Once I get on the next deck, I'll light one of the lanterns, so you can see your way down."

One step at a time, Dutch slowly moved down the ladder. Moments later, with his feet firmly on the lower deck, he felt the interior humidity and flashed his light around the small compartment. "Looks like a small control room down here. No dead bodies," he yelled up to Doug. "Drop me down a lantern without the chimney. I'll light it for you."

With both men safely on the conning tower deck, they shined their lights around the cramped compartment. The bulkheads were painted a dark gray, and the room was full of values, dials, gauges and levers. From all the different names printed on the cloudy instruments, they determined that the boat was German. Leaving the lamp burning, they dropped down to another control room below the conning tower deck, and explored the submarine from the stern to the stem. They looked into all the compartments, which were painted white; all were empty. They found no signs of humanity, living or dead. Most of the berths didn't have mattresses and most of the blankets were missing as well. When they checked inside the galley, they found the shelves empty. In the crew's mess, however, they came upon a bronze plate on a bulkhead. It proclaimed: U-3521 - Type XXI, built Bremen Germany, March 1944. In the companionways, they did notice the bony remains of a few dead bilge rats, and some mold growing on a few of the damp bulkhead plates – the apparent source of the rancid smell.

With their tour complete, they returned to the control room and scurried up the ladders. Once on the conning tower bridge, they kept the hatch open for air exchange.

"What the hell happened to the crew and all their gear?" Doug asked, moving down the outside ladder.

Following him, Dutch answered, "I have no idea. Let's set up the camera on the pier and get some more footage. See if you can climb up to the dock, using the cargo netting, and push the boarding platform across to me."

They spent over an hour shooting more footage of the boat. When they were done, they were set up in front of the dark entry to the other cavern. Pointing his flashlight inside the next cave, Doug asked, "Should we explore?"

"That's why we're here," Dutch replied, turning on his flashlight and pointing it at the dark entry.

As they walked up the steep grade of the narrow, rocky corridor, their footsteps echoed back to them. Soon, they came to a series of large stone niches carved into the volcanic rock. In one of the recesses, they found a few wooden crates stacked upon each other. The boxes were all empty, but Dutch noticed Japanese symbols and the word "Sake" stenciled on one side.

In the harsh beams of the flashlights, Dutch shook his head. "Japanese Sake and a German U-boat? This makes no sense."

Further up the path, they came to another nook that contained five mounds of loose rocks on the floor, with six mattresses stacked against the back wall.

"What the hell?" Doug said, shined his light on the mattresses.

"Look at the size and shape of the rock mounds," Dutch answered. "This is a burial crypt."

Doug backed away from the tomb, and the guys moved farther up the narrow way. Around the next corner, with their lights focused on the corridor, they came to another recess. When they flashed their lights inside the chamber, they froze in place, stunned by what they saw.

The room was near filled with a large number of stacked wooden crates. On the top of the pile, a canvas tarp was draped over it. But their beams of light weren't shining on the crates, as they were standing directly in front of a skeleton seated on the ground, with its ridged, bony back resting against the pile of crates. What clothes it had worn were almost rotted away. The only item Dutch could recognize was the fragments of a white navy hat atop the skeleton skull. Around its leather hatband, a few strands of gray hair could still be seen. The skull and eye sockets were devoid of any flesh, as were its torso and legs. In the left temple of the skull, a small, round hole was visible.

Dutch moved his beam of light to the left side of the corpse. Just below its bony left hand was a rusty Luger pistol resting on the stones, next to a metal box.

The scene silenced the guys for a few moments. Finally, Dutch broke the quiet. "This guy had to be the Captain…but why did he commit suicide? Let's get the movie camera up here. This is unbelievable."

Using the light bar, they filmed inside the niche. It was footage that Dutch had never expected to shoot. When he was done, Doug did the same with his still camera. Then they lost battery power for the light.

As Doug lit both lanterns, Dutch told his mate, "I'll take the light back to the boat for recharging. I'll return with the girls. I want them to witness what we found, so don't disturb the scene. While I'm gone, explore some more."

An hour later, Dutch returned with the girls. They were frightened by the sea cave and spooked at walking up the long, dark corridor of the interior cave. Lois grasped onto the back of Dutch's belt, while Heidi kept her hand on Lois's shoulder. They were as jumpy as a bride on her wedding night. As they moved up the corridor, Dutch showed them the different chambers that he and Doug had found.

When they got to the Captain's room, they found Doug squatted next to the corpse.

"Did you find any more surprises?" Dutch asked, approaching the niche.

"Yeah." Doug stood up. "Just up the way, I found what looks like an outside entrance, but it's blocked with stone rubble. It's totally impassable."

"That's strange." Dutch flashed his light around the chamber. "Why would the Captain want to entomb himself?"

Doug moved to the stack of wooden crates and pulled back the tarp. "I have no idea. Let's see what's inside these crates. My curiosity is killing me."

The girls stood speechless, taking in the terrible scene as Dutch moved to the boxes and helped Doug remove the tarp. Using his flashlight, he examined the top row of crates. He pointed out one box that looked like it had been opened before. They lowered that extra heavy box carefully to the ground and placed it next to the corpse. Then, taking his knife, Dutch pried open the nailed lid.

Pulling back the wood shavings, they found the box was full of gold bars!

Now the guys were speechless, as well.

Doug finally knelt next to the box and lifted out one of the bars. In the lantern light, its color shimmered around the chamber. The bar was marked with a Swastika and twin lightning bolts.

Dutch squatted next to him and pointed his light inside the box. He counted the gold bars, nine in all. Then he noticed three leather pouches.

With the crew watching, he opened each sack and shined his light inside. With the first pouch, he said, "Diamonds," then, "Jewels." And, finally, "Little gold nuggets."

Dutch looked at his mates, who were speechless. "We'll take the pouches and one gold bar back to boat. And we'll take the metal box and the Luger pistol, as well."

The crew just gazed at the treasure. They seemed stunned, lost in their own imaginations.

Standing up, with the leather pouches in hand, Dutch faced his mates and said firmly, "Let's get this buttoned up and get back to the boat. *NOW*."

In the remains of the afternoon, Doug rowed the ladies back to the sailboat, with all the treasure. As Dutch awaited his return on the submarine, with the camera gear, he stared up at the conning tower. The day had been an adventure he would never forget and, more than likely, a turning point for him and his crew. His thoughts soon turned to the sub's long journey and its dead captain. Something tragic had happen on Henderson Island, but he couldn't understand what it had been. He had too many questions, and too few answers. But he sensed, somehow, that he was destined to tell the story of U-3521.

On the skiff ride back to the sailboat, he found Doug as quiet as the skeleton they had stumbled on. His face had no expression and his eyes had a distant look. His friend frightened Dutch a little. Gold could be the biggest evil of them all.

When the guys brought the camera gear aboard, Dutch found a much different mood with the ladies. Lois worked at her stove, while Heidi sat at the table, with all the treasure spread out. Both girls were smiling, and they warmly welcomed their mates.

"You guys must be starved. You didn't have any lunch today," Lois said brightly as they came below. "I'm making special horsdoeuvres, and I have a bottle of champagne in the icebox. The party can start anytime now."

"Hey, fellows, how's it feel to be rich?" Heidi added, holding up the gold bar.

Finally, a smile chased over Doug's lips, and he joined Heidi behind the table. As they emptied out the pouches of treasure, Dutch stowed the camera gear under the port settee. When he was done, he went over to the table and looked down at the piles of stones.

Lois seemed fascinated with the diamonds. She was not only counting them out, but also sorting them by size and color. There looked to be a couple of hundred diamonds on the table, and the same amount of precious stones. Looking more closely at the gemstones, Dutch recognized emeralds, sapphires, opals, pearls and many other types. In the afternoon light, both piles of jewels sparkled on the table. But what he had identified as gold nuggets didn't have the same luster. He picked up a few, and looked more closely at them. Then his expression soured, and he dropped them back onto the table.

"That's disgusting! Put all this gold back into its pouch. I never want to see it again," Dutch said, his voice shaking with emotion.

"Why?" Doug asked, looking up at his friend.

"Those aren't nuggets. They're gold dental crowns and caps from dead people. I'll have nothing to do with Nazi gold. It's the work of the devil."

Doug inspected a few of the nuggets, with an inquisitive frown, and then sadly shook his head in agreement.

"Wow," Heidi said. "Where would they get that many dental caps?"

Dutch glared at her like she was an idiot. "In the concentration camps, from their dead victims. Don't you know anything?"

"Well, excuse me!" she replied indignantly.

Dutch picked up some diamonds and held them in one hand, "This is the stuff that dreams are made of." Then he gestured to the pouch of teeth gold, "That's the stuff nightmares are made of. Bet all the damn loot from the submarine is probably from dead people."

"You don't know that," Doug replied, putting his arm around Heidi. "And don't take it out on her. Maybe you're right about the nuggets. But we have no idea who owned the jewels, and the gold bars belonged to the Nazis, who are long gone. We found them, fair and square, and now we own them."

Dutch sat on the corner of the settee and held up the gold bar. "So you're going to walk into Barclays Bank in Tahiti and sell this gold bar with a Swastika and twin lightning bolts embedded in it? I don't think so. The bank will call the police, and then comes the International Press. Soon, the whole damn world will know about our discovery. Then we'll learn that some country owns Henderson Island, and they'll lay claim to our discovery. Or maybe the new German government will claim it. Or the European Allies, as war reparations. We'd be in the courts for years. That's not for me!"

Lois approached the table with a plate of canapes and four empty glasses. "Let's not get our panties in a twist," she said with a smile, putting the plate on the table. "We'll come up with a scheme to save our treasure."

"Yes," Doug replied with a brighter face. "We can melt down the bars and remove the German markings, then sell them on the open market."

Dutch smiled at his optimistic friends. "That would require a foundry. Don't think there are any of those out here."

Lois returned to the table with a bottle of champagne and popped it open. "Then let's drink to our good fortune and come up with a better plan."

As the crew talked about different schemes, Dutch finally opened the galvanized lid to the metal box. Inside, he found a thick envelope filled with German Marks. Under the envelope was a black-bound ledger, which he leafed through. It was all in German, which he couldn't read, but the handwriting was all the same, with different dates and places. The book looked to be a diary. Under that was the ship's log for U-3521. Folded inside the logbook was the packing slip for the gold cargo, and ten loose pages that looked like a crew roster, complete with pictures. The Captain's information and photo were included as well. His name had been Hans Miller, and the last entry in his diary was dated 20 January 1946.

Dutch was spellbound by the contents of the box, only rousing when Heidi broke into his thoughts to ask, "Why can't we just load the gold aboard and sail it back to the States?"

Dutch looked up at her, not wanting to hurt her feelings again. Unfolding the packing list for the gold, he replied, "From the numbers on these papers, there are 597 gold bars in all. At over forty pounds per bar, that's over twelve tons of dead weight. This boat would sink." He passed around the papers from the box. "Take a look at what else I found. This is the true treasure of our discovery."

"What treasure?" Doug answered. "These are just papers we can't read."

Dutch smiled at his mate. "Think this out. The story of U-3521, and our discovery of it, would make a great book or documentary. We'd get rich from the story."

Only Lois seemed to agree with Dutch, while Doug and Heidi remained fixated on the gold. When the mates finished the bottle of champagne and started drinking wine, Dutch gathered up the papers from the table and returned them to the metal box. He was tired of arguing with them, so he poured himself some Yukon Jack and went topside for a smoke.

In the brilliant amber light of the sunset, he considered his next move. Henderson Island had turned out to be just another reminder of the war he wanted to forget. Was this to be his only destiny?

That evening, after a dinner of beans and franks, the crew continued yapping about schemes and dreams. Dutch had not said but a few words during the meal, and he soon tired of their conversation. Getting up from the table, he gathered up all the treasure and took it into his cabin. When he returned, he stood in front of his crew.

"This is my boat and my decision. For now, we will forget about the gold and raise some capital by selling off a few of the jewels. Then we will use that money to claim U-3521 as salvage, under International Maritime Law. We'll get the submarine repaired and then take it back to the States. Remember, we all signed 'ships article's' back in Honolulu. Those terms and conditions still apply. Trust me, we will all profit from this discovery." He looked at his watch. "It's getting late and I'm dead tired. I'm off to bed."

When Dutch climbed into his berth, he could still hear the muted voices coming from the main salon. Turning on his reading light, he removed Captain Miller's diary from the metal box. Thumbing through the pages, he tried to read some of the words and all of the dates, but it was like a book without a beginning or end.

An hour later, the crew had gone to bed, as well. Crawling quietly out of his bunk, Dutch went to the nook, put on the headphones, and turned on the shortwave radio. Unfolding his map, he looked for any islands of consequence in the area. The only one he found was Mangareva Island, some seven hundred miles west of the Pitcairn Islands.

He dialed in his first frequency, keyed the microphone, and calmly said, "This is the sailboat *Laura* calling Mangareva Island. Please come back." He repeated the words over and over, each time changing to a different radio frequency.

Undertow

When Lois walked into her galley, early the next morning, she found Dutch slumped over in the nook. With the headphones off and his head down, he was fast asleep. She shook him gently, and he came awake with his eyes wide.

"Did you sleep here all night?" she asked.

Dutch scratched his head. "Reckon so."

"Your radio is still on."

Dutch looked around the cabin, then at his watch. "I'm expecting a call."

"Who would call at this hour?"

He smiled at her. "I'll explain later. How about some coffee?"

Waiting in his nook for the coffee, Dutch refolded his map and took a closer look at the Marquesas Islands, some nine hundred miles northwest of Henderson Island. There were four major islands in the group, and Hiva Oa was the seconded largest. Then he thumbed through the *Divers Guide,* and learned that the group was rated as some of the best diving waters in the entire South Pacific. He crossed his fingers, looking forward to the call he was waiting for.

When the coffee was done, he took his mug topside and lit a cigarette. It was another beautiful tropical morning, and he felt good, as if he finally had a firm plan. In some ways, he wished they had never discovered the submarine. In other ways, he relished the challenge of telling the boat's story.

Lois called up the cabin hatch, "You have your call on the radio."

Dutch flipped his smoke overboard and raced back to the nook. Putting the headphones on, he keyed the microphone. "This is the sailboat *Laura.* Come back, Hiva Oa."

As Dutch started talking, Doug and Heidi came into the cabin. All that the crew could hear was one side of the conversation. They were all curious, and didn't understand what was happening.

Twenty minutes later, Dutch signed off and removed the headphones from his ears, with a broad smile on his face. Joining his inquisitive crew in the galley, he poured himself more coffee. "That was Mr. Lyle Chandler, the owner of Chandler and Sons Boatyard and Salvage. I've made a deal with him to come here and tow the submarine back to his boatyard."

Doug's expression darkened. "You made a deal without consulting us? That's not right!"

"As I said last night, this is my boat and my decision. Before you get your dander up, hear my plan."

Dutch told them about what he had learned the night before. He had been lucky to make connection with a radio operator on one of the inter-Island freighters, who advised Dutch that boatyards were few and far between in the South Pacific. Then he'd told him about Chandler & Sons Boatyard and Salvage on the Island of Hiva Oa. That island also had an airport with direct air connections to Tahiti. After thanking the operator for the information, Dutch had spent hours trying to make contact with the company. He finally talked with a woman, who was the wife of Mr. Chandler. She promised that he would call back, first thing in the morning.

"You told him about our submarine?" Doug interrupted angrily.

"No. I'm not a fool. I told him the sailboat's diesel engine had broken down, and that we had bad storm damage to our main mast. When he gets here, I'll tell him the truth, *if* we think we can trust him."

"And if not? Then what?" Lois asked.

"Then he will have made a long trip for nothing," Dutch replied and continued with the explanation of his plan.

Once the submarine was safely moored at the boatyard, Mr. Chandler would give Dutch a price for the repairs. Then Dutch would fly to Tahiti and on to the States, where he would sell enough diamonds and gems to pay for the repairs. "I'm not sure I can sell that many just in LA, so I might have to go to New York, as well."

While he was Stateside, raising capital, Doug, Heidi and Lois would sail the *Laura* to Tahiti and setup a 'barefoot' sailing business on the docks of Papeete. That way the crew could earn enough money to live on, while he was gone. When he returned with the money, they would sail back to Hiva Oa and get the submarine seaworthy, then raise a crew and sail the boat back to the States, where it would be the centerpiece for their story of the discovery of the U-3521.

When he finished telling them his plan, the crew stood quiet, with long faces. Finally Doug asked, "How far away is this island? And what's the cost to get the submarine towed?"

"Hiva Oa is nine hundred miles northwest of here. It will take the tugboat five days to get here. The cost is two thousand dollars for the tow and three hundred for the fuel."

"We don't have that kind of money," Doug answered.

"Yes, I know. I've got enough to pay them for the fuel. And I'll give them a deposit of a few sapphires and pearls, for good faith. Trust me, I have a plan."

"What do you know about this island?" Lois asked.

"Not much. The *Divers Guide* said the island is also known as Paul Gauguin's Island, because he's buried there. They also say the waters are the most pristine in all of the South Pacific."

Heidi looked confused. "And what about the gold?"

"We'll deal with it later, once the submarine is fixed. Until then, what's on Henderson is our secret. Secrecy is everything."

Finally, everyone had smiles on their faces. They were beginning to see the wisdom in Dutch's plan. The submarine could be loaded with the gold.

"So we sit around here for five days, waiting for the tugboat?" Doug asked.

"No. I have more than enough plans to keep us busy. Let's have some breakfast and get started."

After the meal, Doug, Lois and Dutch rowed the dinghy around the North Point of Henderson Island and went ashore in the small surf of North Beach. They crawled up a few embankments and soon found themselves among the palm and scrub trees of the island. There they found an overgrown trail that seemed to led towards the south side of the small mountain where the cave was. The ground cover was mostly vines and weeds. The inland landscape looked arid and sterile, with few signs of life other than a few birds in the trees. But as they moved along the trail, they found a few man-made items: a rusty tin can, a piece of torn cloth, and the sole from an old shoe.

When they arrived at the south side of the mountain, they started searching for the cave entrance. Soon they found, under a thick blanket of vines, the mouth of the cave blocked by a pile of stone rubble. They searched the general area and came upon the remains of a small village, with collapsed huts made from palm logs and bamboo.

Next to the site was a tiny stream that offered only a trickle of water. Inside the flattened shelters, they found a few rotting mattresses, some personal effects, and a few bits of clothing, which lead them to believe that the storm-ravaged little village must have been the bivouac area for the crew. But, if so, where were those men?

As Dutch and his group snooped around further, they found a few burned-out fire pits and some rusty pots and pans. Doug took pictures of all of their finds and then, using a long stick probe, uncovered a deep, rocky pit at the foot of the mountain. He pulled back the growth of vines, aimed his flashlight deep inside and then, wide-eyed, called for his mates.

When they reached his side and looked down, not a word was spoken. The beam of light revealed a deep hole filled with the skeletal remains of numerous bodies.

"I count a dozen skulls," Lois finally said, with a solemn expression on her face.

"But why are all the big bones broken in half?" Doug asked, the beam from his flashlight trembling.

Dutch turned away. "Because someone ate the marrow from inside their bones."

Doug switched off his flashlight and turned away, as well. "Cannibals?"

"It must have been," Lois answered shakily. "They either ate each other or some natives slaughtered the entire crew. I'd say that's why the Captain entombed himself inside the cavern, to save what remained of his men."

When the first shock had faded, Dutch held both flashlights while Doug took pictures of the inside of the pit. Then they walked around the bivouac area one more time, spooked at the thought of what had gone on there in the jungle.

The row back to the sailboat was quiet, with all the mates lost in their own thoughts. Something awful had happened on the island, but they still didn't know *how* or *why*. Still, there was hope that they would learn more when the Captain's diary was translated.

The crew spent that evening speculating on their discoveries and talking about, of all things, cannibalism. It was a hard topic to confront, as no one could imagine the violence of it, or the reason for it.

After a sleepless night, Dutch and Doug rowed back over to the sea cave. Using the storm lanterns, they walked back up the rocky corridor to the gold chamber. Reaching it, they used the tarp from the top of the crates to wrap up the body of Captain Miller, then carried his remains to the crypt room and laid him beside his five mates. For the next few hours, they carried rubble rocks from the entrance back to his grave, and buried him in stones. When they finished there were six identical rocks mounds on the floor of the tomb.

Standing over the stones, head bowed, Dutch said a few words from a POW Camp poem he hadn't thought about in years: "I gave my all without restraint, and rest now with my duty done. I lie in peace without complaint, and apologize to none." He wiped away a tear. "Oh Lord, in life these men were our enemies; in death, they are our comrades. Forgive these sailors for their violent end. Lift up their souls and grant them atonement. Amen"

When Dutch raised his head, Doug asked, "Do you think prayer does any good?"

"It does for me," Dutch replied.

On the way back down the corridor, the two men stopped at the empty wooden crates and pulled apart boxes until they had a pile of wood slats. These they took back to the sailboat. That afternoon and evening, the crew carved and shaped the wood into six crude grave markers. The next day, the guys returned to the crypt and placed the markers on the mounds of rock. Five said 'Unknown Sailor,' and the last one said, 'Captain Hans Miller '46.'

On their return to the sea cave, Dutch said, "We have one final task. We should move all the empty fuel barrels from the other end of the pier to the front of this cave entrance. That way, no prying eyes will ever find the crypt or the gold."

Waiting for the tugboat, the crew spent the next two days diving the area in search of food for their icebox. The ocean floor turned out to be almost as sterile as the land, but they were able to add a dozen fish to their larder.

On the morning of the sixth day, Mr. Chandler radioed and told them the tugboat was only ten miles out. Two hours later, the sea-tug *Mohawk* arrived at Frigate Cove. They dropped anchor a few hundred yards from the *Laura,* and Doug and Dutch rowed the skiff over to the boat to meet the crew.

As they came aboard the tugboat, Lyle Chandler and his three sons stood on the deck to greet them. "Don't see any storm damage to your sailboat," Mr. Chandler said, with an inquisitive face under his white captain's hat.

Dutch smiled at him and held his hand out. "Let's do the introductions first. I'm Dutch Clarke, the Skipper of the *Laura*."

The old man just stared at his outstretched hand. He was a grumpy-looking fellow with a body like a fireplug. His hair was more salt than pepper, and his weathered face read like a road map.

Finally, he reached out and shook Dutch's hand. "Hope you blokes didn't get us out here under false colors."

"I'll explain everything in a few minutes, Captain. This man next to me is my mate, Doug Asbow. On board my sailboat are two more members of my crew."

Doug and Lyle shook hands, and he introduced his three sons. John was the oldest, at twenty five; Matthew was next, at twenty-two and Luke was the youngest, at eighteen. They were all young and handsome, with auburn hair and stout bodies that glistened with muscles in the bright sun.

As everyone shook hands, Dutch asked Mr. Chandler, "Where did you get this tugboat? Don't think I've seen one like it before."

"From the US Navy after the war," the old-timer answered. "Now what the hell is going on here?"

The mates looked at each other, knowing full well that they would have to trust Mr. Chandler and his sons if they wanted their help. "We do have a tow for you, and we want you to take it back to your boatyard for repairs," Dutch said, looking at their faces. "We just couldn't talk about it on the radio. It's an old war relic that still floats, and we are claiming it under the Maritime Salvage Laws."

"What is it?" the old man demanded.

"It's a German U-boat," Dutch replied firmly, watching their faces turn to surprise.

"What's a German submarine doing out here?" Matthew finally asked.

His question opened the door for Doug and Dutch to tell them how they had discovered the U-3521, omitting any mention of the treasure or of cannibalism. They talked for a good long while, in the hot sun. When they finished, John asked, "What happen to the crew?"

"As far as we know, they are all buried on the island," Dutch answered, making eye contact with him.

"We'll have to inspect the boat's condition to see if it's safe to tow," Mr. Chandler said to his sons. "Get the motor launch into the water and we'll go look."

The boys all had eager faces as they jumped to their father's command.

The guys watched them for moment. Then Dutch said to Mr. Chandler, "We'll row back over and get our flashlights. You should bring some light, as well. The inside of the hull is black as a coal pit. Just remember, this discovery is ours, and we want it kept a secret. Do we have an understanding, sir?"

"Aye, we do," he replied.

After stopping off at the sailboat, Dutch and Doug rowed towards the cave, with the motor launch not far behind. With the ebbing tide, neither boat had any trouble crossing the jaws of the cavern. Once inside, the guys stopped rowing just a few yards from the gray hulk, and let the launch come alongside.

"Well, fellows, what do you think of our discovery?" Dutch asked in the obscure light, his voice bouncing off the walls.

The tugboat crew was quiet for a long moment, pointing their flashlights down the submarine and all around the watery cavern. Finally, Luke turned to Dutch and answered, "Man, this old war relic is cool."

Soon, both boats were tied to the sub, and everyone went aboard. Doug showed them the aft hatch and told them that it was rusted shut. Then they carefully moved to the forward deck hatch, where they were told the same. Mr. Chandler directed his boys to get some tools from the launch and see if they could open the hatches.

As they went to work, Dutch, Doug and Lyle Chandler went up the conning tower ladder to the sail-bridge, and down inside the U-3521 to the conning tower deck, with two lanterns lit.

Mr. Chandler was all business as he walked around the small room, flashing his light on all the instruments. Then came some noise, and they saw light coming from the control room below.

Luke crawled up the hatch ladder. With just his head and shoulders above the conning tower deck, he said with great excitement, "The forward hatch is open, Papa. We'll get the aft hatch next."

"Good," Lyle answered. "Walk this old tub from end to end and report back to me."

Luke looked around the conning tower room with wide eyes, then disappeared back down to the control room.

"I like your boys," Dutch said to Lyle. "They've got good Christian names."

The old man scoffed. “The Mormons got to my wife right after we married. They’ve been chasing after my soul ever since. With no luck, I might add.”

“Well, your boys seem to know what they’re doing around boats,” Dutch said.

Mr. Chandler turned off his flashlight and, in the flicker of just the lamp light, answered, “She coddled ’em and I cussed ’em. They turned out just fine.”

They spent hours checking out the sub. The only real problem they found, was that the bilges were almost totally filled with water. The boys didn’t think it was from any leakage, just the high humidity trapped inside the hull. Two of the boys went back to the tugboat and returned with a bilge pump, fans and a generator, to dry out the submarine and drain the bilges.

In the control room, they were able to free up the rudder controls with enough movement that the sub could be maneuvered safely. The entire crew from the tugboat proved to be experts and, by late afternoon, Mr. Chandler decreed that the U-3521 could be towed safely. They would turn the sub around inside the cavern, using the motor launch, then push and pull it slowly out of the cave with a long tow cable connected to the tugboat. According to Mr. Chandler, the extraction would take place at the next ebb tide, at 0730 the next morning. The only catch was that the old man wanted to see the color of Dutch’s money before he’d do the job.

While the boys continued working, Dutch and Doug rowed Lyle Chandler over to the sailboat to settle the money issue. It was a quiet ride, as both mates worried about what the old man’s reaction would be to the truth.

When they got aboard the *Laura*, Dutch introduced the girls to him, and it was clear that he was instantly taken by their charms. He bowed to them and said, “Always wanted to have sweet daughters.”

“I’m going to have a whiskey, Mr. Chandler. Would you like one?” Dutch asked as they sat down in front of the table.

“Yes, don’t mind if I do,” he answered with a friendly nod.

As Heidi poured the drinks, Dutch went into his cabin for his money belt and removed four gem stones from the pouch. As the drinks were served, Dutch made a toast for a safe passage back to

Hiva Oa. Then, in front of everyone, he explained in detail, his plans for raising enough money to get the submarine repaired.

Finally, Dutch opened his belt and removed all of their money. "As you can see, Mr. Chandler, we have only a little over six hundred dollars. I will give you the three hundred dollars today to cover your fuel costs." He placed four stones on the table: two sapphires, one large pearl and a good-sized ruby. "Once the sub is safely moored at your dock, I'll give you these stones, as a security deposit for the tow. The stones are worth a couple of thousand dollars, and you'll still have our submarine, as well. It's worth three or four thousand in scrap, if nothing else. It's a win-win for you, Mr. Chandler."

The old man sipped his drink and looked closely at the stones with a blank face. Dutch could tell he was deep in thought. They heard the motor launch approach and John called out, "We're done, Dad. Do you want a ride back to the *Mohawk*?"

Lyle slid out from behind the table and called back, "I'll be right there, boys." As he stood, he stared down at the money and the stones on the table.

"Do we have a deal, sir?" Dutch asked, also standing.

The old man reached down and took three hundred-dollar bills. "Yeah, we do. I love your old war relic. It reminds me of me – rusty and tired, but with a few more good miles still in her."

The two men shook hands and Lyle Chandler said with a smile, "See you at my dock on Hiva Oa. Bring those stones the next time we see each other."

Dutch walked Mr. Chandler up to the cockpit and watched him get aboard the launch. Then he returned below, with a broad smile on his face. "That old sea dog has a heart. Our submarine is in good hands."

Paul Gauguin's Island

Early the next morning, Dutch set up his camera on the bow of the sailboat. Then he and Doug, with the still camera, rowed over to the sea cave. In the dim reflecting light, they watched and photographed, as the boys turned the submarine around using just their own brute strength and the motor launch. Once the sub was turned into position, the launch went back to the tugboat to get the tow line. Returning to the sailboat, the guys stood on the bow with the gals, ready to film and photograph the slow extraction of the sub.

Everyone aboard the *Laura* held their breath as ever so slowly, the rusty, salt-stained submarine emerged into the bright sunlight. Once it was totally out of the cave, the tugboat increased speed and towed the U-3521 to within a hundred yards of the sailboat. It made magnificent footage, with the sun still low in the sky, the sub's rusting steel plates and white salt lines glistening in the sun. In his viewfinder, Dutch could see Luke standing in the conning tower bridge, waving goodbye. Then Matthew came alongside in the motor launch and yelled, "See you folks at home. Hope you can keep up with us."

The submarine was safe now, and moving again at about five knots in a northwest direction. The sailboat would stay in radio contact with the tugboat all the way to Hiva Oa.

Moments later, the sailboat weighed anchor and was soon under canvas in a brisk south-westerly breeze. With Heidi at the wheel, Lois, Doug and Dutch stood silently in the cockpit, watching Henderson Island slip away in their wake. Something terrible had happened there, something they just couldn't understand. How could anyone ever explain cannibalism?

Late that night, when Dutch climbed the stairs for the cockpit, he asked Lois, "Can you still see the *Mohawk*?"

She handed him the binoculars and pointed in the general direction. He put the glasses to his eyes and, looking out across the water, was greeted by the sight of the running lights on both the tugboat and the submarine. "They must have rigged up that light on the sub with their generator. We're making good speed to keep up with them." He removed the binoculars from his eyes and hung them back on the helm pedestal. "I'll take over. What did the sunset look like?"

Lois took a cushion and told him about the clouds at dusk, while Dutch lit two cigarettes and handed one to her. She puffed on it for a moment and then said, "I want to go back to the States with you."

Dutch was surprised by her request. "Why?"

She smiled in the starlight. "I'd be just a third leg with Doug and Heidi in Papeete. And I know more about diamonds than you'll ever know."

She went on to explain that her American father had owned a few jewelry stores in New Jersey before he retired. When Lois was just a young girl, he had taken her to the New York Diamond market twice a year. "Dad taught me how to deal with the Ashkenazic Jews. They control the market. And he got me interested in the different sizes, grades, cuts and colors of diamonds, and their value. You need me, Dutch."

Dutch puffed on his cigarette. "I don't have enough money to buy your airfare. You saw what we have left, only three hundred dollars. The boat's going to need a hundred, for fuel and food for the trip back to Tahiti. That leaves me with just two hundred dollars to get back to the States."

Lois stood and flipped her cigarette overboard. "That's not a problem. I saw a pearl store back in Papeete, and we have some beautiful pearls to sell."

Dutch grinned at her. "Are you telling me you're an expert in pearls, too?"

"Every girl is an *expert* when it comes to pearls," she answered, and kissed him on his cheek. "I'm going to bed. Wish you were joining me."

Dutch watched her disappear down the hatch. He still wasn't sure he wanted Lois to join him on the pilgrimage. She would only complicate things. But she *did* know more about diamonds than he did, and she was a brash broad. That could mean good salesmanship.

Two days later, they lost sight of the tugboat, falling behind when the winds died out. Dutch had to use the motor all night. The next day, the winds returned but they were adverse, requiring the sailboat to tack with the ever-changing wind directions. Dutch made sun sightings at noon, using his sextant to keep the boat on course.

On the seventh day, the Island of Hiva Oa came into view. The *Divers Guide* called it the Pearl of the Pacific, with its mix of lush jungles, tall coastal cliffs and towering volcanic peaks. The Guide boasted about the black-sand beaches and the nodding palms that made the island home to friendly natives and serious divers from all over the world.

A few hours later, they arrived at the little village of Atuona, with its pristine harbor and jagged cloud-capped mountains. Their arrival was two days after the tugboat. They moored at the boatyard dock, just behind the submarine, which was now draped under green camouflage netting.

Luke greeted them on the dock. “Dad’s up in his office. He wants me to take you to him. We’ve got your sub hooked up to shore power now. It’s real cool, man!”

“Where did you get that camouflage mesh?” Dutch answered, stepping off the sailboat.

Luke smiled at him. “It came with the *Mohawk* when we bought it from the Navy. Dad had it stored in our warehouse.”

With Doug and the girls following, Luke and Dutch walked down the floating dock and up a slight ramp to a large wooden pier. Crossing over the wharf, Dutch noticed stacks of old rusting Marine parts littering the planks. On the shore side of the pier, they entered the dingy boatyard office, where Mr. Chandler was seated behind a cluttered desk. A middle-aged, stone-faced lady sat at a neat adjoining desk. She had a nice figure and looked to be part native, but her demeanor was all business.

“Glad you finally got here, Dutch,” Lyle said, standing with a smile. “I want you to meet my wife, Helen. I think you talked to her on the radio.”

She made an effort to smile as Dutch introduced himself and his crew. With her brown eyes sparkling, she had the manners of a Polynesian as she greeted each person. “Aloha kakahiaka.”

After the introductions, Lyle asked, “Did you bring me something?”

Dutch nodded at him and reached into his pocket, pulling out the four stones they had agreed on.

Helen quickly held her hand out for the gems, and Mr. Chandler nodded in agreement.

She stared a good long time at each stone, using her desk lamp. Finally, a broad smile chased across her pretty face, and she handed the gems to Lyle. “These will do. Nicely done, husband.”

Mr. Chandler looked at the stones and then put them in his desk drawer. “Let’s go down to the submarine,” he suggested, “and I’ll show you what we’ve discovered.”

Their walk-through was amazing. For the first time, the crew saw the interior lit with shore power, not just in the dim glow of their flashlights and storm lamps. The sub was modern and brightly painted inside, and the boys had uncovered many other treasures. In the forward torpedo compartment, they had discovered eight live torpedoes. The officer's wardroom held a complete set of porcelain dishes, coffee cups and eating utensils, all with the U-3521 mark, and the galley was equipped with a stoneware set for the crew. They had found old uniforms and blankets, also with the boat's mark. In the control room, the boys had uncovered the boat's manuals, written in German, for every piece of equipment aboard. In the conning tower's fore and aft gun turrets; they had uncovered two pair of anti-aircraft guns, with thousands of rounds of ammunition in watertight compartments. Everything aboard the submarine seemed neatly organized, as if the crew had simply gone ashore and never returned.

In the engine room, Mr. Chandler explained what he and his boys could and couldn't repair. They could overhaul the diesel engine, put in a new battery system to keep the power on, fix the ventilation system, get the galley's cook stoves repaired, and fix any problems with the running gear. What they couldn't repair was the main electric motor used when the sub was submerged, or its massive battery system, which had been destroyed by the bilge water. Nor could they promise to get any of the old electronic gear working. The boat would sail again, but it would be navigationally blind and unable to submerge.

When they finished the tour, they exited up the aft deck hatch and stood under the camouflage netting.

"First thing tomorrow morning, we'll get the boat out of the water and check out the hull," Lyle said. "The superstructure needs to be cleaned and painted, and any other problems fixed."

"I like your netting," Dutch said, looking up. "We've got to keep this project quiet."

"We'll have to take the mesh off tomorrow. It might get caught up in our haul-out system," Lyle answered. "And there's one other problem we can't fix – disarming those live torpedoes. They could be dangerous."

"What do you think it will cost for all the repairs?" Doug asked.

Mr. Chandler shook his head. "Not sure until it's out of the water. The repairs will be fifteen to twenty thousand dollars, easy, and we'll need six to eight weeks to complete the work. But that's only a guess at this point."

"That's not going to be a problem," Dutch said with confidence. "Over time, this boat will more than pay back those expenses. This U-boat will be the find of the century."

The crew frowned at his comment. "We sure hope you're right, Skipper," Doug said, clearly speaking for them all.

That afternoon, the girls rowed the dinghy across the narrow harbor and walked to the village to buy food and provisions. While they were gone, Dutch and Doug motored the sailboat over to the fuel dock and filled their tanks.

When they returned to the boatyard, John, the oldest son, came aboard and hooked the boat up to shore power. As he worked, the mates learned a little more about Chandler & Sons Salvage. The boatyard had been through hard times for the past few years, and the boys hoped the submarine job would help rescue the company from its financial problems. "A job like this could lead to others, and we desperately need the work," John said with a frown. He was a bright kid with a strong work ethic and a handsome, serious face. Dutch hoped he was right about improving the family business.

That evening, Dutch told his crew that he had decided to take Lois with him back to the States. "She has much more expertise with diamonds than I do, and we need to raise a lot of money. When we get to Papeete, we'll sell a few stones and leave some of that money for you at the Harbor Masters Office. That will finance you until you get a few bookings."

Doug and Heidi didn't seem upset at all that Lois wasn't sailing with them. They both beamed at the chance of being alone on the long sail back to Tahiti.

The next morning, Dutch and Doug shot the last of their film, documenting the submarine being removed from the water and secured inside a large, corrugated-metal workshop. The haul-out was slow and deliberate, with the boys moving the U-3521 above a submerged flatbed skid with a cradle. Once the submarine was in position and secured to the cradle, the skid was pulled up and out of the water on railroad tracks by a diesel winch on the shore.

The underside of the sub's hull was covered with barnacles and strands of seaweed. It was a dirty mess, but the boat was soon out of sight again, and in the expert hands of Chandler & Sons Salvage.

Dutch was disappointed when he heard the last of his film flopping loose inside his camera. As he packed away the gear, he noticed many bystanders watching from the pier. A few of those onlookers had cameras in their hands. He didn't like the audience, but there was nothing he could do about it.

After they learned that the next flight to Tahiti wasn't until Sunday morning, the sailboat remained tied up at the boatyard dock for the next two days. The crew spent their time working with the boys on the submarine in the mornings, and playing tourist in the afternoons. It was time well spent, as the crew had been sailing almost constantly for six months. That first afternoon, they rowed across the harbor and roamed the streets of the quaint little village of Atuona. The locals were friendly, colorful and generous, while the town itself was enchanting. The island's claim to fame was as the resting place for the famous artist Paul Gauguin. After getting some directions, they soon found the cemetery where he was buried. His tombstone was like the story of his life, unusual and fascinating.

Before returning to the sailboat, they sampled the local cuisine at one of the few restaurants in town. While they waited for their meal at an outside table, with rum drinks in hand, they were approached by a short, pudgy man with a Leica camera around his neck. He introduced himself as an Argentine named Nick.

"I watched you filming the submarine this morning," he said with a heavy Latin accent to Dutch. "Do you own that boat?"

"No," Dutch answered quickly. "We were just hired to film its removal."

"Never seen a submarine that looks like that before. Who owns it?" the ruddy-faced guy asked.

"Why do ask?" Dutch replied, getting a little suspicious.

"I'm just a curious tourist," Nick answered.

Dutch chuckled. "We're getting paid by Gold Coast Petroleum out of New Jersey," he answered with a smile. "They've used the sub for years in their oil exploration business."

The pudgy fellow looked down at the crew, slowly nodding. "Thanks for the information, Yanks. Sorry if I interrupted you," he replied, then turned and walked away.

As he departed, Dutch whispered to the table, "My biggest fear is that guy could be a reporter. We've got to keep our story quiet until we're ready."

The next afternoon, they borrowed the boatyard's jeep and drove around the island. In many ways, the landscape of Hiva Oa reminded Dutch of the Pacific Northwest, except for the palm trees. The cloud-covered mountains were tall and majestic, with endless craggy vistas. The coastline, with its many bays and inlets, was breathtaking, and the black-sand beaches were amazing. The island was like no other they had seen and, at the end of the day, they were sorry they hadn't bought more film.

After a farewell breakfast the next morning, they sat at the table and divided up the gem stones into two pouches. One would remain aboard, while Dutch took the other with him.

"If you run low on money, sell a few stones. But don't get greedy and draw attention to yourself or the boat," he cautioned Doug.

After packing the Pan-Am flight bags they had bought in Tahiti, and reviewing Doug's sailing plan, they said their good-byes on the dock. As Dutch stood with Lois, watching the boat motor out into the harbor, he had some misgivings about leaving his beloved sailboat behind. But, deep down, he knew that Doug would care for the *Laura* like his own.

After one last farewell with Helen and Lyle Chandler, Luke drove them out to the airport.

"Where do I buy my tickets, and how much will they cost?" Dutch asked with his fingers crossed.

"If I remember right, it's about fifty US."

"How do I pay?"

The boy grinned, "It's the island way now, Dutch. You pay when you arrive at Papeete."

When they got to the airport, they found an isolated runway, with no buildings and only a few service trucks waiting. Soon, they heard the sounds of an approaching aircraft. Moments later, a vintage DC3 landed.

While the plane unloaded its cargo, the fuel truck filled its tanks, and they said farewell to Luke. He was a fine lad with a smile tattooed on his face.

As the pilot signed a few papers on the tarmac, he yelled for them to come aboard and find a seat. Ten minutes later, with a fresh cargo secured behind the passenger compartment, the Gooney Bird[25] was in the air again. As the plane gained altitude over the island, Dutch gazed out his window, hoping to see his sailboat underway, but found nothing. His view reminded him again how vast the Pacific Ocean was.

Stateside

Two days later, Dutch and Lois sat in the lounge at the Tahiti Airport, waiting for their flight to Los Angles. With cocktails in hand, they celebrated their sales success of the day before. Lois had done the best, selling three nice-sized pearls to the local pearl shop for nine hundred dollars. Dutch had sold four good-sized diamonds to the only jewelry store on the island for three hundred and fifty dollars, and they sold two additional small rocks to a waterfront pawnshop for one hundred and twenty-five dollars. After leaving money for Doug at the Harbor Masters office and buying two one-way, first-class plane tickets home, they still had a little over seven hundred dollars in their poke. Dutch had to admit that he'd been impressed with Lois; she knew her stuff and was one a hell of a saleswoman.

They remained in the bar until their noon flight was called, and when they boarded the jetliner, it was like stepping into the future. Neither of them had flown a jet plane before, and each was a little anxious. Their forward first-class compartment was plush with seats that faced each other, and generous leg room. They drank champagne as the long, narrow-bodied plane lumbered into position for the six-hour flight to Honolulu. Both watched breathlessly, out the window, as the flight shuddered and shook with engines roaring down the long runway before slowly lifting up into the sky. They seemed frozen in place watching the island of Tahiti soon became only a speck in a sea of blue. Their first jet ride was an experience neither would soon forget.

After a few hours layover in Hawaii, the flight continued on to its final destination. They landed in the City of Angels at eight on Wednesday morning, with the sun still low in the sky. Strolling

---

[25] Nickname for DC3

through the terminal with their flight bags, Dutch stopped at one of the pay phones and called the Hollywood Roosevelt Hotel to make reservations. Then he called Professor Eric Jacobs at UCLA. After a few moments of jogging the good professor's memory about the 'Witness to Yesterday' project, he agreed to see Dutch in his office at ten-thirty.

Outside of the terminal, Dutch hailed a taxi and told the cabbie to take them to Cameron's Camera Shop on Wilshire Boulevard.

In the car, he relaxed back in his seat and watched the cityscape speed by. The Fall weather was typical for Southern California, bright and warm. Dutch was pleased to be Stateside again, especially in a town where he had such fond memories.

When they pulled up in front of the camera store, Dutch was surprised it was still there. He hadn't shopped at the store since 1944. Rummaging through his flight bag, he removed the six rolls of black & white film that Doug had shot.

"I'll be inside for a moment," he said to the driver. "Keep your meter on." Then, turning to a yawning Lois, he added, "You stay with the cab. They're hard to find in LA."

She nodded drowsily.

Inside the store, Dutch approached one of the counter clerks and asked whether Ed Cameron still owned the shop. He was sad to learn that Ed had passed way a few years before, and that his son, who now ran the business, was in Hawaii on vacation.

"Do you guys still have a black-and-white film lab?" he asked.

They did, and Dutch dropped off the six rolls of film, with instructions to make a 5X7 print of every printable negative.

As the clerk wrote out the order, he said, "Your order will be ready after four o'clock tomorrow. We're open until six."

Getting back in the cab, Dutch told the driver to take them to UCLA.

Thirty minutes later, they were at the campus. It took twenty minutes of searching before they found Professor Jacobs office. When one of his students finally ushered them in, they found the professor drinking tea at a cluttered desk. His gray hair was disheveled, his white shirt had stains, and his right eye still had the nervous twitch that Dutch remembered. His ornate, wood-paneled office was small, and smelled of stale cigar smoke. Three of the walls had book shelves from floor to ceiling, and the fourth had windows that looked out over the campus.

Looking up from his tea, he greeted them. “Colonel, nice to see you again.”

Dutch moved to the side of the desk with a smile and extended his hand. “Nice seeing you again, sir. Thanks for meeting with us,” he said as they shook hands. “This young lady here is Miss Lois Berg, my close friend.”

The professor put on the glasses that dangled from his chest. Then he peered at Lois over the top of them. “Berg sounds German. Are you?” he asked, staring at her.

Lois moved next to Dutch and extended her hand to the professor. “I was born in Germany but came to the States in ’38, when I was just five years old,” she answered, shaking his hand.

The professor held her hand for a long moment, gazing at her face with obvious approval. Then he stood and moved a chair next to his. “Have a seat next to me, Fraulein. I’m pleased you got out in time.”

As she sat down, he returned to his chair and looked at Dutch. “What can I do for you, Colonel?”

“I have a rush translation job that I was hoping you would help me with.”

The professor took his glasses off and rubbed the bridge of his nose. “Tell me about it.”

Pacing the floor next to the desk, Dutch told him just enough about their discovery of the submarine to peak his interest. He left out any indication of where they had found the sub and made no mention of the treasure or of cannibalism. Then he removed from his flight bag the two books they had found, and handed them to the professor, one at a time. “This is the ship’s logbook. It starts in March of ’44 and ends in May ’45. There are only sixty pages of information that need to be translated.”

Eric flipped through the book quickly. Then Dutch continued, “This book looks to be the Captain’s diary. It, too, has about sixty pages, and it ends in January of 1946. I need the translations typed out in English, with a carbon copy, and I’m willing to pay handsomely.”

The professor leafed through the diary pages and then looked up again at Dutch. “When, and how much?”

Without hesitation, Dutch answered, "Saturday afternoon, because we're flying to New York on Sunday, and three hundred dollars for the work."

Professor Jacobs smiled and lit a cigar, then turned to Lois. "What do you think, Fraulein? Will I like the Captain's story?"

She smiled back at him. "Yes, sir. I think you will."

"Good. I'll get a couple of grad students started on it today. Come back at one o'clock on Saturday," he answered in a cloud of blue smoke. Turning back to Dutch, he asked, "Do you have any pictures of this submarine you found? I have an old friend who was a U-boat Skipper, and I know he'd love to see them."

"I should, on Saturday," Dutch replied, motioning to Lois that it was time to go.

The wait for a taxi took nearly half an hour, and the ride to the hotel started out quietly. Dutch was anxious to read the translations, and hoped no mention of the treasure would appear on the pages.

Lois broke the silence. "You never told me you were a Colonel."

"That was a long time ago," he answered, then grinned. "I think the professor was sweet on you."

She frowned at him. "Why not? Most men are. What's our plan? I didn't know we were flying to New York on Sunday."

"Simple enough. We'll spend the next couple of days selling our gems in Hollywood, on Rodeo Drive or any other swanky place we can find."

"I'll need some money," she answered.

"Why?"

"If I'm going to be selling jewels on Rodeo Drive, I'd better look the part."

Dutch grinned at her. "No problem. Just go easy with the dough."

When they got to the hotel, Dutch registered while Lois walked around the lobby, window-shopping. When they got into the elevator, Dutch handed her one of the two keys.

She looked at both keys, and a wide smile chased over her lips. "You got us just one room, this time. Hooray, Dutch. We're making some progress!"

But when they got to the room and entered, her smile was wiped away. He had taken a two-bedroom suite.

Lois walked through both bedrooms and then returned to the living room, where she found Dutch undressing.

"Why two bedrooms?" she asked, clearly disgruntled.

With his shirt off, Dutch removed his pants and pulled on a pair of walking shorts. "We've spent months cooped up on a tiny sailboat. Now it's time for our own space."

"What the hell are you doing?"

"The valet is on his way to pick up my dirty clothes. I need to look my best for Rodeo Drive, too."

Still scowling, Lois shook her head. "At best, you'll only look like my chauffeur in that outfit," she said, turning for a bedroom. "I'm going to take a hot bath."

"Chauffeur, that's a great idea," Dutch yelled back, as the bedroom door slammed shut.

Dutch heard the water start to run, just as the valet knocked. After giving him an armful of soiled clothes and tipping him a few dollars, Dutch returned to the room and searched out the room service menu. When he yelled through the bathroom door that he was calling down for food, Lois shouted back her order.

After calling room service, Dutch phone Maggie at NBC. She was unavailable, so he left a message with her secretary. Then he called Avis and ordered a car for nine o'clock the next morning. His final call was to the travel agency in the lobby.

Lunch arrived just as Lois finished up in the bathroom. She ate her tuna sandwich and downed her milk quickly, as she was restless to go shopping. After finishing her food, she stood and put her hand out. "Money, please."

"How much?" Dutch asked, eating his steak sandwich.

"Two hundred should do it," she answered.

Dutch protested the amount, but to no avail.

It was dark by the time Lois returned from shopping, carrying a garment bag filled with goodies. When she came through the door, she was greeted by an empty room. Turning on a lamp, she noticed four spent beer bottles on the lunch cart. Taking her garment bag into her bedroom, she hung it up. Then she checked Dutch's bedroom. She found him asleep, sprawled out on top of his bed, with his clothes and shoes still on. Lois grinned at him, shaking her head. "Why do I care?" she whispered, removing his shoes and covering him with the bedspread.

After her departure Dutch opened his eyes and smiled, then rolled over and went back to sleep. No test of the flesh, this night.

By eight thirty the next morning, Dutch was showered, shaved and dressed in his freshly cleaned clothes, drinking coffee. When he heard Lois in the bathroom, getting ready, he called through the door, "Our ride will be here at nine. Meet me downstairs at the main entrance."

She called back, "I'll be there in twenty minutes."

When she exited through the hotel front door, looking like Loretta Young, all eyes were on her, including Dutch's. She was gorgeous, dressed in high heels, dark nylons and a pristine white dress that accented her figure. Her red hair was piled high on her head, and her suntanned face glowed with understated makeup that emphasized her high cheekbones and delicate features. With her sunglasses on, she looked every bit like a movie star. Dutch was speechless.

"Where in the hell is our taxi, and where did you get that silly hat?" she demanded.

Dutch moved away from the car he was leaning on, and took off his gold-embroidered baseball cap with the MGM logo. "I found this and my driving gloves in the hotel's Lost and Found. They were lost, and I found them. Just like the submarine." Then he turned to the automobile next to him and gestured. "Your chariot awaits, Madam."

Lois grinned and moved towards the Black Chrysler Imperial convertible, giving him an inquisitive look. "Did you buy this car?"

Dutch chuckled, while opening the car door for her. "No, just rented it until Sunday. We'll drop it off at the airport."

She got into the backseat, and Dutch went around to the driver's seat. Adjusting his rearview mirror, he smiled at her. "May I put the top down so your public can see you, Ma'am? You look just marvelous this morning."

She smirked back at him in the mirror. "Yes James you may."

"Where to, Madam?"

"Off to Rodeo Drive," she answered in a snooty voice.

That day, the pair roamed the streets of Beverly Hills, visiting only the swankest jewelers. On their first stop, at Steinfeld Jewelers, they sold their only five carat ruby. It was a brilliant stone with excellent color and clarity. During their sales pitch, the movie star and her chauffeur played off each other like professional actors. In the end, they were paid four thousand eight hundred dollars for the stone by a very enthusiastic jeweler. It had been an Academy Award performance.

Shortly after noon, after three more visits to jewelry stores, the couple drove back to Wilshire Boulevard to pick up their pictures. While Lois shopped at a nearby liquor store, Dutch went into the camera shop. He was a little early, so he walked around the shop, admiring the latest in photography. When his order was ready, he paid his hefty lab bill and purchased a photo album designed for the size of prints he had ordered.

As he was about to leave, the counter clerk said, "The lab boys sure loved your pictures. Where did you find that submarine?"

Dutch smiled at the clerk, searching for the right words. "It's just a movie prop for a new project we're considering," he answered nonchalantly.

The clerk gawked at his baseball cap. "Ah! MGM."

That evening, back in their hotel suite, drinking champagne, they counted out their loot on the coffee table. Their sales total for the day was seven thousand, seven hundred dollars. Then they both went through the large stack of photos they had picked up. Doug had done well with the small camera. Most of his shots were correctly exposed and in focus. In the end, Dutch slid more than forty pictures into the album he had purchased.

As Lois leafed through the photos he had selected, Dutch found himself gawking at her like a teenager. Then he realized he was on his third glass of champagne. Too much wine plus Lois wasn't a good idea. Reaching for the loot on the coffee table, he started stuffing the bills into his money belt.

"We're going to need some heavier clothes for New York," he said, handing her two fifty-dollar bills. "I'm going to take a walk and buy some warmer threads. You should do the same."

"I can go with you," she answered.

"No, thanks. I need some space."

Finishing up her wine, she took the bills, frowning. "What am I going to do with you? One minute you're endearing, the next as cold as an iceberg."

Dutch stood with the money belt in hand. "I'll be back in a few hours."

Friday was a repeat of Thursday, although the couple concentrated on the jewelry stores in Hollywood. In all, they visited six stores and two pawnshops. Their haul wasn't as large as the day before, but that evening they counted out an additional four thousand three hundred dollars.

"We'll do better in New York City," Lois said, pouring two whiskeys on the rocks at the sideboard. "I feel a little like Bonnie and Clyde, with all that cash."

Returning to the couch, she handed Dutch his drink. He took a sip and placed his glass on the coffee table. "We'll need to buy some travelers checks before we leave," he answered, neatly stuffing bills into his belt.

Lois snuggled next to him on the sofa and raised her glass. "Here's to larceny!" They toasted each other with smiles. "You owe me a fancy dinner tonight for my performance," she said, pulling him close for a kiss. "No going our separate ways!"

Then came a knock at the door.

Dutch slipped the money belt under the sofa and got up to answer it.

Standing in the hall was a slender young man dressed in a dark suit, carrying a briefcase. He had a crewcut and brown eyes, and he wore black-rimmed glasses. He introduced himself as Mr. Don Haze from the Federal Bureau of Investigation. "I'm looking for a Mr. Clarke," he said, showing his identification card.

A surprised Dutch looked carefully at his credentials. "I'm Clarke. What can I do for you?"

"I'd like to come in and talk to you."

Dutch looked cautiously at him, then opened the door all the way and invited him in.

Lois was still on the couch, with her drink in hand, when Dutch introduced the FBI Agent to her.

"What's this all about?" Dutch asked, joining Lois on the sofa.

"Did you folks sell a five-carat ruby to Steinfeld Jewelers on Rodeo Drive yesterday?"

"Yes, we did," Dutch replied. "Why do you ask?"

"There might be a problem about who the rightful owner of that stone is."

"Have a seat, Mr. Haze. I don't understand," Dutch answered, gesturing to a chair.

The FBI Agent sat down on the other side of the coffee table and pulled out a file from his briefcase. Then he explained that one of the older appraisers at the store claimed he had seen the gem before. "It was back in Poland in 1937. The ruby was the center stone for a tiara owned by a wealthy Jewish family. He claims he cleaned and repaired that tiara, just weeks before the Nazi's came to power."

"How would he recognize that one stone?" Lois asked.

"Evidently, there's a tiny fault on the rear of the ruby. He called it the jewel's signature. Where did you folks get the stone?" the agent asked, looking up from his paperwork.

Lois seemed about to repeat her performance from the store, but Dutch stopped her, knowing that it was *never* a good idea to lie to a G-man.

"We found the ruby as part of a larger cargo aboard a German war relic in the Pacific. We've claimed salvage rights for the ship. Under International Maritime Law, we own the rights to its cargo, as well."

The agent made notes in his file and then looked up. "A German vessel sounds right. Do you have any proof of this discovery?"

Dutch reached for the photo album and showed him the first two pictures: one inside the sea cave, and another of the boat being towed out of cavern.

The agent made additional notes. "May I have one of those pictures for my file?" he asked, still staring at the photos.

Dutch closed the album and shook his head, "No, they are part of our evidence for the salvage rights."

The young agent was stone-faced as he made a few additional notes. "One last question, sir. What is your permanent address and phone number?"

Dutch got up poured himself some more whiskey. "Don't have a permanent address. I live on a sailboat in the Pacific. How did you find us?"

Mr. Haze pulled out a small photo from his file. It was a fuzzy picture of the couple getting out of the convertible in front of the jewelry store. "As part of their security system, they take pictures of all the cars that drive up in front of the store. I traced your license number, and Avis gave me your location. If I have any more questions, how can I reach you?"

"We'll be in New York, next week, staying at the Plaza. After that, we're on our way back to the Pacific."

The FBI Agent got up and shook Dutch's hand, with a nod to Lois. "Thank you for your time, folks. Have a safe trip to New York."

Once he was gone, Dutch breathed easier and Lois looked relieved. But having the FBI nosing around their affairs sucked the wind out of their sails for any further celebration that night.

Early the next afternoon, they returned to the UCLA campus to pick up the translations. When they entered Professor Jacobs office, they found him waiting for them, in a sober mood. He had cleared his workspace and placed both typed translations on top of the originals, with two chairs positioned in front of his desk.

"Have a seat," he said, gesturing to the chairs as they came in. "Your work is completed. I've checked it thoroughly. Your English versions are accurate reflections of the originals," the professor said, his eye twitching.

"Was there anything of interest in the originals?" Dutch asked, pulling out his wallet to pay for the services.

The professor pulled the papers on top of the logbook closer. "As you might expect, the ship's log was filled with facts and figures. From weather to fuel consumption and locations, the book traces the boat's passage from sea trials in the Baltic Sea to wherever you found her." His eyes narrowed. "It also logs references to a Japanese family and a twelve-ton cargo of gold that was brought aboard by the SS in Kiel, in March of 1945. Another entry recounts how the U-3521 almost sank, just off Pitcairn Island, in May of 1945."

He handed Dutch the book and the two copies of the translations. Then he turned his attention to the other stack of papers, on top of the diary. He pulled those documents closer and told the story of the journal, using such words as *horrific, mutiny, murder* and *barbaric* in the course of his long dissertation.

"The truth, Dutch, is that the Captain's story is horrifying. The gold you've unearthed, coupled with his tragic story, is going to earn you enemies all around the world – enemies like the Bonn Government, the secretive Odessa, and all the former European Allies. You're in a dangerous place, my friend, and you're playing with fire."

"Who the hell is Odessa?" Lois asked.

That set the professor off again, this time on a long critique of the SS and Nazi's and its worldwide, underground organization. He concluded, chillingly, by stating, "It has been rumored for years that, in the closing days of the war, the SS sent a submarine with a cargo of gold to the Odessa in Argentina. Now you have their gold, and they will do anything to get it back. They are as ruthless as a rattlesnake, and they have tentacles longer than an octopus. "

The office went quiet. In silence, Dutch got to his feet and paid the professor.

"Did you bring me a picture?" the professor asked, putting the money in a desk drawer.

Dutch gave him an extra photo. "No mention of this treasure to anyone," he said firmly.

"Aye," the professor answered. "When will you be back?"

"Next weekend. Ask your Captain friend if he'll have lunch with me next Saturday. I'll call you when we get back into town."

The walk back to where they had parked was slow and quiet. When they got into the car, Dutch asked Lois, "Did the good professor frighten you?"

"Well, yeah," she admitted, slipping into the front seat.

Dutch started the car and looked at her, his expression serious. "Not all that glitters is from gold. Sometimes it's from the wings of the angel of death."

"Twelve tons of gold will make us all rich. It's worth the risk," Lois answered, as Dutch pulled away from the curb.

He lit a cigarette and answered forcefully, "The gold is our downfall. The story is our salvation."

"Where are we going?" she asked, as Dutch turned away from the campus.

"Burbank. We have an appointment with Ms. Meede. She's the Vice President of Programing for NBC, and a dear friend."

Their meeting with Maggie went well. Dutch gave her the last three exposed reels of 16mm film, then told her about their new discovery while they flipped through the photo album.

Maggie was clearly amazed, and she listened patiently to what he had to say. For safe-keeping, Dutch gave her the album, all of the negatives, extra prints, and the original logbook and Captain's diary, with one translation of each. "Only you and Colonel Ford should read this story, and view the film and photos. This discovery will ignite a firestorm of International News, and I don't want that to happen until the submarine is safely in the States. It's going to be one hell of a story!"

When they were finished, Maggie walked them out, and they agreed to have dinner at the hotel on the following Saturday night, when Colonel Ford would be back in town.

As they said good-by, Maggie kissed Dutch on the cheek. "Maybe we can go dancing after dinner, Dutch. I told you I'd teach you some moves."

When they got back to the car, Lois didn't seem very happy about the kiss or the invitation. "She's too old for you. And I thought you didn't like to dance."

Dutch just smiled at her, since his loyalty would not allow him to tell her the truth about Maggie.

Early the next morning, Dutch dressed in his traveling clothes: penny loafers with no socks, worn jeans, a t-shirt with the image of Marilyn Monroe, his only blue blazer, and his MGM baseball cap. Then, with Lois at his side, he boarded a United Airlines flight for New York City. Dutch supposed he looked pretty out of place in the First Class compartment, but he didn't care.

As the plane gained altitude and turned east, he asked Lois, "Did you call your parents and tell them you were coming home?"

Her expression turned sour. "No."

"Why not?"

"The truth is I just don't get along with my American parents anymore."

"That's a shame," Dutch answered, not wanting to pry any deeper.

Six hours later, they landed at LaGuardia Airport. It was late afternoon, local time, when they deplaned, carrying just their flight bags, and entered the terminal. Inside, they saw a large number of men holding up homemade signs for arriving passengers. One of them read, 'Plaza Hotel – Clarke.'

Now that's first-class, Dutch thought. Approaching the man, he said, "I'm Dutch Clarke."

The older gentleman introduced himself as their driver for the Plaza Hotel, and showed them the way to baggage claim, where Lois retrieved the new suitcase that contained her ever-growing wardrobe. Outside, they walked to a gray limousine, and their driver opened the rear door.

From the shadows inside the car, another man appeared, holding a gun. "Hello, Mr. Clarke," he said, his low voice expressionless. "Get in."

Chapter Eleven

Revelations

Bewildered, Dutch stayed close to Lois, determined to protect her as they cautiously entered the rear door of the limousine. Inside he caught a quick glimpse of man and a woman, each pointing snub-nosed revolvers at them. The unfamiliar pair were seated in the jump seats facing the back seat. The man was burly, dressed in a brown, wrinkled suit with dirty shoes, while the woman was slight, with a black floppy hat and sunglasses. Dutch and Lois were told to get on their knees facing the rear seat. Their hands were fastened behind them with handcuffs, and a blindfold was slid over their eyes.

"Now turn around and sit down," the man ordered firmly. "No talking."

As the car pulled away, Dutch heard the sounds of zippers, and figured that their captors were rifling through their luggage.

"Anything?" the man asked.

"Only these," the woman answered. "I'll have to go through them."

"See if he's wearing a money belt. And get his wallet," the man replied.

Dutch smelled the woman in front of him as she reached into his breast pocket and slid his wallet out. Then she felt around his waist and on top of his clothes. "He's got one," she said. There was a scent about her that Dutch recalled, and he realized that she wore the same perfume that his wife Laura had once used. What was that fragrance called?

She pulled his shirt out from his pants, undid his belt and unbuttoned his trousers. Then she felt around his waist with her gloved hands.

"Do we know each other this well?" Dutch whispered to her.

Finding the rear buckle, she removed his money belt with a rough tug.

Dutch felt a sting on his skin as the belt was slipped out. Why couldn't he think of the name of that perfume? He sat back in his seat, with his clothes still askew.

"Aren't you going to tuck me in?" he asked.

"Shut up. No talking," the woman answered.

What did she look like? He tried to recall that quick glimpse. She had short, dishwater-blonde hair under the floppy hat, and she wore a pair of black slacks and a beige blouse, under a dark blue raincoat. The man had a hat on, as well – a brown fedora. That was all he could recall. He didn't remember a single facial feature of either of their captors.

"Wow, look at those thousand-dollar travelers checks," the man said.

Dutch muscled up some courage. "What we've got here are a couple of common thieves," he said with a smirk, butting his shoulder against Lois, next to him.

"Hey, asshole," the man retorted, "another word and I'll tape your mouth shut. Understand?"

Dutch nodded.

The car drove for a long while. Because of his blindfold, Dutch had no way of knowing the direction in which they traveled, but he heard the sounds of a long bridge. Then, after a few quick turns, he felt the bump of railroad tracks. Now the sounds were those of a waterfront, with a few fog horns and buoy bells.

The car slowed, turned sharply, and drove down a steep ramp. Finally it came to a stop. As they were prodded out of the car, still handcuffed and blindfolded, Lois said, "I've got to pee."

After some hesitation and mumbling, the woman led Lois away. While they waited, the man put his pistol to Dutch's head, unlocked his handcuffs, and told him to tuck in his shirt. "Nothing funny," he added gruffly.

When Dutch was done, the cuffs were locked again. The man pushed him forward, then stopped him again after a few paces, and Dutch heard the man pushing buttons. Then he heard what sounded like a freight elevator moving. They waited inside the lift, with doors open, until they were joined again by Lois and the woman. The slow, noisy elevator soon stopped, and they all walked down a corridor and into what felt like a room.

After some confusion, Dutch and Lois were told to sit down on chairs. As soon as they settled themselves, Dutch heard what sounded like stage lighting being turned on or off. Their blindfolds were removed. The room was totally dark, with the exception of a single bright spotlight shining directly on their faces. As his eyes adjusted, Dutch felt the presence of a man standing behind his chair and another behind Lois. He heard footsteps in front of him and watched as best he could through the glare, as a desk lamp was turned on.

"Welcome, Colonel Clarke," a man said, sitting down behind the desk.

How the hell does he know I was a Colonel? It isn't on my driver's license, Dutch thought. He could hardly see the man, with the bright light in his eyes, so he looked down at the rough wood planking of the floor. "Why are we here in this old warehouse?"

"I've invited you here to tell us more about the submarine you found," the man answered, and Dutch thought he detected a slight German accent.

Dutch raised his head, with his eye lids half-closed. "A gunpoint invitation is a hell of way to start."

"Were there any pictures?" the man asked.

"No," a woman answered, and stepped into the light to whisper into the man's ear.

Through the glare Dutch could hardly make her out, but she seemed to be the woman from the car.

"Tell me about the cargo you found aboard. I have your jewels here in my hand," the man said, holding up the gem pouch.

"I have nothing to say to snatchers."

The man nodded, and Dutch was slapped hard on the back of his head by the man behind him. He fell forward, off the chair and onto the floor with a *thud*. The man picked him up and shuffled him back onto his chair. Dutch could feel blood running out of one nostril.

"This will get painful, Colonel, if you don't cooperate," the man said.

Dutch bent his head to awkwardly wipe the blood from his nose onto his blazer. "I've been interrogated by the best, the Japanese Kempeitai, so I've tasted pain before. I'm no longer a slave to it. Go to hell."

"Yes, I read that you're a hard-ass. Let's see what your lady friend has to say." The man nodded again.

Dutch saw the other man, who appeared to be their chauffeur, raise his arm to hit Lois. "Wait! She knows nothing. She's just a bimbo I picked up in a bar in LA. Don't take it out on her. Take it out on me."

The man put his hand up and stopped the chauffeur. "You lie, Colonel. But there is a lot that you don't know about your lady friend. I have her Ellis Island file here on my desk. She came to American as a Jew, with the name of Bergstein. Being ashamed of that, her American relatives changed her name to Berg."

"Who the hell are you people?" Lois snarled.

Dutch squinted through the light directly at the man. "I'd say Odessa."

The man scoffed, and waved a hand at the shadows. There was a *click* and a spotlight came on against a side wall, while the light on Dutch and Lois was turned off. The light lit a large picture hanging there, a black and white photograph of prisoners behind a barbed wire fence, with smiling SS Officers looking on. The people were emaciated and wore only rags, with fear etched on their gaunt faces. It was a dreadful image.

"We represent *these* people. They demand what is rightly theirs," the man said.

"The Odessa *is* those SS Officers," Dutch angrily said, looking away from the picture. "You are the scourge of the Earth, may you all rot in hell."

The man waved his hand again, and another spotlight, next to the first, clicked on. It was another shocking photo of bodies stacked up like cord wood in front of ovens. The man shook his head. "We don't represent the SS, you fool. It's the victims of the Holocaust that we represent."

"I don't believe you. You're German, through and through. I can hear it in your voice."

The man picked up some papers from his desk, a large brown file and a manila folder. "Would your government give the Odessa your military records and their FBI field reports? No! We are Mossad, Israeli Secret Police, and we are Allies with the American Government."

"Never heard of Mossad. But, if that's true, why all the charades?" Dutch asked.

The man glared at him for long moment. "Maybe I started out poorly," he finally said. "Admiral King calls you a patriot. Is he wrong?"

"How would you know about Admiral King?" Dutch replied.

The man held up the records again. "It's all here, in the records the FBI gave me. So, Colonel, if I can't reason with you with fear, I'll try to reason with you as a friend. Turn on the lights. Remove their restraints," he ordered to the shadows.

The room lights came on and the handcuffs were removed. Rubbing his wrists, Dutch stood, and saw that they were in the middle of large photo gallery composed entirely of pictures from the Nazi concentration camps.

"What is this place? Who the hell are you?" Dutch asked, looking around the room.

"This is the future home of the New York Holocaust Museum. My name is Gil Hirsh. I'm the Bureau Chief for North American Mossad." He walked over to Dutch. "Here is my identification. We are the organization that kidnapped Adolf Eichmann out of Argentina in 1960. I'm sure you read about that in the news. He now awaits trial in Israel."

That did jar Dutch's memory. The Mossad was well respected for its covert operations all over the world. They were renowned for their cunning in capturing Nazi war criminals.

The lady from the car, who wore rimmed glasses, rushed over to Dutch with a damp handkerchief and gave it to him. "For your nose," she said.

Mr. Hirsh introduced her as Jean McDonald, from the Asset Recovery Unit of Mossad. The man in the car and the chauffeur were both field agents. The burly fellow said to Dutch, "Sorry, mate. Didn't mean to hit so hard."

Dutch smiled wryly at him. "Maybe someday I'll return the favor."

Finally Lois stood. "Dutch, I don't trust these people. They lied about me."

Mr. Hirsh stood and moved to Lois with a frown. "Here's your Ellis Island Entry Form. We didn't lie."

With sad eyes, she read the document. "I had no idea. My American family never told me I was Jewish."

Dutch turned to her. "Don't worry about it. We can trust these people. They won't harm us."

Mr. Hirsh asked Jean to show them around the gallery, while he inspected their pouch of jewels. As they walked around the room, Jean's commentary about each exhibit was almost as compelling as the photo itself. She talked as if she had stood behind the camera and felt each image as the photographer did. Jean had a way about her, calm, kind, and cloaked in compassion. She seemed to glow with humanity as she talked about the poor souls within each horrific photo.

When they finished, Lois had tears in her eyes. "I was so young when I came here. I had no idea I was a Jew."

They returned to Mr. Hirsh's desk, where he handed back their pouch. "We are not thieves," he said firmly. "We had to make sure you weren't selling anything else that belonged to the Holocaust survivors. I hope you'll consider what you saw here tonight."

Dutch and Lois were driven to the Plaza Hotel, riding in the backseat of the limousine, facing Gil and Jean in the jump seats. With eyes puffy from weeping, Lois sat quietly. Dutch's head was swirling, haunted by the appalling images he had just witnessed. Until that very day, he hadn't truly understood the brutal scope of the Holocaust.

"I saw you have a copy of the logbook for U-3521," Hirsh said, lighting a cigarette. "The Germans kept impeccable records, so we've known for years that the U-3521 carried a shipment of twelve tons of gold for the Argentine Odessa. It never arrived. I'll bet your logbook would tell us where to look."

Dutch wondered if he could trust him. "Yes, we found the submarine, but you'd lose your bet. The logbook only talks about a Japanese island call Haiku. Try to find that on any map of the Pacific. When we found the sub, there was no gold aboard. If there had been gold, why would I be selling diamonds in New York?"

"That gold belongs to the Israeli people," Jean said, cracking open the car window next to her.

"We Jews are also business men, Dutch," Hirsh added. "Israel will pay you a five percent finder's fee for the gold. That's over half a million dollars for your trouble."

Dutch shook his head. "That discovery involves more than just me, and I can't speak for the others. My only interest is the submarine. I know nothing about a cargo of gold."

It was almost ten o'clock when they were dropped off at the hotel. As they exited the car, Jean said, with a sober expression, "Israel is a much better friend than enemy."

Dutch watched as the limousine pulled away. He and Lois had learned far too many disturbing facts for one night.

After checking in, they went right up to their room. There was only quiet in the elevator, as they pondered the gruesome pictures they had seen. When they entered their room, Lois didn't say a word about another two-bedroom suite. Instead, she went right to the phone and called her American mother. Not wanting to eavesdrop, Dutch went into his bedroom and unpacked. Still, he could hear one side of the heated conversation. There was more sobbing, then some angry yelling, so Dutch assumed that Lois's American mother had confirmed she was indeed a Jew. When she slammed down the phone receiver, she broke into tears and ran into the bathroom. Dutch tried to console her, but she had locked him out. "I was born a Methodist, but that didn't make me a Methodist," he said through the door. Lois didn't answer. "Your nationality doesn't mean a thing. You're still yourself." Still no reply. Frustrated, he concluded, "I'm going down to the bar. If you'd like to talk, join me. If not, I'll see you in the morning. We have diamonds to sell."

The next morning, they had breakfast in their room. Lois seemed to be better. She had a smile on her face, and she was dressed again in her white outfit, looking like her old self. As they ate their meal, she told Dutch a little about the New York Diamond District.

The majority of all diamonds in America came through that exchange. It was a district in Manhattan with over two thousand independent shops that dealt in diamonds or jewelry. The market was controlled by Orthodox Jews, who had fled Europe during the early days of WWII. Most of them had come from Antwerp and Amsterdam.

"They all speak and understand English," Lois said. "But they want you to believe they only understand Hebrew. It's a tactic they use to beat you down, or up, on price. I know some of their tricks and some of their language, so let me take the lead."

That day, Dutch and Lois visited half a dozen businesses in the district, but their sales only amounted to a disappointing thirty-five hundred dollars. The Jews were hard bargainers, and Lois's Hebrew was rusty. The dealers had given them low prices for their gems. By the end of the day, Lois was in a funk again.

Late in the afternoon, when they arrived back at the hotel, they found Jean McDonald waiting in the lobby. She had more information for Lois, and she came up to the room with them. Dutch offered the ladies a drink, but they declined, so he mixed one for himself at the sidebar.

The two women took seats on the sofa, and he overheard the news Jean had brought. Lois's birth mother, Helga Bergstein, was still alive. She lived in Bonn, Germany, where she owned a small used bookstore. Jean told the story of Helga's survival in the concentration camps, and spoke about the death of Lois's birth father in Auschwitz. It was during that tragic tale that Dutch finally noticed Jean as a woman. She was thirtyish and slender. Her shoulder-length hair was almost blonde, and she had a pretty face, with piercing hazel eyes. There was something special about her, as she tried so hard to comfort Lois.

When finished with her news, she stood and said, "I know this all comes as a shock to you, but I just found out today about your mother. Maybe you should go to Germany and reunite with her."

Lois remained on the sofa, shaking her head and weeping. "My whole life has been a lie."

Jean glanced at Dutch sadly, as she moved to the door. "Sorry for the intrusion."

Just as Jean reached to open the door, Lois stood up, wiping her eyes. "You're right, I want to go to Germany and meet my mother. What do I need to do?"

"You'll need a passport and a visa. Do you have these?" Jean asked.

"I have a passport," Lois answered, then added, "but I don't have any money."

"I have a friend at the German Embassy. We can get you a visa yet this afternoon. Pan Am has a midnight flight to Bonn. You could be with your mother tomorrow."

"And I have the money," Dutch added, reaching into his pocket. "Here's fifteen hundred dollars, more than enough to get there and back."

Lois seemed frozen in place by their offers of help. She became teary-eyed again. "I can't take that money. That's half of our sales today. I'd be leaving you in the lurch."

Dutch moved to her with the cash in hand. "This is just an advance on your Ship's Articles."

Lois's expression was hopeful, but Dutch could read doubt there, as well. "So I would still be part of the Articles?"

"Yes, of course. Take the money. Go see your mother. That's a hell of a lot more important than a rusty submarine."

She reached out and took the cash, then kissed him on the cheek. "I'll never forget you, Dutch. Thank you for being my friend."

He stared at her for a long moment. The brash broad was gone, replaced by a confused young woman. Lowering his voice, he said, "I have one question for you. How do you vote? Do I tell them the truth?"

Without hesitation she answered, "Yes. These are my people now."

"We'd better get a move on, if we want to make that plane," Jean prompted.

In ten minutes, the time it took Lois to pack, both ladies were out the door, leaving Dutch alone in his two-bedroom suite. *Wow, how fast things can move*, he thought, and poured himself another whiskey.

By the next morning, Dutch had prepared himself for going it alone, selling in the diamond district. He changed his sales tactics to those of an ordinary tourist who had found a few gems among the personal belongs of his dead uncle. He had written out his spiel the night before, and was now memorizing it with his morning coffee when there was a knock on the door. Opening it, Dutch found Jean McDonald standing in the hall.

"Good morning. What are you doing here?"

"As I said, Israel is a much better friend than enemy. I came to help you sell some diamonds. I know the district, and my Hebrew is impeccable. Would you like my help?"

They spent the next three mornings working together, selling gems in the district. Jean seemed to know many of the Ashkenazic Jew shop owners, and she was often welcomed warmly with a friendly "Shalom." Dutch couldn't understand a word of her Yiddish sales spiel, but she could haggle with the best of them. It was a great performance to watch. By the end of the week, he had over eighteen thousand dollars of fresh money in his belt. But it wasn't all work. In the afternoons, Jean always had someplace else to take Dutch. On that first day they had lunch with the Israeli Ambassador to the UN, in his private dining room. He was a survivor of the camps, and most of the conversation was about the Holocaust. After the meal, Jean and Dutch toured the UN Headquarters and talked about the prospects for world peace. It was an encouraging afternoon, but both had reservations about whether the UN could improve the human condition.

When they got back to the Plaza, Dutch asked Jean to have a drink with him in the bar. She agreed, but only ordered a club soda, while he had his usual whiskey.

"You don't drink?" he asked.

"No," she answered, removing her hat. "Never liked the taste much."

Over their drinks, Jean told Dutch a little of her story. She had been born in New York to a Scottish immigrant family that was Catholic. Her father was a sculptor and her mother a fine-art curator. Jean had been raised with love and respect for all things in the art world. For a time, she worked as a docent in an art museum. In 1955, she had married an Israeli diplomat and moved to Israel. In 1958, her husband was called to active duty with the Army. He was killed in action in 1960, leaving Jean with two infant girls. She stayed on in Israel, after Mossad recruited her for the Asset Recovery Unit. She remained a Christian and lived in Tel Aviv, where her mother-in-law watched over her children when she was on assignment. She didn't think anything about being a Christian in a Jewish state, as she said Israel was a religious melting pot.

Dutch found her story both tragic and compelling. She, like he, had lost someone they loved. But she had moved on with her life, apparently without feeling sorry for herself. He respected her for that.

On the second afternoon, she took him to an art gallery that had an exhibit of concentration camp art. Jean knew every piece, and gave a passionate description of each scene. The art's subject matter was almost as appalling as the photos. When it came to art, Jean was an insightful docent to have around.

Dutch spent each evening alone in his suite, counting out the daily receipts, making notes in his ledger and thinking about the Holocaust. He realized that he was being manipulated by the Mossad; they were playing him like fiddle. But he didn't care. The Nazi gold had always been tainted. It was time to resolve that issue.

On Dutch's last day in New York, he and Jean finished selling their gems in the district, and had lunch with Mr. Hirsh. They met him at a bistro in the theater district. It was a quaint downstairs restaurant with many dim corners, so no one could see them talking together. After ordering some food and drinks, it was there, with a single candle burning on their table, that Dutch gave away twelve tons of gold.

He told them the true story of their discovery, and explained his plans for the submarine. Neither of them seemed surprised with his decision or truthfulness. He concluded by saying, "So I'll take you up on your offer of a five percent finder's fee for the gold. But my crew is going to play hell with me for giving away their dreams."

"Maybe not," Hirsh said, as the waiter brought their food. After the server departed, he continued, "You can take Jean back with you. She can help convince your crew that you did the righteous thing. And she can oversee the transfer of the gold cargo to an Israeli ship."

Dutch pulled on his bottle of beer. "What do you think about that, Jean?"

"I'll go where I'm needed. I've never been to the Pacific before."

"I still have Lois's return airline ticket for Tahiti," Dutch said. "So you'd have to travel as her."

"Good idea," Gil said, eating his corned beef sandwich. "Your code name will be Lois Berg, and I'll be Uncle Harry. We'll communicate via short wave radio, through our center in San Diego. We'll speak only Hebrew, using our standard code."

They spent the next couple of hours working out dates, places and the terms for the Israeli payment of the five percent finder's fee. When all the details were finalized, Jean wrote an agreement in English, while Mr. Hirsh wrote out the same agreement in Hebrew. Both men signed the agreement, with Jean as a witness. Signing the documents was Dutch's ultimate expression of trust.

When they finished, Dutch asked Gill, "Will you send an Israeli Navy ship for the transfer?"

He shook his head. "Probably not. Our Navy is small, and it's on the other side of the globe. We'll find some Israeli freighter for that task."

Dutch stood to leave. "I have some phone calls to make." Turning to Jean, he continued, "See you at the airport tomorrow morning at nine o'clock. The flight leaves at ten."

"What kind of clothes should I bring?" she asked.

Dutch smiled at her. "Casual and light. That means shorts and bathing suits. We'll be spending the holidays in the tropics."

Shadow Government

Argentina can be an intoxicating place, with its diverse peoples and enthralling history. It is the eighth largest country in the world, with some of the tallest mountains on the planet, expansive deserts, and an impressive coastline. From the beauty of its snowcapped volcanoes and emerald waters to the stark, windswept remoteness of Patagonia, Argentina never ceases to impress. But its history is also filled with civil unrest, strong-man dictators, political tension and ever changing governments. These conditions were exactly why the Odessa considered Argentina the jewel in the crown that would become the Fourth Reich.

After the untimely death of SS Colonel Rolf Kolb in 1945; the Scorpion, A.K.A Nicole Lopez, assumed command of the Argentine Odessa. She ruled with an iron skirt and built upon

Colonel Kolb's network of safe houses all over the country. The early discovery of copper had lifted the financial future of the group, and the Scorpion wielded this money wisely, with political bribes and influence peddling. By the 1960's, she had a near monopoly on all Argentine copper, and her 'behind the scenes' powers stretched from local city halls all the way to the highest levels of the central government. Those who ruled Argentina both feared and respected her. Also, by this time, there were thousands of former SS members and Nazis living under the protection of the Odessa. These men, and a few women, owed their livelihoods, their safety and their futures to the Scorpion, and all had pledged their blood loyalty to her. She was the face of the Fourth Reich.

Nicole Lopez maintained offices in downtown Buenos Aires. The reader board inside the building lobby said 'Headquarters, South American Mining Company' but, in fact, it was from here that the Scorpion ruled over the Argentine Odessa.

It was a warm, bright November morning as Nicole Lopez worked behind her massive mahogany desk in a plush, top-floor suite that overlooked the presidential palace and the Plaza de Mayo. The years had been good to her, she had retained a trim figure and her bronze skin still glowed with youth. She had always been a beautiful woman, and now the gray streaks in her near-black hair made her look distinguished. She had always been a flirt, and remained the same, despite her age. Most men thought of her as an ideal lady with brains, personality and looks. Little did they know she despised all men; her only true love had been Eva Peron, the wife of President Juan Peron, before her tragic death from cancer in 1952. Nicole could still charm the stripes off a tiger and persuade most men to do her bidding. But those who knew her well thought differently. She had a temper with a short fuse, and a mouth that would shame any sailor. And she was a murderer. Over the years, she had killed not only Colonel Kolb, but numerous other threatening rivals. After Adolf Eichmann was kidnapped from Argentina, she had overseen the execution of the two informants who had turned him into the Mossad. Her name, the Scorpion, was well chosen.

The intercom on her desk buzzed. "Ms. Lopez? Señor Wattenberg would like to see you."

"Send him in," she answered.

Wattenberg had been a U-boat Skipper during the war, and had escaped American captivity in 1945. Now in his early forties, he still carried himself like an officer in the Kriegsmarine. The Captain was a valued member of the Odessa, and acted as an inner-circle military advisor to the Scorpion.

Nicole smiled at him as he entered the room with his briefcase. She gestured for him to take a seat. “Good morning. What can I do for you, Captain?”

“I had breakfast with Nick Flores, this morning. He’s one of the political editors for the Buenos Aires Herald. Do you know the man?”

“No, but I read an editorial by him a few days ago. He isn’t very happy with our new President. I liked what he wrote. Why do you ask?”

“Right after the national elections, last month, he and his wife took a short vacation to the South Pacific. They stayed on some island called Hiva Oa, in French Polynesia. While they were there, he saw a submarine tied to a salvage company’s dock. He was able to take a few pictures of the boat being removed from the water. He showed me those pictures, and I thought you should see them, so I borrowed his negatives and had some enlargements made.”

Nicole grinned at the Captain. “Sounds intriguing. Let me see.”

Wattenberg opened his briefcase and handed her three eight-by-ten inch, black and white photos. The Scorpion stared at the pictures, side by side, a for long moment.

“It’s a submarine class I’ve never seen before,” the Captain said, standing to lean over the desk. “If you look closely at the top of conning tower,” he added, pointing to one print, “just under the rust and salt streaks, you can make out what looks like the boat’s numbers, painted in white.”

Nicole opened a desk drawer and removed a large magnifying glass. She bent over the pictures and her eyes grew wide. “Yes, I see what you’re talking about. U-3-5-2, what?”

“I think it’s a one, U-3521. That’s the submarine we waited for aboard the *Hercules,* in 1945. That’s the boat that carried our cargo of gold. But where is the gold now?” he mused, watching her face.

Nicole reached for her intercom and flipped a switch. "Have Señor Klein join us. And hold all my calls." She flipped the control off with a smile. "You're right, Captain. That's our gold boat. Are they scrapping it?"

"No. Señor Flores told me it's in for repairs. He said the boat was owned by an oil company out of New Jersey. I'll check out the company today."

Moments later, SS Captain Hans Klein joined his comrades. He was in charge of security, as well as acting as the official Odessa enforcer. Hans Klein was a sadistic, ruthless man, and a wanted Nazi war criminal.

After looking at the pictures with the magnifying glass, he concurred with his comrades. "But where is the gold?" he asked.

The Scorpion took a cigarette out of her purse, slipped it into her black ivory holder and lit it. "These pictures are a month old. Send a couple of agents to the island. I want that boat searched. You can't easily hide twelve tons of gold, and I want to know where the boats going after the repairs. See to it now. I want that cargo!"

As both men stood, Nicole looked up at Captain Wattenberg. "We will need a Navy ship to go after that submarine, a boat and crew with a sting. Find out what's available in the Argentine fleet."

The Captain shook his head, "That's going to be impossible, now that President Arturo Illia has taken power. We don't have any influence with his new government."

"Leave that to me," the Scorpion said, and smiled. "I have my ways."

Last Patrol

The next morning, as the jetliner gained altitude and turned west, Dutch asked Jean, "Have you ever crewed on a sailboat before?"

She shook her head, looking uneasy. "Never even been on a sailboat before."

"Can you cook?"

"Yes, actually. I'm a darn good cook."

"Good," Dutch answered, smiling. "Look out that window. See how fast we're moving? Sailing is the direct opposite. Out on the sea, time seems to stand still. I hope you'll like it."

"My concern is sea sickness. Any advice?"

"Just keep your eye on the horizon. You'll get your sea legs soon enough."

"Can I ask you a personal question?"

"Sure," Dutch answered, sipping his coffee.

"What was all that 'Ship's Articles' talk about?"

"Ever read Moby Dick?"

"Yes, in school. Didn't like it much."

"It was all about sailors and shares. When Lois came aboard in Honolulu, she signed Ship's Articles that granted her a small percentage of any profits the boat makes."

"Wow. She did well with your discovery. Are you two an item?"

Dutch shrugged. "We spent many a night together under the stars, so yes, in some ways we were an item. You'll see. There are no secrets aboard a sailboat. What's the name of your perfume?"

"Chanel No.5. Why do you ask?"

Dutch told her about his wife using the same perfume. That opened up a discussion about his personal life. Dutch found Jean an enjoyable companion. She was a bolt of brightness, with an agile mind and a great sense of humor.

They arrived in L.A. late in the afternoon, and took a cab to the Hollywood Roosevelt Hotel. While registering, Dutch was given a package that Maggie had sent over. When he got into the elevator, he was chuckling.

"What's so funny?" Jean asked.

"The desk clerk welcomed my wife and I back to the hotel. Gave us the same room we had last week. The only problem is, I have a different 'wife,' this week! Guess that's common here in Tinsel Town. Wives just come and go."

"Watch out, Dutch," she warned, and snickered. "I'm not so easy to dump!"

When they got to the room, Jean went to unpack while Dutch went to the small desk and wrote out a list of items. When he was done, he phoned for the concierge. While he waited, he poured himself a drink and made some phone calls. When the porter arrived, he gave him the list and a hundred dollar bill, plus a twenty-dollar tip.

"I'll need these things by tomorrow."

"Yes sir," the porter answered with a smile.

When Jean came back into the room, Dutch opened the package from Maggie. It contained the submarine photo album he had asked her to send over. He proudly showed it to Jean. As she looked, wide eyed, at the pictures, Dutch called down for room service. They spent the evening talking about the fate of the submarine and the transfer of the gold.

The next day, Dutch and Jean had lunch with Professor Jacobs friend, Wolfgang Zimmerman. Wolfgang had been a legendary sea wolf, one of the fortunate few U-boat Skippers to survive WWII. He had been laid up in a hospital, with a broken leg, during the closing months of the war. He was also fortunate to have been captured by the Americans. When the admirals at the Pentagon learned of his imprisonment, he was quickly brought to the States, where he taught submarine tactics to the US Navy. He and his American wife now lived in Ventura, where they owned a horse ranch. He was a string bean with a weathered face, deep-set eyes, and a commanding voice.

Dutch told him of their discovery and allowed him to see the pictures, but made no mention of the treasure, or of cannibalism. The old U-boat Captain was practically drooling as he flipped through the album. He recognized the type XXI sub right away, and called it a wonder weapon. "I was supposed to have one of those, but then I crushed my damn leg in an auto accident."

Dutch talked about the repairs being made and his plan to raise a local crew to sail the boat to the West Coast. "We can't submerge, but the diesel power plant is being totally overhauled. Our destination is the Columbia River."

Wolfgang stared at the open album with a far-away look on his face. "I've dreamt about one last patrol, ever since the end of the war. Now you're making one. Do you need an old sea dog who knows his way around submarines?"

"Are you volunteering?" Dutch asked.

"Yes," Wolfgang answered firmly. "And, if I get on the phone, I can raise two or three more old comrades for your crew."

"No Nazis," Jean said.

"No! These will all be men that I vouch for," the Captain answered.

Dutch smiled at Wolfgang. "Make your phone calls. I'll buy the airfares to Tahiti and give each man five hundred dollars when the submarine is moored on the Columbia River. And, there is an extra five hundred for your help."

Jean inserted, "They will all need US Passports, and we'll need their names for airline tickets and for my Uncle Harry."

"Who the hell is Uncle Harry?" Wolfgang asked.

"He's one of my partners," Dutch answered. "Do we have a deal?"

Captain Zimmerman extended his hand like a lightning bolt. Over a second round of drinks, they worked out all of the details. Dutch relaxed, pleased to have an experienced sea wolf for his passage to the States.

As they rode the elevator up to their room, Dutch asked, "Why the mention of Uncle Harry?"

"Simple, security." Jean answered. "We want to know all the players in this exchange. No room for former Nazis or current Odessa."

When they got to their room, they found two black canvas duffel bags waiting, with a note from the concierge.

"What's in the bags?" Jean asked.

"Special holiday provisions for the islands," Dutch answered, and took the duffel bags into his bedroom.

When he returned, he walked toward the front door. "I've got to go buy some film. I'll be back in few hours. We're having dinner with Maggie and Colonel Ford downstairs at seven. They are NBC executives and my dear friends. You'll like them."

"How do you explain me?" Jean asked.

"I'll tell them the truth."

"Not about me! No mention of me being a Mossad Agent."

"Fine, I'll leave that part out. You're just a crew replacement for Lois."

Jean frowned. "I didn't bring anything to wear for a dinner party."

"Nor did I," Dutch answered, reaching into his pocket. "Here's fifty bucks. I bought clothes for Lois. I guess I can do the same for her replacement."

"I don't want your money, Dutch. I have my own" she replied, with fire in her hazel eyes.

Dutch smiled at her. "That's a fresh breeze – a truly liberated woman! Be back in a few hours."

When he returned to the room, carrying two shopping bags, he heard Jean in the bathroom, getting ready. After turning on a light, he took the bags into his bedroom and repacked all the film and new camera gear he had bought into the duffel bags. Changing clothes, he put on his best pair of slacks, his blue button-down shirt and his only blazer. Then, returning to the front room, he poured himself a drink. When Jean joined him Dutch did a double take, almost spilling his whiskey. She wore a black strapless cocktail dress, with nylons and high heels. Her makeup was perfect, making her eyes glow, and she had a single strand of pearls around her creamy neck. She looked stunning.

"Will this do?" she asked. "I was told shorts and bathing suits."

"Guess I forgot to tell you," he answered sheepishly. "You're a knock-out in black. My friends will be impressed."

They arrived downstairs at the dining room right on time. Dutch tipped the maître d' ten dollars and secured a quiet booth just off the dance floor. A few moments later, when Maggie and Colonel Ford joined them, Dutch stood to greet them.

Maggie gave him a big hug, and the Colonel hugged him as well, while they shook hands. Then Dutch introduced Jean to his friends.

As they slipped into the black vinyl booth, Maggie asked, "What happen to other lady friend?"

"Lois had some family business in Europe. I was fortunate to find Jean in New York as her replacement."

After they ordered drinks, Maggie asked Dutch, "Is Lieutenant Asbow still with you?"

"Yes, he's still my mate."

"Good," she replied. "I have something for him." She reached into her purse and gave Dutch an official-looking envelope with Doug's name on it. "This came to my office three days after you sailed for Hawaii. By then, it was too late."

Dutch removed the document inside, and saw that it was a Notice of Wage Garnishment. He folded the notice and put it in his pocket. “I’ll give it to him. He’s got a few ex-wife problems.”

“Yes, I can see that,” she answered, with a disapproving gaze.

After the cocktails arrived, Colonel Ford asked, “Can we talk freely?”

“Yes,” Dutch answered. “Jean knows it all.”

He reached into his breast pocket and gave Dutch a three-page typed summary of all of the cut-away footage the network planned to use in the ‘Witness to Yesterday’ project. The total footage used was just over six minutes. That meant a usage fee of over eighteen thousand dollars.

“The final editing won’t be completed until May,” the Colonel said, sipping a martini. “You’ll be paid this June, although, the programs won’t air until next year. Your underwater footage of the Battleship Arizona was outstanding.”

“How did our submarine footage come out?” Dutch asked.

He chuckled. “Wow, is about all I can say! Your discovery is going to be a firestorm of International news. While we never pay for news, we do hope that you’ll extend, to NBC, the exclusive rights to break your story worldwide. It would be great for you, and a big break for our fledgling News Division.”

“Tell him about the documentary project, Colonel,” Maggie inserted with a proud smile.

Colonel Ford reached into his breast pocket again and brought out an envelope, which he handed across the table to Dutch. It was a check. “NBC would like to buy the ‘right of first refusal’ to your story of discovery, for three thousand dollars. You write it and we’ll produce it. What do you say, Dutch?”

Dutch beamed and extended his hand to his old friend. “Sounds good to me, Colonel.”

“Great. Let’s get this party started. I’m buying,” Colonel Ford said firmly.

They spent the rest of the evening celebrating the prospects of Dutch’s story being produced as a major network documentary. The food and drinks were fabulous, the conversations fascinating, and Jean seemed to fit in like a glove. When the dance band started, Maggie had Dutch on the floor, swinging his hips like a teenager. Her long ago days of being a professional contract dancer in Hollywood was still apparent and Dutch enjoyed watching her moves.

When a slow dance started, Maggie pulled Dutch close and whispered in his ear, "I notice you never recruit ugly crew-members. Who is this Jean really?"

"She's a replacement for Lois," he answered innocently.

She chuckled in his ear. "That lady doesn't know a jib from a mainsail. Who is she? We don't have secrets, remember?"

Dutch hesitated, not sure what to say, but he couldn't lie to her, so he told her the truth. Just as he finished, the music stopped, and people started filtering off the dance floor.

Still in the middle of the room, Maggie murmured, "She doesn't look like an Israeli Secret Agent. So, you're giving away all your gold?"

"It doesn't belong to me. It belongs to the Israeli people."

Maggie pulled him close, and kissed his cheek. "You're doing the right thing again, Dutch. I'm proud to be your friend."

"Well, don't tell anyone, especially the Colonel. He'll think I'm a fool."

Late on Sunday morning, November 17, 1963, Dutch and Jean boarded a Pan Am flight for Tahiti. Dressed in his traveling clothes again, Dutch had sore feet and a cotton mouth from the night before.

As the DC8 gained altitude and turned southwest, Jean said, "That Maggie is sweet on you. You guys danced the night away. Good thing that Colonel Ford was so interesting or I would have been bored stiff. Why don't you do something about that gal?"

"She too old for me, but I tried, many years ago. She's had the same lady friend for over twenty years now."

"Oh," Jean answered, with a perplexed look. "That's tough competition."

"But a great fantasy," Dutch replied with a wishful grin.

After a lengthy layover in Hawaii, they arrived in Papeete early on Monday afternoon. When they deplaned down the outside boarding stairs, Dutch smelled the scent of the tropics again, and was pleased to be back. After getting their luggage at baggage claim, they went through Customs, where Dutch was obligated to pay a hefty duty for his two duffel bags. Between the airline overweight fee and the duty, the bags cost him over a hundred dollars. No matter; the contents were precious to him.

Hailing a cab, they were taken to the harbor. But Dutch's sailboat was nowhere to be seen. Lugging their baggage to the Harbor Master's Office, they learned that the boat was out on a charter.

"They should be back around four," the Harbor Master told them. "Leave your bags here, Dutch. I'll keep an eye on them."

With the weather mild, and a few rain squalls threatening, Jean and Dutch walked to town and had lunch at a small café. After their meal, they went to the local post office, where Dutch rented a box. From there, they walked to Barclays Bank. He opened an account with the three-thousand-dollar check Colonel Ford had given him. Now that Dutch had both a mailing address and a bank account number, the Israeli Government would have a way to deposit their finder's fee.

It was nearing four o'clock when they returned to the Harbor Master's Office. Standing on the dock, watching out to the bay, Dutch spotted his sailboat just inside the breakwater.

"Here's the *Laura* now," he said to Jean, pointing towards the harbor.

"Was that your wife's name?"

"Yes," he answered shyly. "You probably think me a romantic fool."

Jean turned to him, the light of the low sun on her pretty face. "No, not at all. I love the way you loved her."

They watched from the office as Doug motored the boat next to the transit dock and Heidi secured it fore and aft. Soon, two couples got off the boat, with smiles and beach bags. Doug said farewell to them, and they walked up the gangway for the shore.

Doug and Heidi wore identical looks of surprise when they looked up from washing down the boat and spotted Dutch and a strange woman approaching, luggage in hand.

All work stopped, and the crew was reunited. Doug and Heidi looked great, as both glowed with dark suntans. Dutch introduced Jean, saying only that Lois had gone to Europe on family business.

"Jean is much like you were, Heidi, when you came aboard," Dutch said. "She's a tenderfoot, with skills we can use. I hope you will accept her, just like we accepted you."

"No problem," Heidi answered, with a friendly smile. "Is she our new cook?"

"Yes," Jean answered quickly.

"You should have sent us a telegram. I've got the boat booked through Thanksgiving," Doug said.

"That's what the Harbor Master told me," Dutch answered. "I told him to cancel all the charters. We're sailing for Hiva Oa tomorrow afternoon. We'll be spending the holidays on the island."

Doug frowned. "Why?"

"I've got the money for Mr. Chandler, and lots of news from home. Trust me. You'll want to hear what I have to say."

Doug still scowled. "I like this charter boat business. I'm good at it."

Dutch smiled at him. "Well, my friend, when you get your share of the money, buy a boat of your own and have at it."

"Alright, Captain Bligh. We'll do it your way," Doug answered, finally smiling.

They brought the luggage aboard, and Dutch showed Jean where she would be sleeping in the bunk berths.

"It's cramped and small, but you'll get used to it. If you find any of Lois's personal effects, give them to me. I'll see she gets them back."

"When are you going to tell them about the gold?" she whispered.

"After we shove-off."

The next morning they bought provisions, filled up the tanks, and paid off the Harbor Master. The sailboat cleared the harbor early the next afternoon. Once outside the breakwater, they set the sails, and the boat heeled over in a brisk wind. Dutch stood at the helm of his beloved sailboat again, delighted to be underway.

Doug sat in the cockpit with coffee in hand. "Are you doing the midnight watches again?"

"Sure. Heidi is showing Jean around the boat. When they're done, she'll take the wheel."

The evening before, Dutch had showed his crew the contents of his duffel bags: two canned hams, one cured smoked turkey, four bottles of Yukon Jack, and four bottles of champagne – gifts for the boat, to help celebrate the holidays. For more practical reasons, he had also purchased a used Bolex 16mm hand-held camera, along with a light bar and enough film to document their passage back to the States.

Over dinner that evening, Dutch learned that Doug and Heidi had done very well with their 'barefoot' sailing business. They had made a profit of over five hundred dollars in just a few short weeks. Dutch shared his sales ledger with them, as well. They were dumbfounded by his expenses and amazed by his profits.

"We'll celebrate the holidays in style," Dutch told them. "I'm going to radio Helen Chandler and have her rent us a bungalow for our stay."

He also shared with them what he had learned about their cut-away footage and the money for the 'right of first refusal' agreement. They seemed pleased with the news, and he could see that each was starting to calculate their share of the money.

With Tahiti in their wake, Heidi and Jean joined the mates in the cockpit and took a seat.

"What do think about our sailboat?" Dutch asked.

"That little galley is going to be a challenge," Jean answered. "But I'll learn my way around it. When do we stop tilting over?"

The crew chuckled, and Heidi replied, "When we're in port. Don't worry. You'll get your sea legs."

"We need to talk privately," Doug said with a serious face. "About what we found and what we're going to do about it."

"Do you mean the gold?" Dutch answered.

Doug glanced at Jean with a frown, and then looked at Dutch. "You told her?"

"Yes, she's knows it all," Dutch replied, lighting a cigarette. "She's part of my solution."

"Damn you, Dutch! You had no right. She's not getting any of my share," Doug answered, with fire in his eyes.

"Jean, get your pictures," Dutch replied, and then turned to his crew. "While I was gone, I learned who truly owns that gold."

That started the conversation that Dutch had dreaded since New York. Both Doug and Heidi had gold fever. They had not experienced what he and Lois had learned about the Holocaust. So, with the help of Jean and her concentration camp photos, Dutch told them what they had learned. His story was long, and filled with compassion for the victims. Jean helped, with vivid descriptions of each image, and additional stories about the survivors and the dead. Heidi listened and looked intent, while Doug seemed bored. Dutch ended his story by telling them Jean's true identity and the offer of a finder's fee from the Israeli Government. "The gold belongs to the Israeli people, and I have agreed to give it to them."

When he concluded, Heidi had tears in her eyes, and Doug's face was red with anger.

"The hell with you, pal," he finally said. "I survived the Jap camps, and I'm owed that damn money. Why can't we be rich? We found it, fair and square."

"Here's the deal," Dutch replied. "Before Lois went to Europe, she voted to give Israel the gold. I voted the same."

Heidi wiped away a tear. "I vote with Dutch and Lois."

Doug stood up, shaking his head, and paced around the deck, clearly frustrated. But finally he came aft again. "All right. I guess the cake is baked. I'll be just a little rich. Guess that's better than being a little poor. I'll vote with Heidi."

Over the next few days, the boat fell into its usual routine. Jean mastered the tiny galley, and her meals were simple but tasty. She also found her way around the nook, and was soon sending and receiving messages from Mr. Hirsh. On the radio, she spoke only Hebrew, and the crew seemed to like having a secret agent aboard, although Doug didn't like her speaking only Hebrew, as he couldn't understand her. "I sure hope you trust this bimbo," he said to Dutch, one night at the wheel. "For all we know, she could be selling us down the drain."

Dutch took a sip of coffee. "She's not a bimbo, pal, but I understand your doubts. We spent a lot time together, dealing diamonds in New York. She will have my back all the way home. This I know as a fact, and she'll have your back as well. Trust me, Doug, you can take THAT to the bank."

During the days, both Heidi and Doug gave Jean sailing lessons, and soon she was standing her own 'fair weather watch' at the wheel. During this time, Dutch stood his midnight watch, enjoying the solitude of being under the stars again.

On the third night out, Jean joined Dutch in the cockpit with her nightly hot tea in hand. "Just got off the radio with Uncle Harry. Captain Zimmerman and his mates have been checked out. No problems. He's also found an Israeli freighter in San Francisco that has agreed to take on the cargo. They can be at the rendezvous point by January 10th."

"That will work," Dutch replied. "We'll have to leave Hiva Oa before the New Year. It's seven to nine days to Henderson Island."

"When will Captain Zimmerman and his friends arrive?" she asked.

"January 2nd. They can move into the bungalow we're going to rent. Mr. Chandler will put them to work on the submarine. We'll be back after the middle of the month, and shove off for the States."

"Uncle Harry also wants me to sail with you and the submarine. You might need my Hebrew, if we encounter any problems."

Dutch smiled at her in the moonlight. "Wolfgang won't like it, having a woman aboard, but then I'm the Commodore. Thanks for your help with my crew. Doug took the news better than I thought."

"Heidi got it right away. Doug just took some time." She cocked her head. "Is it true that Paul Gauguin is buried on Hiva Oa?"

"Yes. I'll show you. It's a mighty weird tomb."

As was his habit, each evening before his watch, Dutch stopped in the nook and used the radio directional finder to confirm the boat's general location. So it was that late Friday evening, after warming up the equipment, he slipped on the headset and dialed in the local radio station on Papeete. This was the only station in the islands with enough power to be heard out at sea. He soon found the correct frequency, but the radio reception was filled with static. They were sailing at the outer limits of the station's power. He fine-tuned the station as best he could, then dialed in the directional finder. Once he had written down his final bearings, he reached to turn off the radio…but stopped in his tracks, realizing that there was something wrong. The station on Papeete wasn't playing music, which was its format. Dutch pushed both cups of the headset against his ears. He could only make out a few garbled words, spoken in English, from what sounded like the BBC. The announcer gave the date and mentioned JFK…and then Dutch heard the word 'assassinated.' His heart froze. Unable to believe his ears, he quickly dialed in KSFO, a powerful radio station out of San Francisco that they often received far out to sea. It's reception was better. Long-faced and shaking, Dutch heard the horrible news that President John F. Kennedy had been assassinated in Dallas, Texas, on the morning of November 22, 1963. Dutch was filled with sadness; and his eyes teared up as he heard the somber music and listened to the shocking words. The news was still sketchy; no one seemed to know who had done it, or why. Vice President Lyndon Johnson had taken the oath of office and was now President. Dutch listened, stunned, to every tidbit of news. His head filled with dark thoughts about the safety of his country. When there seemed to be no more details that he hadn't already heard, he slipped the headsets off, not sure what to do next.

"Hey, Dutch," Doug called from the cabin hatch. "It's after midnight, pal. Are you going to relieve me?"

"Yes, I'll be right there," he shouted back, and exited the nook. Dumping out his coffee in the sink, he poured three fingers of brandy into his cup – something he never did when the boat was underway. Then he climbed the stairs to the cockpit.

"Not like you to be late," Doug said from the wheel.

Dutch took the helm, tears stinging his cheeks. "The President is dead."

"What!" Doug quickly turned back to Dutch at the wheel.

"It's all over the news. That's what I was listening to, in the nook."

"Wow. Are you alright?"

"Yes. You go below and listen. This could be the work of the Russians."

Doug moved quickly to the hatch, then looked back at his mate. "I'll keep you informed."

With the deck to himself, Dutch tied off the helm and stared up at the moon. Lighting a cigarette, he recalled the few patrols he had made on PT boats during the war. Years later, he had learned that JFK had been the Skipper of PT109, operating in the same waters where he had sailed. Dutch had respected the man, and known he was right for the Presidency. In 1961, John F. Kennedy had gotten his vote. With teary eyes, he held up his coffee cup. "Life is short and death sure. Oh, Lord, guide Lieutenant Kennedy on this, his last patrol."

Chapter Twelve

The Scorpion

Ruling Argentina in the Twentieth Century was as elusive a goal as ruling the weather. The powerful factions within the Republic included the Catholic Church, fifteen different political parties, the wealthy industrialists, and the Buenos Aires ruling class. These conflicting constituents were an obstacle for any fledgling government, and required a strong leader with a vicious bite and a clear vision.

One such strong administration was that of Juan Perón, who came to power in 1946. He and his popular wife, Eva, ruled successfully for six years. Like royalty, this couple was beloved by the people, and were shrewd stewards of a booming economy with an ever-growing middle class. Unfortunately, Eva died from cancer in 1952. After her untimely demise, Juan Perón never fully recovered from his grief. He resigned his powers in 1955 and went into self-imposed exile in Spain.

After his administration, Argentina had five different governments in as many years.

Early in 1963, the Argentine Navy revolted, attempting a coup to replace the civilian government with another military strongman. The revolt was short-lived, without the support of the Army and Air Force, causing a major setback for the Navy and occasioning the removal of most of its commanding admirals. By mid-year, however, National Elections had been called, and in October those elections brought to power the reform government of Arturo Illia. This new president captured the office with the slimmest of majorities, and started his term with shaky control of his own government.

Against this backdrop of confusion and intrigue, the Scorpion and her henchmen plotted the recovery of their SS gold.

When Captain Wattenberg entered the plush office, on the morning of November 15th, he found the Scorpion on the phone.

She waved him in and pointed at a chair, while continuing her conversation. When she concluded, she hung up the receiver with a smile.

"That was Vice President Perette. He is a buffoon," she said, her eyes flashing. "But he's my buffoon! What do you have, Captain?"

Wattenberg handed her a folded paper. "Another report from our agent, Carlos on Hiva Oa. He snuck aboard the submarine but didn't find any gold."

The Scorpion read the document carefully, not once but twice. "Do we know who this Dutch Clarke is?"

The Captain chuckled. "Some rich oilman out of New Jersey. He's due back on the island any day now. The rumor around the docks is that he's returning from the States with money to overhaul the diesel engines. In his last report, Carlos found out that the sub's electric motor is inoperable, so the boat can't submerge. The owner plans to cruise the U-3521 on the surface, all the way to Long Beach, California, in January. But there's no gold aboard."

"Uh-huh," she answered, still staring at the document. "Our agent says the entire battery system for the electric motor has been removed from the boat. Where would those batteries have been kept?"

"Under the deck plates in the engine room. Why?"

"How much space would be under those deck plates, without the batteries?"

The Captain nodded with a grin. "A lot of room, more than enough for twelve tons of gold."

The Scorpion folded the document. "We'll board the boat, or sink her in shallow waters, and then dive onto her to remove the gold. Send a cable back to Carlos. Have him return to the submarine and look under the deck plates. That's where our gold is."

"Yes, Ma'am," the Captain answered. "How is it going with the Navy?"

"Yesterday, I had a meeting with the new Commanding Admiral, Daniel Alberto. The morale aboard our ships is at an all time low, so he's open to the idea of a training mission to the western approaches of Panama. Tonight, I'm dining with Vice President Perette and the Senate President. Our Company will offer to underwrite such a training cruise, for the good of the Navy. With any luck, we'll have a ship and crew before the month is out."

"Good," the Captain answered. "We'll have to be underway by the first of the year if we want to intercept the U-3521. What happens if Carlos can't get aboard the submarine again to check under the deck plates?"

The Scorpion lit a cigarette, and its blue smoke circled her attractive face. "Not to worry. Captain Klein has gotten word that Mr. Clarke is recruiting a few former U-boat sailors for his passage to America. One of his new recruits will be working for us. He'll report the boats position and disable her in shallow waters. We will *not* lose this cargo again."

The Exchange

After the crew learned of the assassination of President Kennedy, spirits aboard the sailboat dropped faster than a barometer in a typhoon. With somber moods, they spent the next few days huddled around the nook radio, scanning the airways for whatever news tidbits they could find. The crisis seemed over, but the shock of the President's death hung over the *Laura* like a black mist. The only rational conclusion to be drawn from his tragic death, they all finally agreed, was that one lone, crazy assassin had changed the course of history. It was a crying shame.

Early on the seventh morning out of Tahiti, the sailboat approached the darkened outline of Hiva Oa. With the eastern horizon crimson, Dutch turned the boat into the wind and reefed his sails. Once the canvas had been tucked away, he started the motor and turned the boat again for the island. Just behind Hiva Oa, tall, murky clouds stacked up in the morning sky, producing flashes of lightning and rolling claps of thunder. It was an awesome welcome back to paradise.

As Dutch stood at the wheel watching the show, Jean came on deck with coffee mugs in hand. She gave one to him and stood next to him, watching the view. "The power and the beauty of the Pacific are beyond my wildest imagination," she said, and sipped her brew.

"Foul weather or fair, she is a seductive mistress. Of all the islands in the Pacific, the Marquesas Islands, with their blatant beauty, plentiful bounty, black sand beaches and mirror clear waters are the pearls of paradise."

Jean turned to Dutch, with early morning sunrays dancing in her hair. "The President's death has been like a shroud on us. I felt so helpless, out here at sea."

Dutch drank his coffee with frown. "Yes, I know. But today is the dawn of a new day. Let's embrace it and move on."

As they approached the island, Dutch pointed out the little village of Atuona. "That's where Gauguin is buried. I'll show you his weird grave." As they motored past the town, Dutch noticed that all of the French flags were at half-staff. Kennedy's assassination had made its mark, all the way across the Pacific.

By 0730 on the morning of November 27th, the sailboat was secured to the salvage company dock, and Jean was in her galley, cooking up spam and eggs. After their meal, the guys and Jean walked up to the deserted docks and headed for the repair shop, while Heidi remained aboard to take a fresh-water shower.

"Where is everybody?" Jean asked, walking across the dew-covered planks.

Doug chuckled. "Out here, we're on island time. The work day starts when the locals get the notion."

Inside the corrugated-metal building, they found their submarine still standing large on the cradle, although it looked totally different. All of the rust and salt stains on the deck plates had been removed, revealing the raw iron under the corrosion. The hull had been scraped clean of barnacles and seaweed, and the underside of the boat looked ready for finishing.

As Dutch rubbed his hand across the smooth steel plates of the hull, a stranger approached them from behind. "What the hell are you folks doing in here?"

Dutch turned toward the voice, startled. "Who are you?"

The burly Polynesian held a baseball bat in one hand, and was slapping it onto his open palm. He was huge, and his pocked face looked angry. "The question is, who in hell are you?" he answered, his brown eyes afire.

"We own this submarine. We've come to inspect the work that's been done," Dutch said.

The Polynesian took a few steps forward, still glaring at them. "I'm the guard here, and nobody told *me* you were coming."

Dutch heard the shop door open on the other side of the sub. There were footsteps. Then Luke came around the bow of the submarine, into view of the confrontation. "Sam, back off," he shouted, moving quickly to the crew. "These are friends."

The Polynesian glared at Dutch for a moment more, then extended his hand with a sudden smile. "Just doing my job, bub. I like your submarine."

Dutch was pleased to see Luke again, who introduced Sam to them by saying, "We caught a guy inside the boat, a few weeks ago. He claimed to be just a curious tourist. But he returned a few days later, and we kicked him out again. There's a lot of valuable copper here in the shop, so Dad hired Sam and his brother Adam to watch over the yard when we're not working."

After introducing Jean to Luke, Dutch asked, "How's the work going?"

Luke beamed with pride. "The boat is ready for painting. Let's walk around the hull. I have a few questions."

As they inspected the boat, Luke pointed out all of the repairs that had been made to the hull. One of the propeller blades had been fixed, the rudder had been straightened, and all of the interior fuel tanks had been scrubbed clean. "We've lubricated all the running gear, and it's ready for paint. What color do you want?" Luke asked.

"What color was it, under the rust?" Doug asked.

"A dark blue-gray," Luke answered. "And we found small, white boat numbers near the top of the conning tower. Do you want those, as well?"

"Yes, dark blue-gray and white numbers," Dutch answered. "We'll make her look like she just came off the factory floor."

As they finished up with the hull, Luke's brothers, John and Matthew, came into the shop. They were overhauling the twin diesel engines, and the crew went aboard to inspect their work. Dutch was pleasantly surprised with all they had accomplished. Both engines were torn down to deck plates, waiting for new parts.

"Did you bring us money? We've got to get these parts ordered," Matthew said, standing in the engine room.

"Yes, that's not a problem," Dutch assured him.

Matthew smiled and rubbed his hands together. "Good. Dad will be pleased to see you."

"I bet he will," Dutch answered with a grin. "Has he come to work yet?"

"Yes, we rode in together this morning," John answered.

Dutch turned to Doug, "Show Jean around the submarine while I go pay off Mr. Chandler."

Dutch found Lyle and Helen in the cluttered boatyard office. They were surprised to see him so early in the morning. "We didn't even notice your sailboat at our dock," Helen said with a welcoming smile. Then her expression turned sober. "Sorry to hear about your President Kennedy. He was a great man."

"Thank you, Helen," Dutch said sadly. "I think I owe you folks some money."

Both their faces brightened. Reaching into his pocket, Dutch brought out his American Express Travels checkbook. Opening it, he signed two of the checks and handed them to Mr. Chandler. "This is for the tow." Then he reached into his other pocket and brought out a slip of paper, which he handed to Helen. "This is for you. It's a receipt from Barclays Bank, showing that I deposited fifteen thousand dollars into your account, last week."

The couple seemed stunned. "It's a lot of money," Dutch continued. "And I've got you covered with whatever else we need."

Lyle had a distant look on his face as he muttered, "That's the most money we've had in that account for years."

Helen finally found her voice, as well. "I have your gems right here," she said, opening her desk drawer. "They're hard to give back," she added as she handed Dutch the four jewels. "I've enjoyed admiring them each morning."

Dutch smiled and handed back a sapphire and a ruby to her. "These are for you, Helen, for trusting me. Thank you for that."

Her eyes got teary and she looked away, while her husband beamed at the desk next to her. "Thank you," she whispered, grasping the two stones. "These will always remind me of you."

"Did you rent us a bungalow?"

She turned back to Dutch. "Yes. It's just half-mile down the road, on the way to the village, three bedrooms and two baths, with a view of the harbor. Two hundred a month, plus a hundred-dollar cleaning deposit."

As Helen searched in her purse for the keys, Dutch reached for his checkbook again. Signing over a five-hundred-dollar traveler's check, he said, "We'll take it for two months. Tomorrow is our Thanksgiving, so we'll be taking the day off."

"If that's case," Mr. Chandler answered, "we better go over the parts I need to order."

Helen found the keys and handed them to Dutch. "Hold on, husband. Before you boys get wrapped up with your 'wish lists,' I wanted to invite Dutch and his crew for Christmas. Because of them, we're having a good, old-fashioned Hawaiian luau to celebrate."

Dutch beamed. "Thank you, Helen. We'll be there. Can I bring something?"

"Nothing at all," she answered. "And please, no alcohol. I don't want the boys exposed to the devil's brew."

Nodding his head, Dutch noticed Lyle winking at him. "Not a problem. We'll respect your wishes."

Dutch and Lyle Chandler spent the next few hours going over all of the paint, supplies, parts and equipment needed to complete the job. To this final list, Dutch added a new VHF radio with a directional finder, and a modern Depth Sounder. "We'll also need thirty tons of diesel fuel in January, and food for a crew of ten for two weeks," he concluded.

"Make out your list of food needs and give it to the village market," Helen answered. "They'll be cheaper, fresher and better than our vendor in Papeete."

When Dutch was done in the office, he walked back to the shop and found Doug taking pictures, standing over Luke's workbench.

"Where's Jean?" he asked, approaching them.

"She went back to the sailboat. You should see what else Luke is working on."

The metal bench was cluttered with weapons and a large wooden box.

Luke proudly picked up a long-barreled rifle, holding it with both hands. "Remember the anti-aircraft guns we found? I've dismantled all four rifles, cleaned, oiled them, and then put them back together again. They're ready to fire."

"How did you learn to do that?" Dutch asked.

Luke beamed. "From the boat's manuals. I can't read a word of German, but there were a lot of pictures."

He was a smart kid, and Dutch was impressed with his initiative. "Did you test-fire them yet?"

"No," he answered sheepishly. "I wanted to shoot a few seagulls, but Dad wouldn't let me. He said it would scare the townspeople."

During their absence, Luke had also discovered the boat's gun locker. Inside the safe, he had found a few other small arms and, of all things, a black walking stick with a silver skull handle. "I have no idea why this was locked away," he said, holding the cane so Doug could take a picture.

"What's in the wooden box?" Dutch asked.

Luke grinned. "That's very special," he answered, opening the lid. "I found this inside a locked compartment in the radio nook. At first, I thought it was just a typewriter. But then I looked at the booklet inside the box. It's a fully working Enigma machine."

"What the hell is an Enigma machine?" Doug asked.

Dutch bent over the workbench to see it better. "It's a top-secret cipher device that the Germans used during the war," he answered.

"Wow," Doug said, taking a few more shots. "Luke, you've got a lot of treasures here."

Dutch looked at his mate. "*We've* got a lot of treasures here. It's all part of *our* story."

Doug grinned and nodded. "Yeah, *we* do."

Early that afternoon, the crew borrowed the yard's jeep, and moved into the bungalow. The Polynesian-style house was located between several tall shade trees, and looked almost brand new. The road side of the cottage had spectacular mountain views, while the water side had a deck with endless views of the harbor and the Pacific. The spacious interior was neat and clean, and was fully appointed, right down to pots and pans, and dishes in the cupboards. The furniture was a bright floral overstuffed rattan, with a cane-and-glass table that could seat six. Doug and Heidi took the master bedroom, while Dutch and Jean took the two spare bedrooms and shared the adjoining second bath.

After the crew was settled in, they drove to the village, where the girls bought some groceries for Thanksgiving. While they shopped, Dutch and Doug talked to the owner of the market, and gave him a typed list of their food needs. The proprietor was delighted to fill their order, and they worked out the delivery dates and payment. When everyone was finished, the crew walked around town, introducing Jean to the quaint little village.

On their way back to the bungalow, they stopped by the cemetery where Gauguin was buried. As they all stood looking down at his unusual lava stone grave, Jean asked Dutch, "Why do you think his tomb is weird?"

Dutch squinted and cocked his head. "It's so out place, in shape, texture and color from all the other markers. It's as if he wanted to stand out from everyone else."

Jean beamed. "Very good. His tomb is like his synthetic style of work. He was famous for his bold shapes, colors and texture. He was a post-impressionist like no other artist."

"It's still just bizarre to me," Heidi added.

Jean walked around the large tombstone, telling them about the greatness of Paul Gauguin. She knew his style, and told many lively stories of his life and times in Polynesia. Jean was like a walking art encyclopedia, and Dutch found himself admiring her smart, quiet knowledge.

With the solitude of the bungalow, Dutch slept in until just after nine the next morning. Still drowsy, he got out of bed wearing only his white skivvies, and reached for his shaving kit. Opening the bathroom door he shuffled to the pedestal sink and turned on the hot water. After washing away the sleep, he lathered up his soap mug and brushed the lather onto his face.

Taking his straight razor, he was about to begin shaving when he glanced at the medicine cabinet mirror and saw the reflection of some of Jean's colorful undies, hanging from the shower curtain bar behind him. Turning with the razor still in hand, he moved to her bedroom door and knocked. "Jean, are you in there?" No answer. He opened the door.

Her room was empty.

"Jean," he shouted to the house. "I can't take my shower. Your underwear is in my way."

Jean shouted back from the direction of the kitchen, "I'll be right there."

Returning to the bathroom, Dutch adjusted the mirror door so that he could see better, and began shaving, with a grin.

Jean rushed into the room, wearing only a short, blue silk kimono, and quickly removed her panties and bras. "Sorry, Dutch. I forgot all about them."

"Don't worry about it," he answered, and finished up one side of his face. Then he noticed in the mirror, that Jean was staring at his near-naked body. "What are you looking at?" he asked.

"Is that some kind of tattoo on your arm?"

Dutch turned his shoulder to the mirror. "No, it's just an old scar from a bear clawing."

With her arms full, Jean moved closer and touched his shoulder lightly. "Wow. You'll have to tell me about that," she said. "Does it hurt?"

"No," he answered, then concentrated on shaving his chin. When he looked in the reflection again, Jean was staring directly at him. "*Now* what are you looking at?"

"Ever since I met you, I've wondered how you shaved that hollow in your chin."

Using the very tip of his razor, Dutch carefully scraped his deep cleft. "I usually do this alone," he said, staring back her in the reflection. "I was surprised to see your sexy underwear. You're such a quiet gal."

Her face flushed, and she turned for her bedroom. "*Filles tranquilles sont les filles les plus agréables*," she said, opening the door.

Dutch wiped the soap off and turned to her. "What the hell does that mean?"

She gave him a strange look. "It's French. 'Quiet girls are the most enjoyable girls,'" she translated, and left.

Dutch stared after her. Had she just flirted with him?

Thanksgiving turned out to be the laziest day Dutch could recall in years. The crew had absolutely nothing to do. They played cards, talked and read, cover to cover, two American news magazines that had been published before the President's assassination. During all this time, Dutch found himself strangely fascinated with Jean. He kept sneaking glances at her, making conversation with her and offering to help in the kitchen. *Why?* He thought. *I'm not falling for a woman who packs a pistol in her purse, with two young children at home. Impossible!*

In the afternoon, they enjoyed a semi-traditional Thanksgiving meal of smoked turkey, mashed potatoes, gravy, yams and pineapple spears, along with two bottles of champagne. It was a scrumptious meal; worth every penny Dutch had spent getting the food in-country. But, doing absolutely nothing all day could become boring, as well.

With the sun low in the sky, Dutch told his mates, "I'm going to walk down to the sailboat and get my transistor radio. Maybe, after the sun goes down, we can get some news from home."

Part of his mind hoped that Jean would offer to walk with him, but that didn't happen, and Dutch couldn't decide whether he was disappointed or relieved.

For the next four weeks, the crew worked each day on the submarine. The guys helped Luke paint the hull and deck plates with one coat of a reddish marine undercoating and two finished color coats of blue-gray. While they worked on the exterior, the ladies scraped mold off of the interior bulkheads, and painted the compartments off-white. As they painted, the brothers, John and Matthew, completed the rebuild of the two diesel engines. It was a big job, but rewarding work.

On the weekends, the crew explored the area. They sailed to all four of the major islands in the group, and dove in numerous crystal-clear inlets and bays. Jean learned how to snorkel, and then to dive. She quickly fell in love with the undersea world.

The fishing proved to be outstanding, and each Monday morning they would share their weekend catch with the Chandler family. The Marquesas Islands or, as the natives called them, the Mysterious Islands, were indeed the pearls of paradise.

On a bright, warm Christmas Day, the crew walked to the village. The Chandler family home stood just outside of town, on a flat parcel of land. It was a typical, wood-frame island bungalow, with a metal roof, and striking views of the harbor and mountains.

Helen greeted them at the front door. "Mele Kalikimaka," she said with a friendly smile. "Would you like to see our home?"

The house had four bedrooms and two baths, with thin bamboo walls, and woven rugs on the wood floors. It was neat, clean and well-appointed with nautical artifacts.

"Lyle and the boys are out back, roasting a pig," she said when they finished the tour in the kitchen. "We'll eat in an hour or so."

"Can we help?" Jean asked.

"Yes, you can help me cut up some fruit," she answered. "You boys help yourselves to some punch in the icebox and go outside with the others."

Dutch and Doug poured themselves some juice into coconut shells, and moved outside to watch the pig roast. They found the brothers and father sitting in lawn chairs next to a burning fire pit. "Where's the pig?" Doug asked.

Matthew pointed to the pit. "Under the coals, cooking."

Lyle got up from his chair and greeted the mates. "Good, you've got yourself some punch. Now let's step around the corner of the house. I have something to show you."

The mates followed him to the side yard. "See this green plastic cistern?" Lyle asked, with a funny look on his face. "It catches all of our rain water and stores it in this large tank. We use the water for our baths and showers. It's a nice, cool place to store the water." He bent down and removed the top lid. "If you take the top off, you'll find a small rope inside. Pull it up, and at the other end of the rope you'll find an earthen jug of Pineapple Vodka." He uncorked the crock and poured a hefty amount into the mate's coconut shells. "Help yourself while you here. Needless to say, Helen doesn't know anything about this."

Dutch took a sip. "Wow, this stuff is white lighting. Where do you get it?"

Lyle chuckled. "The boys and I distill it at the shop. That's how we make extra money."

Doug took a drink and licked his lips. "Good hooch. Sure makes the punch taste better."

That started their wonderful luau with the family. Soon, the backyard was filled with jovial friends and neighbors. At one point during the day, Dutch counted over forty guests, most of whom were natives. It was a gala time, with island music, songs, and people of all ages dancing in colorful grass outfits. The food was endless: roasted pig, fresh fish, rice, squid, chicken, sweet potatoes, tropical fruits, and Hawaiian sweet bread. It was a spread not soon forgotten by the crew or the villagers.

During the festivities, that afternoon, all three of the brothers approached Dutch individually and volunteered to crew for the voyage back to the States. Dutch told them all about the deal he had made with the Germans, and offered them the same five-hundred-dollar bonus and airfare home. The brothers seemed excited about the prospect of sailing a U-boat to America, but he also told them that it would be up to their father whether they went or stayed.

Late that evening, in the twilight of the setting sun, the crew walked back to their bungalow. As they walked along, Dutch was quiet.

"Why the long face? Didn't you have a good time?" Doug finally asked him.

Shaking his head, Dutch answered, "Very good, although, the locals asked too many questions about our submarine. I didn't like that."

"That's only normal," Jean answered. "The island has never seen a boat like yours before."

"This time next month, we'll be on our way home," Heidi added.

Dutch lit a cigarette. "I sure hope you're right."

On Friday, when they returned to work at the boatyard, Dutch found Mr. Chandler in the sub's wardroom, drinking coffee and going over paperwork. Dutch thanked him for the luau, then handed him a typed list of nine items that needed to be finished while the crew was gone to Henderson Island.

"My punch list is fairly simple," Dutch said, pouring some coffee.

Lyle looked over the list. "Don't see any problems here." Then he looked up. "I understand you offered my boys five hundred dollars each, and airfare home, to crew this boat to the States. That's a lot of money, Dutch."

"They volunteered first. Then I told them about the deal I made with the Germans, and offered them the same. What do you think?"

"It's more money than they make in a year," Lyle answered. "But I'm not sure I want all three of my boys put at risk in this submarine. I'm still thinking about it."

"I understand," Dutch replied. "By the way, do you have any dynamite here in the shop?"

Lyle's expression turned curious. "Why?"

"There's a cave on Henderson Island I want to close up. It's a tomb of dead German sailors. Doing that will require a couple of sticks of dynamite."

Lyle got up from the table, flipped on the intercom, and called Matthew to the wardroom.

Moments later, when Matthew stepped inside the compartment, his father asked, "Do you remember that reef we dynamited a few years ago? The shoal where the big yacht went a ground?"

"Yes, I remember the job," Matthew answered.

"Do we have any of that dynamite still in the shop?"

"Sure. There are half a dozen sticks still in the box. Why?"

"Dutch needs a couple of sticks to blow up a cave on Henderson Island."

Matthew turned to Dutch. "You're a powder monkey?"

"No," Dutch answered, shaking his head. "I've never used the stuff."

Matthew frowned. "Bad idea, Dutch. You need somebody like me for that job. I've been working around explosives all my life." He put his fingers together. "It's all about how you plant your charges and how you detonate the dynamite. It's dangerous work."

Dutch looked at Lyle. "It needs to be done. Once it gets out where we found this submarine, that island is going to be crawling with treasure hunters."

Mr. Chandler poured himself some more coffee. "We can spare Matthew for the next few weeks. You take him with you. It will cost a few dollars extra, but it's the safest thing to do."

"Is that okay with you, Matthew?" Dutch asked.

"Yes," he said quickly, with a smile. "When do we leave?"

"Monday morning. By the time we return, the sub should be ready to sail home."

That evening at the bungalow, Dutch told his mates the *why* of Matthew joining them on the voyage to Henderson Island. They weren't overjoyed with the news.

"Where is he going sleep?" Jean asked.

"There's an extra berth in your cabin," Dutch replied.

Jean shook her head with a scowl. "I don't think so. Having a twenty-two-year-old sleep in that small cabin with me is bad idea, way too many male hormones."

"I didn't think about that," Dutch replied, scratching his head. "How about if he sleeps on the main cabin settee?"

Doug chuckled. "We don't have a lee cloth for that couch. He'll be rolling out of bed all night. Why don't you and Jean 'hot bunk' it while we're underway. Then Matthew can sleep on the settee when we're at anchor."

Jean looked confused. "Explain 'hot bunking' to me."

The guys smiled at her and did just that.

Monday morning, December 30th, they sailed for Henderson Island. Dutch motored the boat out of the Hiva Oa harbor. Then he and Doug set the sails. The weather was warm, the wind brisk, and the boat heeled over as they turned southeast.

Late that night, with the sky full of stars and a crescent moon in their wake, Jean joined Dutch in the cockpit with her evening tea in hand.

"Did you and Matthew get moved in?" Dutch asked from the wheel.

"Yes," she answered. "Thanks for making room for me in your cabin. I still feel a little funny about this arrangement."

"Don't worry about it. Hot bunking has been done at sea, for thousands of years."

She took a sip of her brew. "You've got a lot books in your headboard. Have you read them all?"

"Yes, so please feel free to borrow any you like. I call it my little sailboat lending library."

From the cushions, Jean looked up at him. "Here's what I don't understand. This is supposed to be the Twentieth Century, where everything is moving fast – everything except sailing. It moves so slowly. Why do men still sail?"

Dutch lit a cigarette with his back to the wind, and replied, "As long as man remains a curious animal, he'll take to the sea and search for himself. That's the way God intended it."

Jean stood. "Good answer. I guess you're right. It's just a silly tradition. Well, I'm off to bed. Can I get you anything?"

"My rain slicker, please," Dutch answered.

Jean looked up into the starlit night. "There's not a cloud in the sky, Dutch," she answered.

He smiled at her. "The squalls will be here in an hour or so."

She moved to the cabin hatch. "How do you know that?"

"Simple – the clouds at sunset and the barometer in the nook."

She climbed down a few steps, then turned back to him. "You're a good skipper, Dutch. I'll get your jacket."

New Year's Eve came and went without much fanfare on the sailboat. The only thing Dutch noticed from the helm that night, was a few distant flares in the night sky, shot from ships well over the horizon. Those silent bright flashes were a reminder to him of the tragic death of Present Kennedy, and he hoped for better days in 1964.

On the evening of January third, Mr. Chandler radioed the sailboat to inform them that Wolfgang Zimmerman and his three German comrades had arrived on Hiva Oa. They had moved into the rented bungalow, and Lyle planned to put them to work on the submarine the next day. "They were like children when they toured your boat," he told Dutch. "They all spoke English and seemed excited about what they called a 'wonder weapon.' Sure hope you can trust these fellas." Dutch reassured him, and thanked him for the information.

Late in the afternoon on January eight, the *Laura* dropped anchor in Frigate Cove. The winds had been contrary during some of the passage, and the boat arrived two days late. Jean had been on the radio with the Israeli freighter, they were only a day and half ahead of its arrival.

The next day, Dutch and Doug hauled the camera gear to Henderson Island and filmed what they had found only a few months before. That tragic part of the German crew's story needed to be told.

In the afternoon, they took Matthew with them and removed the empty fuel barrels that blocked the secondary cave's entrance. Then they went to work inside the cave, with more filming of the tomb and the chamber of gold. Matthew was speechless at what he saw, and asked many questions about the gold and the graves. Dutch answered him as vaguely as he could.

That evening, on the sailboat, Dutch talked to his crew. "Tomorrow, Jean and I will witness the transfer from inside the cavern. I'll use the hand-held camera to document the removal. Doug, I want you and the big camera setup on the bow, to do the same while the exchange is happening."

Doug and Heidi listened with frowns on their faces, while Matthew looked confused.

"What are we talking about?" he finally asked.

Doug shook his head and drained his glass of Yukon Jack. "In all his wisdom, Dutch is giving the twelve tons of gold to the Israelis. It makes no sense, but that's what's happening."

"We've been over this before," Jean answered firmly. "Everyone has voted."

"Yes, we have," Doug replied, pouring another whiskey. "But now it's reality."

"We're keeping one gold bar, all the jewels, the story of our discovery, and the submarine," Dutch answered, glaring at his mate. "In a few months, we'll be swimming the high tide of good fortune. Let's thank our lucky stars."

On the morning of January tenth, the Israeli freighter *Goliath* dropped anchor in Frigate Cove. The exchange went flawlessly. The ship sent three motor launches to the sea cavern, with seamen and officers who loaded the boats, under the supervision of Jean and Dutch, with the heavy crates of gold. Each skiff made three trips from the cavern to the freighter, where the cargo was stacked on the deck and opened for inventory. To the very last crate, Dutch added the pouch of gold teeth and crowns. "This belongs to the Israeli people, as well," he told the Captain. After the final count, paperwork was signed and the Captain gave Dutch a receipt for

596 gold bars, each weighing approximately 40 pounds, as well as for the eight-pound pouch of 'other gold assets.'

The Skipper of the *Goliath* and his crew couldn't have been more friendly and professional with Dutch and Jean. When they left the freighter late in the afternoon, the Captain handed them a canvas bag filled with Israeli goodies, including cheeses, dried fruits, crackers, nuts and two bottles of their national drink, Aviv Vodka.

As they rowed back to the sailboat, with the ship weighing anchor, Jean commented, "Your treasure will boost our gold reserves, strengthen our currency, and promote better International trade. Thanks for trusting us, Dutch."

"Never had much use for that tainted Nazi gold," he answered, frowning at the ship while he rowed. "As the old saying goes, with God's word as my map and His Spirit as my compass, I'm sure to stay on course."

Jean's hazel eyes twinkled. "I wish more people felt like that."

The next morning, Doug set up the film camera on the sailboat bow, while Dutch and Matthew rowed over to the sea cavern with the half-box of dynamite they had brought from the shop. Using a flashlight, the young lad searched the granite walls of the cave for cracks and faults. After selecting where he wanted the charges set, he used a hammer and chisel to deepen the stone holes. When he finished, he put four sticks of dynamite on the inside of the cave and two sticks on the cavern side of the opening.

"You're sure we need that much dynamite?" Dutch asked, watching him work.

"Yep," he answered, placing firing caps inside each stick of the explosives.

When he finished, he ran fuses from the four inside sticks to the two sticks on the cavern side. Then he ran a long fuse from the cave entrance to the stone wharf. "We'll light the fuse from the dinghy. We'll have about five minutes to make it out of the cavern."

While Matthew double-checked all of the connections, Dutch rowed back out to the chamber's jaws and shouted to Doug to standby. "When you see us again, wait a minute and then roll the camera."

Returning inside the sea cave, he rowed to the stone wharf and waited. He watched as the lad rolled three empty fuel barrels under the long fuse, to keep it off the damp stones.

When Matthew finished, he turned and looked at the cave entrance. "This will work." Getting onto the dinghy, with the end of the long fuse in his hand, he said, "When I say 'go,' row like the wind. This fuse is old. If it's dried out, it will burn fast."

"That's nice to know," Dutch answered sarcastically, oars in hand.

Matthew lit the fuse and watched it burn for a few seconds. "Alright, go," he said, with excitement on his face.

Dutch hadn't realized he could row so fast. The boat was out of the jaws of the sea cave in less than three minutes, and on its way toward the sailboat in five. Then they heard one muffled explosion, and Dutch stopped rowing. They heard a second, louder blast, and then nothing. Dutch started rowing hard again. Seconds ticked away, and then an ear-splitting explosion rolled across the water like thunder. Smoke, soot and dust filled the air above the sea cave, and the cove shook as the entire sea cavern slowly collapsed in upon itself. The implosion sent boulders crashing into the water, causing huge waves to roll across the cove. The resulting surf almost swamped the dinghy.

As the waves subsided, with part of the mountain now in the sea, Doug yelled from the sailboat, "Wow, that was great!"

On the still-pitching dinghy, Dutch watched the cloud of dust hanging over the rock rubble in the cove, then turned to the lad. "Think you used enough dynamite, Matt?"

Last Voyage

When the sailboat arrived on Hiva Oa, they found Luke waiting on the company dock and the U-3521 back in the water, with the camouflage mesh reinstalled. The passage from Henderson Island had been a grueling affair, with contrary winds and two powerful storms hindering them and delaying their arrival by several days. As Luke secured the lines, Dutch stood in the cockpit, which was awash in warm, bright sunshine.

"Nice to see you," he said to the lad. "Those storms were hellish. We're pleased to be in calm waters again."

"The first storm missed us, but we got some heavy rain out of the last one," Luke answered, securing the aft line. "Your German crew is working inside the boat. They sure know their stuff when it comes to submarines."

Dutch stepped off the sailboat. "Let's go see what they've accomplished."

Aboard the submarine, Dutch found Lyle Chandler and Captain Zimmerman in the freshly painted wardroom, with German manuals spread out on the table. The tiny compartment had two small black fans swirling to keep the stale air moving.

Both men seemed pleased to see his return. Wolfgang looked just like Dutch remembered him, tall and slight, with a booming voice.

"What do you think of our boat?" Dutch asked him.

Zimmerman smiled with a faraway look. "Good old-fashion German engineering. If we'd had weapons like this in '43, we would have won the Battle of the Atlantic."

"Have you taken her out for sea-trials yet?"

"Yes, twice," the Captain replied. "Yesterday, we even submerged the boat to decks-awash. She's quick to helm, and her speed is phenomenal. It should be a fast passage home."

Lyle handed Dutch a slip of paper. "Your fuel and food will be here tomorrow. Here's a list of what's been repaired or replaced while you were gone."

Dutch read the list, and saw that everything looked completed, "What about the new radio and depth sounder? Have they been installed?"

"Yes," Lyle answered. "The Germans have also got the snorkel repaired, and the problems with the ventilation system fixed. They've been a big help."

"Good. Let's go meet the rest of your crew," Dutch said to Wolfgang.

As they were about to leave the compartment, Luke broke his silence. "Father, are my brothers and I crewing with the boat to the States?"

Lyle looked at his son as he got up from the table. "You and Matthew can go along. Matt knows the diesel engines, and you're good at the helm. John will stay behind and help me around the yard."

"How many will that make?" the Captain asked.

"Eight," Dutch answered.

"That's a real skeleton crew," Wolfgang replied wryly.

"The passage should take two weeks. I figured we'd need a crew of ten, three on, six off, with Jean as the cook. So we'll need a couple more sailors," Dutch answered.

The Skipper frowned. "A woman aboard is bad luck."

"Not up for discussion, Captain. She's coming aboard as our cook," Dutch replied firmly.

"No problem," Luke added with excitement. "Sam and Adam Lani would love to come along. They've never been to the States before."

"Who are they again?" Dutch asked.

"The guards we hired to watch over the shop," Luke answered.

"Sure. Why not? These local boys are big and burly," Dutch replied.

In the crew mess, Dutch met the rest of the Germans. He liked two of them right away. John Hahn had been the Chief of the Boat on Zimmerman's last command. He was pudgy, with a friendly moon-face and a firm hand grip. Torpedo Chief Carl Huffman was much like him, except for his fireplug size and huge arms. Then there was Samuel Beck, Wolfgang's last Executive Officer. He seemed cold, with short-cropped blonde hair, shifty blue eyes, and a small red birth mark on his right cheek. His handshake was like a noodle, and he avoided direct eye contact with anyone he spoke to. Dutch was less than impressed with Mr. Beck.

"What are you guys working on now?" he asked.

Chief Hahn gestured to a manual on the table. "I'm trying to get the old radar and sonar systems to work again."

"I'm just finishing up in the torpedo room," Chief Huffman added. "I've got most of the mechanisms operational."

"And I'm checking intake and exhaust valves for the ballast tanks," Samuel answered.

Dutch grinned at the Germans. "Good. Just remember, we're not embarking on a battle mission, just a simple passage to the States. Get packed up and moved aboard. We'll shove off in a couple of days."

That afternoon, back on the sailboat, Dutch told his crew about his plans to shove off. "The submarine will have a crew of ten, while the sailboat will just have you and Heidi," he told Doug. "Should I recruit more help?"

"Maybe you should," Doug answered. "It'll take us over a month to make it home."

Jean frowned at the mates. "That's not going be necessary."

"Why?" Doug asked.

Jean smiled mysteriously. "Let's just say other arrangements have been made. Tomorrow afternoon, two new crew members will arrive here from Papeete."

"What the hell is going on?" Dutch demanded. "I know nothing about two new crew members."

Jean looked at him. "Uncle Harry just confirmed the arrangements to me late last night, when we were still at sea. Here's the plan…"

The next day was consumed with taking on fuel, water and food provisions for both boats. As all of that activity unfolded on the company dock, Dutch noticed many curious locals watching from the wharf, some of whom had cameras in their hands. He didn't like the audience, but what could he do?

That afternoon, Dutch and Jean secretly moved all of their personal belongings from the sailboat to the submarine. Dutch moved into the Captain's cabin, while Jean took the XO's quarters, just across the companionway. The Germans took the other four officer's compartments, while Luke, Matthew and their two friends found crew quarters close to the galley. As this was happening, Luke drove to airport and picked up the new crew members. It was Uncle Harry's plan to send them two sailboat replacements for Dutch and Jean. "The *Laura* arrived on the Island with a crew of four," he had told Jean on the radio. "And it will depart with the same."

Late in the afternoon, when Luke returned from the airport, he helped the new crew to the sailboat and made the introductions with Doug and Heidi. Both were startled and stunned at who stood before them.

Doug chuckled. "Dutch and Jean have got to see this! Let's take them to the submarine and introduce them to the Skipper."

They all walked to the sub and went aboard. As they moved down into the bowels of the boat, Doug heard Dutch's voice coming from the wardroom. Stopping outside the entrance, he told the new crew members to wait in the passageway. Moving inside the compartment, he found Dutch and Jean going over paperwork.

Dutch looked up from the table. "Do you need something, pal?"

Doug smiled at his mate, "Thought you might like to meet our new crew members. Can I bring them through?"

"Sure," Dutch replied.

Doug went to the companionway and waved in the couple. When they entered the cabin, Dutch and Jean's jaws dropped, and their eyes bulged. Standing before them were a man and woman who were absolute look-a-likes of Dutch and Jean. It was as if they were looking into a mirror. The man wore a straw hat that covered a face that Dutch would know anywhere. His facial features were perfect, right down to a deep cleft in his chin. And his body type, age and dress were also identical. The lady was the same for Jean, slender and attractive, with a duplicate body figure and similar facial features, including her piercing hazel eyes.

Dutch found it spooky as hell to be staring at himself! "Where did you guys come from?" he finally asked.

The man answered, "Central Casting. We're both actors. We were hired by a guy out of San Diego. He sent us here. Is this right?"

Jean chuckled. "Uncle Harry. He loves everything theatrical."

"Yes, you're at the right place," Dutch answered the man. "How did you get our look so spot-on?"

The man reached inside his coat pocket and brought out a folded black and white picture. Handing it to Dutch, he said, "This is what we had to work with. We're both makeup artists, as well."

Dutch looked at the picture; it showed him standing with Jean outside of his New York hotel. He handed it to Jean. "You guys are the perfect diversion. Doug, take them to town tonight for dinner, and spread the word that the boat is sailing back to Papeete for more parts. That will keep any press off balance until we leave tomorrow night."

"I'll join you," Luke inserted. "I know everyone in the village, so I can help get the word out."

“But can either of you sail?” Doug asked.

The man nodded proudly. “Yes for me. I own a small sailboat.”

The lady frowned. “No for me, but I’m a quick learner. Can we see your submarine? I’ve never been on one before. ”

Dutch asked Luke and Jean to show the newcomers around the boat, while he Doug and Heidi said farewell. Moving to the sidebar, Dutch poured three whiskeys and handed two of them to his mates. “Those doppelgangers are a hoot. I hope they are as much help to you at sea.”

“They’ll do fine,” Doug answered, taking his drink. “Tomorrow I’ll turn southwest, as if we’re sailing back to Tahiti, and then circle around the northern Marquesas Islands. I figure it will take me four weeks to make it to Long Beach. Is that where you want us to stay?”

Dutch sipped at his drink. “Yes, get us a slip at Alamitos Bay Marina. I’ll join you when I can.” Reaching into his pocket, he gave Doug three hundred dollars. “This should hold you over until I see you next.” Dutch’s gaze honed in on his comrades. “But above all else, my friends, have a safe trip home. Heidi, I’ll miss your haircuts. You can give me a trim, the next time we meet.”

The friends hugged each other, with tears in their eyes.

Late that night, Dutch climbed the sail tower for one last cigarette. As he stood alone on the bridge, he heard the yard’s jeep return from the village. There was laughter and giggling as the crew stumbled down the ramp for the sailboat. As he watched from his dark distance, they went aboard the *Laura,* still chuckling. Then there was quiet again, with only the gurgling of the harbor. Dutch had a knot in his stomach as he gazed upon his beloved sailboat. She had come so far, with so few. Now for her final passage home.

Late the next morning, Dutch and Jean kept out of sight on the submarine as the sailboat departed. From the cover of the camouflage mesh, they watched some of the locals taking pictures from the wharf. It was a beautiful, clear day, and Dutch felt confident that the ruse had worked.

By late that afternoon, all the submarine crew had come aboard and were busy making final preparations for getting underway. As these activities were happening, Dutch and

Wolfgang worked in the wardroom, making out a duty roster for the voyage. Each standing watch would have three crew members. The watch commanders would be Dutch, Wolfgang, and Mr. Beck. The helmsmen would be Luke, Chief John Hahn and Chief Carl Huffman. The three floaters, or deckhands, would be Matthew and the Lani brothers. Action stations were assigned for all the crew, and emergency procedures spelled out. The timetable concluded with some simple passage rules about smoking, drinking, and avoiding lewd language in front of Jean. The roster came together surprisingly well, and Dutch was guardedly pleased.

That evening, Dutch helped Jean cook and serve her first meal for the crew. It was a simple but tasty menu of German bratwurst, sauerkraut, potato salad and French bread with Hinano beer. It was consumed by the men in good spirits and with hungry appetites. Jean seemed pleased with her first meal, as she had dreaded cooking in the boat's all-electric galley.

After dinner, Dutch passed out the duty roster, he and Wolfgang went over it in detail. The crew digested the information, with few questions and no grumbling.

"Any other news?" Wolfgang asked as he passed out flashlights.

"Yes, my Captain," Chief Hahn answered. "Today, I got our radar system partially working. It only works on the low settings, which is just a twenty five mile range, not the fifty miles I was hoping for."

Wolfgang smiled at his old Chief. "Good work, John. It's better than sailing blind. Now let's all go topside and remove the camouflage netting. We'll be underway within the hour."

As Dutch stood on the dark dock, watching the crew remove the mesh by flashlight, Lyle Chandler and his wife Helen approached him.

"Here's that receipt I promised you, Dutch," Lyle said, handing him a slip of paper. "Thanks for settling up with us today. Once the news of your submarine gets out, I have a feeling we're going to get very busy, so get our boys back to us as fast as you can."

"No more than a couple of weeks," Dutch replied, shaking his hand. "I hope the publicity rewards your business for years to come."

Helen hugged Dutch, just as the submarine's motors came alive. "Send my boys back safely to me," she whispered in his ear.

He assured her, with a kiss on her cheek.

At 2130 hours, under the cover of darkness, and with no running lights, the U-3521 slipped out of Hiva Oa, slowly heading due south. Two hours later, the boat turned north-northeast, heading for open waters, and increased its speed to 15 knots. It was four thousand miles to American waters, and another twelve hundred miles to the Columbia River. Dutch's plans and dreams were coming true.

As usual, life aboard the boat soon took on a routine. Dutch had the midnight watch again, with Mr. Beck relieving him at 0800, while Wolfgang stood the swing watch. Mechanically, the submarine purred along, with only some occasional tweaking. There were a few minor leaks and some sea seepage between a few of the watertight hull compartments, but Chief Hahn soon had the problems under control.

While the submarine had been in for repairs, the Chandler brothers had uncovered many tidbits of memorabilia, hidden deep inside the bowels of the boat. All these treasures had belonged to the original German crew, and were placed in a wooden crate for safe keeping. The items included old snapshots, letters from home, crew art, Navy medals, German paperback novels, and numerous other souvenirs. The current crew loved the contents of the box, and spent many off-duty hours in the mess hall, going through the keepsakes and talking about home. Others of the crew played cards, read, and wrote letters. Some even jogged up and down the boat. They all seemed content with the food, the voyage, and each other.

At the beginning of Dutch's second midnight watch, Jean called up to him, asking permission to join him on the bridge. After she climbed up the tube rungs, he helped her through the deck hatch. "Watch your step. It's cramped quarters up here," he told her.

With no running lights on, the bridge was as dark as a coal pit. The only illumination came from one small lamp burning under the bridge cowling, and the glow from the instrument panel. She moved to the other side of Dutch as her eyes adjusted. "It's as small as a doll house up here. Why is it so dark?" she asked, looking up at the sky.

Dutch lit a cigarette, with his back to the wind. "It's a cloudy, moonless night. What brings you up here for your first visit?"

"Have you seen anyone using the new radio?" she asked.

"Not that I've noticed. Why?"

"Late last night, I used the radio to contact San Diego. When I turned the set on, the frequency was dialed in on Channel Ten, and I changed it to Twenty-Eight and made my call. After I signed off, I changed the frequency to channel Twenty-Two. Tonight, when I turned it on, it was set on Channel Ten again. That seemed odd to me. Who else would be using the radio?"

Dutch chuckled. "So you're the person who always changed the sailboat's radio to Twenty-Two. I wondered about that. Why do you do it?"

"It's just a habit. I like to know who is using the radio."

Dutch smiled at her in dark. "Secret agent stuff, huh?"

She grinned. "Maybe."

"I'll keep an eye out," Dutch replied. "How did you like our doppelgangers? I thought they were a little spooky."

Jean moved back to the glow of the open deck hatch. "The world doesn't need two of me. One is enough. I'm going to bed."

Dutch helped her step down to the tube ladder. "Thanks for the visit. Come back anytime. But if the French are right about shy girls being the best girls, then there would be twice as much of you to enjoy."

Jean smirked at him in the dim light, and shook her head. "Goodnight, Dutch."

After being relieved of his watch on the sixth morning out, Dutch found Luke in the control room, studying the chart on the navigation table.

"Looks like we're in the middle of nowhere out here," he said with a hopeful smile. "Can I test-fire my anti-aircraft rifles today?"

Dutch considered the question. The anti-aircraft guns on the Type XXI submarine were located inside two amour-plated gun turrets, forward and astern of the sail bridge. Each battery had a small compartment for a single gunner, as well as two twin 20 mm automatic rifles. The only accesses to the turrets were from small amour-plated hatch doors located under the cowling, fore and aft, of the conning tower bridge.

Looking over Luke's shoulder, he saw that it was all open water. "I don't see why not. But take it up with Wolfgang first. He'd be the best to have on the bridge when you test your guns. And alert the boat before you fire them off."

Luke's face lit up. "Okay, I'll talk to him when he gets up."

Dutch nodded at the lad and shuffled off for breakfast and bed.

Wolfgang had agreed to allow Luke to test fire his guns and so, that afternoon, not long after the Captain started his watch, Luke eagerly joined him in the sail bridge.

"I'll test the aft turret first," he explained, crouching down below the bridge cowling and creeping towards the amour-plated hatch door. Then he stopped. "Son of a bitch," he mumbled to himself as he opened the access door and crawled inside the tiny compartment.

He remained inside for only a few minutes. When he crept out to the bridge again, he wore an angry expression, and he said nothing. Crouching under the forward bridge cowling, he visually checked the forward hatch, and shook his head. Then he turned to exit the tower. "I've got to talk to Dutch. I'll be back later," he said abruptly, and left Captain Zimmerman standing there, looking startled and confused.

Luke found Dutch in the wardroom, having his morning coffee. When he walked into the room, he pulled the green curtain closed.

"Thought you were test-firing your rifles today," Dutch said to him.

With a stern, angry look, Luke reached into his pants pocket and drew out a small slip of cardboard and two short lengths of hemp cord. Placing them on the table, he announced, "We have a saboteur aboard."

Dutch looked at him, then at the items. "I don't understand. What's this stuff all about?"

"Back home, when I reinstalled the guns, I checked and doubled-checked them. Everything was ready for testing. This afternoon, I found out that somebody had been inside the turrets, tampering with my guns. Both rifles in the aft battery had these hemp cords stuffed deep inside the barrels. If I *had* fired the rifles, *BOOM*, the entire turret would have exploded, killing me and ripping off the top of the conning tower. Your submarine would be dead in the water right now."

"What the hell," Dutch muttered angrily, lifting the rope cords. "What made you so suspicious?"

Luke picked up the slip of cardboard. "This matchbook cover. After I reinstalled the guns, there was no way to secure the compartments, so I slipped this cardboard between the door and the jamb at the bottom of each hatch cover. If the matchbook was gone when I came back, I'd know someone had been inside the turrets."

"Where did you learn that trick?" Dutch asked, staring up at the lad.

Luke forced a grin. "From Mike Hammer, a character in one of Mickey Spillane's books. He used matchbook covers in doorjambs to alert him if someone was in his hotel room."

"So a piece of cardboard saved your life?"

"Well, that and the hollow sounds the breeches made when I dry fired the guns today. It didn't sound right, so I checked barrels and found the cords. We've got a traitor in our midst, Dutch. What are we going to do?"

"Did you check the forward turret?" Dutch asked, his mind reeling.

"No, but I saw that the cardboard was gone."

"Well, there's one thing for sure. If Captain Zimmerman allowed you to test fire the guns while he was still on the bridge, he has no part in the plot. Let's go up and show him what you discovered, and check that forward compartment."

Their confab with Wolfgang on the bridge went from bad to worse, as the Captain learned what was happening on the boat right under his nose.

"I'm sure you suspect one of my men," the Captain said as the plot was explained to him.

"I don't know," Dutch answered. "These are just the facts. Only you, I, and Mr. Beck have been on this bridge since leaving Hiva Oa."

"That's true," Wolfgang answered. "But the watch commanders are often relieved to use the head and get some food."

"Yes," Dutch said. "But this tampering took some time. Let's check the other gun battery."

Luke inspected the forward turret and returned to the bridge with more bits of rope and another matchbook cover, confirming their suspicions.

"What now?" Luke asked, holding out the evidence in the late-afternoon sun.

"Whoever is behind this plot would be quite worried if they heard the rifles firing without any problems," Wolfgang said with a scowl. "Let's make them nervous."

"Good idea," Dutch agreed. "How long will it take you to clean and triple-check your rifles again, Luke?"

"Half an hour per turret," Luke answered.

"Let's do it," the Captain said. "It will be dark soon, and we'll put on a lightshow."

As Luke worked in the gun batteries, Dutch and Wolfgang came up with a plan to find and entrap the culprit.

An hour later, just before the test firing, Dutch left the bridge to go below and observe the crew during the test. Soon, the Captain's voice came on the intercom, alerting the boat to the test firing and inviting the crew to come out onto the aft deck to watch. Almost everyone aboard went topside – everyone except Mr. Beck, who Dutch could not find anywhere.

The test-firing was short, loud, and flawless. As the crew returned below, Dutch noticed Mr. Beck exiting the head with a magazine in hand, looking frightened. He made a beeline for his compartment. Dutch followed, but Beck closed and locked his cabin door.

Standing in the companionway, Dutch rapped on his door and shouted, "Mr. Beck, the Captain wants to see you in wardroom now!"

After the third knock, Beck opened his door, red-faced. "Why?"

"Just report to him *now* in the wardroom. It's important," Dutch answered sternly.

As the Exec moved down the passageway, Dutch slipped into his stateroom and used the intercom to tell Wolfgang that Beck was on his way. Then he carefully rifled Beck's cabin, searching it for incriminating evidence. Shortly thereafter, he joined Wolfgang and Mr. Beck in the wardroom.

With Luke in the conning tower to stand the Captain's watch, Wolfgang sat at the wardroom table, drinking coffee, with Mr. Beck standing before him. Walking up to the table, Dutch put down what he had just found – a short length of rope that was the same size, color, and texture as the hemp cord Luke had recovered from the guns. There was also a small, blurry snapshot of a bearded man dressed in prison garb, and a ten-pound bag of table sugar.

The Captain handled the exhibits while glancing at his old Exec with hatred in his eyes.

"Well, Mr. Beck?"

Beck said nothing, his gaze downcast, fixed on the deck plates at his feet.

The Captain rose and approached him, placing one hand on his shoulder. "You tried to kill me today, old friend. Should I do the same to you? Or will you come clean and perhaps live to see another day?"

Beck's eyes filled with tears, and his body quivered. "When I heard those rifles fire, I knew I was doomed. But I had no intention of killing you, my Captain," he said, his voice shaken by sobs. "I was told to disable and disarm the boat before late tonight. Then they would release my brother from an East German prison."

That opened the flood gates. For the next half hour, Mr. Beck spilled his guts. He had been approached, at a German social club in Houston, by a man who told him that his brother, Ralf, was still alive in East Germany. Beck, who hadn't seen or heard from his brother since the end of the war, believed the stranger. He was then told to volunteer with Captain Zimmerman and, on the sixth day of their passage, to be prepared to immobilize the boat in any way he could. Afterwards, his brother would be released from captivity.

Wolfgang listened and shook his head. "That 'long-lost relative' scam had been used by the East Germans for years. I've seen this very picture many times before. More than likely, your brother is long dead," he told his old friend.

Mr. Beck's eyes welled up again, at the Captain's explanation that all of his efforts had been for naught. Wolfgang continued to interrogate him, drawing out all of the details of the plot. When he finished, he asked Dutch whether he had any questions.

"Yes," he answered. "Other than our AA guns, what else have you tampered with on my boat?"

Beck glanced at Dutch and then looked away. "Nothing, tonight, I was going to sabotage your torpedo tubes."

"When is the Argentine warship due here?"

The Exec shook his head. "I have no idea."

Wolfgang moved to the intercom and called all off-duty crew to the mess hall. Turning back to Beck, he said, "I have one last question. Why is Argentina interested in this boat?"

The Exec frowned, wiping his eyes. "I was told there is Nazi gold aboard." He looked from the Captain to Dutch and back again. "What is going to happen to me?"

Wolfgang glanced at Dutch, and then answered Beck. "We'll go tell your story to the crew and see what they have to say."

The meeting with the men was short and loud. Dutch told them about the happenings of the day, while Wolfgang related the details of his interrogation of Mr. Beck. The crew was stunned to hear of his betrayal, and quickly turned their anger at him. At first, the consensus was to throw him overboard. Then their anger grew into more graphic death threats and lewd suggestions. With the group in the mess hall in a lynching mood, Jean stormed out of the galley and begged for the Exec's life. She told the crew her true identity and why she was on the boat. They were bewildered and dismayed to learn that they had an Israeli spy aboard, but she compared Mr. Beck's plight to that of the victims of the Holocaust.

"The Jews were lied to, as well, by their own countrymen. The traitor needs to be interrogated by Mossad," she pleaded. "He's worth more alive than dead. He knows the identities of the US German agents, and that information could save lives."

Her calm, firm words seemed to reawaken a thread of rationality in the crew.

"This is not the time for revenge. It's the time for truth," she concluded.

The crew responded to her wisdom, and soon agreed that the Exec could be restricted to his cabin until other arrangements were made. Mr. Beck sobbed at his deliverance.

Captain Zimmerman asked Dutch openly about the rumors of Nazi gold.

"Check anywhere you like," Dutch answered both the Captain and the crew. "There is no Nazi gold on this boat," he pledged.

Wolfgang nodded at him, and said, "This boat is hereby placed on high alert. We will all work twelve on and twelve off until we are out of danger. We have no idea when the threat will come, or from which direction. Therefore, all eyes on our radar. We'll increase speed to twenty knots and turn northwest for deeper waters. Chief Huffman, load your tubes with four torpedoes. This boat still has a sting."

Late that night, when Dutch reported for his midnight watch, he found the Captain in the dark control room's radar nook.

"Do you see anything yet?" he asked him.

"No. The waiting game will be the worst of it," he answered, hunched over the round, green screen. "I'm going to turn in shortly. Wake me if we get a hit."

Dutch talked with Luke at the helm, and had Matthew replace the Captain in the radar nook. Then he climbed the bridge to start his watch.

All that night, as he nervously scanned the moonless horizon with his binoculars, he had an unsettled feeling of doom. Deep inside, he worried about the outcome of any skirmish with the Argentine warship. Was the submarine worth the lives that such a clash would put at risk?

Just before 0300, Matthew called the bridge on the intercom, his voice startling Dutch. "We've got a hit off our starboard beam. It's just inside our range," the lad said calmly.

Dutch keyed him back. "Wake up Wolfgang."

A few minutes later, Captain Zimmerman climbed up the tube ladder and joined Dutch. "Now the game of hunter and hunted begins. How do you want to handle this, Dutch? It's your boat. Do you want to do the maneuvering?"

Without hesitation, Dutch answered, "No, sir. You're in command, Captain."

"Good," Wolfgang replied. Keying the intercom, he began spouting orders for everyone below. The alarm was sounded, and the entire crew took their battle stations. The boat changed course to due west at flank speed, with Matthew calling out the bogey's position every few minutes.

An hour later, the hunter had closed the distance to way under twenty miles.

"We can't out run him," Wolfgang said, with binoculars to his eyes. "I'm guessing from the size and speed of the target that we've got a destroyer on our ass."

With the night sky still as black as a coal mine, the Captain changed course again to due north.

"What's our speed?" he asked Chief Hahn on the intercom.

"Twenty-four knots," was his answer.

"Send Luke up here to man the guns," Wolfgang keyed. "Secure all the hatches, have the torpedo room standing by, and take the boat down to decks awash."

As the boat slowly submerged, Dutch could hear the creaking and moaning of the deck plates. Moments later, with Luke in the bridge, the sea rushed the length of boat and curled up in white water on the conning tower.

Matthew told the Captain that the bogey had changed course as well, and was within a ten-mile range. Wolfgang sent Luke to the dark aft turret, with instructions to hold fire until ordered. With that old copper taste in his mouth, Dutch heard the lad moving around inside the turret, clearing his weapons and preparing them to fire. *It must be like a tomb in there,* Dutch thought.

Matthew's voice came over the intercom, saying, "Bogey five miles out." At that moment, the southern horizon lit up with three bright flashes like lightning bolts. Seconds later, three tall water plumes erupted, a few hundred yards behind the submarine.

Zimmerman held his binoculars tightly to his eyes. "I can't see the target yet."

Then a rocket shot high above the ship, and a night flare exploded. As the phosphorous light slowly fell back to the sea, Wolfgang got a good look at their pursuer.

"Where did that light come from?" he asked, glaring down the lens of his binoculars.

"Out of nowhere," Dutch replied, with his glasses to his eyes.

The flare dropped into the sea, and the dark gloom returned. Three more flashes exploded and, seconds later, more water plumes erupted, this time closer to the boat. Both men ducked behind the bridge cowling for cover as water drenched the tower.

Standing again, Wolfgang said, “We’ve got a Fletcher-class WWII destroyer with an Argentine flag dogging us. That type of tin can was all over the Atlantic in ’43.”

“Can we out run her?” Dutch asked.

“No. They’ll chase us down with ease.”

From the general direction of the destroyer, a signal light flashed off and on. The pursuer was sending a message.

Using his binoculars, the Captain read the code.

“My Morse is a little rusty,” he said, “but they want us to heave to and be boarded.”

Just then, another night flare lit the sky, just above the destroyer. The destroyer was three miles out and closing fast.

With the bright light on the target, the Captain shouted, “Luke, open fire. Aim for the ship’s bridge.”

The sounds and smells of twin automatic rifles filled the air. Every fifth bullet was a tracer, leaving light streaks of red and yellow glowing in the dark morning sky. Luke adjusted his aim. Seconds later, he found his mark, just as the destroyer turned and steamed, at full speed, directly for the submarine. When the light died out and the target went dark again, Luke ceased firing.

Wolfgang reached for the intercom. “Chief, prepare to dive to periscope depth, and change our course to due east at flank speed.” Then the Captain turned from the intercom and cried, “Luke, get out of your turret now!”

As Luke scurried out of his battery, more five-inch shells screamed across the sky. They erupted close to the boat just as the lad slid down the tube ladder. Dutch followed him down, noticing the first amber light in the morning sky.

Wolfgang was the last man down, screaming “Dive!” while he secured the bridge hatch. Once on the control room deck, he ordered the snorkel activated, and reached for the overhead intercom. “We can safely travel a short distance with the diesel engines and the snorkel, but not long,” he said to the room. Keying the microphone, he continued, “Chief Huffman, flood your torpedo tubes and stand by to open outer doors.”

“We’re at periscope depth, sir,” Chief Hahn told him.

The Captain moved to the periscope and looked at his watch. "Reduce speed to ten knots and come right twenty degrees. The morning sun will soon be on our stern."

The control room held its breath, as they heard a few more shells explode in the water on their port side. Moments later, the Captain raised the periscope and followed it up, his eyes glued to the peephole. Quickly, he swiveled the instrument around, then stopped. "I've got the destroyer. It's a mile off the starboard bow. Come right fifteen degrees. Have Chief Huffman open the outer doors."

As this information was being relayed to the torpedo room, the ocean shook with a loud, dull explosion that rippled through the water like an earthquake. Wolfgang jerked his head back from the periscope lens. "What the hell?" he said. He looked through the peephole again, and then pulled back. "Dutch, take a look and confirm."

Dutch moved to the periscope and put his eyes to the lens. In a heartbeat, he glanced away from the peephole with a smile. "I confirm that the destroyer is on fire and sinking."

Within seconds, the entire submarine knew about the sinking, and everyone aboard breathed a sigh of relief. But how could it be? They hadn't fired a single torpedo.

After the crew in the control room confirmed the scene though the periscope, Wolfgang ordered the boat to the surface. Once topside, all the hatches were opened for ventilation, and everyone aboard went on deck to see for themselves.

Jean joined Wolfgang, Luke and Dutch in the sail bridge, while all the other crew stood on the forward deck, gawking seaward. In the calm amber morning light, the still-smoldering wreckage was over a mile off their bow.

"Maybe one of my bullets started a fire aboard the ship that ignited a powder magazine," Luke said, watching the destroyer's bow slowly sink into the sea.

"No," the Captain replied. "I saw the explosion in my periscope. It was low and on the other side of the ship."

With binoculars in his hands, Dutch added, "We should search for survivors."

Without warning, water boiled off the starboard beam. They all turned in that direction and heard hissing air and gurgling seas.

Then, seemingly out of nowhere, another submarine popped to the surface, a hundred yards off of the U-3521. The boat was pure black and had strange markings on the conning tower.

"What the hell is that?" Wolfgang asked as the submarine came to rest on the water.

Jean turned to him with a grin. "That's the INS Tannin[26], half of the Israeli submarine fleet, and my ride home."

Shouting in Hebrew, the Captain of the Israeli submarine called out across the water to Jean. They called to each other for a few moments, and then she translated. "They jammed the destroyer's sonar. It didn't notice because of their hot pursuit of us, so he got a lucky shot. We are to return to our original course at once and leave the area. The *Tannin* will remain behind and provide whatever assistance they can to any survivors."

"We'll catch up with you," the Captain shouted in English. "Clear this area quickly."

The revelation of the *Tannin*, answered many questions about the night flares and the sinking of the ship. The sub and its sister ship, the INS Rahav[27], had been dispatched from Israel to protect the gold shipment home and to escort the U-3521 safely to American waters. Only later did Dutch find out that three high-ranking members of the Argentine Odessa had been aboard the destroyer, including a person called the Scorpion. All three had died when the ship went down.

Betrayal

Four mornings later, the submarine was safely inside American waters on the southern approaches of the West Coast. It was only then, that the two submarines made radio contact. Arrangements were made for transferring Mr. Beck and Jean to the *Tannin*.

A few hours later, the Israeli submarine surfaced, just a few hundred yards off the U-3521. Both boats reduced speed to five knots and came alongside. Rope lines were established between the two conning towers, and a breeches buoy was rigged.

---

[26] A sea monster in Hebrew mythology

[27] Hebrew for 'rage' in medieval Jewish folklore

A clearly agitated Mr. Beck was the first to be strapped into the seat. With his hands bound, he cursed everyone aboard the sub for sending him to Israel. Once the breeches buoy was swaying above the rushing white waters between the two boats, his anger quickly turned to fear. Little did he know that the *Tannin*'s next port of call was San Diego, where he would be interrogated by Uncle Harry, and then, more than likely, released to return home to Houston.

In the warm morning sun, Jean was next in the buoy. Dressed in street clothes, with her red felt hat on, she turned to Dutch and said, "I made fifty sandwiches. They're in the cooler. That should keep the boat going for a few days."

Dutch smiled at her. "You're a real trooper. Stay safe."

She motioned for him to come closer. "You're a bright light in a dark sea of humanity. Kiss me goodbye, and then come see me in Israel. I'll show you why shy girls are more fun."

With both crews watching, he lifted the brim of her hat and gave her a quick kiss. She pulled him back for another, more passionate embrace. Then, with the men yelling and whistling, the breeches buoy started slowly moving across the water.

Dutch, amazed by her boldness, called after her, "I'll come and see you when I can. But I'll have to bone up on my art history first."

She waved at him one final time, and shouted back, "I told you, Israel is a much better friend than enemy." Then she landed safely aboard the *Tannin*.

A few minutes later, the two submarines parted and went their separate ways. Dutch watched sadly from the bridge, as the Israeli boat turned for San Diego. He was tempted to plan a trip to Israel to see Jean, but in three days he'd be on the Columbia River. When would he find the time?

As the U-3521 headed north up the coast, Dutch raised an American flag that he had brought aboard from the sailboat. Thank God, the boat was finally safe.

Early that afternoon, Dutch and Wolfgang met Luke and Chief Huffman in the wardroom, where they told them to disarm all the weapons aboard. The firing pins of all the automatic rifles were to be removed and saved, while all the detonators on the torpedoes were to be removed and thrown overboard. It was illegal for private parties to have such devices in American waters.

That afternoon, Dutch turned his attention to using the ship-to-shore radio services, and started making phone calls. His first call went to Colonel Ford at NBC. Dutch told him their current location and the ETA of their arrival on the Columbia River.

"Let's lift the news embargo at noon on Saturday, February the eighth. By then, the submarine should be tied up at the docks of the Warrenton Boat Works," he said on the phone.

The Colonel answered with a stern warning about dealing with the press. "You're about to swim with piranhas who will eat you alive if they can. Most of the news crews are as cut-throat as Jack the Ripper, so answer their questions truthfully but with short, simple responses. Never embellish or volunteer anything, and for god-sakes don't trust any of them," he cautioned. Later that evening, Dutch shared the Colonel's warning with his crew.

He also told Dutch that he had talked with two publishers in New York City concerning a book about the discovery in the South Pacific of tainted Nazi gold. Both publishers were very interested, and had compared the project to that of the Kon-Tiki expedition. "We'll need to get the documentary script done first, and then the book manuscript. I know a good ghostwriter who can help you with both," he told Dutch.

They made plans for meeting in Burbank in a few weeks, and then signed off. Dutch liked everything that he had heard, except the part about a ghostwriter. He was determined to write the story of the U-3521 in his own words.

His next phone call was to Ralph Higgins, the owner of Warrenton Boat Works. He explained to him, in very general terms, that he was returning to the Columbia River with a large boat that needed some attention. He described his docking needs and told him that news media would be coming to greet the boat.

"This should be great for your business," Dutch told him. "Please ask Rolf and Alice Klep of the Maritime Museum to join us as well. The boat I'm bringing has a lot of history to it. We should be at your dock late on Saturday morning."

Ralph warned him that the weather had been miserable and Bar conditions sloppy. He offered to send a River Pilot out to the boat before it crossed the Bar. Dutch thanked him but declined, and asked him instead to make reservations at the Hotel Elliott for his crew.

As they finished, Dutch said to Ralph, "You might want to alert your local newspaper of our arrival. And tell your Mayor that the sleepy little fishing village of Astoria is about to become the center of world news. See you on Saturday."

Dutch's last phone call was to Skip and Louise in Alaska. He told them part of his story, keeping the details vague, and invited them down to Astoria to witness an event he called 'as historic as the Kon-Tiki expedition.' They agreed to fly down.

That evening, with the sun low in the western sky, two small, high-winged planes flew over the submarine. Both held cameramen, who filmed the boat underway. Dutch watched them for a few minutes, knowing full well that media coverage had started.

On Saturday morning, February the eighth, in between rain squalls, the submarine came into view of the Columbia River Light Ship. This sentinel of the river was flying flags of a small-craft warning, with her fog horn bellowing. Dutch turned the U-3521 due east and approached the Bar in ten foot swells, with a tall line of thirty-foot, steel-gray waves crashing from shore to shore.

With all the deck hatches secured, Wolfgang stood next to Dutch on the bridge. Looking out across the mouth of white water, he yelled over the wind, "This looks like an entrance to Hell."

Dutch yelled back, "The second most treacherous crossing in the world."

He took the seas head-on at ten knots. The decks soon curled with water, while the wind-driven waves were taller than the conning tower. The boat fell into deep troughs, with pounding surf all around, and then rose up on the waves to ride their crest, with a high view of the next line of gauntlets. At times, the bow was totally out of water; at other times, so was the stern. The bridge was drenched by sneaker waves that tried to roll the boat over. But Dutch remained in control, and he had the boat in calm seas after only twenty minutes of a white-knuckle ride across the jaws of the graveyard of the Pacific. Once on the inside estuary, the skies brightened with a few patches of blue, Dutch noticed other boats and a Coast Guard Cutter watching their arrival.

Wolfgang turned and looked back at the boiling sea. "Impressive seamanship. What is the world's worst crossing?"

Dutch smiled at him. "The Amazon River."

Under clearing skies, just before noon, Dutch maneuvered the submarine next to the company dock in Warrenton, Oregon. It was the same mooring where he had started his odyssey, ten months before. The wharf and docks were crowded with gawking people as Luke and Matthew threw out lines to Ralph Higgins and two of his employees, who helped secure the boat to the floating dock and then moved a raised boarding platform next to it.

Dutch scurried down the outside tower ladder and went to the forward deck where, dressed in his Yap hat, a loud Hawaiian shirt, and khaki shorts, he motioned for the stunned crowd to gather. As they did so, he counted half a dozen reporters and two film crews moving towards him. He had thought there would be more. Then he noticed Skip and Louise in the crowd, and he waved at them.

When everyone was within earshot, he spoke, introducing the U-3521 to the world for the first time. He told them the short version of how the boat had been discovered and how it was repaired on Hiva Oa. He then introduced his crew, and told the audience about what he described as an uneventful passage to the Columbia River. "My crew and I are dog-tired from two weeks at sea, so we'll have an in-depth news conference here on the boat tomorrow morning at eleven. Until then, thank you for coming."

One reporter shouted, "What was the name of the island where you found the submarine?"

Dutch answered without thinking, "The Japanese called it Haiku."

"What happened to the German crew?" another reporter shouted.

"We believe they all perished on the island," Dutch answered.

One of the boatyard workers asked, "What happened to your sailboat?"

"It's on its way back to the States as we speak."

"Aren't you cold, dressed in that outfit?" someone else shouted.

"Yes," Dutch answered with a smile. "I'll have to buy some long pants. Please, no more questions until tomorrow."

As the horde thinned, Dutch invited his special guests aboard, along with the local newspaper and the NBC crew. He gave the group a personal tour of the boat and finished up in the crew's mess, where fresh coffee and cookies were waiting.

As everyone helped themselves and talked with the crew, Dutch approached Rolf and Alice Klep. "What do you think of my boat?" he asked them.

Alice grinned from ear to ear. "What a historical find. Thanks for sharing it with us."

"Did you get your Maritime Museum open?"

"Yes," Rolf answered proudly. "We're in the old City Hall."

Dutch smiled at them. "I'd like to loan you this submarine. You can use it as a fund raiser by selling tours aboard the boat. The more people that file through, the more money the Museum makes. What do you think?"

Their mouths dropped open, as if they couldn't believe their ears. They looked at each other, and hugged. "Yes," Rolf said with excitement.

"You'll need to find a better moorage, one with a parking lot and a covered wharf. Hopefully, you'll have long lines waiting to see my boat."

"What do you get out of this?" Alice asked with a raised eyebrow.

"Right now, nothing," Dutch answered. "A place to park my boat, until it's needed in a film documentary NBC is producing."

"I know the perfect place to moor this boat," Rolf inserted. "I'll make some phone calls this afternoon."

Dutch and his crew did interviews with the guest reporters giving them the run of the boat until early afternoon. After a late lunch of pizza and beer, Ralph Higgins used the boatyard's pickup to drive the crew to the Hotel Elliott. After Dutch signed the men in, he went up to his room, and found that Skip and Louise had the adjoining room. The three spent the afternoon together, drinking martinis, catching up on family news, and listening to Dutch talk about his ten-month adventure in the South Pacific.

That evening, when they dined at a bistro across the street, they read the local newspaper, which was filled with pictures and stories about the arrival of U-3521. When they returned to their room, they watched the NBC Nightly News from New York, and the lead story was about the submarine. The opening footage was that of the boat underway in the setting sun, just off the California coast. The narrator likened the discovery of the U-3521 to that of the Kon-Tiki expedition, calling it the most thrilling story of the century. Skip and Louse were impressed, but Dutch recognized Colonel Ford's fingerprints all over the story, and he felt a little embarrassed. Right after the news, he excused himself for bed.

"Our flight is early in the morning," Skip said. "Let's have one last nightcap before we say goodbye."

The next morning, the phone calls started coming at five AM. Somehow, the news hounds had tracked Dutch down to his hotel, and the switchboard was soon swamped. In the course of the morning, he talked to newspapers, radio stations, magazines, and television stations from all over the country. Nearly all of the media were sending crews to Astoria.

Later that morning, when Ralph Higgins returned to the hotel to pick up the crew, Dutch learned, not too surprisingly, that the Coast Guard was waiting at the boat to do a routine inspection of the submarine and to interview the men. As all the crew got into the pickup truck, Dutch made sure they had their paperwork. The three Germans had valid US Passports, while the four lads from Tahiti had French Polynesian documents, and Dutch had his own passport. He felt confident that all the papers were in order.

When they arrived at the Boat Works, he found a Coast Guard launch tied up to the submarine, and a young Lieutenant JG waiting with two Petty Officers on the aft deck. Dutch introduced his crew and invited everyone below. The Lieutenant interviewed the men in the mess, while Dutch showed the Chiefs around the boat. As he did so, he told the Petty Officers that all the weapons aboard had been disarmed and that all the detonators had been removed from the torpedoes. "This submarine no longer has a bite," he said proudly. "It's as house broken as a well-trained puppy."

The Petty Officers showed little or no reaction, and kept taking pictures and writing down information.

When the tour was completed and the interviews done, the Lieutenant handed Dutch a Coast Guard Citation that listed the violations they had found: no approved life jackets were aboard, the boat carried dangerous high explosives that posed a threat to navigation, and the four crewmen from Tahiti didn't have visas to enter the United States.

"These violations must be fixed before the boat can sail again," the cocky young officer told Dutch. "Sign the ticket and fix the problems, or the next citation will have a monetary fine."

While Dutch agreed to secure proper life jackets, he loudly protested the other items on the list, and refused to sign the ticket. He reminded the young Lieutenant that, under the International Maritime Laws, entry visas for transit crews were not required if they returned to their home ports within seventy-two hours. And he reiterated again, that all weapons and torpedoes aboard had been disarmed. With a frown, the surly young officer made notes on the citation and then gave a copy of the unsigned ticket to Dutch.

Dutch read what he had written: *Boat Captain uncooperative.*

"Why are you being such a hard-ass about this, Lieutenant?"

The officer glared at Dutch. "I watched you cross the Bar yesterday, with small craft warnings flying on the Light Ship. What are you, some kind of sea cowboy?"

Dutch glared back. "This isn't a small craft. This submarine was engineered to sail in all sea conditions, anywhere in the world."

The officer sneered and rolled his eyes, then returned to his launch and motored away. From the aft deck, Dutch watched them depart in a light drizzle, and mused on why the Coast Guard had dug in their heels.

Because of threating weather, Ralph Higgins moved the eleven o'clock news conference into his company warehouse. His people built a large raised platform at one end of building that looked out over open doors to where the submarine was moored. Here Dutch and his crew could easily be seen and heard. By the time the conference started, the crowd of reporters had grown from yesterday's handful to more than thirty.

Dutch introduced himself and his crew to the audience and then told them the short version of how the boat was found, repaired and brought to the Columbia River. As he spoke, news cameras rolled, and still camera flashes filled the warehouse. He went on to tell the crowd about the documentary film that was planned, and about a new book that would outline the details of the discovery. When finished, he asked for questions.

The first few inquiries were the usual, about the boat and his crew. Then a reporter shouted a question that stunned him. "The Argentine Government claims your submarine torpedoed and sank one of its destroyers in International waters, nine days ago. Is that correct?"

Dutch smiled at the reporter. "That would be hard to do. We departed Hiva Oa with eight torpedoes aboard, and we arrived here in Astoria with same amount," he answered, making no mention of the Israeli submarine or the gold.

"So you're saying, unequivocally, that you didn't have a run-in with a warship in International waters?" a lady reporter demanded.

Dutch glared at her. "Nine days ago, in the middle of the night, we were fired upon by a ship we could not see. And yes, we answered fire with our 20mm automatic rifles, before we ran away. But at no time did we torpedo or sink any ship in International waters." Hearing muttering from the audience, he held up his hand, "Please feel free to talk with, and interview my crew. They will confirm my statements."

They did just that for the next hour. The crew was swarmed with questions, as was Dutch, as they underwent on-camera interviews. In many ways, it was a dreadful experience; some of the reporters *did* act like piranhas, although others were friendly and professional. But Dutch surprised himself, enjoying his time in the limelight.

That afternoon, the crew and Dutch gathered up forty used life jackets from around the boatyard, and stored them aboard the sub. Then they sparked up the boat and moved it to the new moorage that Rolf and Alice Klep had rented. It was the ideal location, right next to where the Astoria–Megler Ferry boat came and went a dozen times a day. The floating dock was two hundred and fifty feet long, with ramps at both ends that lead up to a large, covered, open-air wharf.

When the submarine arrived at the moorage, they found Rolf Klep and some volunteers hard at work, positioning two elevated boarding ramps on the pier. Wolfgang maneuvered the boat with the bow pointing down-river, and then backed it into the dock.

After the crew fastened docking bumpers on the starboard side, the Captain nudged the boat against the quay and ordered the mooring lines set.

"What do you think of our sign?" Rolf called out from the dock.

When Dutch looked up, he noticed that other volunteers on the wharf were hanging a large canvas banner that read: Daily Tours of This Submarine $2.

"I like it," Dutch answered with a smile. "You can bring your docents aboard to learn about the submarine. The crew is flying home tomorrow, so this is the time."

That afternoon, some of the crew went to work, clearing the boat of all personal belongings, including the food in the refrigerators, which was given to the volunteers. Meanwhile, the German members walked around the boat with the Museum instructors, teaching them how it was to live aboard a U-boat. While that was happening, Dutch walked to town and picked up the airline tickets for the next morning. Then he made arrangements at Thiel Brothers Restaurant for a gala farewell party that night, where he would pay off his crew.

As he walked back towards his hotel, he stopped in a stationary store and purchased a portable electric typewriter and a ream of paper, to start on the documentary script. When he got back to his room, the first thing he typed was the answer to the age-old question of war: why had some lived, while so many others had not? `Only by the grace of God can those who lived find a more purposeful life.`

Early the next morning, Ralph Higgins and Dutch drove the crew out to the airport. The ride was as quiet as tomb. All of the men except Luke had hangovers and cotton mouths. On the tarmac, Dutch shook hands with them all again and promised to send them copies of the photos taken at the party. Then the crew climbed aboard a Western Airlines DC4 and departed for Seattle and, from there, connecting flights home. The voyage had turned out to be a true adventure, rich in friendships and filled with memories.

The next days and weeks flew by. Dutch stayed at the hotel, talking to the press and fulfilling interview requests. The lines of tourists waiting to tour the submarine were always long. The attraction proved to be a big success for the Museum. In the evenings, Dutch pecked away at his typewriter developing a script he called *The Voyage of Atonement*. He also planned a second story, called the *Voyage of the Lost*. This would be the tragic story of the German crew.

He enjoyed the discipline of writing, and the vivid flow of recollections. His only regrets were that he was a hunt-and-peck typist with poor spelling habits.

February 20, 1964, proved to be the day when Dutch's life turned upside down, again. On that day, Rolf Klep at the Museum received a registered letter from the US Coast Guard. Inside the envelope was a Federal Court order allowing the Coast Guard to confiscate the U-3521. Under the laws of the War Powers Act, the boat had been deemed a danger to navigation and a threat to American well-being. The date of seizure was to be 0900 the next morning. Rolf immediately telephoned Dutch and called the City Attorney.

Dutch quickly walked to the Museum. With his head swimming with questions, he read the court order for himself. Afterwards, he and Rolf walked to City Hall and met with the Mayor and the City Attorney.

Both parties read the documents with long faces and quiet reflection. The submarine attraction had helped put Astoria on the map again, and both hated to see it go. The only suggestion the attorney made was to get a Federal Court order to quash the Confiscation Order. But that would take weeks to prepare and file.

"The bottom line," the Mayor said, "is that you can't declare war on the Coast Guard. You'll have to relinquish the boat to them until it's worked out in the courts."

Dutch and Rolf could not believe their ears, so they walked over to consult another lawyer in town. But he was as pessimistic as the City Attorney, and advised them to fulfill the court order without protest. His parting words would be etched in Dutch's mind for years to come: "Only fools fight the Federal Government in their own Federal Courts."

When the pair returned to the Museum, Rolf asked, "So what do I do now?"

Dutch looked at him sadly and answered, "Get your volunteers to remove everything from the boat that's not tacked down, and bring all the items to your warehouse for safe keeping. I'll get on the phone and start making calls for help. There has got to be some way to stop the Coast Guard."

By the time Dutch returned to his hotel, it was getting dark. He spent the entire evening in his room, calling out for help. His first phone call was to Colonel Ford at NBC. The Colonel listened patiently to what Dutch had to say, and asked a few questions, while extending encouraging words. "The story of your submarine is all over the news. It has ignited an interest again in WWII and the tragedy of the Holocaust. The news that our own government is confiscating the U-3521 will just add fuel to your fire of publicity. I'll have news crews on the docks, early tomorrow morning. They'll document the seizure, and I'll see that it's plastered all over tomorrow night's national news. The country won't stand for this!" The last thing Colonel Ford did was give Dutch the home phone number of the network's attorney. "I'm not sure he can help you, as he's not a Maritime lawyer, but see what he has to say."

Dutch thanked the Colonel and hung up the phone, with a sinking feeling that he could not stop the taking. Later that night, when he did reach the network attorney, the only interesting thing he learned was that most Federal Court orders had a two-week waiting period, giving the plaintiff time to respond. No such provisions had been made in his Confiscation Order. The lawyer then referred Dutch to a Maritime attorney in Long Beach. Other than that, he offered no encouragement about being able to stop the seizure of the submarine.

Dutch also called Admiral King in New Jersey, only to find that he was in the Caribbean, on vacation. He then called two other attorneys that he found listed in the yellow pages, but both offices were closed. That was when Dutch gave up and crawled into bed, with three fingers of Yukon Jack.

Sleep came hard and late that night, as Dutch's sadness turned into anger. He knew, deep down, that he had lived up to all of the Maritime Laws, so why was the Coast Guard out to get him? Tossing and turning, he dozed off a few times, but that was about it. When his wake-up call rang at eight thirty the next morning, he stumbled out of bed and numbly dressed, without giving a thought to his attire. The last thing he put on was his light-weight windbreaker and a baseball cap.

Without a word to anyone, he went downstairs and started walking towards the wharf, in a rain storm he did barely noticed. His rambling mind was still filled with so much anger that he could not feel the wind-swept downpour on his face.

The U-3521 had survived the ravages of North Atlantic storms, the fury of Pacific typhoons, and a passage that almost circumnavigated the globe. The boat had sunk just off Pitcairn Island, only to resurrect itself and outlive its crew in a dark, damp sea cave for almost eighteen years. It had survived the repairs, the scrutiny of Mossad, and an attack by the Argentine Odessa. The boat represented the best and worst of mankind, and yet, on this very morning, Dutch's own government would rob him of his discovery. It was a damn crying shame.

With his hat and jacket soaked through, Dutch looked like a drowned bilge rat by the time he reached the covered wharf. As he marched through the crowd of onlookers, he ignored the news crew filming the event, and scarcely heard the words of Rolf Klep, who assured him, "We got everything off the boat. It's all safely at the Museum."

With glazed eyes, Dutch turned at the first ramp, back out into the weather and down to the dock.

Someone behind him shouted, "Is he going to kill himself?"

The submarine mooring lines had already been removed, and a tugboat was pulling the boat out into the river, with the Coast Guard Cutter standing by. The U-3521 was towed out into the shipping channel and downriver for a half mile. Then it was carefully turned upriver for its journey across the Bar to Bremerton, Washington.

As it passed Astoria again, with the Cutter leading the way, Dutch dropped to one knee and raised his drenched, clenched fist high over his head. He wanted to extend his middle finger to the Coast Guard, but he couldn't bring himself to do it. Instead, he shouted over the weather, "You sons of bitches, this betrayal will not stand! Your day of atonement is upon you."

VOYAGE END

Epilog

Torpedoed by his own government, Dutch soon turned his disappointment into a determination for revenge. He didn't have long to wait. While the sea tug still had the submarine under tow, the news of its seizure flashed across the nation with headlines like 'Coast Guard Takes Treasure,' 'Treasury's Darkest Day' and 'CG Steals History.' The negative stories about the Coast Guard and the Department of the Treasury continued for weeks.

Along with this fire storm of publicity came support from the most unlikely allies, including an attorney out of Tacoma, Washington, by the name of Melvin Bell. He was a grumpy old seadog with forty years of experience in Maritime Law. After reading the story of the confiscation in his local newspaper, he telephoned Dutch and asked a flurry of questions. Dutch mailed him copies of all the documents he had.

A week later, Bell phoned back and offered to take on Dutch's case against the Coast Guard. His *pro bono* services came with two stipulations: Dutch would have to appear and testify honestly in all court appearances and depositions, and he would have to stick with the litigation, whether winning or losing the appeals, all the way up to the Supreme Court if necessary. Dutch quickly agreed with his terms.

As they talked further, Dutch asked him why he had offered to take the case for free. Bell's encouraging answer was that he was committed to maritime justice. "I can't stand by and allow the Coast Guard free rein in confiscating ships without consideration of Maritime Law. We'll get your submarine back. In the meantime, get on with your life," Mr. Bell told him. "This might take years but, in the end, we will prevail."

By the end of the month, Dutch's beloved sailboat was safely moored in Long Beach, but Dutch stayed on in Astoria to finish the documentary script. When it was done, he flew down to Burbank for meetings with Colonel Ford and a reunion with his old crew. It was wonderful to be aboard the *Laura* again, sharing the news of both passages back to the States. As it turned out, the two doppelgangers had proven to be able sailors and agreeable companions.

Doug and Heidi had heard, and seen, some of the submarine publicity when they first arrived in port. In fact, they had been interviewed by a NBC news crew when they tied up at the marina. Both were astounded by the news coverage and wanted to learn more about the seizure. Dutch told them what he knew about where the boat was, and the status of the lawsuit. He stressed that he had a world-renowned Maritime Lawyer, but that only time would tell if they got their submarine back.

"I have a question for you," Doug asked of Dutch. "I know where you hid the jewels in your cabin, but for the life of me, I couldn't find that one gold bar we kept back on Henderson Island. Where the hell is it?"

Dutch got up from the salon table, opened the sole cover hatch for the generator, and reached inside the compartment. He fumbled around for a few seconds, then pulled out a large, oily rag and opened it up. Inside the cloth was the gold bar. "Do you mean this?"

Doug rolled his eyes. "It's been right under our feet, all the way home!"

A few evenings later, Dutch and his crew had dinner with Maggie and Colonel Ford. During the meal, the Colonel shared more good news. The network liked Dutch's documentary script and had agreed to produce the project. The crew would be paid twenty thousand dollars for their story, and would own the final film equally with the network.

"This offer, of course, assumes that you all will assist in the production of the film," the Colonel said.

The crew whole-heartedly agreed.

"When will our documentary be released?" Dutch asked.

The Colonel grinned. "Next year, a month before the 'Witness to Yesterday' project. Your story will get the conversation started about WWII." He handed Dutch an envelope. "Our 'Witness' project is almost totally complet and ready for release. Here's the payment for your footage. I pried it out of accounting early, as I thought you folks might need some folding money."

Dutch looked inside the envelope and found a check for eighteen thousand, seven hundred dollars. "You're one smart man," Dutch answered, smiling, and passed the check around the table.

The next day, Dutch opened a checking account and made the first of many distributions for the crew, under the terms of the 'ships articles'. Finally, his mates started to realize their good fortune in finding the U-3521. Doug was pleased with his share and used some of the funds to hire an attorney to secure his divorce. Heidi bought a bus ticket home and spent a long weekend with her parents. Dutch mailed Lois' check to her American parents in New Jersey, and hoped it would find its way to her in Germany. He was proud as hell of that first distribution, which also included the funds he had deposited in Papeete.

The next few months flew by, with the crew working on the documentary almost every day at NBC. In the evenings, Dutch and his typewriter pecked out the book's manuscript. With the help of some staff writers at the network, the book was finished in just ninety days. Working with a New York publisher, it was scheduled for release two weeks before the airing of the documentary in May of 1965.

Maggie read the book manuscript before it was sent off to the publisher. She liked it very much, but had a warning for Dutch. "Your book tells the *true* story, right down to cannibalism, the gold treasure, and the Argentine destroyer. Have you told the Israeli Government about the release of your book?"

Dutch hadn't even thought about the Israeli Government since his arrival back in the States. But he knew Maggie was right, so that evening he contacted the American Mossad, using the radio frequency Jean had used. Soon, he was talking directly with Gil Hirsh, who didn't seem concerned about the contents of Dutch's book. "We've always known the truth would come out, sooner or later. By the way, your finder's fee was deposited into your Papeete bank account two weeks ago. I'll relay your message to my government."

When Dutch was finished on the radio, he poured himself a drink, smiling broadly. It was time for another distribution for his crew.

Just before the end of 1964, Mr. Bell won the submarine case at their first appearance in a Federal Court. The Judge correctly ruled that Dutch had been denied his due process when the Confiscation Court Order was issued without the customary two-week waiting period for a response.

The Treasury Department immediately appealed the judge's ruling to a higher court and sent Dutch a government check for $2750.00. Across the front of the check it read, 'Estimated salvage value U-3521.' On the reverse side it read, 'Endorsement represents agreement to all terms and conditions of the Department of Treasury.' After talking to his attorney, Dutch never cashed the check. Instead, he issued a press release about the judge's ruling, along with a copy of the check as what he called 'hush money.' This reignited another round of negative press stories about the Coast Guard and the Treasury Department. But fighting the government was like wrestling an octopus.

In early May of 1965, their book was released with an impressive national marketing campaign. For weeks, Dutch and his crew traveled around America, doing public appearances and book signings. In late May, the documentary film was televised, and in June the 'Witness to Yesterday' project aired to excellent ratings and critical acclaim. Just as all this was happening, the British, who owned Henderson Island, and the French Government, who considered it part of French Polynesia, announced a pending lawsuit against Dutch Clarke. They claimed he had removed, without permission, a submarine and an unspecified amount of gold treasure from their territory. They were demanding the return of both the boat and the gold. This International news drove up the television audience and rekindled the publicity for the U-3521.

A few days later, the Argentine Government announced a similar lawsuit for Dutch's part in the sinking of its destroyer in International waters. Right after that, the Israeli Government announced their involvement in receiving the cargo of gold, and in the accidental sinking of the Argentine ship. With the Israeli statement of complicity, all of the complaining countries quickly withdrew their lawsuits. These developments added even more fuel to the publicity campaign and the plight of Dutch's confiscated submarine. It was coverage that no money could buy, and books sales quickly turned from brisk to the top of the New York Times Best Sellers list. How sweet the taste of retribution.

During 1965, Melvin Bell won his second appearance before a Federal Court. Again, the Treasury Department immediately appealed the judge's ruling to the next higher court. On the phone, Bell said, "They've got their spurs dug in on you, Dutch. I think the boys at Treasury hope you'll give up and walk away. But if you don't, the nine black robes of the Temple of Justice will decide this case."

With book royalties and fees flowing in, the crew found other opportunities for making money. College campuses around the country started inviting them to make presentations about their discovery. The compensation was great, with all expenses paid. Ever so slowly, the crew members of the *Laura* were becoming cult-like celebrities.

Late in 1965, Doug secured his divorce, but along the way he got subdivided by all of the attorneys. Dutch received legal papers and a Court Order that required him to pay half of all future payments for Doug to his ex-wife, Trudy Asbow. He resisted the Court Order at first, but then his attorney advised him not to get involved. Reluctantly, Dutch directed that all future crew distributions include twelve and half percent for Doug, and the same for his ex-wife Trudy.

Early in 1966, the crew spent most of its time traveling the country, doing book signings and making presentations at college campuses. During this time, they met tens of thousands of people, young and old, all eager to hear their story. Their events were mostly packed, and they did hundreds of local press interviews, which helped them sell carloads of books.

In early summer, Dutch took a long weekend off from the book tour and traveled to Maryland, where he was joined by Skip and Louise from Ketchikan, and by Jack Jr's mother from California. On Saturday, June 11, Dutch's son Edward and his godson, Jack Jr., graduated from Annapolis. With patriotic music playing and flags waving, it was a gala event that included rousing speeches from famous politicians and colorful military leaders, all spouting 'Duty, honor, country.' During the ceremonies, Edward received his gold bar as a Second Lieutenant in the USMC, while

Jack Jr. received his gold bar as an Ensign with the US Navy. After the ceremonies, a thousand young midshipmen, dressed in their summer white uniforms, threw their hats into the air and screamed their relief at completing their studies at the Naval Academy. It was a proud, impressive sight to behold.

That evening, at a fancy local hotel, Dutch hosted a graduation party for his boys and friends. It was a well-attended catered affair, with an open bar and tables filled with fine foods that lasted long into the night. Many of the guests knew who Dutch was, and had read his book. They asked the usual questions and got the usual answers about his adventure and why he had given away all that Nazi gold. The young, new officers he met that evening were a remarkable and handsome bunch, all eager to make their own marks on the military and on the war in Vietnam.

He encouraged their young ambitions but warned them off of the war. "Only fools are eager for war. It's the wise man who's eager for peace."

From the looks on their faces, he knew that his words of warning mostly fell on deaf ears.

Both his own boys had been assigned to flight-training school after graduation. With the war heating up, it was an assignment Dutch feared, and he did his best to warn the boys, as well. But they both had a fire in their bellies for war, and Dutch knew from his own youth that trying to dissuade them would be a waste of time. Instead, he invited the boys to use his boat in Long Beach, and proudly gave them each a thousand dollars as pocket money for their upcoming thirty-day leave.

"We'll be on tour for the next couple of months, so the sailboat is all yours," he told them. "There are plenty of pretty girls around the marina."

With a sheepish look, Edward replied, "We both have girl friends in New York City, Dad. That's where we want to spend our shore leave."

Dutch grinned at his guys. "Anchors away, boys!"

In July, after months of being on the road, the crew returned home. They were all weary of the traveling and hordes of people, and looked forward to the solitude of the sailboat. But as the summer faded away, Doug and Heidi went their separate ways.

With their new-found fortunes, they both had opportunities to follow their own dreams. Dutch fully understood, wishing them well on their next adventure in life.

With his crew gone, Dutch went to work, writing his second book, *Voyage of the Lost.* This novel would be about the German crew of the U-3521 and what became of them. The new project would be filled with history but riddled with many unknowns, requiring him to use his own imagination in writing his first historical fiction manuscript.

Late in the year, the Supreme Court agreed to hear the case of Dutch Clarke vs. The United States Department of Treasury. The oral arguments were scheduled for the spring of 1967. Melvin Bell invited Dutch to join him in Washington DC for the arguments, and Dutch quickly accepted.

In March of the New Year, the government announced that, effective on April 1, 1967, the United States Coast Guard was being transferred out of Treasury to the newly-formed Department of Transportation. Within hours of the news, his attorney telephoned and speculated that, with the transfer of the Coast Guard, a proper settlement might be achieved with Treasury. He asked Dutch to fly up to Tacoma so they could draft terms and conditions for such a settlement.

"All I want is my boat back," Dutch told him on the phone.

"That's not true," Bell answered. "What about lost revenue for the Museum? And what if they don't return your submarine? Then they owe you all the expenses of finding, repairing, and sailing the boat to the States. Then there are all the legal expense, and all the time we spent on the case. Trust me. I know what I'm doing."

"I thought you were doing this *pro bono*?"

"I am for you, Dutch, but not for the Department of the Treasury."

Dutch chuckled. "I'll be there tomorrow, with my ledger book. It has every expense we paid during the voyage."

In May, Dutch flew out to Washington DC for the oral arguments. When he checked in at his hotel, he found a message waiting from Mr. Bell, instructing him to be on the steps of the Supreme Court Building at ten the next morning.

The cab ride through the city, early the next day, was a wonderful experience. The sun was warm with the scent of a late spring, and the town seemed engulfed in cherry blossoms. When the taxi pulled up in front of the Supreme Court Building, Dutch couldn't believe his eyes. The architectural style, with its sixteen marble columns and magnificent oval plaza, helped harmonize the iconic Justice Building with other nearby congressional buildings. It was a stunning shrine to the American way of life.

Paying off the driver, Dutch moved across the open-air pavilion and up the long flight of marble steps leading up to the portico and the Great Hall. As he approached the top, he noticed the massive Corinthian pillars and the paneled carving of Lady Justice, holding a sword and scales.

Just inside the shade of the columns, he found Mr. Bell waiting with his briefcase in hand. "Good morning, Dutch. What a gorgeous morning to be here with the guardians of the law. We start the oral presentations at ten-thirty. You can sit with me and my associates at the plaintiff's table."

Dutch shook hands with his attorney. "This should be a very interesting morning."

"Yes," Bell smirked, "a very interesting morning. By the way, I have someone who would like to meet you. Do you mind?"

Dutch glanced around at the crowd in the marble portico. "No, not at all."

Mr. Bell smiled and waved his hand in the air. One of the tourists, standing by a carved panel, turned and walked towards them. She was an attractive lady dressed in a beige silk blouse with a dark brown skirt. She had a shapely figure and wore a large spring bonnet that covered her amber hair and part of her face. When she stood in front of the men, she lifted the brim of her hat and removed her sunglasses. Dutch about fainted; it was Lois Berg!

"What the hell are you doing here?" he stammered.

She smiled and kissed him on his cheek.

"She telephoned me last week," Mr. Bell said. "She told me who she was, and that she had read in the newspapers about the oral arguments, and wanted to know if you would be here. I told her you would, and this morning she took the train down from New York."

"Is that alright, Dutch?" Lois asked, with a hopeful look on her face.

"Of course," Dutch answered, all in a flutter. "But I almost didn't recognize you with clothes on." He paused. "Oops. I didn't mean it like that! On the sailboat, we mostly lived in our swimsuits," he explained to his attorney.

Mr. Bell chuckled. "I understand Dutch. She can sit with us at the plaintiff's table."

Just then, one of his associate lawyers rushed up and announced, "Our time with the Supreme Court has been canceled. According to the clerk, Treasury is settling the case out of court."

Mr. Bell frowned. "We'll see about that. Dutch, you and Lois go back to the hotel. I'll telephone, or come by, when I know more about what the hell is happening."

Lois grabbed onto Dutch's arm, smiling brightly. "That's fine with me. We have some catching up to do."

It was indeed a morning to remember. During the cab ride back to the hotel, Dutch felt as giddy as a teenager to be sitting next to Lois again. He kept looking at her and then turning away, not wanting to embarrass himself. He couldn't understand why he was so taken with her.

When they got to his one-bedroom suite, she made a comment about not needing two-bedroom suites when he traveled without her. Lamely, he replied, "But it's not as much fun."

After opening up the window blinds and calling down for room service, they came to rest on the sofa. Lois removed her hat, and let her amber hair fall to her shoulders. She looked marvelous. While they waited, they started a far more serious conversation. Her birth mother had passed away three months before, and Lois had buried her next to her birth father. She had considered keeping the family's used bookstore, but decided that Germany wasn't really her home, so she had sold the business and returned to the States, where she had made peace with her American parents. "I've lived with them for the last couple of months now," she told him. "But it's still a little awkward."

"Are you working?" Dutch asked.

"No, I've been living off the generous 'ships articles' you've been sending me. What's happened to Doug and Heidi? I haven't heard from them in over a year."

Dutch chuckled. "I guess Heidi caught Doug with one too many coed's during our book tour. They've gone their separate ways. Doug bought a sailboat and returned to Papeete, where he's running a bare-foot sailing business of his own. Last I heard Heidi had bought a restaurant and bar in downtown Bakersfield. I think she's doing very well."

"And what about you, Dutch? I understand you became sweet on Jean."

Dutch lit two cigarettes and passed one to Lois. "It didn't work out. She had two young children back home. I'm too damn old to be a father again, or to live in Israel."

Lois took a drag from her cigarette. "Not even if they were your own children?"

"With my malaria, that's impossible. I would if I could, but I can't."

Room service knocked, and Dutch got up to get the door. Lois watched him go. "Stranger things have happened," she said, giving him one of her looks.

Over sandwiches and drinks their conversation continued.

"So, where are you living, and what are you working on?" she asked.

Dutch opened a bottle of beer. "I bought a classic old Victorian house, and I just finished my second book."

"Wow. You bought a home in LA?"

He took a swig of his brew. "No. I did buy some acreage in the Hollywood Hills, but my house is on the shores of the Columbia River. It was built sixty years ago by a sea captain named Handover. It's in sorry shape and needs a lot of work. But it's got a widow's-walk and tall turrets with dynamite views of the Bar, all the way up-river to Astoria. That's where I hope to write my next novel."

"So you're going to be a writer?" Lois asked with fondness.

"Yes. I have a great publisher, and I know the drill now for selling books. Next week, I'm sailing the *Laura* up the coast to the Columbia River, where I'll live aboard while I'm remodeling the old Handover place."

"Do you have a crew for your sail north?" Lois asked.

"I was going to sail it solo," Dutch replied. "Are you volunteering?"

"Yes," Lois answered quickly, her eyes flashing. "I'd love to sail with you again. When do I have to be in LA?"

"Saturday. I'll pick you up at the airport. It will be just you and me, on a leisurely trip up the coast. I'll show you the great Pacific Northwest."

Mr. Bell came to the room in the early afternoon, bringing news, along with papers that had to be signed. Treasury had indeed offered a full settlement of the case. They were frightened that the Supreme Court would order them to return the submarine, and that was a big problem for them because the Coast Guard had inadvertently listed the U-3521 as surplus and obsolete, after which the boat had been towed out to sea and sunk during missile testing of a new weapons system. The boat was gone for good.

"That's why they settled for everything we asked," Mr. Bell said proudly.

The settlement was all written out in legal terms for Dutch to sign. The sailboat and crew would receive three hundred thousand dollars for punitive damages, their time and expenses of finding, repairing, and transporting the U-3521 to America. The Maritime Museum would receive thirty thousand dollars for the lost revenue of not having the submarine, and Mr. Bell and his law firm would receive one hundred thousand dollars for their time and legal fees.

Dutch felt sad, signing the final agreement. He really only wanted his submarine back. But that was impossible now.

Mr. Bell had one final paper for Dutch to sign. It was a short agreement that he would cease and desist from any future negative comments, stories, or news footage about the United States Coast Guard. Dutch smirked as he signed the document. "They started it," was all he said.

"I know you're disappointed about your submarine, Dutch," Mr. Bell said, folding up the signed papers. "But your case has made legal history, and you beat the government in their own courts. You should be very proud, lad."

Late that afternoon, Dutch hailed a cab and drove Lois to the train station. He had hoped she would stay the night, but she told him she had other business at home. "I'll be in LA on Saturday morning," she promised, boarding the train. "We can be at sea in the afternoon."

"Don't you want to see LA?" Dutch asked as the train started to move away.

She smiled and blew him a kiss. "I want to see you and your boat, not another big city."

The next Saturday, under a clear blue sky, with the winds out of the southwest, they were underway by early afternoon. Their first port of call was to be San Francisco, and then up the coast, stopping along the way at other ports.

Lois came on deck, wearing tan shorts and a yellow silk blouse, with a mug in her hand. "Here's some fresh coffee. I spiked it with some brandy."

Dutch tied off the helm and took the mug from her. "On this day, I'll break my own rule and have a drink while underway. How long can you stay?"

She smiled, taking a cushion next to Dutch. "Until you send me away." Then her expression turned serious. "There's something else, Dutch. Something I should have told you, back in Washington, DC. When we arrived in New York City to sell our jewels, I was pregnant. I was going to tell you, but then my life turned upside down when I found out who I really was. When I got to Germany, in my third month, I had a miscarriage. The local doctor said it could have been from the stress of traveling, or of finding out my true identity, or maybe it was just one of those things that wasn't meant to be. But I thought you should know, Dutch, because it was your baby."

Dutch stood mute, looking down on her, his mind racing. "Are you sure it was mine?" he stammered.

She stood and kissed him, with one eyebrow raised. "Well it sure wasn't Doug's, or any of those native boys. You're the only lover I had on our voyage. That's why I wanted to come back into your life. You're as virile as a teenager."

Lois moved to the cabin hatch, then turned back to Dutch. "Did you sleep with Jean?"

"You know that I don't kiss and tell," he answered sheepishly.

Lois frowned.

"But I can tell you this," he continued. "You're still only the third woman I've ever loved."

She flashed him a look. "Good. I like that. I'll get some lunch started."

Dutch could hardly believe what he had just learned. His manhood had returned, and Lois was back in his life again.

As he stood at the wheel of his beloved sailboat, with the wind in his hair and the warm sun on his face, he felt gratified with his life. He had returned the tainted Nazi gold to its rightful owners, and rekindled worldwide awareness about the Holocaust. He had found satisfaction from own his government, and truthfully told the story of the men and mission of the U-3521. During the passage, he had come to terms with the death and memory of his loving wife Laura, and with his own complicity in the death of his best friend, Jack Malone. *Life doesn't get any better than this*, he thought, watching the seagulls soring high above the boat. His voyage of atonement had come full circle.

###

Acknowledgments

If you want to sail across the vast Pacific Ocean, you'll need a seaworthy boat and a skilled crew. If you want to write about such a journey, you'll also need a skilled crew. Writing a novel like 'Voyage of Atonement' would have been nearly impossible without the skilled supporting cast that helped my storytelling take shape.

As with all of my historical novels, I let my characters move the story, while history dictates the direction and substance. 'Atonement' is generously sprinkled with kernels of historical truths and glimpses into another time when life was simpler, with bright horizons.

During the writing of this novel, I am grateful to have had a wonderful team of professionals, friends, and family who helped and supported my efforts.

For the front cover art, I was fortunate to acquire the rights from Parisian artist Michel Guyot. He is a gifted and world-renowned illustrator and painter of the weapons of war.

Judith Myers, story editor, has collaborated on all five of my novels. She has a magic touch with language and is a joy to work with. Her savvy advice is indispensable. Judy knows my writing weaknesses and somehow, like an anchor, she can reel me back into a safe harbor.

Kudo's to both of my proof readers. Kate Miller provided a second look at punctuation, and enthusiastic feedback on story development. Steve Wright provided another set of keen eyes to double and triple check every word. Their comments and thoughtful observations were invaluable and deeply appreciated.

For sailing terms and methods, I turned to my old friend, David White, a renowned sailor. David was one of the first to sail solo around the world, and became the founder of an international sailing competition. I thank him for his attention to each chapter and detail.

My wife, Tess, has always been the first to read my stories and provide non-stop encouragement and unwavering support. Her constructive feedback keeps me focused, and her heartfelt enthusiasm keeps me hopeful. She is also my walking, breathing spell-checker. Without her I couldn't write myself a parking ticket. Her faith, grace and loving kindness have co-authored my life.

Having said all this, it's my name on the title page, and I am responsible and accountable for every word. Any errors, misinterpretations, or mistakes are solely mine.

Appendixes

Boats Underway

U-3521

The *Laura*

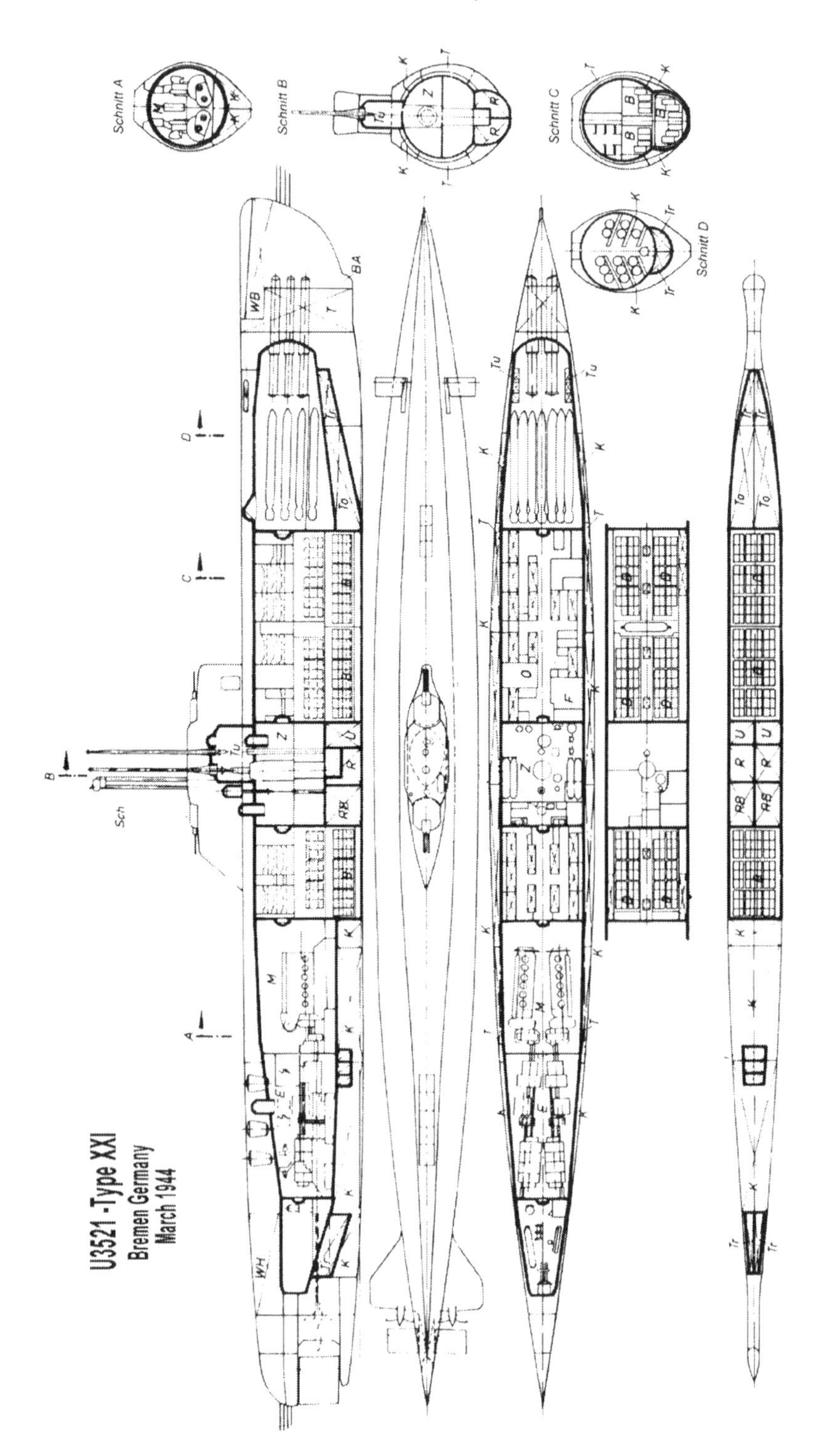
U3521 -Type XXI
Bremen Germany
March 1944
Schnitt A
Schnitt B
Schnitt C
Schnitt D

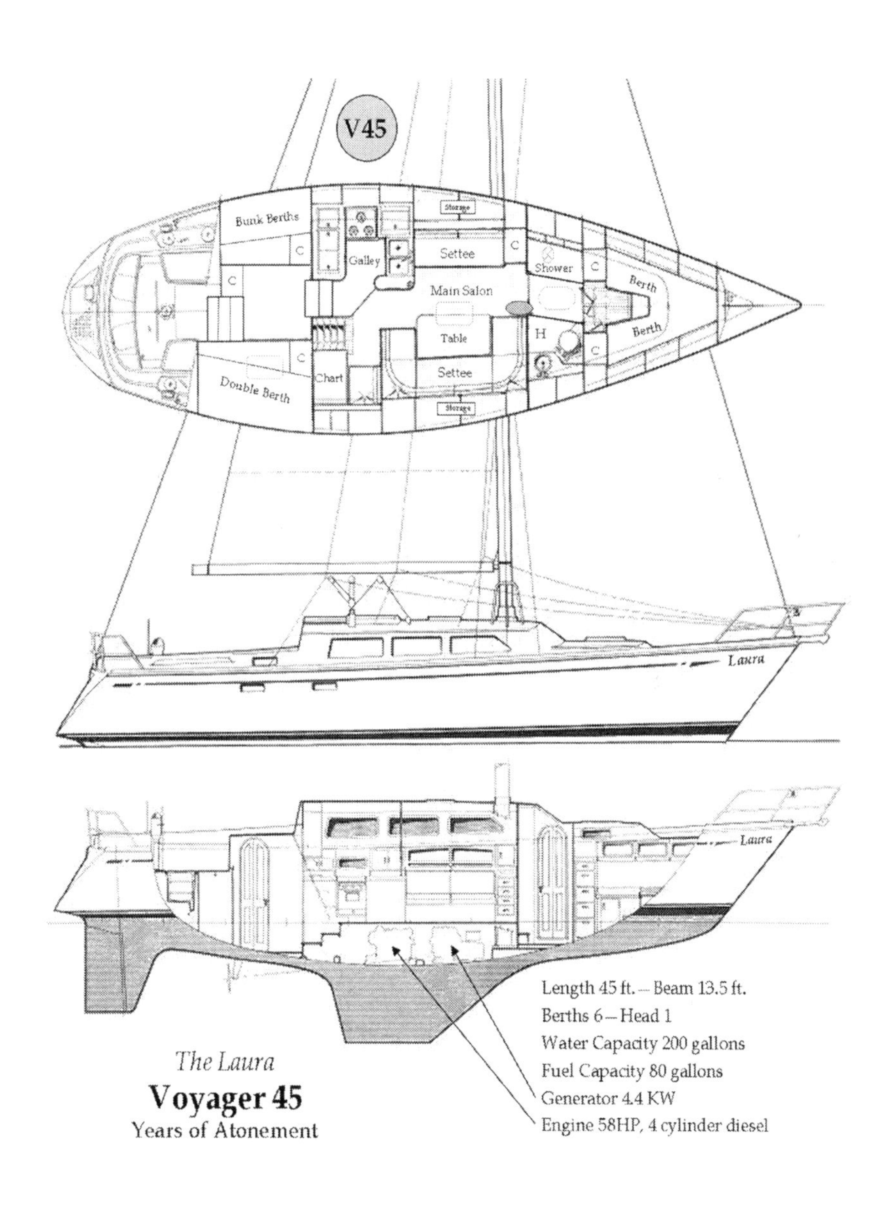
V45
Bunk Berths
Galley
Storage
Settee
Main Salon
Shower
Berth
Berth
H
Table
Chart
Settee
Storage
Double Berth
Laura
Laura
Length 45 ft. — Beam 13.5 ft.
Berths 6 — Head 1
Water Capacity 200 gallons
Fuel Capacity 80 gallons
Generator 4.4 KW
Engine 58HP, 4 cylinder diesel
The Laura
Voyager 45
Years of Atonement

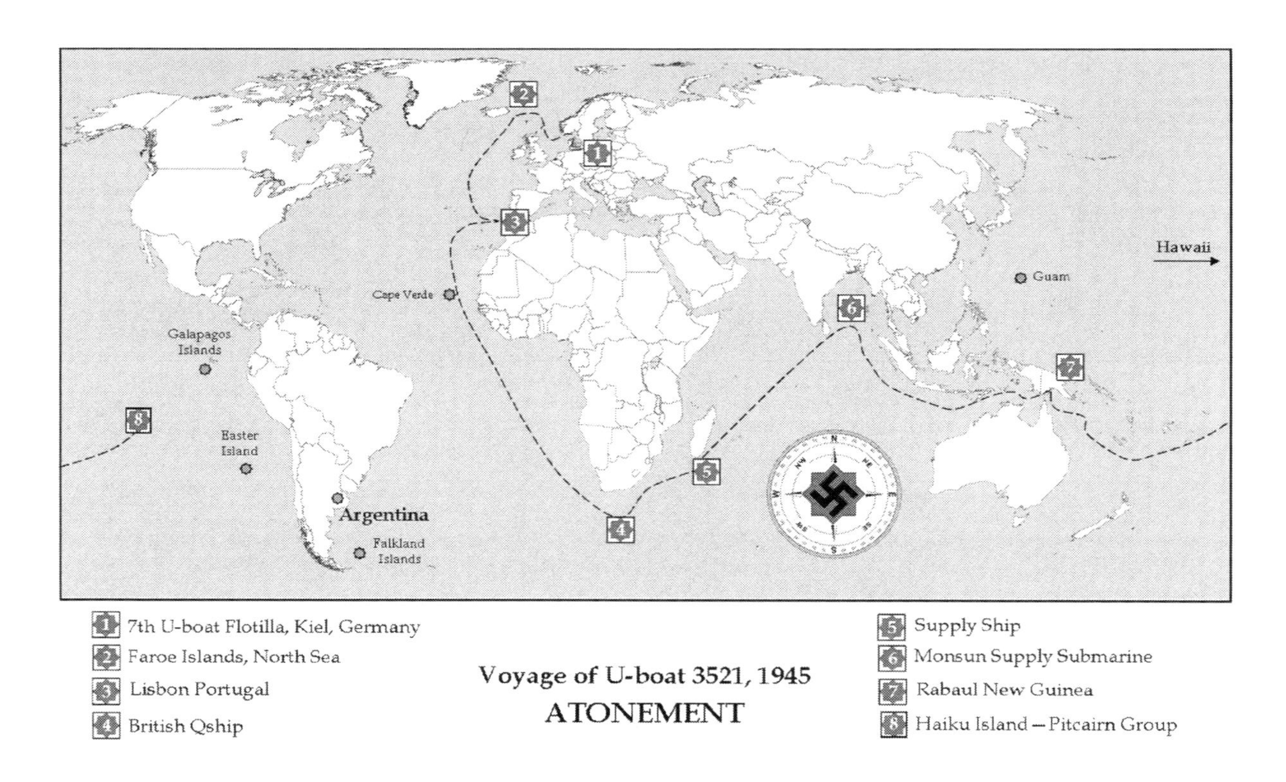
Hawaii
Guam
Cape Verde
Galapagos Islands
Easter Island
Argentina
Falkland Islands
1 7th U-boat Flotilla, Kiel, Germany
2 Faroe Islands, North Sea
3 Lisbon Portugal
4 British Qship
Voyage of U-boat 3521, 1945
ATONEMENT
5 Supply Ship
6 Monsun Supply Submarine
7 Rabaul New Guinea
8 Haiku Island — Pitcairn Group

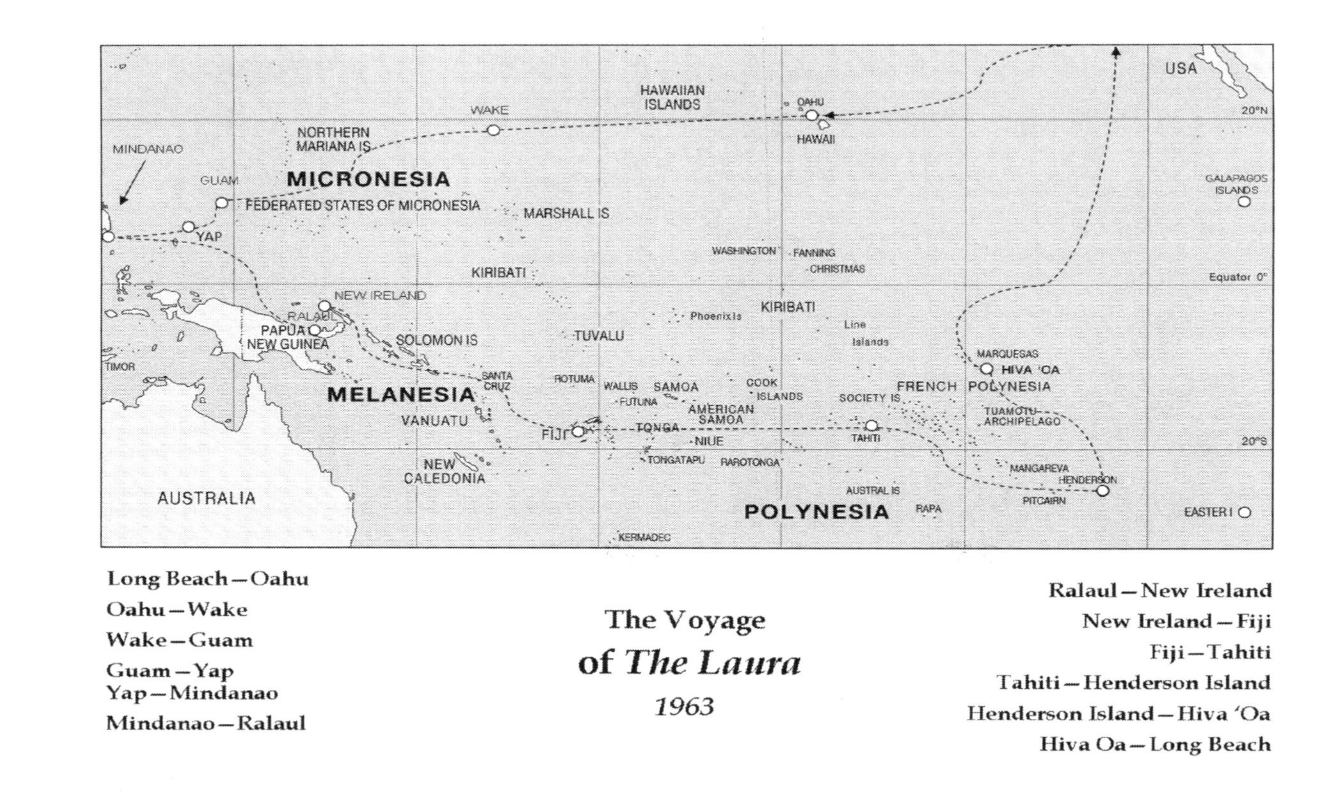
USA
HAWAIIAN ISLANDS
OAHU
HAWAII
WAKE
NORTHERN MARIANA IS
MINDANAO
GUAM
MICRONESIA
FEDERATED STATES OF MICRONESIA
MARSHALL IS
YAP
WASHINGTON
FANNING
CHRISTMAS
KIRIBATI
NEW IRELAND
RALAUL
PAPUA NEW GUINEA
SOLOMON IS
TUVALU
Phoenix Is
KIRIBATI
Line Islands
TIMOR
SANTA CRUZ
ROTUMA
WALLIS
FUTUNA
SAMOA
COOK ISLANDS
AMERICAN SAMOA
MELANESIA
VANUATU
FIJI
TONGA
NIUE
TONGATAPU
RAROTONGA
SOCIETY IS
TAHITI
FRENCH POLYNESIA
MARQUESAS
HIVA 'OA
TUAMOTU ARCHIPELAGO
MANGAREVA
HENDERSON
PITCAIRN
NEW CALEDONIA
AUSTRALIA
AUSTRAL IS
RAPA
POLYNESIA
KERMADEC
GALAPAGOS ISLANDS
EASTER I
20°N
Equator 0°
20°S
Long Beach—Oahu
Oahu—Wake
Wake—Guam
Guam—Yap
Yap—Mindanao
Mindanao—Ralaul
The Voyage
of The Laura
1963
Ralaul—New Ireland
New Ireland—Fiji
Fiji—Tahiti
Tahiti—Henderson Island
Henderson Island—Hiva 'Oa
Hiva Oa—Long Beach

About the Author

Brian D. Ratty, a retired media executive and graduate of Brooks Institute of Photography, also holds an honorary Master of Science degree. He and his wife, Tess, live on the north Oregon Coast, where he writes and photographs that rugged and majestic region. Over the past thirty five years, he has traveled the vast wilderness of the Pacific Coast in search of images and stories that reflect the spirit and splendor of those spectacular lands. Brian is an award-winning historical fiction novelist of five books.

Why I write

I write what I like to read, historical fiction rich with bold characters and powerful storylines. I shy away from gratuitous violence and descriptive sex; instead my stories portray adventure with vivid descriptions and believable plots. My goal is to whisk my reader away to another time, another place and another frame of mind… the results being a suspenseful and brisk read. **Readers Wanted!**

For more information: www.dutchclarke.com/

Other Brian Ratty Books

The Early Years: Trail of Discovery
Foreword Magazine: Book of the Year
Amazon Breakthrough Novel Awards
If you enjoyed Jack London's classic 'Call of the Wild,' you'll love 'The Early Years.'

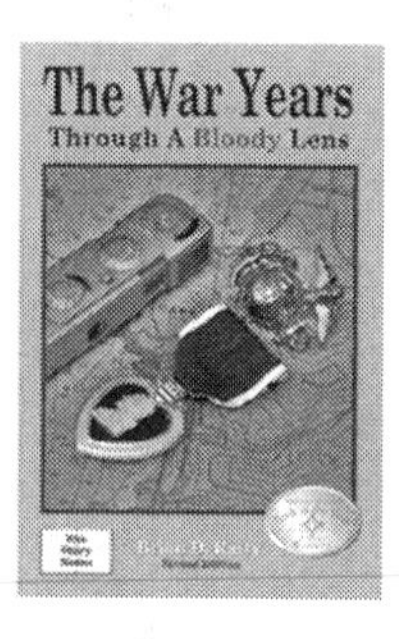

The War Years: Through A Bloody Lens
Foreword Magazine: Book of the Year
Eric Hoffer Award-winner
If you enjoyed 'The Band of Brothers/Saving Private Ryan,' you'll love 'The War Years!'

Tillamook Passage:
Two Worlds - One Destiny
Eric Hoffer Award-winner
Tillamook Passage is a rare view of the Oregon Coastal Indians. Don't miss this book!

Destination Astoria: Odyssey to the Pacific
Readers Choice—Five Stars
If you enjoyed the classic novel 'The Last of the Mohicans,' you will love Destination Astoria.

Made in the USA
Columbia, SC
01 July 2017